WHEN RIVERS COLLIDE

Adventures of a Victorian Soldier - Book 2

M. J. TWOMEY

eBook ISBN:978-1-954224-00-1

Visit my website to join my mailing list and access information on new releases and updates. Feel free to email me or send a message via the website.

www.mjtwomey.com

This book is a work of fiction. The scenes with actual people from these historic events are fictional. The place names used reflect names used in the nineteenth century .

CHAPTER ONE

The good Anglican worshippers seated in the wooden pews—men with pork chop sideburns in somber suits, mingled with women in feathered hats overseeing squirming children—despised Samuel Kingston. They despised him for killing one of their own, the Fifth Earl of Baltimore. They despised him for marrying a colored woman who was also a Catholic. And no matter what God or the reverend said this morning, none of this was likely to change soon.

Samuel tugged at his collar and tried to concentrate. He was there to pray. Afterward, he would speak with the reverend about this guilt that was destroying him—if his courage held. He'd attempted to approach the reverend before but lost his nerve. He couldn't back out today, not after requesting a meeting.

High in his marble pulpit, Reverend Welby slid his wire spectacles up on his head and squinted down at his small congregation. "That concludes today's service. Remember to pray for our brothers and sisters in Ulster; may the Lord protect them from the rioting papists."

Samuel's eyes cut to the iron-studded door and the spring day waiting outside. Too late to escape. He stepped back to let his siblings, Jason and Emily pass into the aisle. "Wait for me outside, please."

Emily squeezed his elbow as she brushed by. "More prayers, Brother? Why? You spend more time on your knees than the rest of us together. Or are you planning to donate some of that fortune you brought back from Nicaragua to the church?"

"Just a theological question, that's all." He faked a smile.

The church was too warm inside, and the cloying smell of polish, burning candles, and sweat added to Samuel's discomfort. The congregation flowed from the sanctuary with a subdued shuffle of feet knocking kneelers and quiet coughs. Waiting for Reverend Welby to reappear from the vestry was like waiting for the headmaster in boarding school. Samuel quailed when the cleric finally appeared in his customary black suit, adjusting his white collar as he approached with pigeon-toed steps. He looked about fifty-five, but who could tell? Samuel had known him forever.

Reverend Welby slipped into the pew beside Samuel. "Master Kingston. How's your new wife? Is it . . ."

Samuel missed the rest. The tinnitus was louder than usual in his left ear; the ever-present hiss of rushing water a constant reminder of shattering his eardrum in Crimea eighteen months before. "Pardon, Reverend, I didn't quite catch that."

"I asked if Sofia is your wife's name."

"Yes, Reverend. Sofia."

"Settling in, I hope? Quite a change, even the weather. She must find Ireland cold after Nicaragua."

"Not at present, Reverend. I believe this is the hottest April I ever experienced."

"And the baby? Must be due soon."

"Any day now." No more stalling. He'd just come out and say it." Reverend, it's about my Father's—"

"Have you considered what I said about the christening?" Reverend Welby fidgeted in the pew.

Samuel shrank inside. No matter how he avoided it, this conflict kept finding him.

"You must raise your child as a Protestant."

This damned baptism was diverting him from discussing his guilt . . . but reverend was right. He must raise his child in the faith the Kingstons had always followed. But Sofia was adamant about a Catholic baptism, and he'd grown tired of the argument, tired of tiptoeing around it like a warhorse in the drawing room.

He tilted forward; hands draped limply over the pew in front of him. "She knows I'm devoted to our church . . . how much my religion means to me, but Catholic doctrine is clear and demanding. We're at an impasse, and it's a contentious one."

The reverend raised his eyebrows.

"I've been out of sorts since returning from the war in Nicaragua." Samuel fidgeted with his worn bible.

The reverend frowned at the tattered bible. "We're talking about the baby's baptism here, not a war on the other side of the world." Samuel hadn't mistreated the good book; it had belonged to Mother and was a reminder of he carried on all his travels. It had been with him on every campaign.

"I'll have a word with Sofia, Reverend." Another thing to worry about, but now he'd ask for help with his feelings about Father; he might never pluck up the courage to do it again. "But I came to you to ask about my guilt for causing Father's death; it's unbearable. Everything reminds me of him—the land, the house, the monument Jason built for him . . . all are reminders that I failed him . . . that he died alone in Nicaragua when I should have saved him. And now this conflict over religion . . . I can't bear to lose Sofia too."

Reverend Welby's bushy eyebrows wormed together, and his features softened. "You can't blame yourself for John's death. That's on Lord Baltimore. But if you fail to save this baby's soul, that's on you."

"But I-I don't want—I mean, it's not my choice to raise our child this way, but I hardly think a baby's soul—"

Reverend Welby stopped tapping his fingers on the back of the pew in front of him. “I’m sure your young wife’s better than most, but Catholics are suspicious, indolent people. They worship false idols . . . saints.” Reverend Welby’s hands curled. “And their Virgin Mary . . . Can you fathom that for paganism? If you allow them to claim this innocent soul, you’ll both be denied the joys of heaven.”

This was eighteen eighty-six. Samuel seriously doubted that he was responsible for sending anyone to hell, but the reverend sounded so certain. Could he really be jeopardizing his unborn child’s soul? He covered his face with his hands. “I love her so much, but I love the Lord too. I don’t know what to do.”

The reverend placed a hand on his shoulder. “I believe you do, my son, and you’ll make the correct decision.”

Samuel peered through his fingers.

“I’ll pray for you.”

CHAPTER TWO

Rings swished across the curtain rail, and daylight flooded Samuel's gummy eyes.

"You're not going to lie here all day again?"

Another *whoosh* as Sofia opened the curtains of the second bay window. He groaned and pulled the covers over his head. He just wanted to stay in bed today . . . to be alone.

Her hard boots clacked along the wooden floor in quick steps approaching the bed. "So tell me, Samuel, what did you say to Father Mulcahy? Some parish priest he is, refusing to baptize our baby without your consent."

Of course, Father Mulcahy had to back him, after Samuel had delivered a ton of Father's grain to the starving refugees at the workhouse in Skibbereen in the height of the famine. One baby's soul was a small price to repay Father's support of Catholic peasants back in those terrible times. Samuel squeezed his eyes tightly. But now he faced another argument about the baby's religion. It never ended.

"Our child will be born in two months, and God forbid something should happen to it before it's baptized. Do you want our baby to end up in limbo?"

The Romish Doctrine concerning purgatory and limbo is a fond thing, Reverend Welby had told him, *but rather repugnant to the Word of God.* Samuel turned his face away. Such vainly invented beliefs didn't come from the scripture, and they made him uncomfortable. She had no right to muddle his child with them. "Limbo! There's no such place as limbo; that's a ridiculous notion. It's unreasonable not to consider my right to raise the child as a Protestant."

The atmosphere chilled.

"Unreasonable?" she switched to her native Spanish as she always did when she was angry.

He shouldn't have said anything at all. Now they would argue, when all he wanted to do was curl up and sleep again.

"This is not a nicety; it's the law of my church." Sofia picked his socks off the floor. "I'm going to ask you again, Samuel. What did you say to Father Mulcahy?"

"Nothing. We've not met in ages."

"And yet he refuses to baptize our baby without your agreement." She flipped through the pairs of trousers hanging in the closet "You'd best talk to him and sort this out."

He sat up and gathered the bedclothes about him. "Perhaps Father Mulcahy's hesitant because the family has helped him out in the past, when we delivered grain to the poorhouse during the famine. But you and I, Sofia, must come to an agreement. I've rights—"

"You drag me over here to a strange country and demand that I raise my child as a heathen? I've a good mind—"

"Sofia, Sofia . . . Not now. I don't feel well. I don't wish to discuss this now." He collapsed back onto the pillow.

Petticoats rustled as she tossed his trousers onto the bed and sat beside them. The haze of rose-scented woman stirred him despite their conflict. "You never want to discuss it. Get out of bed. Filipe will be here any minute, and I don't want him to see you like this."

He'd forgotten her brother arrived today. He closed his eyes.

"I'll see him tomorrow. He'll be here for months, and I need rest now."

"He looks up to you, and you better not disappoint him."

Another reminder of Nicaragua, the place he was desperate to forget. She stooped to kiss him, and he turned away, curling his fingers in the blanket as he drew it up to his neck.

She lunged off the bed. "What's the matter with you? You haven't put a hand on me in months." She touched her swollen belly. "Is it this? You think I'm ugly now?"

He was being unfair. "Of course not, my love. You're beautiful, and with child, you're perfectly radiant."

She plucked at her skirts. "But something's bothering you. All you do is sit in the drawing room and stare at the sea. Or you hide in your bedroom. At least get up so Molly can tidy the room."

He groaned.

"Samuel! You stink. Get up and bathe. I'm tired of living like this." She slammed the door behind her.

He sat up, hating himself. She didn't deserve this—none of them did. He had to get up.

Get up, then.

He threw his bare legs over the mattress. The wooden floor was smooth and cold on the soles of his feet. She was right: The bedroom stank of stale whiskey, cigarettes, and sweat.

He slinked out of bed and padded to the bathroom where Peadar, the footman, was filling the bath.

"There you are, Master Samuel, nice and hot, just as you like it." The veteran soldier looked at Samuel's four-day stubble and tutted. "Would you like a shave, sir? And those bags under your eyes . . . I could fetch a cold—"

"No need," Samuel snapped. "Clear off and leave me in peace."

But the bath did little to ease the ache in his left leg, a constant reminder of the Crimean War in '84. Hard to believe it had been two years now—the memories, the pain, the regrets made it seem like yesterday. Stropping the razor was too much bother; he viciously scraped the stubble from his chin, missing a spot or two, and climbed from the tub, sloshing a gallon of water across the wooden floor, vaguely aware of hooves clattering up the driveway.

His breeches were too tight to button, and the next pair didn't fit either. He flopped back on the bed and stared at the cornice. A boy's laugher tinkled up from the courtyard, and he threw an arm over his eyes. Filipe was a good kid; he'd make an effort to welcome the lad. Besides, Sofia would be angry if he didn't come down. The only breeches that fit were the ones crumpled on the floor. He dragged them on. Sofia would berate him for wearing rags. Why did he need to dress up? He never left the house anymore.

He reached under the mattress for his tobacco and rolled an uneven cigarette. He scored a lucifer with his thumbnail and squinted at the smoke as he took a deep drag. The smoke burned his lungs and made him cough. Christ, when would he get the hang of it? He blew out a stream of smoke. Yes, he needed that. It took time to finish dressing; everything took longer these days. Finally, he pulled on his slippers and shambled onto the landing.

Averting his eyes from Father's portrait over the stairs, he winced at the lilting brogue drifting up from below. He didn't want to face Padraig's concerned expression; he didn't want to see any of them. He'd have to find an excuse to escape dinner early. Damned Fred Kiernan, the bugger needed to get moving and finish the new house. Samuel was pouring money into it, but the walls were rising no quicker. They needed to move out of Springbough; he longed for the quiet of his own space.

He paused in the dining room doorway. Even with the purple saber scar across his nose, Padraig was still handsome. His unruly mop of straw-colored hair and freckled face assured his popularity with girls, and he certainly took advantage of that. At twenty-two years old, he was the same age as Samuel, but he looked almost as young as fifteen-year-old Filipe, seated beside him at the dining room table.

Filipe had Sofia's honey-colored eyes, and they brightened when he caught Samuel dithering in the doorway. He jumped to his feet and dragged a hand through his black hair. "Samuel, *felicidades* on your marriage. *Ahora somos familia*—now I'm related to the hero of the Battle of La Virgen."

Filipe spoke Castilian, the language of the Spanish elite and unusual for a Nicaraguan, but not surprising, as his father owned one of the largest haciendas in Central America. He also spoke English perfectly.

Samuel waved a hand. "Hero, my backside. We won that battle for the wrong faction. I should have shot Walker, not fought for him. Nicaragua would be far better off." He trudged to his chair. "Not my problem anymore. The lot of them can drown in the San Juan River, for all I care."

Filipe's eyes narrowed. "What do you mean? Papa says William Walker's a visionary. He will make Nicaragua greater than—"

"Poppycock!" Padraig said with a sneer. "That leech will enslave every one of you and—"

Sofia's silverware clunked on her plate. "*Por favor*, no politics. Let's enjoy our lunch, Filipe. And you're in Ireland now; practice your English."

Samuel shrugged. Padraig's father, Jerry Kerr, had fought with the Royal Irish Dragoons in the Peninsular Wars and met his wife in Talavera. He'd managed the Kingston estate for years, and when Samuel's mother had died in childbirth, María had nursed Samuel along with Padraig, who was a month younger than he was. She'd raised the boys to be fluent in both English and Spanish, and the conversation could continue in either language as far as Samuel was concerned. In fact, he'd prefer no talk at all.

Padraig fiddled with his teaspoon. "How are you, Samuel? I see little of you these days."

Samuel twisted his wedding ring and looked out the open window at the paddock.

"Are you dodging me?" Padraig grinned. "We must go hunting again. Your mare's getting fat."

Poor Belle. Perhaps Filipe could exercise her. The sea breeze fluttered the curtains with a pungent twang of seaweed and salt. "Been terribly busy around here."

"Jason and Dad are in the stables, and Mam's fussing in the kitchen. Apparently, no food's good enough for Sofia's little brother. She'll drive the cook crazy." Padraig rolled his eyes then peered more closely at Samuel. "You all right?"

"Course I am. Why wouldn't I be?"

Sofia tugged at her green blouse and looked away.

How could Padraig be so dense? Father lay in a jungle grave half a world away, and he knew it was Samuel's fault. He had to know what was wrong.

But Padraig nattered on. "Filipe is telling us about the war. When Costa Rica declared war on Walker's filibusters back in November, I thought President Mora was all talk. Costa Rica is a fart of a country with a population of fewer than one hundred and twelve thousand people."

Of course, know-it-all Padraig would have that fact on the tip of his tongue. Samuel didn't care about Costa Rica. He glanced at Sofia, pouring more tea for her brother. He'd better not slip away early, not if he wanted peace that evening.

Filipe shoveled a third spoonful of sugar into his tea. The Nicaraguans were gluttons for the stuff. "Papa said Costa Rica wants to seize control of the San Juan River. If the Costas build the canal, they'll get the profits instead of us. That's why President Mora marched four thousand men into Nicaragua and captured Rivas."

"I'll bet that pissed Walker off." Padraig swirled the red wine in his crystal glass.

"Of course not," Filipe said. "Nothing scares General Walker.

He counterattacked, but he hadn't a hope with six hundred men against two thousand Costas."

"The Costa Ricans control the south now?" Padraig looked ridiculous as he put down his wine and lifted a china teacup, pinching the fragile handle between a beefy finger and thumb.

Filipe puffed out his chest. "No way. They drove us back, but we slaughtered eight hundred of them as we retreated. Walker's *yanquis* know how to fight. Papa says we'll take Rivas because disease drove the Costa Ricans back to their own country."

"Oh, the cholera," Padraig said.

"It decimated the Costa garrisons in San Juan del Sur, Rivas, and La Virgen, and it forced President Mora to retreat. They won't come back." Filipe raised his chin. "Every day, more volunteers arrive from the United States to reinforce Walker. If the Costas return, we'll hammer them."

Samuel grimaced and looked out the window. Walker may have hoodwinked Colonel Valle and Filipe, but it wasn't his problem anymore. He felt Padraig's eyes on him and looked up. His childhood friend was, indeed, observing him. Padraig better not start fussing again.

"The disease has been a terrible burden for our people," Sofia said soberly.

"Hundreds of Costa Ricans died from cholera while waiting for ships in San Juan, and only five hundred made it home." Filipe chortled and slapped the table. "The joke was on President Mora. His men brought the disease back to Costa Rica, and it killed another ten thousand people there. He won't be in such a hurry to invade us again."

"Enough!" Samuel pushed away his plate. "I'm tired of hearing about Nicaragua."

Filipe's grin wavered, and his eyes bounced from his sister to Padraig. "I was only explaining how we were the ones who really beat the Costa Ricans, not the other way around, as the American newspapers reported. Papa said it was all part of Walker's genius plan to lure them to their deaths. We were the deciding force."

Sofia's lips curled. "'We'? What do you mean, 'we'?"

"Papa allowed me to fight with Colonel Machado's company," Filipe said. "I wish I'd been with the Americans. That coward Machado fled the plaza as soon as the Costa Ricans fired on us."

Sofia bit back an exclamation and clasped both hands tightly in her lap. "Why's Father still supporting Walker? He knows Walker intends to repeal the abolition of slavery."

"That's propaganda," Filipe said. "Walker's considering a form of indentured servitude to get the country back on its feet, but it'll only be temporary."

Samuel glanced at Sofia. Her nostrils flared as she stared at her plate.

"And what then?" Padraig asked.

"Father says we must support Walker against the traitors who've invited every country in Central America to invade us."

Sofia huffed. "Then they've tricked you, little brother. Father supports Walker out of fear he'll lose his estates if Walker falls."

"That's not true!"

"It most assuredly is," she replied. "What do you think, Samuel?"

"We're safe here in Ireland." Samuel looked at his hands. "I don't care what happens over there. Change the topic."

Padraig looked down at his plate, and Sofia shook her head. They ate to the hollow tick of the clock for an awkward minute.

Filipe turned his attention to Padraig. "Do you really have a steamboat or were you teasing me on the ride down from Cork?"

Padraig bumped him with his shoulder. "I do. I called her the *San Carlos*, because I used some of Walker's gold to purchase her."

Filipe hooted. "I can't believe you robbed a fortune in gold from the filibusters. That makes us enemies." He grinned mischievously.

But taking the gold hadn't stopped Walker; the man had nine

lives. Samuel slammed his cup down on the saucer. "No more about that, please, Filipe. I'm serious."

Filipe shrugged. "So how big is your steamboat, Padraig?"

"Sixty feet long, big enough to motor far offshore for the big catch." Padraig pointed to the sun-speckled sea beyond the paddocks. "Hundreds of years back, when the O'Driscoll clan ruled in West Cork, they made a fortune from the sea. This boat will change how fishing's done in these parts. If it works, I'll buy a fleet of them."

Sofia murmured something approving behind her napkin.

"Yes, we should go see!" Filipe twisted to his sister. "Can we go out on his boat? Please?"

"We could take her out tomorrow, if you wish," Padraig said.

Filipe looked at Samuel. "Will you come along? You must. It'll be great fun."

Samuel pushed back from the table with a grunt. Filipe's arrival was a raw reminder that Father's body lay in a lonely grave far from home. "I've things to do."

He ignored the disapproving eyes that followed him as he dropped his napkin beside his plate and slouched from the dining room. He would retreat to his ledgers. At least the numbers wouldn't prattle endlessly of the past.

But weeks later, Samuel wasn't so sure the numbers hadn't aligned to plot against him too. He groaned and looked up from the ledger. Rows and rows, with hardly a difference between them. It was so confusing. Outside, another June day panted beneath the clear blue sky. Christ, it was sweltering. With all the money the builder was spending on the new manor, it should've been finished, yet they hadn't even started on the roof.

It was almost ten by the clock over the fireplace. He'd summoned the builder, Fred Kiernan, who should've been here by now. Kiernan had better have a good reason for the additional expenditures and be able to present a convincing plan for getting construction back on track.

The whack of wooden swords and intermittent grunts coming from outside were most distracting. Did Padraig have to train Filipe in the courtyard? He'd told them to ride to Oak Tree field for that. Jesus, they were giving him a headache.

Filipe's high-pitched squeal of laughter, piercing like a needle, was the last straw. Samuel flung his pen onto the ledger, spitting turquoise ink across the ranks of numbers. He couldn't work like this; he'd put a stop to these ridiculous antics.

He stalked downstairs, unmoved by the aroma of fresh-baked bread from the kitchen and sparing no greeting for Cookie as she bent over the cast iron cookstove, and stepped into the yard.

White shirts clinging to their sweating bodies, Padraig and Filipe advanced and retreated across the worn flagstones with dancing steps, thrusting and warding with the heavy wooden sabers Samuel had used as a child. Fencing and riding every day since he'd arrived nearly a month ago had added muscle to Filipe's gangly frame. He stamped forward and cut at Padraig. Padraig warded off the blow and sent his saber whistling down at Filipe's knee. Filipe blocked. The boy had fast hands.

Padraig dangled his blade between them. "Come on, get past me."

Filipe grinned and slashed at Padraig's horizontal blade. Padraig twisted his wrist, and Filipe missed his saber.

"Not fair!" Filipe skipped back a step. "How did you do that?"

Padraig's blade was already back in between them. "I'm watching your eyes. You signaled that move. Try again."

Filipe brushed his long black hair from his forehead and hacked at Padraig's suspended blade again. Padraig dipped his wrist, and Filipe's blade missed. Filipe gave up that move and attacked with rapid slashes, high and low, and the ash weapons thunked as they cut and parried.

A weight settled inside Samuel. This was a waste of time. All his weapons training and seven years of campaign experience hadn't saved Father when it mattered. This was vanity.

"Padraig, I told you to train in the Oak Tree field." He knew he shouldn't be so petty, but they should've respected his wishes, damn it. "I can't concentrate with that racket. If you dislike the Oak Tree field, you'd think you could find somewhere secluded on a fifteen-hundred-acre estate."

Padraig's jaw fell slack as the fencers halted. "This is where you and I always practiced."

Typical. Samuel crossed his arms. "I don't care."

Padraig lowered his saber and took a step closer. "You've been acting like a wasp since . . ." He flicked a glance at Filipe and returned his eyes to Samuel. "Look, can we talk? I need to—"

Wheels rumbled and tack jingled down the driveway as a gray mare pulled a two-wheel trap into sight. Samuel tilted his head at the diversion. He didn't need to chitchat with Padraig.

"There's Kiernan at last," he said. "Late, as usual. Be good fellows and train elsewhere."

He hoped they would move off as he rounded the house to greet the driver who dismounted and left the mare in the care of Mickey Spillane. Samuel had known Fred Kiernan for the last fifteen years, and he never seemed to age. He looked forty, but he could've been anywhere between thirty and sixty.

Samuel shook hands. "Mr. Kiernan, thanks for coming."

"Good morning, sir." Kiernan broke eye contact.

"I hope you bring good news about the progress," Samuel said. "I'm eager for my child to grow up in its own home, out from under his uncle's feet."

Kiernan opened his mouth but closed it again.

Samuel steeled himself for a round of excuses. "Is something the matter?"

"I've received an alarming note from Boyd, manager at the Trustee Saving Bank."

Kiernan gulped and rubbed his chin. "Your bank has refused to honor your last money order."

Samuel's skin tingled from the back of his neck across his face. "Are you certain?"

"I'm sure it's some mistake," Kiernan agreed. "But I must be paid."

"It's an error. I assure you, I've more than ample funds." He, Sofia, and Padraig had stolen a fortune in gold Louis Greenfell that his aristocrat cronies had sent to Walker in return for the filibuster's promise of vast estates in Nicaragua and his promise to allow the use of slaves to work the land—money meant to fund Walker's filthy war.

Kiernan drew a letter from the breast pocket of his rumpled overcoat. "Here, read it for yourself if you like."

Samuel skimmed the letter, his finger tapping energetically. Sure enough, the bank said his funds were unavailable.

"I'd like to help you out, Mr. Kingston, truly I would," Kiernan said, "but if I'm not compensated, I must stop working on your home. I've expenses. Men to pay."

This was preposterous. Samuel was the richest man in Clonakilty now. "No need for that. I'm sure it's a stupid mistake." He glanced at his pocket watch. "Ten thirty. I'll ride to Cork and sort this out. You must keep your men at work."

Kiernan showed his palms and shrugged. "These are tough times, Mr. Kingston."

Samuel sighed and pinched his nose between his fingers. How was this possible? He still had close to two hundred thousand pounds in the bank, enough to buy half of West Cork. "I promise you'll have your payment this very evening."

"I'll stay on the job until tomorrow, but if it's not sorted by then, we must stop."

"Look, this is nonsense." Samuel grabbed Kiernan's sleeve. "Even if there were some bizarre issue at the bank, my brother's credit—"

"The entire county knows there's a hefty lien on Springbough Manor." Kiernan shook Samuel's hand off and stepped toward his trap. "Your brother's in no position to help you."

"Jason's affairs are none of yours, sir. Your business is with me. If you don't work on my home, I'll find somebody else."

Kiernan opened the door to the trap, and his face slackened. "Sorry, Mr. Kingston. Everyone's struggling since the famine, and I've a family to feed. As you say, it's probably a mix-up by the banker in Cork. I'll wait until tomorrow."

"Very well."

"I wish you luck in the city. Good day to you."

Padraig and Filipe were still watching as the builder cracked his whip and the trap lurched away.

Samuel waved his hand. "It's nothing. Get on about your business. Filipe, before you go, please ask Mickey to saddle Belle. I must ride to Cork."

"I'll come with you," Padraig said. "You won't reach town until late afternoon, so you'll have to ride home in the dark, and the roads aren't safe these days. Not with highway men roaming the county."

A ten-hour inquisition was the last thing Samuel needed. "I'll be fine."

"Let me come, please?" Filipe asked.

"You should stay with Padraig."

"Please? I want to see the city."

"I said no." Samuel spun on his heel. First the damned bank, and now Filipe.

Padraig drew him aside. "What is it, really? You've not been the same for months . . . since Nicaragua, in fact."

Samuel had heard it all before, from Sofia, from Jason, and from Emily. He shook his head. "Nothing . . . Nothing. I prefer to ride alone. Jesus, I survived the Charge of the Light Brigade and fought one thousand Nicaraguans in Rivas. You think I can't handle a highwayman?"

Padraig didn't look at him but gave a small nod and strode

back to Filipe. "That's enough for today. We'll go to the Oak Tree field tomorrow."

Filipe appeared at Samuel's elbow as he stalked toward the main house. "Please take me with you. I've never seen the city. Padraig plucked me off the steamer in Queenstown and hustled me here."

Samuel kept his eyes on the cobblestones. "It's not his fault. I told him to bring you directly here."

"But—"

"You can't come. Go clean up, Filipe. You're a sweaty mess."

Belle threw up her head and whickered a greeting, her mane shimmering like coal in the sunlight.

Samuel hugged her wet muzzle. "Sorry, old girl. I've been neglecting you."

He nodded to Mickey Spillane and mounted.

"She's as fit as a fiddle, Master Samuel. "Mistress Sofia exercises her every day, even in the rain."

Samuel's eyes narrowed. Was that some sort of admonition? He feigned a smile. "Thanks. Tell Mistress Sofia I'll be back some time tonight."

The sun's warmth was a stranger on his face, but he forgot his woes as he reveled in the smooth rhythm of Belle's gait in the summer air. The sleek mare needed no guidance as they trotted westward around Clonakilty Bay, where the sea, calm and blue, and the flooding tide spat tiny silver-crested wavelets onto the gray sand. Gulls wheeled in the cloudless sky and hurled their high-pitched cries into the balmy air. The hedgerows sagged with juicy blackberries, ripe for the picking, and the last of the yellow daffodils waved farewell from the fields.

Samuel looked to the rolling green pastures and fields of ripening crops and sighed. He loved Springbough Manor, but it was time to leave the nest. Even together, the three farms he bought with the Nicaraguan gold were small compared to Springbough Manor's estate, and his home would be smaller too. The new estate would be infinitely more secure than Springbough, and that was what mattered. The outer walls would be ten feet high, and double steel gates would guard both entrances. His family would be well protected, so important now that the baby was coming.

A baby . . . If it was a boy, would he be six feet tall and broad-shouldered like his father? He'd certainly have a dark complexion, for Sofia's silken skin was the color of honey and Samuel was dark as a Spaniard. *Eyes as dark as a pint of Guinness*, Cousin William used to jest. *Black Irish*. But the baby might have Sofia's—

A sixth sense honed by years of combat raised the hair on the nape of his neck. He was being followed. He glanced over his shoulder. The rutted road was empty, but that prickle in his scalp was a warning. He halted Belle, dismounted, and feigned tightening his girth to steal a glance behind him.

Back where the boughs of beech trees arched across the road, shaking hands, a rider trotted into the sunlight-flecked tunnel, then hastily backed out of sight. Samuel's heart skipped a beat. He mounted and spurred Belle down the road. Half a mile ahead, the laneway leading to the ruined cottage would offer a hiding place.

He reined in at the ruined building and moved closer, where thorny bushes laden with blackberries smothered the entrance. He prodded Belle behind the briars, petting her warm, damp neck. The warhorse was a real jewel. She would remain quiet.

Hoofbeats grew louder, and Samuel rose in the saddle. His Navy Colt was locked away at home, damn it, now that he'd sworn not to bear arms again. Not after Nicaragua. If this was a highwayman, his only defense would be surprise—and Belle. The clever Jerry Kerr had trained her to bite and fight.

Harness jingling, a familiar chestnut mare ambled into sight, her rider's face shadowed beneath a wide-brimmed hat.

Samuel released his pent-up breath. “Filipe!”

Filipe flinched in the saddle, reached under his frock coat, and halted. “Samuel?”

“Bloody hell, what are you doing?” Samuel nudged Belle onto the road. “Following me?”

Filipe’s hand flickered back to the reins. “I want to go to Cork. I thought if I trailed behind a while, you would relent.”

“You shouldn’t have come.” Samuel brushed away a fly and looked back down the empty road. “These roads aren’t safe for a foreigner. Robbers would kill you for Goldie, and Sofia will be furious you took her mare.”

“Please don’t send me back.”

“God damn you, I don’t need this distraction,” Samuel snarled. If anything happened to the boy, he’d never forgive himself, and he’d endured enough of that shade of guilt already. He spurred Belle ahead without waiting for an answer. “Fall in, then, but don’t let me hear your nattering the entire way to Cork. Mark my words, you’ll pay for this when we get back tonight.”

The offices of Allen and Norton, the Kingston family’s solicitors in Cork City, enshrouded its occupants in an aura of old parchment, leather bindings, and dust.

Peter Norton plucked at his gray pork chop sideburns and gave Samuel a deep sigh. “There is nothing we can do. The Earl of Lucan is the legally appointed representative of the Nicaraguan government here, and his claim states you stole that gold from them. The magistrate insists the bank freezes those funds until the court addresses the dispute. I can—”

“William Walker is not the Nicaraguan government,” Samuel said. “He’s little more than a pirate that the Democrats were foolish enough to hire for their civil war, and now he pulls the strings of the puppet president, Patricio Rivas.”

Norton looked at him blankly.

Samuel dragged a hand through his hair. It was impossible. No one in Ireland had ever heard of Nicaragua, never mind the civil war.

Norton raised his eyebrows. "Perhaps if you gave some background, I could help."

Samuel stilled his foot tapping under the table. This wasn't Norton's fault. "Everything I say is confidential? Strictly between us?"

"Of course." Norton tapped his forehead. "Every word goes into the vault."

"Good." Samuel looked at the door. "Nicaragua's location in Central America, with a narrow isthmus dividing the Caribbean from the Pacific Ocean, makes it the fastest route between the East and West Coasts of the United States. You may have heard of it for that reason."

Norton shrugged vaguely.

"The opposing political parties there are the Democrats and the Legitimists, like the Whigs and Tories here. I can't see much difference between their policies. I think they're fighting to control the wealth. One faction will conquer a district, then confiscate the land from their opponents."

He took out his tobacco tin. "Three years ago, when the Democrat Party candidate won the election for the position of supreme director, the Legitimists claimed election fraud. Civil war broke out. The Democrats invited William Walker to raise an army of American volunteers to fight for them, but they brought a cuckoo into the nest, for Walker believes in manifest destiny. He planned to annex Nicaragua and add it to the United States, just like Texas, but once he tasted power, he grew determined to take it for himself."

Samuel finished rolling his cigarette and paused to lick the paper.

"The expectations for responsible men of leadership are

evidently different there and, dare I say, a bit backward," Norton said with a sniff. "Not like here."

"Oh, there's plenty like here over there," Samuel said. "Walker partnered with a British consortium, mainly Anglo-Irish aristocrats, including the Earl of Baltimore—Louis Greenfell—the Earl of Lucan, and the Earl of Sligo. Some British, too. Lord Paget, for example."

Norton's face crumpled. "That can't be. These are reputable men, powerful men. You mustn't say such things. What—"

"I have proof," Samuel said. "Baltimore framed Father for treason. You'll remember that?"

"Of course I do, but what has that to do with—" Norton's eyes bulged. "Oh, so the rumor is true."

Samuel raised an eyebrow.

"You killed Lord Baltimore?" Norton asked.

Samuel's hands curled together. "He kidnapped Father and dragged him off to Nicaragua. Father died alone, devastated by cholera." And if Samuel had acted faster, Father would still be alive today.

Norton put his palms on the table. "So, you killed Greenfell?"

"Yes." Samuel rummaged in his pocket for matches. "But in a fair fight after I learned he kidnapped Father. I had to stop him delivering a fortune in gold to Walker."

"Why would Greenfell give gold to Walker?" Norton's eyes flicked to the door. No wonder, such intrigue never happened in Cork.

"Greenfell and his crony lords sent three hundred thousand dollars to Walker in Nicaragua to fund—"

"Three hundred thousand dollars!" Norton tugged his jacket firmly in place. "That's a king's ransom; you could buy up half the county."

Samuel's ears reddened. Norton made him sound crooked. "Listen. They paid Walker that gold in return for his promise to give them thousands of acres of land confiscated from the legitimate owners. In short, they tried to steal a country. Worse, the wretches insisted that Walker abolish the slavery ban so they could bring slaves from Africa and turn the native population into thralls later. Walker planned to use that gold to fund his war, so I confiscated it to stop him."

Norton scoffed. "That can't be so. Good men of the union would never—"

"I have their correspondence."

Norton sat back to absorb this information. "So you discovered what they were about, and that's when you went after the lot of them?"

Samuel nodded curtly. "I turned on Walker, even though I knew it might cause Father's death." He lit his cigarette and dragged on it. There it was, the truth. Father had died because of Samuel's high-and-mighty principles.

"You took the gold, sold it, and deposited the money in the bank." Norton gave a small yelp. "That's why Lucan and the others are helping Walker come after you . . . but why now? Why not a year ago?"

"I already threatened to publish my evidence of their involvement in this land theft and slavery if they moved against me. That frightened them, especially Lucan, which is why I'm puzzled why he's acting now." Samuel sagged back in the seat. "What can you do? That's my money, the spoils of war. You're my solicitor. It's urgent you get it back for me." He stabbed a finger at the documents on the table. "I need access to my funds to pay the builder for expenses, and there's the matter of the debts on Springbough. I promised Jason I'd settle those."

"I'll get to work on it." Norton gathered the documents into a neat pile. "But in the interim, you must find another way to cover your expenses. The court can tie up your funds for years."

"But I don't have another source of income. I resigned my commission in the Seventeenth Lancers," Samuel said. "You know my affairs, you know that. They'll come after Jason and Springbough now too. I need that money back."

"Lord Lucan is a powerful man. We may not win against him."

Samuel drummed his fingers on the polished desk. One thing at a time. "How long can we stall the debt on the estate?"

Norton wiped his glistening brow with a silk handkerchief. "Baltimore's heir is a young rake from Sussex named Bentley. I know nothing more about him, but he should take title within the next twelve months. I'd guess he'll call in the debt on Springbough then."

Samuel shook his head. "This will devastate Jason. I assured him I'd clear the debt as soon as Baltimore's heir showed up."

"That can't be too far away now, I'm afraid."

Samuel slammed a fist onto the desk. "That bastard Baltimore still haunts me from the grave." He rose decisively. "Contact Lucan. Tell him I'll send Baltimore's papers to the London Times unless he releases my money. He and his conspirators won't survive the scandal."

"The Baltimore papers?" Norton's eyebrows shot up.

"My wife found the incriminating correspondence—their references to buying stolen land and bringing back slavery—in Baltimore's possession, that's why I call the evidence the Baltimore papers."

Norton rose as well, fussing with his pince-nez glasses. "My God, you're playing a dangerous—"

"I've held these papers as insurance against exactly this event. Now it's time to put them to work. Do it."

Filipe sprang up from his seat in Norton's reception room and followed Samuel. "May we walk around now? I want to go into that fancy hotel where we stabled the horses—the Imperial, is it?"

Samuel ignored him and stalked in the direction of the stables. The little pest should've stayed in Clonakilty.

"Samuel? Can't we go see? I'd like to tour the city."

"We're going home," Samuel said. "The horses have only had two hours' rest, but that must suffice. If we leave now, we'll still have daylight most of the way."

"But we're right here—"

Samuel's scowl silenced the boy.

Once clear of the carts rumbling into town to the markets, Samuel held the horses to a steady pace. Why would Lucan choose to move against him now? He knew Samuel still possessed the Earl of Baltimore's papers, outlining their plan to revoke the 1826 act abolishing slavery and buy African "apprentices" from the French colonies. Publication of that correspondence would ruin Lucan. Why would he move against Samuel with those risks at stake?

As the last light leaked from the evening sky two hours later, he took the lonely road to Clonakilty after passing through Bandon Town. Still ruminating on his troubles, he scratched the back of his head; the swarms of tiny midges were as irritating as mosquitoes. Filipe sulked beside him. He hadn't spoken since they left Cork. Samuel shifted in the saddle to ease his stiff thighs. This was the first time he'd ridden a long distance in months, and damnation, he was out of condition.

A masked rider burst from a gap in the briars ahead with a pistol in hand, its muzzle a black dot aimed at Samuel's breast. "Halt, or I'll shoot!"

Hooves drummed on the road behind them, and Samuel craned around. A broad-shouldered man in a top hat had ridden from behind the ditch to block their escape.

Samuel raised his hands slowly. It was hopeless to resist.

The man in the top hat rode closer. "Can't believe we took the great Captain Kingston so easily." He snorted and waved his pistol. "Off yer horses, both of yous." The scarf covering his nose and mouth muffled his speech.

They clearly knew him, but Samuel didn't recognize the voices at all. "What do you want? I've—"

"Shut you yourself up and dismount," Top Hat roared. "You too, boy. Who the hell are you? Billy, yous said he'd be alone."

This was no random robbery. Samuel looked about for more men or other travelers.

Filipe spat in the mud. "Go to hell. I'll do nothing for you."

Billy lunged forward and struck Filipe across the face, knocking him from the saddle. Filipe hit the dirt with a thud.

These men meant to kill them. The scene about to unfold flashed before Samuel's eyes. He'd failed once more to protect his own family: first Father, now Filipe.

Samuel caught the acrid stench of Billy's body odor as the highwayman dismounted and approached Filipe.

"Don't harm the boy." Samuel swung down for the saddle. "I'll do whatever you ask."

"Kill them, now," Top Hat said. "The others will soon finish their raid on the manor."

Filipe rolled onto his back, and flame lit the dusk as a pistol blazed in his hand. Billy crumpled to the ground and dropped his own pistol. Samuel lunged for it.

Scooping up Billy's pistol, Samuel shot Top Hat in the head, and the highwayman tumbled out of the saddle with a grunt.

Filipe was frozen two feet away with a smoking pistol, lips quivering, slowly sweeping his head right and left. Top Hat was prone on the ground; a cup of blood leaking from the hole in his head.

Samuel stooped over Billy, who was moaning in the mud. There was a black stain on his shirt, and the smell of coppery blood wrinkled Samuel's nose. It was a fatal wound. "Who sent you?"

Billy's blue eyes dulled.

Samuel shook him roughly. "Who sent you?"

Blood dribbled from the corner of Billy's lips, and he coughed. He clutched Samuel's hand feebly, and his eyes glazed over. He was gone; Samuel would get no answer here.

Suddenly cold inside, Samuel whirled on Filipe. "Where did you get that pistol?"

"I told you, I'm a soldier just like you," Filipe said. "I brought it with me."

A fifteen-year-old soldier. Just what they needed. "Jesus, you're your sister's brother."

Filipe turned away and vomited.

Samuel's mind raced. This was no random highway robbery, and the one in the top hat had said there were more of them at the house. He tugged Filipe's sleeve. "We must go. Hurry, reload the pistols. Search for a cartridge box."

Warm blood smeared Samuel's hand as he lifted a cartridge box slung under Billy's coat. He loaded Billy's pistol deftly and shoved it into his belt.

He glanced at Filipe. The boy's hands were trembling, and he was spilling powder as he poured it down the barrel of his pistol. Samuel took the pistol and finished reloading it, all the while firing glances to the west. His family could be in danger that very moment.

Belle stood patiently waiting, but the other horses had disappeared during the fracas. Samuel shoved the second pistol in his belt. "Wait here. I'll be back for you."

"But, Samuel, I can help!"

No time for that; the boy would be safer here on the road than getting in the way of whatever was happening at home. Samuel vaulted into the saddle and heeled Belle into a mile-eating canter, panting and cursing his lack of fitness. It was still an hour's ride to the manor.

Please, God, let me be in time.

Darkness hid the ruts in the road. Belle could trip and break a leg. He clicked his tongue as the nimble mare stretched out, her muscles flexing under him as clods and gravel flew from her hooves. Dusk faded to night while they hurtled through shards of moonlight that stabbed through the trees, his worst nightmare unfolding in his imagination. He'd caused Father's death, and now he was about to fail the rest of his family.

Belle snorted like a bellows as she crested a hilltop. Orange flames flickered against the inky sky north of the moonlit bay.

Springbough Manor was burning.

CHAPTER THREE

Vultures soared and wheeled between the church spires of Rivas, sunrise pinking their wingtips like a bloody omen. Colonel Benjamin Fry shifted on his haunches to ease the cramps in his legs and strained to hear anything besides melodious bird calls and leaves crunching as forty-nine men wearing the blue hatbands of William Walker's Army of Nicaragua slid through the undergrowth. Most were recent volunteers from America—failed gold prospectors, veterans of the Mexican American War, farmers, townsfolk, even two Texas Rangers. Men between the ages of fourteen and fifty-odd, all risking their lives for the promise of five hundred dollars a month and five hundred acres of land once Walker won control of Nicaragua.

He scrubbed a grimy hand across his face. But many of them could be dead before the sun rose again. Nothing was going as planned. It was the tenth of April already, and the Costa Ricans still had the upper hand. Their president himself, Juan Mora, had invaded the Nicaraguan town of Santa Rosa with three thousand men. But if Fry could snatch the president from his temporary headquarters in the town, Walker could force the Costa Ricans to surrender.

A squirrel's chatter in the tree overhead snapped Fry back

into the undergrowth with the prickly leaves and insect bites. The muddy road before him led into the central plaza and the bivouac of General Juan Mora, commander of the Costa Rican invaders and president of the Costa Rican republic. The acrid stench of raw sewage and cooking fires hovered in the sticky air. Fry spat to clear the sour taste from his mouth and scanned the shutters of the outlying adobe buildings. He smiled bitterly. If sweet Jane were alive, she'd have scolded him for spitting like a common soldier. The buildings and narrow streets were empty. Thousands of enemy soldiers were in the town, but not a single sentry was in sight.

A church bell in the town clanged six times. Time to move. No sentries, no patrols . . . It shouldn't be this easy, but he could wait no longer. He caught Captain Dawson's eye and chopped a hand forward. The command whispered down the line, and bushes crackled as men climbed to their feet.

He dashed for the adobe buildings bordering the town, so much farther away than they had seemed earlier. His failing legs pumped as his heart pounded. Any second now, he expected a storm of bullets.

He crashed against the nearest wall, gasping air into his starving lungs. By the time his chest stopped heaving, the street was still empty, and the only sounds were the *thumps* of boots as his men piled in around him.

Dawson flattened against the powdering adobe next to him. "God damn this place, sun's just up and it's a furnace already. No sign of the greasers?"

Fry swat at the mosquito buzzing his ear. "Quiet as a whorehouse in Vatican City. But they're here, sure as shooting. The captured spy swore President Mora was in the house of a widow named Francesca Carrasco. On this side of the plaza, opposite the powder magazine."

"Fat lot of good his information did the spy. Walker hung him anyway." Dawson plucked off his wide-brimmed hat and peered around the corner. "What now?"

"We'll give the other rifle companies five minutes to get into position, and then we go in for the president." He checked his pocket watch and glanced back at the men. "Two teams. You take the left side, and I'll take this one. Don't dawdle. We may have surprise on our side after all."

He risked a peek around the wall. A white sleeve flickered into view at the next corner, and a glowing cigarette stub flipped into the street. "Did y'all see that? A sentry."

"Where?" The stench of Dawson's body odor was overpowering as he peered around his commander.

Fry slung his rifle and drew his Arkansas toothpick. "Never mind. I'll handle him. Keep your virgins quiet."

Stooping low, he eased around the corner and stepped onto the elevated boardwalk. There was no sign of the sentry. A child squawked in a nearby house.

Fry tiptoed across the uneven boards, wincing at every creaking step. He swung around a marble column into the doorway and clamped a hand over the startled sentry's mouth. The man grunted as Fry drove his narrow blade up under his chin, blood spilling down to soak his hand and sleeve, lending a metallic tang to the humid morning air. The man's face contorted, and his widened eyes glazed over as he collapsed. Fry caught the musket falling from lifeless hands and let the wiry body slide to the ground.

Another figure in white broke from an entranceway several houses up and sprinted back toward the plaza. "*Yanquis*! *Estamos bajo ataque*."

"That's set the cat among the pigeons." Fry returned his sticky blade to its scabbard and beckoned his men. "Come on, you lazy bastards, let's go cut some greaser tail."

He dashed up the street, his breath rasping in his lungs and sweat stinging his chafed private parts. To hell with this furnace of a country. The Costa Ricans would shoot back any time now, but they met no resistance as they raced to the cobblestoned plaza. Was it that easy? It had better be. His legs were wobbling after the two-day march from Granada; he didn't need a hard battle. With only six hundred and fifty men, Walker required surprise on his side. This small army needed a win.

He stopped at the edge of the plaza to get his bearings. To his left was a hotel, and the warehouse to his right stretched to the terraced shops that lined the south side. The ruins of a stone cathedral and a convent to the west would provide cover. Men whooped on the east side of the plaza, and he craned around to see Lieutenant Kane leading a cluster of riflemen to capture two brass cannons beside the shadowed verandas of the shops. The pompous ass seemed to have forgotten the aim was to capture the Costa Rican president. There was no sign of Kane's commander, Colonel Sanders. More's the pity.

Stale alcohol wafted on Dawson's breath as the captain joined him. "Look there. They captured some guns."

Fry raised a hand to halt his company. "They'd better leave them there and get on after Mora." That street beside the small canteen should take them right to President Mora's billet. "There—Colonel Sanders finally has his men advancing again."

Puffs of smoke erupted from the buildings on either side of Sanders's company, and muskets cracked as a hail of lead chopped down several of the leading riflemen.

Fry pulled back against the warm adobe. "The greasers have cut loopholes in the walls and they're firing on Sanders from the houses over there." There had to be another route. He tapped Dawson's shoulder. "Come on. This street should take us around them. We can attack the Carrasco house from the other side."

He raced across the plaza, his men huffing and cursing behind him. But before they reached the second street, rifles barked in the distance. Bullets ricocheted off the cobblestones and two of his men pitched over, screaming. He threw himself down and hit the ground hard, landing beside a rifleman with a gruesome wound in his back. Jesus Christ, minié balls. He threw an arm up to shade his eyes and scanned the rooftops. The enemy marksmen up there could pin the attackers down.

He eased his head around to survey the plaza. A bullet slapped the cobblestones and a stone chip grazed his cheek. He tried to ignore the stinging pain, blinking rapidly to clear the dust. A wisp of smoke puffed from the archway of a church tower four blocks away—another marksman, likely a European mercenary. Few Costas had rifles, and far fewer could shoot with that accuracy. Out in the plaza, his men were easy marks.

"Back up and find cover. This place is a killing ground." He tucked in his elbows and crawled backward.

Shouts and the tramp of boots issued from the southern side of the plaza. Led by Colonel Natzmer, the Second Rifles were flooding into the shop verandas on the east side, kicking in doors and darting into buildings. Seconds later, tongues of flames licked out from the windows and rifles barked as they fired on the enemy loopholes. Bullets pocked the walls around the jagged openings, chipping up clouds of dust, but the muskets kept firing from within.

At least it was a distraction. If they were going on, they should go now.

"Forward. Follow me." Fry raced across the plaza and skidded into the dubious cover of a narrow street.

His eyes skimmed the plaza. Willy stood at one of the windows manned by Colonel Natzmer's men, there was no mistaking the gaudy, red bowler hat, his son had begged for it on his fifteenth birthday, and Fry's heart sank.

"Christ, son, get back," he murmured. The boy was going to get himself killed—his only child.

Fry dashed into the plaza. Bullets plowed the surrounding mud, gouging plaster from the wall behind him, one tugging at his sleeve as he leaped back to cover, heading toward Willy. *Lord God, spare him out there. He's only sixteen.*

He lunged forward, but someone pulled him back and shoved him against the wall as gunfire thundered and men screamed in the square.

"Don't, Colonel," Captain Dawson said. "It's suicide."

"It's Willy. Gundry promised to keep him safe, but my boy's out there in the midst of it." Fry's head spun. He should never have allowed Willy to switch to Gundry's company.

He shrugged off Dawson and peeked around the corner. Bullets kicked puffs of red dust from the wall around the window sheltering Willy. A rifle poked out, and Willy fired again.

Fry fought back rising nausea. He shouldn't have brought Willy to Nicaragua. He searched the smoke-hazed plaza for Walker's native company. Those useless greasers should've arrived long ago, and he needed more men to support Willy and his comrades. To extract Willy.

He cast his eyes up at the blinding blue sky. *Dear God, protect him from harm and I promise to be a better man, not to drink, not to fornicate.*

A single rifle barked in the distance, the marksman in the church tower. Fry propped himself against the corner and aimed his carbine at one arch in the tower—a forlorn hope—and pulled the trigger. The butt kicked against his shoulder, and smoke plumed from the barrel. Perhaps it would keep the marksman's head down.

Rifleman Brady brushed past him, his eyes on a fallen comrade writhing and crying in the dusty square.

Dawson grabbed for him but missed. "Come back, you damned fool."

Geysers of dust puffed around Brady, bullets exploding the cobblestones. One struck the prostrate soldier in the head. Brady made an unlikely midair turn and sprinted back toward the uncertain safety of the corner. He shrieked and pitched forward, blood from his neck spattering his shirt. His wide-brimmed hat rolled across and landed at Fry's feet.

Fry swallowed the saliva flooding his mouth. Would that be Willy's fate as well? *Dear God, it couldn't be.* He whipped off his sweat-soaked hat and pressed his cheek to the wall; the warm adobe smelled of mildew and dust. One American rifleman had climbed into the tower of the ruined church and was sniping at the Costa Ricans, but the filibuster rifle fire around the plaza buildings was sporadic. The crouching Americans seemed reluctant to advance against the thousand Costa Rican muskets bristling on the west of the plaza. Colonel Walker had grossly underestimated the enemy's strength.

Fry wove a hand through his hair. He couldn't blame his countrymen, but they'd have no chance of capturing President Mora now, not against those odds.

As bullets pecked dust from the walls and pelted the cobblestones, General Walker cantered into the plaza, bellowing at the hesitant Light Infantry. "Are you men cowards? Conduct yourselves like Americans, for God's sake. Where's your frontier spirit?"

Bullets whipped the air but miraculously missed him. Debris and dust powdered his clothing and his horse white, but the general was icy calm in the storm of gunfire.

"Up and at 'em, men," he shouted. "Don't let the world hear of you cowering before a meek and inferior race."

Fry flinched. General Walker was in mortal danger.

"For God's sake, General, get out of there!" He wouldn't watch his golden goose shot from the saddle. He jinked into the plaza, expecting at every step a bullet that would blow him back. His breath burned in his lungs by the time he seized the lathered reins of General Walker's mount.

"Fry! You fool." General Walker halted his swinging sword. "I almost took your head off."

Fry dragged the horse from the plaza.

"Leave me be." General Walker sawed the reins brutally. "We must advance. Someone must lead these cowards."

Muskets blazed from loopholes all the way along the street, filling the air with lead, madness, and peril.

The lapel of Walker's coat ripped in Fry's fingers as he dragged the general from his horse and held him tightly. "Not now, General, they'll hit you for sure."

A middle-aged woman ran into the plaza leading a score of

Costa Ricans and charged the brass cannons abandoned by Sanders's men. It could be the widow Carrasco, an ardent *Legitimista*. What a fearless woman.

Hundreds of muskets blazed a gale of lead as the Costa Ricans laid down covering fire, and Fry cringed as bullets hammered clay from the adobe wall beside him. The Costa Ricans reached the guns intact, and the woman and soldiers fired at any filibuster who aimed at the officers jamming spikes into the cannons' touchholes.

Fry lifted his rifle with flighty hands. He couldn't shoot this woman, so he pointed his rifle at an officer as bullets exploded dust from the wall around him. As he ducked back, limbs shaking, he cringed in the maelstrom of powder and shards of clay. This was the end. They couldn't miss—but then again, if they were firing at him, they couldn't fire at Willy.

The ring of steel on steel clanged louder than the musketry as the two officers hammered spikes into the touchholes of the cannons. As soon as they drove the spikes home, the sabotage party scurried back whence they'd come. Every one of them made it back to the widow's house alive, their mission a complete success.

So that's where the president must be.

Angry bellows came from the left, where Major Markham and a score of riflemen charged across the plaza and plunged down the street leading to the Carrasco house. They withered like scythed barley beneath a barrage of bullets in the narrow street, and the survivors ducked behind two ammunition carts and dragged them back as shelter.

"Cover them, men." Fry fired his rifle at the loopholes and reloaded as fast as he could, the barrel and breech hot in his hands. Acrid gun smoke stung his eyes, reeking like brimstone. He wiped his eyes with a grubby hand as the survivors of Markham's ill-fated group crouched behind the ammunition carts, rolling them back as they dragged their wounded to the cover of a dry goods store.

General Walker frowned. "Brave, but foolish. We've lost the advantage of surprise. Hold this corner while I check on the other companies. We must retake the initiative."

Fry shook his head as the general ran back at a crouch. General Walker was brave but clueless. He was younger than Fry's thirty-six years, but unlike Fry, the general had never served in the army. Fry may have dropped out of the Naval Academy, but he had later worked his way up from private to lieutenant in the Voltigeur Regiment during the Mexican-American War. The inexperience showed. Any fool but General Walker could see that the Army of the Republic of Nicaragua's goal was hopeless. The Costas vastly outnumbered the ARN.

All morning long the crash of muskets spiked and faded around the bloodied square as each side sought the advantage. Fry and the survivors of his fifty-man company clung to their corner at the edge of the plaza, doling out more punishment than they received, but a thousand enemy muskets were firing back. Fry couldn't advance. He dispatched Dawson and a dozen men to the red tile rooftops of the stores behind them. They sheltered behind the hips of the roofs, rising and firing into the western quarter, before dropping into cover to reload, but the enemy was entrenched behind their walls. They'd have to winkle them out.

Fry left ten men to hold the street and led the rest south, parallel to the plaza. They would have to dislodge the Costa Ricans the hard way. Musket fire crackled from the houses they passed. He halted at the gable wall of the last house on the terrace bordering the south side of the plaza and beckoned to Lieutenant Grieves, a nineteen-year-old from Tennessee. "Punch a hole in this wall and fire at the enemy within."

The freckled lieutenant's jaw dropped. "Punch through, sir? It's—"

"It's clay, Lieutenant . . . just mud." He drew his bloody knife and gouged a chunk from the adobe wall. "We'll dig several holes large enough to shoot through. With luck, we'll drive the bastards out."

The ARN attacked the wall with bayonets, hammers, spades, and even rocks. Tom Culbertson, a wiry ex-slave from the East Coast, hacked through all but the last inch of clay in one of three holes, and another two were ready a few moments later. Fry did not understand where Culbertson had found that axe but he'd made kindling of the wall.

Fry drew his revolver and stood opposite Culbertson, pistol cocked. "Now, Culbertson."

Culbertson drove the axe through the wall, and Fry stooped and fired his revolver at the men inside. A bullet hit the adobe beside him. He flinched but kept firing, encouraged by the screams inside, until his hammer clicked on an empty chamber. He ducked aside to reload as his men stepped up to pour lead into the building. Screeches greeted their efforts.

He finished reloading, removed his slouch hat and placed it over the jagged opening. A shot rang out, and his hat sprouted a single hole. Only one enemy left.

He peeped inside, blinking at the dust. One white-clad soldier was frantically reloading his musket. Fry shot him in the head.

"Sergeant Wulchak, take two men and fire the thatch on the roofs of the next terrace," he ordered. "Smoke the bastards out. The rest of you, inside. We'll work our way along the terrace, wall by wall."

Wulchak brushed his lank blond hair back from his sunburned face and waved a sloppy salute with fingers as fat as sausages. "Aye, sir. Right away, sir."

Fry wriggled through the hole into smoke and dust and gagged on the stink of saltpeter and blood. Five bodies lay on the blood-slicked floor, and a wounded soldier sat against the wall, his youthful face contorted as he whimpered. The Costa Ricans didn't take prisoners, and Fry didn't have time for that either. He shot the boy in the face, splattering the wall with blood and brains.

He grabbed the axe from Culbertson and hacked at the wall of the adjoining house. It was going to be a long, hot, and deadly day.

By the afternoon, sweat-streaked dust coated Fry's face, aggravating the stings where clay shards had grazed it. He'd punched his way through four houses, but the enemy had overwhelmed them and driven them back to the second house. From time to time, he'd scanned the buildings for Willy, but out where the sun hammered the combatants and curdled the dead in the gore-drenched plaza, there was no trace of the boy. He pictured Willy dead in a building close by.

There was a flurry of movement in the street behind the Carrasco house where President Mora quartered. A hoard of Costa Ricans was pouring into town. Reinforcements.

Fry let out a windy sigh and closed his eyes. It was time to retreat, but there was no sign of General Walker. Smoke rolled across the plaza, dimming the flames in the buildings burning all around them. Fry sagged against the window, sweating from the heat, his grazed flesh stinging and his gullet raw from coughing and shouting. He was down to his last five rounds. Neither side had ammunition to waste on blind shots into the darkness. It was hopeless; there were too many Costa Ricans and more still arriving.

A little after midnight, he sent Dawson to find General Walker and slumped against the warm adobe wall, struggling to keep his eyes open. They'd been fighting for almost twenty-four hours. Was Willy safe? His limbs trembled. He'd never been afraid in battle, but this time was different. Willy was out there. In danger.

He pinched the end of his nose. He should never have filled the boy's head with bunkum about the glory of war. When Willy had shown up unexpectedly as he waited for the steamship in

New Orleans, he'd been thrilled, saddened, and furious all at the same time—delighted to see the boy again, shocked to hear that Jane had died of pneumonia, furious that Willy had run away from the orphanage in Kanawha County, where they sent him after his mother's death. When this battle was over, he'd put Willy on the first steamer out of Greytown. The lad was going home to West Virginia, and Fry would shoot Walker if he tried to stop him.

Dawson's face was so black with powder that Fry barely recognized him when he returned.

The captain's bloodshot eyes blinked furiously. "I thought you were dead. It's hell out there."

"Not yet. But we can't hold out. I've only five rounds left, and we've lost six men."

"We're leaving," Dawson said. "Walker ordered a retreat. If we're still here by daylight, they'll slaughter us."

Fry gave a cursory nod. "Did you see my Willy with Gundry in Colonel Natzmer's lot?"

Dawson's eyes darted to the plaza and back. "I'm sure he's fine. Walker gathered the wounded in the ruined convent. Colonel Natzmer took one in the leg during that stupid charge. I didn't see Willy with the injured, so he must be with his company. Don't worry, he's as tough as his old man."

Fry flopped back against the wall. "You're sure?"

"Of course I am. Listen, each company must retreat down the street they're defending. Walker reckons if we're quiet, we'll be ten miles down the road before the enemy knows we're gone. You'll see Willy on the way."

Fry looked away to the flames lapping the crumbling buildings, the shadows at their feet like dancers making pagan sacrifices of the broken bodies and shattered dreams. "I'm going out there first. I must know for certain."

"Are you mad? The sharpshooters are still out there, French and German mercenaries. They can shoot the eye out of your head at two hundred yards, even by the miserly light of them burning buildings." Dawson gestured to the men collapsed along the walls. "Gundry's one of our best. That's why you let young Willy join him, and I've seen with my own eyes your boy wasn't with the wounded. So he's fine. Your duty is to these young fellows here, to get them home. Every one of them is somebody's son."

Fry bit his lip. Dawson was right. He must do his duty, not follow his heart. Willy would survive. He swallowed and pushed to his feet. "Gather your stuff, boys, and wrap any equipment that rattles. Time to move out—and we can't make a sound."

The snaking shadow of Walker's defeated army materialized ahead in the moonlight on the muddy road to Granada. Fry checked his watch again. Almost four in the morning. It had taken his company forever to catch up with the main column. He needed to know Willy was safe.

Six Rangers cantered from the trees bordering the trail with a clatter of hooves and jingling tack.

"What company, fellas?" called a rangy captain.

Fry lowered his rifle. "Colonel, if you please. I'm a senior officer, Company A, First Rifles."

"Sergeant Brewster, sir. Sorry, sir, it's been a long day. Any more behind you?"

Fry shook his head wearily. "Captain Gundry's company? Seen them?"

"Middle of the column up ahead. Gundry didn't make it. They couldn't find him when we moved the wounded out."

Time seemed to grind to a halt. "How many of his men survive?"

Brewster scratched at his chin. "Hard to say, it being dark and all, but I reckon we've some five hundred men in the column, counting the wounded. Gundry's lot got the worst of it when they made that mad charge across the square. No cannons are worth the price those boys paid, even if they're made of brass."

Without another word, Fry sped up into an exhausted jog. Dawson could bring the men along. Sweat streamed down his back, stinging his abraded flesh, as he pushed past staggering men to the column of horses carrying the wounded and the dead. He slowed to scan the pain-filled faces. Some were still boys. Black flies furred their gaping wounds and buzzed around bodies dangling across saddles.

Blasted minié balls . . . they tear a man to pieces. His limbs shook as he rushed from body to body. Willy wasn't here. He slumped and pressed his palms to his face. Thank God, Willy was with his company.

He fell back among the downcast men. "Gundry's company. Where are they?"

"Over here," called a voice up ahead. "Who's asking?"

"Colonel Fry. I'm looking for my lad, Willy." Even drained as he was, his deep voice rose easily above the chirp of crickets in the hot night.

No response breached the grunts and mutters of exhausted men. Sucking muggy air in ragged gulps, he jostled through the battle-shocked volunteers, ignoring their curses.

A round-faced youth with dust coating his long hair glanced at him and turned away. He knew that kid. What was his name?

"You! Hold on there." He caught the boy's shoulder and spun him around.

The boy's eyes were bloodshot. Tear tracks striped his powder-blackened face, and blood seeped from a deep cut on his cheek. "Sorry, sir, he's gone. I didn't want to be the one to tell you."

Fry stumbled back, numb all over. Gone? Willy couldn't be dead. He was all he'd left in this world. "What do you mean, gone?"

The boy's face spun before his eyes. "He took a ball in the

belly at a house back yonder. We done all we could for him. Put him in the convent with the rest of the wounded."

He clung to the boy to steady himself. This couldn't be happening. "Where's Willy? Not with the wounded; I already saw that."

"I dunno, I—please, no more. Can't take it. Mammy . . ." The boy slumped to the ground. "Mammy."

Fry glanced up the column. General Walker would know.

He found the commander at the head of the line with several officers. The general turned in the saddle as Fry approached, alerted by the curses and shouts as Fry shouldered past the weary men.

His gray eyes met Fry's. "Colonel, shouldn't you be with your men?"

"My boy, Willy. I'm looking for Willy."

The general's features softened, and he dismounted. "I didn't know you'd a boy with us, Colonel."

"Willy wanted it kept quiet so he could carve his own path."

"And he's missing? Who's his commander?"

"He serves under Captain Gundry. Willy was wounded, and one of his lads took him to the convent."

"Then he must be back in the column with the wounded," Walker said.

"He's not. I checked."

Walker placed a bloodstained hand on his shoulder. "What does he look like?"

Fry shivered and wrung his hands. "B-baby face lad wearing a red bowler hat, a gaudy—"

"Dear God, Colonel." Walker looked away. "I remember him. A brave fellow . . . He was too badly injured to move him. We left him and several others in the convent."

A heart-wrenching moan escaped Fry's lips.

"I left a note for General Mora," Walker continued, "asking him to care for prisoners and reminding him we've done the same in the past."

Fry clawed at his dusty collar as bile bubbled in his stomach. "They're savages. Have you forgotten what happened to our wounded in Rivas? They burned them alive in the plaza, all the men you left behind."

An aide-de-camp trotted up. "General, we must keep moving."

Walker ignored him. "Colonel Fry, it was Nicaraguans who committed that crime. Today we fought Costa Ricans."

"They're all savages down here," Fry repeated. "They won't heed your requests about prisoners, General. I'm afraid my boy is dead."

Walker touched Fry's arm. "If, God forbid, that is so, we'll avenge him."

An ache flared above Fry's right temple, deep inside. "Oh, I will, all right. I'll kill every greaser that stands against us."

"If you want revenge, the war is here," Walker said. "True. But the reason we're losing is in Ireland."

Fry tilted his head.

"Samuel Kingston," Walker said. "He's the reason our enemies are multiplying."

Walker was talking bunkum. "I don't know a damned thing about Samuel Kingston, sir, or what he has to do with the Costa Ricans.

"He stole victory and progress from us all, Colonel, and it's time he paid for his betrayal," Walker said. "You could leave this hellhole, go back on a secret mission for me, and reclaim what's ours."

The general's brittle reply told him everything he needed to know about their adversary. Fry sucked on his dry teeth and squinted down the road before finally nodding. "My son didn't deserve to meet his end on this filthy soil. Perhaps you'll fall to the side with me as we proceed, General, and share with me what we must do about this Kingston. Whoever he is and whatever he's done, it sounds as though he owes us, and now it's time to repay."

CHAPTER FOUR

Belle's muscles pumped beneath her supple coat and her breath exploded in an urgent rhythm as Samuel raced her past the paddocks in the orange glow over the manor buildings. They banked around the corner of the house, her steel shoes gouging sparks from the cobblestones. Samuel reined her in and vaulted from the saddle. The stables were on fire.

He drew both pistols from his belt, cocked them, and charged into the house. "Sofia! My God, where are you?"

In the drawing room, María Kerr was leaning over Sofia, who was stretched out on the couch, her face deathly pale. Padraig lay sprawled on the bloodstained rug with his head in Cookie's lap, blood dribbling from his blond hair.

Icy fingers brushed Samuel's insides. "Sofia! Is she . . .?"

"She's not injured." María was as pale as white limestone. "She's in labor. The baby's coming early. It's the shock."

He flopped to his knees beside the couch, pistols rattling together on the rug. "I'm herruge, my darling. Everything will be fine." He looked at María with wide eyes. "Padraig?"

María ran a blood-spattered hand through her mousey hair. "They hit him on the head, but Jerry said he'll come around. Jerry's helping the men fight the fire in the stables."

Sofia moaned, and Samuel squeezed her clammy hand. He'd been a fool to ride to Cork. His lips trembled as he looked at María. "Are you sure she's . . .?"

"*Mijo*, she's fine. Your baby's coming early." She straightened. "You must help Jerry and Jason keep the fire from the house. It's time for me to move Sofia upstairs to her own bed."

Sofia tugged at his hand. "Thank God you're here. They . . . they robbed us."

He stroked her forehead. "Hush now. Concentrate on bringing our baby into this world. I love you, my darling."

Sheila, the kitchen maid, tottered in, water sloshing from the basin in her hands. "Sarah's bringing clean towels and linen, Mrs. Kerr. Where shall I put this?"

"Upstairs in the bedroom." María nudged Samuel away. "Go help Jerry, or the house will burn down around our heads. Jerry's already sent for Dr. Heinz. We'll take good care of them both."

Samuel stroked Sofia's clammy cheek and brushed her long hair back from her face. He'd kissed her plump red lips a thousand times; now they were parched and gray, parted as she panted. Could this be the first time he touched her in months? He was such a cad. Their petty arguments over the baby's religion were so irrelevant now.

Her slim hand gripped his. "I'll be fine, Samuel. Go help the men."

He shifted back on his heels and rose. "I'll return as soon as I can."

In the yard, long shadows flickered through the firelight. Samuel recognized men, women, and children from the estate's holdings, most lugging pails through the intense heat, all bleary-eyed and sooty. Flames crackled and spiraled through the stable's groaning roof, sending up a rain of sparks like orange snow. The heat scorched his skin as he approached Jerry Kerr, who was marshaling a human chain with the authority unique to a sergeant major.

"Jerry! The horses?"

Jerry didn't look back, deafened by the cacophony of groaning timber, hissing flames, and frantic shouts. Samuel tapped his shoulder. Jerry's soot-blackened face crinkled with relief, and he pulled Samuel close with sooty hands. He smelled of smoke and sweat.

"The horses?" Samuel shouted again.

"We got them out, none harmed," Jerry replied. "Bastards fired the stable to stop us from following them, I guess." He cuffed a scrawny youth gaping at the flames. "Brendan, don't stand there like a fool. Get in the line beside Mickey Óg, quick now."

Samuel wiped sweat and ash from his eyes. "Who did this? Who would—"

"Not now. Get over there and help Jason beat the flames back from the grain shed. If we can hold the fire line, we'll only lose the stables."

Samuel tied his handkerchief over his nose and joined the head of the line that stretched from the pond beyond the paddocks to the yard. Jason stood at the water's edge, captaining the human chain passing sloshing buckets up the line. Tall, spare, and covered in ash, he was the master of Springbough Manor. A peaceful man who shunned violence, he was solid and a block of granite, always at home, always there for the family in time of crisis. Samuel grimaced. Not like Samuel . . . who never seemed to be there when they needed him and always arrived too late.

Samuel blinked at the sparks dancing like a cloud of fireflies in the starlit sky and grabbed bucket after bucket, heaving bejeweled arcs of water over the crackling flames lapping the stable walls and charring the rafters to black bones. Each time the dying building shuddered, and the flames changed hue, his spirits sank lower. Losing Springbough, even a part of it, was like losing himself.

He worked tirelessly, ignoring his aching back and blistered hands, all the while flicking glances at the main house. How was Sofia faring? The baby? He should run back and check on her—

but no, his duty lay here fighting this fire. He would despise himself if he let the family home burn. And so he battled on, smoke burning his throat and pain stabbing his lungs from constant coughing. He heaved slopping pails, though it was hopeless, and shouted encouragement to the line of smoke-blackened, slack faces.

An hour later, clusters of flames still escaped the burning stable, but they were holding the line. Then the black rafters creaked and collapsed. Sparks *whooshed* twenty feet into the air as the tenants jumped back with excited screams.

"Keep going," Samuel shouted. "We've beaten it."

The minutes dragged and every muscle ached as he swung pail after pail. His hands were red, and sweat soaked his scorched clothing. He tossed another pail of water on a tuft of flame and passed the dripping pail to Benny Murphy. It was humbling to see these people—*their* people—fighting as hard as he was to save the manor. His lungs expanded despite the smoke's assault. Father had been right. These were their people, and the Kingstons should sacrifice everything for them.

Then it was over, the last flame quenched in the sizzling, smoking ruins of the stable, and Samuel covered his face with grimy hands. They'd thwarted the fire's ravenous lunge for the main house.

He hugged Jerry. "Well done, Jerry. Please thank the tenants for me. I must see to Sofia."

Jerry's sparse crown was black with soot. "Go on, lad—but don't you worry. She'll be fine."

He waved at Jason, who was still captaining the team drawing water from the pond, and staggered back to the house. His feet ached as he hurried upstairs, trailing smutty footprints and stinking of acrid smoke and stale sweat.

On the landing, a screeching wail as unfamiliar as it was welcome nearly brought him to a halt. He burst into the bedroom. His mouth opened in wonder at the pink baby nestled in Sofia's arms, and he rushed to them, heedless of everything else, warm tears streaming down his face.

Sofia was pale and wane, but she greeted him with the smile that always lifted his heart, a smile he'd not seen in months—or perhaps that he'd only failed to notice.

"A boy," she said.

María cut him off as he reached for his son. "Look at the state of you. You'll make the baby sick. It's a bath for you this instant, *mijo*." Her black eyebrows shot up. "The fire?"

"We were lucky," he said. "We lost the stables, but nothing more. Thank God for the tenants. Without them, we'd have lost everything."

"And without your father, they'd have starved to death back in the famine," she said. "They love your family, Samuel."

But there wasn't time for a bath or to linger with his wife and son; there were too many unanswered questions. He pounded down the stairs again, sent Mickey Spillane to collect Filipe, and hurried to the drawing room.

"There's the proud papa," Padraig croaked from the couch. "Congratulations. Let's hope he doesn't look the least bit like you."

Relief melted away some of Samuel's tension. "How's your head, old man?"

Padraig looked at the dried blood on the cloth he'd been holding to his head. "It's stopped bleeding. Another scar for my noggin. If I ever become as bald as my dad, I'll be a frightful sight."

Samuel put a hand on Padraig's shoulder. "Thank God you're all right. What happened?"

Padraig swung his arms in an arc. "Thieves. We were in the front room of the lodge when we heard a scream from the manor house. Dad and I rushed up here and collided with four masked men darting from the porch. One of them pistol-whipped me in the ruckus, then they overpowered Dad."

"Bastards locked me in the library with Jason," Jerry said.

Jason arrived and collapsed into a chair. "It began when they broke through the front door and covered Sofia and me with pistols."

"Tied them up," Jerry added.

"Well, they tried," Jason said with a grin. "While they bound me, Sofia attacked."

Samuel looked from one face to another.

Jason shook his head and smiled. "She's a wildcat. One of the backhanded her, and she fell. I think that's what brought on labor."

Samuel slumped into an armchair. He could've lost them both. "This wasn't random. Two men attacked us on the road. They knew me by name."

"One was American," Padraig said. "I heard him shouting orders as I went for him."

Samuel's body heated. "An American. Why would an—"

"Pulled the handkerchief from his face too, and I got a look at him," Padraig said. "Evil bastard with a long face and beard. I'd know him again to be sure. I'll kill the wretch when I see him next."

Samuel twisted his wedding ring and glanced at the doorway. This wasn't a burglary. It was sounding more like . . . "Where exactly did they go? What were they after?"

"The study," Jason said. "I heard them tearing the place apart. I looked in there just now, it's a mess, but everything's still there. They took nothing of value from the house, not even the silver candlesticks from the dining room."

Jason wouldn't even have known where to look. Samuel pushed wearily to his feet. "I'll check."

The study floor was littered with ledgers and books the raiders had pulled down from the shelves. Papers were scattered everywhere, quivering in the breeze puffing through the open window.

Samuel's legs turned to jelly as he clumsily picked his way through the jumble of books and toppled ornaments to the cabinet beneath the window. The doors were open, and the folders strewn on the ground. He pawed through them looking for the leather binder and flipped it open.

Baltimore's documents were gone. He'd lost his shield against the wrath of the lords.

Six days since the attack, and the useless Royal Irish Constabulary had no news of the raiders. Samuel hesitated, fingers hovering over the dusty trunk in Springbough's gunroom. At least one of them had been an American. He must have been William Walker's man, and the only thing they'd taken was the Baltimore papers. Samuel had to retrieve them. He'd sworn when they returned from Nicaragua that he'd never go back there, even thinking of Father dying over there made his heart ache, but last week's attack had left him no choice but to offer his help to Cornelius Vanderbilt in New York. He needed money, and Vanderbilt, the richest man in the world, had tried to hire him before. He wet his lips, eased the lid open, and the hinges creaked in protest. His Navy Colt and 1853 pattern light cavalry saber lay as he had stowed them. The fourteen-and-a-half-inch revolver was a killer, with its hexagonal barrel and cylinder engraved with warships in the Battle of Campeche. The smooth touch of the walnut handle quickened his pulse despite the dark memories it summoned. He'd slain many men, but not enough to save Father. If only he'd found Baltimore's hacienda quicker . . .

He'd lain awake all night, reviewing his options for the twentieth time, while the warm breeze carried the stench of charred timber and smoke through the open window as he sweated on the damp sheets. The coming days promised only money problems and humiliation, and the solution had become self-evident: Accept the dubious proposition Cornelius Vanderbilt had made a year ago—if the offer still stood.

He reached for the dusty cartridge box, revisiting his choice to tangle with William Walker again. He loaded the first chamber by rote. What choice? Like the last time he left Clonakilty for Nicaragua, he had no choice at all. He belted on his cavalry holster and shoved the revolver inside; its weight was a familiar friend.

Padraig appeared at the door in a felt hat and a battered canvas coat that reached the tops of his riding boots. "Ready?"

He nodded.

Padraig leaned against the door jamb. "You sure about this?"

Samuel clipped down the holster flap and pulled his calf-length coat around to conceal it. "The debt's due when Bentley takes title to Baltimore's estate. We've lost the money." Father had accumulated that debt to feed his many tenants during the famine, and the previous Earl of Baltimore, Louis Greenfell, had bought up the debts and tried to ruin the Kingstons. "I started this when I shot Louis Greenfell's brother."

"Don't be stupid." Padraig moved into the room. "You were fifteen back then, and William Greenfell forced you into that duel. Besides, I shot William too when the wretch tried to shoot you after he conceded the duel. You hit his knee, and I winged him."

"You saved my life that day. But I should never have taken the challenge." Samuel sighed heavily.

"That family was bad to the bone," Padraig said. "William recovered and tried to murder you when we returned from Crimea. A cess on them all, I say. Both brothers kept coming after you and caused your father's death. I'm glad you slew them. But I thought that was the end of it. Now, another one has popped up."

"Yes. Bentley." Samuel grasped the worn hilt of his saber and pulled it six inches out of the scabbard, part of his old ritual before battle. "But he's a distant relative and doesn't appear to hold a grudge. His solicitor says he'll accept payment on the debt, and that'll be the end of it. In fact, I was going to buy the

Baltimore estate from Bentley after paying off the debt. But now . . . Samuel let his sword hand drop.

"Why risk your life?" Padraig asked. "Springbough's Jason's now, not yours. He inherited the debt with the estate."

"I promised him I'd pay off the debt. It's a drop in the ocean compared to the fortune we brought back. I can't let him down now. Besides, Springbough's been in the family for a hundred years, and I want to keep it that way."

"Here, I'll whet that blade for you." Padraig extended a hand for the saber. "Will Vanderbilt pay us enough to cover that debt?"

"He was willing to pay me anything to remove Walker from power last year," Samuel said. "Vanderbilt lost millions when Walker gave his concession to operate the Trans Nicaraguan Route to Morgan and Garrison and he swore to destroy Walker. The richest man in the world can pay a high price for revenge. He's my only hope."

Padraig rasped the sharpening stone over the saber's blade. "He made that offer a year ago. We're probably too late."

Samuel sighed heavily. "We believed Walker couldn't fight on when we stole his gold, that he could no longer fund his army, but we were wrong. Now we must try another angle; we must help Vanderbilt."

"Surely a man of Vanderbilt's resources doesn't need the help of two Irish—"

"He said himself he needs my unique knowledge of Nicaragua and Walker to bring the bastard down."

Padraig fixed his eyes on Samuel. "And Sofia? How does she feel about this?"

Samuel turned away. "I don't want to talk about that."

They filed up the stairs in silence and walked outside, where Jason stood frowning by the Berlin coach. Like Samuel, his eyes were as dark as old cognac, but he was fairer than Samuel, who bronzed with any nod from the sun.

"I didn't mean that it's your responsibility to save this old place," Jason said. "It's my estate. You mustn't risk your life for it. In any case, it's too late. Bentley's solicitor just delivered notice that they'll foreclose in four months if I don't pay the debt in full."

Lucan and his aristocratic cronies were behind this. Samuel was sure of it. They were working with Walker and got to Bentley. His head suddenly pounded. Four months gave him little time . . . not enough time. He'd return home to find his family in the street, worse off than the famine victims. He forced a smile. "Then we must hurry."

"God bless you, Samuel." Jason hugged him. "I'm sorry I gave you a hard time about your promise to deal with this awful debt. I'd no right. Please take care over there."

Samuel struggled to control his thickening voice as he met his brother's gaze. "No, Jason, you were correct. I promised to clear Father's debts and save the estate, and that is what I must do. This has been Kingston land for over a hundred years. We must keep it, no matter what it takes. It's New York. What harm can befall us there?"

Filipe sat up front on the coach, babbling to the driver with a sparkle in his eye, none the worse for his gruesome encounter the week before. Killing a man hadn't seemed to bother him at all.

Padraig inclined his head toward Filipe. "Why are we bringing him?"

"Sofia will have her hands full with baby John," Samuel said. "I know Filipe can be difficult, but you said he's more than handy with weapons, and he proved himself with the pistol the other night."

Padraig flipped his hat into the coach. "They start them young in Central America."

"It's that damned civil war," Samuel agreed, climbing inside. "Think about it, though. I was his age when I joined the Lancers, and you joined them when you were sixteen."

"A generation of bloodthirsty little bastards." Padraig rapped the coach's panel. "Let's roll."

Samuel twisted the wedding ring on his finger and glanced back at the front door where Jerry and María watched them gravely. Sofia hadn't come to say goodbye. Last night's argument had been hurtful. The coach lurched ahead, and his heart shrank as he sank back into the seat.

The faint odor of mildew made its presence known beneath a proper veneer of leather soap.

Padraig, however, was still laughing and waving out the window. He swiped at his unruly mop of blond curls and flopped against the leather seat with a grin. "Jaysus, 'tis fine to be off on another adventure, but I'll miss them all at—" He regarded Samuel's down-turned face and frowned. "What's the matter? You've been odd all day."

Samuel poked his tongue against his cheek. He didn't want to talk about it, but Padraig would keep on prying. He pinched the bridge of his nose.

"Come along now," Padraig said. "Out with it. I insist you tell me."

"It's Sofia." He wrung the tail of his coat. "Since the baby was born, she's . . . She's so cold. It's like she doesn't care if I stay or depart."

"She gave birth to John a week ago. Mam says having a baby can addle a woman's brain, put them all out of sorts." Padraig bumped his shoulder. "You've not been brilliant company yourself these last few months."

"What do you mean?" It was easy for Padraig to judge him. Padraig waltzed through life without giving a damn.

"We've been through much together," Padraig said. "There's nothing you need to hide from me."

The coach swayed out of the courtyard, past the beds of red roses and into the driveway. Beyond the fence in the paddock, Belle tossed up her head, whinnied, and cantered with them until she disappeared behind a blur of oak trees with the last of spring's daffodils streaming like a smudged yellow ribbon at their spreading roots.

He missed Sofia already, and John . . . He sighed. He'd not had time to acquaint himself with his infant son. All he remembered was a warm, cuddly ball. "It's been going on for a while. She wants to baptize the baby as a Catholic and refuses to consider my side." Samuel closed his eyes.

"I'm not a religious man," Padraig answered slowly, "so I wouldn't care what religion my kids are. I'd have shut my gob and given in just for the peace of it. But I know you're devout."

Samuel rubbed his legs. "That's just it. I don't see what the rush is. She wants to baptize John this week, and she got furious when I insisted that she wait until I return to discuss it further. I want to wait until John is old enough to decide for himself, but she won't compromise. She's convinced he'll go to limbo if he dies unbaptized. What rubbish."

Padraig pulled a face. "Better not let Mam hear that. She'd take the belt to you. Terribly fond of her saints and statues, she is."

"That's my problem with the Catholic doctrine, all this fantasy stuff and worshiping saints instead of God. I don't want her filling John's little head with that."

"It's not all Sofia's fault, though."

Samuel shot him a sharp look.

"To be honest, you've practically ignored me and the family for months—Sofia, too," Padraig said. "Hiding in your bedroom like a sulky child . . . For Christ's sake, look at yourself. You're overweight and out of condition. Even young Filipe up there could thrash you with a saber."

Samuel gaped at Padraig miserably. He was right.

"We need your head in the game if we're to fix this," Padraig said.

"The thought that Father is dead is eating me away," Samuel croaked. "I should've done more."

Padraig sat back. "Are you nuts? Your father was dead before we discovered Baltimore's place, and we did all his kidnappers asked. That would've been a rescue, had the cholera not already taken him."

"Perhaps not. Perhaps—"

"Samuel . . . That epidemic killed thousands over there: Nicaraguans, Costa Ricans, Americans, Europeans. It's the bloody devil's lottery, and it's still going on. Thank God we're going to New York and not back to Nicaragua."

Samuel sighed.

"You'd better snap out of it."

The passing trees were flush with leaves in the summer sun. This was easy for Padraig; he hadn't left Jerry to die alone among strangers.

The leather squeaked as Padraig shifted forward an inch. "I'm your brother, Samuel, not by blood but in arms. I love you, and I won't permit you to self-destruct like this." He seized Samuel's hand. "You did all you could, and your father is sitting up there bursting with pride for you. You're the man who almost stopped the tyrant, William Walker, for God's sake. And now we're going to finish the job."

They'll foreclose in four months, if I don't pay the debt in full. Jason's last words came back to Samuel like a slap. "We must do more than that; I must recover the Baltimore papers. Bentley is about to foreclose on Springbough. Lucan put him up to it; I feel it in my bones. He'll keep coming after us now that I don't have that dirt on him." He didn't want to return to Nicaragua; that place was a raw, painful reminder of his failure. "I think Walker's man stole the papers for Lucan or he'll take them to Walker in Nicaragua."

Padraig's mouth dropped. "The latter, that's it. Walker wants your dirt on their lordships, he wants to extort them or something."

A single black and white magpie flew past the window with a harsh ascending call and a raspy chatter.

"Oh no, a single magpie." Padraig stuck his head out the

window and craned around. “Just one, we don’t need his sorrow.” Padraig saluted the bird.

One for sorrow, two for joy. Samuel cringed as he recalled the old rhyme. It would take more than a salute to stave off his sorrow. A year ago, Cornelius Vanderbilt had offered him a fortune to return to Nicaragua and help the allied armies of Costa Rica, Honduras, and Guatemala to overthrow Walker, but Samuel had refused, not because he’d just become a wealthy man himself but because the country reminded him of his failure to save Father’s life and he couldn’t bear that. Now he might have to chase the Baltimore papers all the way to that place he dreaded.

CHAPTER FIVE

The open carriage clattered to a halt at the two-story West Fourth Street office building, and the teamsters behind them cursed roundly as the driver hauled on the reins, the cries echoing down the line of carts and carriages snaking between the tall stone and brick buildings. Their curses blended into the cacophony of street hawkers, barking dogs, and construction noise.

Samuel stepped out of the carriage. Men in expensive suits and ladies shaped like handbells in their stiffened dresses and bright bonnets wove through workers in drab, tattered clothes.

"Everybody seems miserable here." Samuel slipped a silver coin from his pocket.

"Wouldn't you be?" Padraig straightened his tweed flat cap. "The place is a madhouse, and it stinks of dung and burned wood. No wonder they're all wrinkling their noses."

Filipe bounded out last, stepping on Samuel's foot. "It's incredible! Look at the height of those buildings."

Samuel flinched and pushed him away. "Behave, or I'll have the cabby haul you back to the hotel."

"We're really meeting Cornelius Vanderbilt," Filipe repeated with a silly, overawed grin. "They call him the Commodore—you know, because he owns so many ships."

Samuel looked around. "Be quiet. This is no game. Padraig and I will speak with him. You won't be seeing him."

Filipe sucked in his lower lip and looked away.

"Speak Spanish from now on," Padraig warned the boy. "It's less likely eavesdroppers will understand us. Blast me, it was the devil getting you to speak English in the old country, and now you won't shut up."

Samuel squinted at the building then looked back at the driver. "Is this it? There's no sign or anything."

The cab driver rolled his eyes. "Everyone in New York knows where the richest man in the world works." He flipped his reins and the cab lurched away, iron hubs clattering on the cobblestones.

Padraig pointed at hundreds of hats hanging in the windows of the second floor. "Look at all those—place looks like a milliner's shop. I guess if you've more money than God, you need to wear lots of hats."

Wearing a different hat—yes, that was something he could do. Samuel would do whatever it took to save the family estate and finish his own manor. "Let's see what kind of hat Cornelius Vanderbilt has for us to wear."

Filipe raced up the steps to the entrance, and Samuel followed lightly behind him. He hadn't moved this effortlessly in months. For three hours every day of their ten-day voyage, he'd fenced with Padraig and Filipe, sweating off the extra weight. He tugged his lapels straight; his best suit fit properly again. Loosening up on the ocean liner had broken the ice of his inactivity.

Samuel pulled Filipe back. "Take off your hat and stay close." He swung the brass-trimmed door inward and ushered the others into the anteroom.

"Wow!" Filipe ran to the steamship paintings on the walls. "Are those his boats?"

A wrinkled clerk at the high wooden desk guarding the double doors to an inner office looked up. "May I help you?"

"Samuel Kingston and Padraig Kerr," Samuel said.

The clerk pointed a bony finger at six wooden chairs lining the wall. "Take a seat, please. I'll advise the Commodore you're here." He knocked on one of the double doors and entered Vanderbilt's office.

Padraig and Filipe sat down while Samuel paced the room, mentally rehearsing his proposal until the clerk opened the door and beckoned them in.

Samuel shook a finger at Filipe. "Don't move."

More paintings of steamships lined the office walls inside, and four scale models of steamships sat on the marble mantelpiece above the fireplace. The sparse office was redolent with cigar smoke and ink. Samuel raised an eyebrow at the stuffed striped cat resting on a rolltop desk in the corner and bet himself that there rested an interesting story.

Cornelius Vanderbilt sat at a long, uncluttered desk, scratching away with a stylus. He brushed back his gray mane with a bony hand. "Captain Kingston, Lieutenant Kerr, I'm curious why you're here. The last time we spoke, young Kingston, you'd no interest in helping me. But then, you'd recently become an extremely wealthy man."

Samuel flinched. "Sir?"

"It's my business to know what's going on in Nicaragua." Vanderbilt rose and extended a hand. "Welcome to New York. What can I do for you?"

Vanderbilt didn't need to know that Walker and his Anglo-Irish allies had frozen their money. "Regrettably, Walker seems to be winning his war in Nicaragua," Samuel said. "We thought perhaps you would appreciate some experienced advisors to help you stop him."

Vanderbilt's bushy gray eyebrows drew together and released. "What exactly are you proposing?"

Samuel wrung the brim of the hat in his hand. "Well,

we thought . . . I thought . . . What I'm saying is, I've reconsidered your offer and I'm willing to go to Nicaragua and guide the opposition in their effort to defeat Walker."

Vanderbilt looked at Samuel with narrowing eyes. "That dog don't hunt anymore, boy. I gave you your chance. Now I'm doing it without you. As soon as I round up enough rifles, I'm sending them down to arm Walker's opponents. I need not waste money on you. And remember you agreed in writing to keep our communications secret. Leak one word of my plans, and I'll destroy you. I don't want it known that I'm acting against Walker." Vanderbilt picked up the stylus again. "I bid you good day."

Vanderbilt wasn't a forgiving man, as Walker was soon likely to discover, and Samuel had just learned. Samuel's steps were quick and twitchy as he departed the office deep in thought. He wasn't giving up; too much depended on it. If he couldn't convince Vanderbilt to hire him, he'd have to retrieve the Baltimore papers, and whoever the American was who had stolen them would return through New York. Most likely, the wretch was still in New York as the steamer only sailed from New York to Nicaragua once a month. If this man was connected to Walker, Frank Brogan might know where to find him. Brogan was an immigrant to New York from Samuel's own county of Cork, who Vanderbilt had brought down to Nicaragua to captain one of his steamboats on the San Juan River. Samuel had rewarded Brogan handsomely for aiding his escape down the river a year ago, and Brogan would help him.

Padraig shot Samuel a bitter smile as they stepped back onto bustling West Fourth Street. "What now? We wasted a fortune getting here for nothing."

The endless streams of pedestrians surged around them as Samuel floundered, sweltering in the summer heat. The scent of cooking meat mingled with the stench of the city as coaches, carriages, and loaded wagons creaked and rattled in all directions. Filipe bounced from foot to foot, gawking at the towering arches and colorful stores.

Samuel snorted disconsolately. "This city's a madhouse. Let's find somewhere quiet."

Padraig's face lit up. "A pub?"

"Why not? But closer to our hotel, where there's less chaos." Samuel nudged Filipe ahead. "Stop gawking and walk in front where I can watch you." Here at least was one responsibility he could reliably keep track of.

He caught Padraig's elbow as they threaded their way through the crowd. "We must convince Vanderbilt we're useful in other ways."

Padraig pulled off his felt hat and wiped the sweat from his brow. "More chance the old goat will shave off his ridiculous pork chops than hire us now."

"Well, Walker's losing men daily in skirmishes, and more are dying from disease . . . It's in the papers. He constantly needs more."

"The promise of five hundred dollars a month and of two hundred and fifty acres of land in Nicaragua gets volunteers lining up," Padraig agreed, "but they can only reach Walker three ways: steamships from San Francisco, New Orleans, or from here on a Morgan-Garrison steamship."

"It's a bottleneck."

"But how does it help us?"

Samuel sidestepped a brown dog licking scraps off the street. "So the Morgan-Garrison Nicaragua Line carries the volunteers down there for free, payback to Walker for giving them Vanderbilt's rights to operate the Nicaraguan route."

"That affects weapons, too," Padraig said. "Walker's getting rifles and even artillery from here."

"I heard that New York is stopping the recruits from sailing," Filipe said over his shoulder. "They said the district attorney had over two hundred filibusters removed from a boat here back in December."

A one-legged man standing in the shade of a doorway rattled coins in a tin cup. "Spare something for an old soldier."

Samuel stopped and dropped a copper coin in the tin. "But hundreds are still getting through. The government's going through the motions to conceal its support for Walker from the British. In truth, they want Walker to annex Nicaragua for the United States, just like Texas."

"Fat chance of that. Wait, Filipe." Padraig caught the boy's elbow. "But Walker wants Nicaragua for himself. What's your point?"

Samuel strode on. "If we can bring Vanderbilt a plan to disrupt Walker's supply of men and arms, he might pay us handsomely."

"Didn't I just say 'fat chance'?" Padraig shook his head and gestured at the overpass rising from intricate steel columns on either side of the street. "This place . . . Unbelievable that a road in the sky can carry all that traffic. Frank Brogan told me about it, but I thought he was making it up."

Energy surged through Samuel, and he grabbed Padraig's arm. "That's it! Frank Brogan. I was thinking about him a moment ago . . . he might even know how to find the wretch who robbed me. For certain, he'll know what's going down to Nicaragua. We must find him."

Samuel darted ahead, waving for a cab.

"Where are we going?" Filipe cried, bounding after him.

"To the docks. Where else would you find a ship captain?"

The stench of putrid fish and salt swelled as the cab swayed onto Market Street and clattered west toward the East River. The public house on the corner of Cherry Street with LISTING

SCHOONER on the peeling sign outside seemed a likely place to begin.

Samuel tapped the driver's shoulder and pointed. "Right there, please."

"A pub, perfect," Padraig said as Samuel paid the driver. "It's long past noon back home, so a tankard or two is overdue."

Drunken chatter washed over him when Samuel ushered them inside. Tobacco smoke made his eyes water, spiraling in wispy curls to swirl across the nicotine-stained ceiling and catching the light seeping through the dusty stained-glass windows. Patrons clamored for service with tankards outstretched above the drinkers slumped along the scarred wooden bar. A dozen heavy wooden tables littered with shot bottles and tankards propped up men and women aged beyond their time.

Filipe goggled at an old man with a mottled scalp and white pork chops who was croaking a dirty shanty in the corner. Samuel snagged the boy's collar and tugged him closer.

"Boats arrive day and night," he said. "These places must always be full."

He pushed onto a long bench beside a couple of leather-faced sailors playing dice, then slid closer still to make room for Filipe and Padraig. The men scowled at the intrusion and promptly ignored them.

A middle-aged barmaid waddled up and plunked three sloshing tankards onto the blade-notched bench. "There ya go, boys, finest beer in the house. Want food?"

Samuel frowned at the dark ale. "Thank you. We're fine for now."

She pushed a strand of oily hair back from her face and waited, perhaps for a tip.

He coughed. "Ah, mistress, we're looking for a friend of ours. Perhaps you know him? A young captain named Frank Brogan?"

Filipe flicked a glance from Samuel to Padraig and slid one

tankard to the edge of the beer-slopped table. He took a big swig and pulled a face.

The barmaid rolled her eyes and gestured at the surrounding patrons. "Would you look at 'em? Most 're so drunk they don't know their own names. How the hell should I know who they are?"

Filipe cut another glance at Samuel and lifted his tanker. His Adam's apple flicked as he gulped it down. He must think Samuel was blind; well, Samuel would set him to rights in a minute.

The woman nodded to the hoary singer in the corner. "Old Declan's worked the docks since Noah's ark moored on the East River. He might know your man."

Samuel bobbed his thanks and slipped her a coin. She threw him a wanton wink and rustled away.

Samuel bumped his tanker against Padraig's to catch his attention. "I'll talk to Declan. You circulate, see what you can discover."

Padraig glanced around. "Sure, I can't talk to them. I don't know them at all."

Samuel leaned to one side and pulled out his tobacco. "It's New York. Half the folk here will be Irish." He glared at Filipe. "Don't move an inch until I return."

Old Declan watched Samuel approach with one bloodshot brown eye; the other was cloudy gray. When Samuel stooped to greet him, he halted his song. That was a relief.

Samuel offered him tobacco. "I'm looking for a captain by the name of Frank Brogan. Tall, dark-haired Irishman in his mid-twenties."

"That snotty accent of yours sounds like money." Declan pointed to his tanker with a liver-spotted hand. "You can buy me a drink, young feller."

"Certainly. Mind if I sit a minute?"

"Free country since we kicked you English out." Declan's voice was eggshell-brittle, and Samuel strained to understand him.

"Well, I'm Irish."

"Irish, are ye? That's different. Mam came from Longford. Know it?" The black sacks sagging onto his cheeks wobbled as Declan rubbed his rheumy eye.

"Never been that far north." Padraig signaled the barmaid, but she avoided eye contact.

"How you know this captain?"

He looked around, but nobody was paying attention; the patrons were too drunk for that. "I worked with him on the steamships in Nicaragua."

Declan perked up. "Nicaragua, is it? You one of them filibusters?"

"No, no, nothing so exciting," Samuel said. "We captained the riverboats. Brogan figured things were getting hairy, with the native troops shooting civilians and cholera everywhere, so he went home. When things got worse, I followed him. I'm hoping he can help me find work."

"From what I heard, he didn't do badly down there." Declan smacked his toothless gums. "He's the only one who came back rich. My drink?"

Samuel glanced at the barmaid for the tenth time. She looked away. He rose and flapped his arms. The barmaid rolled her eyes and stomped over.

"Need to wait your turn," she carped. "What's your hurry?"

"Terribly sorry, but Declan here is parched." He jangled two coins and handed them to her.

She placed her hand on her hip, reminding Samuel of a plump teapot; all she needed to do was tip sideways and pour. "You want one too?"

He shook his head. "I still have one over there."

"Not anymore. Your son drank it."

Samuel's head snapped around. Filipe caught his eye and looked down.

"He's not my son . . . And he shouldn't be drinking." He shot another venomous glance at Filipe.

"Just one, then. Humph." The barmaid left.

Declan's flappy cheeks wobbled. "Fine, buxom girl. Were I twenty years younger, I'd ride her like a gull on a gale."

What a wretched image. Samuel wrung the brim of his hat. "So you know Frank Brogan, then?"

"Who?"

"Frank Brogan."

Declan wiped drool from the corner of his crinkled lips with a gnarled hand. "Brogan operates the prettiest tug in the harbor."

Now they were getting somewhere. "Where can I find him?"

"The *Macaw*. Black hull with a red strip on pier 42, three blocks south of here. Where's my drink?"

"It's coming, thank you." Samuel rushed back to their table. He was going to kill Filipe.

Filipe pushed away the two empty tankards, shifted in his seat, and looked down.

Samuel shook his shoulder. "You shouldn't be drinking."

Filipe's eyes glistened. "Why not? I'm fifteen. I drink at—"

"Watered-down wine, maybe. That beer is potent, and you swilled down two tankards. Get up, we're leaving."

Samuel beckoned Padraig, who sat with a couple of rough-looking men in woolen sweaters.

Filipe wobbled to his feet, and Samuel nudged him toward the door. "Damn it, Filipe, you drink again and I'll toss you into the river. We don't have time for this."

Outside on the bay, square riggers and schooners heeled on the fresh southwesterly wind with off-white sails taut as drums, eager to escape sooty Manhattan. Squat steamers paddled the green-gray river, trailing flat tails of smoke from their funnels.

Padraig looked askance at Filipe. "What's the matter with him?"

"The little twat swilled down my beer with his own," Samuel growled. "He's drunk. You should've been watching him."

"Don't blame me, he's your bloody relative." Padraig chuckled. "It's not my fault the little runt would drink from a whore's boot."

Samuel glowered at Filipe, who was ogling a group of ladies across the street. "Any news on Brogan?"

Padraig shook his head. "Everyone told me to talk to the old codger. Discover anything?"

"Brogan has a tugboat now. Pier 42, several blocks south."

They found the *Macaw* tied up to a small pontoon behind one of many piers crammed with vessels three and four deep. Old Declan hadn't lied; she was a fine craft.

Brogan appeared from the wheelhouse with widening eyes. "What the—Samuel Kingston! And Padraig. What are you doing here?" He tipped back his oil-stained flat cap and hastened to the entry port.

Samuel waved. "Business. How are you? I see you invested wisely. Nice boat."

"Thanks to you," Brogan said. "I owe it to you, really. Well, don't just stand there—come aboard."

The friendly, talkative Brogan hadn't changed since he'd carried Samuel and Padraig across Nicaragua on the San Juan River in an Accessory Transit Company steamer. They'd become friends after discovering he'd emigrated from Cork toward the end of the Great Famine after losing his wife. They sat aft in the cockpit to enjoy the sea breeze that stirred the soupy air. Seagulls wheeled in the sky, crying forlornly and diving for scraps in the scummy water.

"Tough break, losing all that money, especially after the risks you took," Brogan said once Samuel had filled him in. "But you came at a good time if you want to impress Vanderbilt, that old shark."

"A good time?" Samuel sat back on the wooden bench and crossed his arms.

"Remember, I worked the river in Nicaragua before their civil war started," Brogan said. "I know a lot about both factions, so I keep my eyes and ears open for a chance to turn that into a few bucks."

"And sooo . . .?" Padraig asked.

"Vanderbilt believed Walker would bring stability down there," Brogan said, "and that's always good for business."

Samuel took out his tobacco. "But now Walker has cheated him by assigning the Nicaraguan Transit Route rights to Garrison and Morgan."

Brogan nodded. "Vanderbilt has sworn he won't rest until he destroys Walker, no matter what it costs. Word on the street is both sides are looking for rifles and artillery to ship down there."

Padraig cocked his head to one side. "Who, exactly?"

Filipe was snoring gently in the shade of the enormous white paddlewheel, and Samuel scowled. They should've left him in Clonakilty.

"Domingo de Goicuría, for one," Brogan said.

"The rich Cuban involved in the Cuban uprising?" Samuel asked.

"The very man, he's with Walker," Brogan said. "George Law also—just to spite Vanderbilt, I'll bet."

Now they were getting somewhere. Samuel offered Brogan his tobacco tin. "Who's George Law?"

"'Live Oak' George Law owns the mail line that operates between here and Chagres in Panama. His business took a hit when Vanderbilt opened the Nicaraguan route, so he and Vanderbilt don't get along." Brogan spread a cigarette paper and pinched some tobacco. "Law bought thousands of obsolete muskets from the US Army and hired an Englishman by the name of Henningsen to bore them to take minié rounds. Rumor has it he's selling them to Walker's people."

Samuel's pulse quickened, and he bumped Padraig's shoulder. "Unrest in Nicaragua would suit this Law chap."

Padraig nodded. "Travelers would avoid Nicaragua there and use his Panama route instead."

Samuel looked out over the river. There might be something he could do here to win Vanderbilt's favor. "You know where they're boring out these guns?"

Brogan rolled his cigarette between oil-stained fingers. "Hundreds of Irish work around the docks, many are Fenian supporters eager for a rebel rising back in Ireland, and the sniff of rifles has them shooting their mouths off. Henningsen is boring the rifles in a waterfront factory on the river. Why?"

"How are they moving the weapons down to Nicaragua?" Samuel asked.

Brogan licked the paper and sealed his greasy roll. "I heard in the pub they barge them downriver and hide them in cargo on the Morgan-Garrison ships. I know for a fact they sent two cannons to Nicaragua that way as well."

A sharp puff of smoke from Brogan's cigarette overpowered the smell of tar, oil, and salt.

Padraig squirmed on the thwart. "Samuel, you're not thinking of stealing guns?"

Samuel pushed up his sleeve. "We could hurt Walker this way. If Vanderbilt wants rifles, why shouldn't we be the ones to sell them to him?"

Brogan looked from Samuel to Padraig and back again.

Samuel locked eyes with him. "Find out when they will move the next lot of rifles, Brogan."

Brogan exhaled hard, and the wind whipped the smoke away. "If you do this, I want in."

"Why? You're all set here."

Brogan looked down at his callused hands. "The Kingston family saved our lives back in the famine. If you hadn't delivered that grain to the workhouse in Skibbereen, we'd have starved, my young lad, my sister, and me. I want to help you."

"And we're glad to have done it," Samuel said, "but you don't need this."

"Competition's tough in the harbor, and I pumped near every penny I brought up from Nicaragua into the *Macaw*. Sure, I could use the money."

Samuel downed a gulp of the warm beer Brogan had given him and held out a hand. "Well then, damned glad to have you. We'll need your local knowledge."

"Hold your horses." Padraig had picked up a frayed rope end and was splicing it. "We can't do this on our own. We're too few. How are we going to carry off thousands of guns? Just three of us? It's a mad plan."

"Four." Samuel nudged Filipe, who still slept in the paddle-wheel's shade, with his foot and grinned.

"Damn it, Samuel, this is no laughing matter." Padraig threw down the rope end and stood. "I don't want to hang as a thief."

"I'm sorry. You're right." Samuel sighed heavily. He was doing it again . . . jumping into action without considering the consequences. "It's too dangerous; we don't have enough reliable men. It'd take a half-dozen carts to haul the guns away and at least eight men. But I don't know what else we can do, except find that bastard who stole the Baltimore papers." He looked at Frank. "Are you sure you don't know the thief Padraig described, a fellow with a long face and a beard?"

Brogan shook his head. "That could be half the men in the country."

Samuel's shoulders dropped. "Then we're out of—"

"Watch out!" Someone roared from the port side.

A barge passed within three feet, and its stern brushed Macaw's gunwale, rocking her. The tug towing the barge slowed, and a man dashed back to its blunt transom. "I'm sorry, the boy's learning. I shouldn't have taken my eyes off him."

"Damned farmer." Brogan dashed to the gunwale and looked

down. "Lord, that was lucky, it struck the fenders and didn't even scratch her." He waved to the man on the tug. "No damage this time but, for God's sake, teach him out in the roads."

A barge, that was the answer. Samuel sat on the edge of his seat. "We don't need men and wagons. We can wait until they load the barge and steal the damned thing. It doesn't take many to hook a barge to your tug and tow it away."

Brogan looked after the departing tug spitting sparks and smoke into the smudged sky. He slapped the gunwale "You're right. And I've a couple of reliable men. In fact, one of your Nicaraguan soldiers is here in New York, too."

Samuel looked at Padraig, who perked up.

"Emanuel Chavez."

Padraig spluttered on his cigarette. "Chavez? Here in New York?"

Chavez was one of the Euronicas who'd helped him defeat the Earl of Baltimore a year ago. He was an enigma, a conscript who could read; Samuel never understood how such a learned man had ended up in the Democrat army. "Why did he leave Costa Rica?"

Brogan shrugged. "Not much of a talker, that one."

"No kidding," Padraig said.

"I suspect there's a woman involved," Brogan said. "Word has it he's been asking around after a woman."

Padraig let out a low whistle. "Well, I'll be. I never figured Chavez for a dirty dog."

Samuel kicked at him. "Shut up and let Brogan talk. So what's Chavez doing now?"

"He must still be looking," Brogan said. "For all New Yorkers' talk of equality, fellows like him, dark as a block of mahogany, find little opportunity to work. He does odd jobs for me."

Samuel stood up. He'd be delighted to see Chavez again. "Where can we find him?"

"Up at Five Points. It's the roughest slum in the city where the emancipated slaves and the Irish live, and not in harmony, mind you."

Samuel smoothed his frock coat. They would need Chavez. "Do you have an address?"

"It's a four-story tenement on Cross Street, no place for strangers with your skin color," he said. "I'm known there. I'll take you, but Padraig better keep quiet. The African descendants don't like the Irish there."

Padraig flipped his cigarette overboard and crossed the deck. "Not looking for a cabin boy, are you? The little don's hands are soft, but they'll surely toughen up." He winked and nudged Filipe with his boot. "On your feet, Filipe. We're leaving."

It was only a mile, but the stench of human waste and decay increased with every step. In the garbage-strewn streets, threadbare men of all races jostled outside the public houses, where women withered from a lifetime of misery peddled their wares or themselves.

Brogan halted at a street crammed with two- and three-story timber shanties. "Cross Street. Chavez lives up there."

Beside Samuel, Filipe looked up in bemusement, perhaps befuddlement, at the tattered laundry flapping between the rough-hewn buildings and belched. He was a pallid shade of green. Samuel shoved him into the littered alleyway, avoiding eye contact with the grizzled men measuring them from shadows thrown by the tenements a block away. He touched the butt of the Colt in his waistband. They stood out too much here.

"*Capitán* Kingston! *Qué esta haciendo aquí.*" Emanuel Chavez waved from a window on the second story of a weathered building down the street before disappearing inside. The burly Nicaraguan appeared on the street a few moments later and flashed a grin. "What brings you here, señores?" he asked in Spanish. "Five Points is not safe for gentlemen."

Samuel's troubles seemed a little lighter at the sight of the man he'd known as a quiet conscript in Nicaragua. He shook Chavez's hand and answered in Spanish, confident that even Brogan had a good grasp of the language after his years in Nicaragua. "Looking for you. Have you time for a chat?"

Chavez gestured around him. "In this place, we've only time . . . Until it runs out."

"Come with us. We need to talk." He caught Chavez's muscled arm and drew him toward the East River. "Why'd you leave Costa Rica? With the gold you had, you were sitting pretty."

Chavez stepped around a fly-furred dog's carcass. "I wanted to find an old friend, but this is an awful place for a colored man. As soon as I stepped ashore, the police took my money—an entry fee, they said."

"What rats!" Padraig cried. "Police are as bad here as they are in Ireland."

"Since then, I've struggled," Chavez said. "No jobs for a dark-skinned man. Honest to God, *Capitán*, as soon as I have the price of a ticket, I'm returning to Nicaragua."

Samuel took Filipe's elbow as they threaded through the throng of immigrants and rickety stalls and wagons packing the narrow street. So many people. A ruddy-faced man with cords of muscle straining the seams of his sack coat kicked a pig rooting in the garbage, and it raced into the raucous crowd with a squeal.

The stranger tipped back his dented John Bull hat and stepped in front of Filipe. "You frightened my pig, greaser. Now you have to pay me for her."

Filipe's beer-bright eyes narrowed. "I'm N-Nicaraguan, not from Greece."

"We don't allow no Italians into the Five Points." The stranger seized Filipe by the shoulder and shook him. "You're a greaser. We don't want your kind here."

Filipe blanched and vomited chunks of creamy chime on the

man's rumpled jacket. Six thugs drinking nearby guffawed as the man dropped Filipe with a curse.

"There you go, Murphy," called a tall man with an untidy beard and bloodshot eyes. "You sure shook the guts out of that greaser."

Hackles up, Murphy swung back to Filipe.

What kind of bully picked on a boy? Samuel drew back and punched Murphy in the face. Pain crackled through his knuckles.

Murphy's companions lunged to their feet and pushed through the crowd. The tall man hurled his tankard onto the cobblestones and punched Samuel in the face. Samuel tasted blood, then crooked a hand around the tall man's head and drove it down to meet his rising knee. The man's nose flattened with a crack, and Samuel threw him backward.

Padraig had apparently punched one of the ruffians in the stomach and was holding the others off, hands lifted like a prize-fighter. "What kind of Irishmen are you lot to be attacking your own? I'll show you, you gombeens."

Crimson drops dribbled from Murphy's upper lip as he staggered back and drew a hunting knife. But Samuel wouldn't pull his Colt; killing someone would bring the law down on them. He spread his arms, prepared to meet Murphy's advance.

Filipe slashed Murphy's forearm with a fat little knife produced from nowhere. "This greaser has teeth too, *yanqui*."

Murphy yelped and dropped his blade. Samuel punched him on the chin, barreling him over a fruit stand.

Chavez charged the four remaining hard cases with a piece of timber torn from a meat stall, snarling and jabbing the nearest man's gut as if he held a bayonet. Whirling the four-foot weapon, he slammed it against the next man's head. The man crumpled as his bowler hat flew into the crowd.

The last two thugs backed up, snarling curses.

Samuel grabbed Filipe's wrist to stop him from stabbing Murphy in the belly. "Enough! Let's go."

Nobody moved. Brogan stood still, arms hanging loosely at his sides. Padraig and Chavez hovered over the men they had felled with their fists up.

"Come on. We don't need a fuss with the coppers." Samuel shunted Filipe into the crowd and directed him down a narrow alley, away from the furor. "Who gave you that knife?"

"I bought it in León last year."

Samuel cursed under his breath. "I can't believe your father let—"

"Left here at Chatham Street," Brogan panted from behind. "Then right on Market. That takes us back to the docks."

Chavez wiped the sweat from his glistening head. "Just like old times, eh, *Capitán*? When we whooped the *Legitimistas* at La Virgen Bay."

"Did you see me take that one down?" Filipe whirled into a crouch. "I was on him like—"

Samuel spun him around. The boy was a menace. "What did I tell you about weapons? If you'd killed that Irish bastard back there, you'd be facing a hangman now. No guns, Filipe. No knives. Not even a stick from now on."

Padraig slapped his thigh with a bemused smile. "Told you he was a bloodthirsty sprat. But he may have saved your life back there."

Samuel shot him a disapproving glare. "I had my Colt."

"Gentlemen, we have urgent priorities." Brogan steered Samuel left into Oak Street. "This way. There's a place we can talk."

The interior of The Bitter Oak bar greeted Samuel with an almost physical wall of stale ale and sweat from its patrons, mainly sailors and stevedores. Once seated with a lukewarm beer at a sloppy table across from Filipe, where he could monitor him, Samuel brought Chavez up to speed on their mission and asked about the other Euronicas, their native Nicaraguan company that had deserted from Walker's Democrat army.

"They could be better." Chavez took a long pull on his beer.

"In Costa Rica, the people discriminated against us because of our darker skin. Thank God for you, for the gold you sent, because it's hard to find work there. The boys are homesick, and it's eating them up that we helped Walker into power."

Samuel looked away. "We didn't know then Walker planned to remove the ban on slavery."

"Nevertheless, *Capitán*, we won that battle for Walker," Chavez said. "It's hard to live with that."

"Well now you have a chance to do something about it," Padraig said.

Chavez rubbed his chin. "What do you mean? What are you—"

"Frank Brogan! How the hell are you?" A tall stranger in his mid-thirties ducked into the nook, beaming at Brogan.

"Well, I'll be—Sylvanus Spencer." Brogan shook Spencer's hand. "When did you get back?"

"Couple of days ago."

Brogan slapped Spencer's shoulder. "Sylvanus worked with me in the Accessory Transit Company. He captained the *Machuca*, another steamer on the San Juan River."

Samuel perked up. Perhaps the newcomer had useful information. "Samuel Kingston. It's a pleasure to meet you. Why don't you join us for a drink?"

"Don't mind if I do. Whiskey, please. Let me fetch my associate." Spencer touched the brim of his bowler hat and hurried to the entrance. The thickset man who followed him back to the table had a neck so short his square head seemed to rest directly on his shoulders. "May I present Clifford Webster, another Englishman."

"We're not bloody Englishmen," Padraig said. "We're Irish."

A flush crept across Spencer's cheeks, and his hand flew to his black mustache. "I beg your pardon. I assumed from Mr. Kingston's accent . . ."

"Don't mind him." Samuel glared at Padraig—this was not the time for touchy nationalism—and extended his hand to

Webster. "The belligerent Irishman is Padraig Kerr. That's Chavez with the permanent suntan, and the young lad is Filipe. Please, sit."

Webster smiled around the table and nodded at Padraig. "I understand your ire. Believe you me, it disgusts me how the English treat the Irish. That's one reason I left Britain."

Padraig brightened and gripped Webster's hand. "Peace, then."

"What news have you from Nicaragua?" Samuel asked.

Spencer unbuttoned his jacket. "From my point of view, nothing good. When Walker gave Vanderbilt's trans-Nicaragua concession to Morgan and Garrison, they fired me, and poor Clifford's business as a migration agent in Granada hasn't profited from the wave of immigrants coming to Nicaragua from the United States. It seems William Walker dislikes Clifford."

Padraig raised his glass to Webster. "Any enemy of Walker is a friend of mine."

Clifford licked his lips and smiled uneasily, glancing out into the room. Spencer seemed a reliable chap, Samuel thought, but there was something about Webster and the way he kept looking over his shoulder.

"How can Walker take Vanderbilt's concession?" Samuel asked.

"President Rivas was nothing more than a puppet, Walker really—"

"Was?" Samuel raised his eyebrows.

"Oh, you wouldn't have heard," Spencer said. "Walker just held a sham election. Now, he's the President of Nicargua."

Samuel froze, his whiskey glass almost at his lips. "My God. When?"

"A couple of weeks ago," Spencer said bitterly.

Then Walker had won, and he'd destroy Nicaragua. "This is a disaster." Samuel swayed back in his chair. This changed everything. It was far too dangerous to travel to Nicaragua now, even in pursuit of the Baltimore papers.

"He'll make slaves of us all . . . sell our country to the highest bidder." Chavez dropped his head onto his hands.

Filipe wasn't paying attention. He was cleaning off the dried blood like it was rust on his knife.

Spencer had been observing Filipe with a deepening frown, and he shifted his seat further back from the youth. "Perhaps it's only short term. Vanderbilt's a powerful man. He won't let Walker get away with stealing his business. The allied army may defeat Walker and things will return to normal. After all, Walker's stretched thin. He's fighting Costa Rica, Honduras, Salvador, and Guatemala now."

Padraig scoffed. "Doubt it. The Costa Ricans have retreated to San José and given up, and American volunteers are pouring into Nicaragua to swell Walker's army. Soon he'll be impossible to beat."

Samuel reached over and touched Filipe's wrist. "Put that knife away, you're making people nervous . . . There's one certain way to stop Walker,"

Spencer's eyebrows wriggled together as he looked at Samuel.

"If the allies seized control of the San Juan River, they would cut off Walker's access to more volunteers and arms," Samuel said.

Filipe slid his short dagger inside his coat. "The Costas already tried to capture the river forts by following the Sarapiquí River through the jungle to where it joins the San Juan River. But Walker's filibusters were too smart for them. They ambushed three hundred Costa Ricans in the jungle and trounced them."

Damn it, Samuel didn't want Filipe drawing attention. These two shouldn't know he was the son of one of Walker's commanders. Samuel kicked him under the table, and Filipe's face darkened.

"That true, Mr. Spencer?" Samuel asked innocently, but his mind was in turmoil. The Baltimore papers were beyond his reach now, and his only chance of saving Springbough for Jason was Vanderbilt.

Spencer nodded. "I heard the Costas made such a ruckus cutting a path through the jungle that scouts from Walker's Hipp's Point fort heard them, and the filibusters drove them off."

"No wonder, after hacking their way through the rainforest, The Costa Ricans must've arrived too exhausted to fight," Padraig said.

Samuel tipped his cigarette ash on the sawdust-strewn floor. "I'd have built rafts and floated troops down the San Carlos River to the San Juan. One of my Euronicas, Quintero—" Samuel glanced from Padraig to Chavez. "Remember him? Small, wiry guy, missing several teeth? He said the San Carlos River is navigable all the way to its confluence with the San Juan River."

Spencer slid his chair closer. "You might capture the outpost at Hipp's Point. It's only a mud redoubt. But El Castillo? Its walls are four feet thick and fourteen feet high. Inside, the keep is fifty feet tall. And if you attacked from the northern side, you'd have to cross a ravine and charge up the steep hill while under fire all the way. For that to work, you'd have to surprise them."

Samuel caught Padraig's glance. They knew that fort well; he'd rescued Padraig from its dungeon a year ago.

Padraig bobbed his head. "It would be hard to attack from the river, too. The fort's guns would sink any steamer before she was clear of the river bend."

The men were all nodding. Samuel dragged on his cigarette. "It's an old fortress, and I know where the walls are weak. I broke in there last year to rescue Padraig."

Stunned eyes turned to him.

"I'd take a couple of men over the curtain wall in the middle of the night, eliminate the guards, and open the gate for the rest of our army. Once we captured the fort, we could keep Walker's lone star flag flying to lull the next riverboat into docking."

"That might work." Spencer shrugged and showed the palm of his hands. "But it's not our problem, is it?"

He'd no time for such idle speculation. Samuel was running out of options. He needed to get moving. He faked a broad smile. "Well, that's never going to happen, and my friends and I have work to do."

The tension drained from around the table, and chairs scraped the stone floor as they rose to leave.

As they headed to the door, Samuel caught Padraig's elbow and held him back. "Vanderbilt's our only hope now. We need those rifles."

CHAPTER SIX

The waning moon shed sliver light on the murky waters of the East River and backlit the forest of masts and funnels screening Manhattan's warehouses on the other shore. Even with her black hull, the *Macaw* would stand out when she crossed to meet Samuel on the Brooklyn wharf. He blinked rapidly and looked at the clouds hovering off the southwest shore. If they arrived, it would be dark enough to give his plan a chance.

He turned to Padraig, squatting against the factory wall beside him. "It's too bright. If those clouds don't move in, we'll be in trouble."

"Wind is southwesterly. It'll blow them in, Brogan was certain of it." The discordant sound of clanging metal, whirling engines, and intermittent whoosh of venting gas from the nearby factories shielded Padraig's voice.

Samuel glassed the river with his spyglass. Law's warehouse lurked in the haze of industrial smoke, a long rectangular building set back twenty yards from a wharf on the East River. The lone barge tied up on the left side of the wooden jetty beneath a cross-like loading derrick had to be the one they sought. "No sign of the guards."

"Brogan's contact reported six on duty every night," Padraig said. "They're probably walking the perimeter. Or sleeping."

Samuel caught the faint beat of drums and off-key voices blaring an Irish ballad behind them. Torches materialized on the street, casting spindly shadows as two dozen figures marched up Pine Street toward the factory.

Samuel twitched and undid the top button of his shirt. "Right on time. Let's hope Chavez has turned out his kind as well." It was a crazy plan—reckless—but it was too late to back down now.

The boisterous throng bellowed ethnic slurs as they approached, hobnailed boots ringing on the cobblestone street and orange light from the factories flickering on their boozy faces. More shadows wielding wooden poles and makeshift weapons erupted from a side street with a roar and fell upon the marchers.

A clash of wood, curses, and yelps of pain filled the air as the two gangs crashed together. It didn't take long for the melee to rumble down Pine Street to the dray-wide double doors of the factory, where George Law had bored the barrels of two thousand decommissioned US Army muskets. The factory door opened, and several bewildered guards stepped outside, swinging clubs and iron bars.

A tic shivered Samuel's left cheek. There was no turning back now. Boots crunched gravel behind him, and he whirled, reaching for his Colt.

Dressed in black, Chavez was almost invisible.

Samuel relaxed. "Fine riot, Chavez. Now it's time to go."

Chavez seemed wholly calm; nothing ever shook the man. His white teeth flashed in the darkness. "First time the African descendants and the Irish got paid to fight. At Five Points, they do it for free."

The boundary wall stood in comfortingly deep shadows, but the spikes along its top made Samuel hesitate. The clink of broken glass and loud jeers sounded in front of the factory. That would occupy the guards.

Padraig produced a rope with a large loop tied at one end, whirled it expertly, and lassoed a spike on his first throw. He'd sailed since he was a child and knew about ropes. Samuel handed him a heavy blanket which he slung around his neck before stepping into Chavez's clasped hands. Samuel eyed the street. There was still no sign of the guards. Padraig steadied himself against the wall, climbed onto Chavez's shoulders, and tossed the folded blanket onto the spikes. He cursed and swayed sideways when the blanket missed the spikes, his boots gouging into Chavez's shoulders. The second try. The blanket settled on the spikes, and he pulled himself up. He straddled the wall, cushioned from the spikes by the blanket, and peered into the yard.

"All clear."

There was another roar from the front of the building, and the mob surged toward the front doors. The guards bellowed and tussled to drive them back.

The rope coiled down and struck Samuel on the shoulder. He passed a crowbar and dark lantern up to Padraig and boosted Chavez up. Chavez's boot crunched his shoulder, the sole cutting into his flesh. It was a relief when Chavez grunted and the weight lifted off him. Samuel grabbed the coarse hemp and pulled himself up. He smelled tar as he lowered himself with the rope on the other side, crouching on the gravel in the shadow of a pile of scrap metal where Chavez waited. At Samuel's tap on the shoulder, the burly Nicaraguan sprinted across the wharf into the cover of the boathouse and out of sight.

"Holy Mary, Mother of God, watch over us." Padraig dashed after Chavez.

The disturbance Chavez had purchased was waning, barely audible above the tinnitus in Samuel's left eardrum. It wouldn't be long before the guards returned. He flicked a glance at the factory and dashed ahead. Metal clinked on metal, and he heard a *snap* as he skidded around the boathouse. Chavez had jimmied the lock off the gate guarding the wharf.

The path was clear to the steel barge riding low on the river. The brackish water stank of piss and rotten eggs. The clouds had drifted over the moon, but Samuel still spotted the silhouette of Brogan's tugboat drifting mid-river, a faint glow atop her funnel. That was bad news; if he could see her, others might.

"Keep watch," he hissed and approached the barge at a crouch.

The barge was a solid steel island and didn't budge as he stepped aboard and unhooked the brass dark lamp from his belt. He lifted the circular lid three times, beaming light across the river as the camphene fumes tickled his nose.

A shadow popped from a hatchway, and Samuel tensed.

"Crates of musket rifles," Chavez said, "just as *Capitán* Brogan promised."

"Untie the springers."

Chavez's eyes widened, white orbs in the darkness. "Huh?"

Samuel pointed out the lines that held the barge from moving fore or aft. "Then undo the stern line but hold it with a wrap around the cleat." Samuel gestured to the stern.

A dog growled over by the boathouse, followed by a curse from Padraig. The growl erupted into snarling and then baying. Samuel glanced at the silvery moonlight spilling from the bow wave of the approaching tug. There wasn't time, but Padraig needed help. The guards must have heard the commotion for certain.

He leaped ashore, skidding on the cinders and metal shavings strewn on the wharf, and raced to the boathouse. Padraig was squirming on the ground, hands around the neck of a gray dog the size of a wolfhound. The dog's foam-flecked teeth snapped inches from Padraig's face. It clawed at Padraig's gut with its powerful forelegs then corkscrewed and ripped into his sleeve.

Samuel grabbed an oar leaning against the wall and swung at the raging beast with all his might. The dog screeched and threw back its head. He struck again, and his heart skipped a beat as something in the dog's back snapped. The dog yelped, twisted into a spasm, and went limp.

Padraig's face was deathly pale as he hurled the dog aside. "We're screwed now. The whole bloody harbor heard that. Get aboard and take the tow line. I'll hold them here."

The metal deck of the barge rang under Samuel's boots as he ran to the bow, taking care not to trip over cleats or hatches. The *Macaw* surged in and turned parallel, her engine roaring, and she shuddered into reverse. Her screw churned the water and she spurted back and forth in the tiny space until her bow faced out across the river. The engine slowed to a gentle pant as Brogan held her in place. *Macaw* would haul the barge up the Hudson River where Samuel and the others would unload the rifles at the warehouse he had rented two days earlier. All that remained was to sink the barge beyond the outer harbor—another task to accomplish this very night . . . if Samuel's plan worked out at all.

Filipe jumped up and down on the tug's foredeck as a crewman swung a messenger line underhand toward the barge. Samuel snatched it with clammy hands and hauled it in. The thin rope wrenched back, burning his hands as it took the weight of the thick tow cable attached to the other end that was fed overboard from the *Macaw*.

"The barge," someone shouted from the shore. "They're stealing the barge!"

Pain lanced through Samuel's palms, but he clung on, and the looped cable from the *Macaw* splashed through the water as he hauled it across to the barge. A pistol crashed behind him, and someone yelled. Padraig must be firing to keep the guards at bay. Saltwater on the hard hemp cable stung Samuel's raw palms, and he gritted his teeth as he hauled it over the bow, dropped the spliced eye over the large cleat, and belayed the messenger rope over it to secure it in place.

Two pistol shots erupted onshore. Orange tongues blazed about a hundred yards back from the wharf.

"Cast off." He circled his arm in the air. "Padraig, get aboard."

Loud curses, running feet, and the crack of a pistol sounded close by. Boots crashed on the deck as Padraig landed aboard the tug. Four men raced onto the wharf, roaring and shaking their fists.

The *Macaw*'s engine gunned, the tow cable snapped taut, and the barge's bow twitched away from the jetty as her stern crashed against the wharf. Samuel was hurled to the deck. The barge corkscrewed into the river, following the thrashing wake of the *Macaw*'s powerful screw.

A gunshot rang out, and metal pinged off the gunwale beside Samuel as he pressed against the cool deck. The barge was gyrating wildly as the *Macaw* accelerated into the center of the river. By the time the guards had reloaded, the barge was a quarter mile offshore, and Brogan slowed to allow it to catch up.

A bearded sailor leaped across from the tug with a messenger rope paying out behind him. His boots clanged on the deck. "I'm here to rig a towing bridle, sir."

Samuel drummed his fingers on the gunwale, eyeing the figures milling on the wharf. If Law's men had access to another boat, they were in trouble.

Within minutes they got underway again, with the barge tucked close behind the *Macaw*'s stubby stern. The moon broke from the clouds at the confluence of the Hudson and East River. To port, the lights on Governor's Island and Ellis Island winked against the night sky. Samuel dared to hope his crew was in the clear.

A boat powered from the dockyard south of Law's factory and sped up past the vessels moored along the Brooklyn wharfs, peeling a glittering bow wave before her. Samuel's heart skipped a beat. He'd rather face an army than a hangman's noose in

Brooklyn, a likely prospect if they were captured. Black smoke and sparks spurted from the steam launch's funnel as she sped across the East River in their wake. Half a dozen men gathered at the bow with clubs dangling in their hands.

Padraig stuffed his reloaded Colt into his waistband and met Samuel and Chavez on the rolling stern. "Now we're rightly screwed. It's going to be all-out war."

Samuel shook his head. "We can't fire on them. We're the pirates here, and if we harm someone, we'll hang for it."

A sheen of sweat glistened on Padraig's forehead. "Then we'll take bare knuckles to them."

Samuel squeezed his fists. "Damned right. Here's what I want you and Chavez to do."

After finishing his instructions, he dashed to the bow, ignoring the spray from the gap between the barge's bow and the *Macaw*'s stern.

Filipe was hanging over the taffrail of the *Macaw*.

"Did you see the boat?" he called.

"I'm jumping over. Catch me."

Samuel jumped for the *Macaw*'s elevated stern. Water boiled in the gap below, and then he was across, crashing into the tug's transom. He grabbed the taffrail and scrambled for a hold.

Filipe grabbed his wrist and heaved as Samuel clambered up and toppled onto the deck with a grunt.

"We fight." Filipe drew a brace of pistols.

"Put those away," Samuel said with exasperation. "I forbade you to carry *armas*, you bloodthirsty lunatic. Follow me." He beckoned at two crewmen. "You fellows, too. Follow me."

In the wheelhouse, Brogan was calmly conning the tug. It was hard to rattle a man who'd operated a steamboat in the middle of Nicaragua's civil war.

"What shall we do?" Brogan asked.

"No guns," Samuel replied. "We'll see if we can surprise them. How long before they catch us?"

Brogan glanced aft and down at the semaphore. The brass

lever was hard over to starboard at Full Ahead. "We're making about five knots to their six. I'd say ten minutes."

"Take us south into Upper Bay. There's more room to maneuver there and less likelihood we'll be seen from shore. My lads and I will hide. Perhaps there's a chance we can surprise them."

Brogan craned around. "Are you joshing me?"

"You've a better idea?"

Brogan shook his head and tried in vain to jam the semaphore lever farther over as he pointed the bow between Governor's Island and Ellis Island. The ebbing tide and current from the Hudson had helped them maintain a lead, but now the steamer was in the channel and receiving the same assist. The men on her foredeck hurled abuse and threats at the *Macaw*, shaking fists and clubs. Two tongues of flame licked out from the pursuing steamer, desperate shots that kicked up water behind the tug.

Padraig and Chavez ran to the barge's bow, and Padraig tossed the signal lamp across to Samuel, before both men jumped from the barge across to the *Macaw*.

Samuel pointed to the wheelhouse roof. "Hide up there and attack when I act. Chavez, slip around to the port side of the wheelhouse out of view.

Leaving them to get into position, Samuel hurried to the engine room ladder. Hot air rising from the hatch flooded his mouth, tasting of grease and smoke. The clatter of the shaft and flywheel below was deafening, and the stench of fumes and bilge water nauseated him as he searched the workbench for the bottle he needed. He hastened back into the fresh air.

Filipe waited impatiently, shifting his weight from one foot to another. "What about me?"

Samuel held out his hand. "Give me those blasted *pistolas*."

Filipe handed over the guns and spread his legs in a wide stance. "I can fight with you."

Samuel's nostrils flared. This boy was impossible, "No. Sofia will be furious when she hears you're involved. Tell Brogan to heave to—and remain in the wheelhouse, whatever happens. I mean that. Whatever happens." He placed the pistols in a locker and headed aft.

The engine's roar faded to a pulsing pant, and the *Macaw* lost headway until the barge bumped against her stern. Both vessels halted, rocking on the ocean swell. The river steamer surged alongside them, moonlight glinting on her brass portholes. Two of her crew were already pointing pistols at the *Macaw*'s wheelhouse.

A burly man in a John Bull hat and dark suit hung over the starboard gunwale and cupped his hands. "Keep your paws where we can see them, you damn pirates. We're coming alongside."

The hulls crashed together, and three men leaped across with the leader, one with a bow line, another with a stern line. Their hard soles crashed on the deck plates.

Samuel hurled the bottle of kerosene onto the steamer's teak deck and sent the signal lamp sailing after it. The breaking glass tinkled and flames exploded against the steamer's wheelhouse.

Padraig leaped from the wheelhouse roof onto the leader's shoulders and drove him into the deck.

Chavez ran from behind the wheelhouse and rammed a paddle into another boarder's stomach. "Take that, *yanqui*."

On the steamer, Law's men cursed and scrambled around the dancing flames. They would quench the fire, but in the meantime, it would keep them busy.

Filipe erupted from the *Macaw*'s wheelhouse; firelight flickered on the leather blackjack he slammed against the third man's head. Before Samuel could reach this man, Chavez felled him with a blow to the back of his neck.

"Stop." Samuel hauled Filipe off his unconscious opponent. "Don't kill him. Padraig, Chavez, *ayudame*, we'll toss them overboard. The steamer will be too busy firefighting and fishing the buggers out to chase us."

They swung the first man like a pendulum and heaved him

overboard. With Filipe and Chavez's help, they soon offloaded the remaining boarders the same way. Samuel nodded to Brogan, still dragging on his cigarette in the wheelhouse. Brogan slammed the semaphore to Full Ahead and the tug's engine roared, vibrating the deck as she spurted forward with her funnel spewing black smoke and embers into the starlit sky.

In her wake, yellow flames on the steamer cast grotesque, shifting shadows of the figures fighting them. Samuel sagged against the guardrail and pressed his hands to his thighs so nobody would see them tremble. *Thank you, God, for getting us out of this.*

Filipe was grinning wildly and chattering to Padraig. He should never have agreed to bring the boy, but Sofia had insisted.

"—how I slugged that *payaso* back there? Did you?" Filipe was jumping up and down as he jabbered to Padraig. "Wow, I can't believe it."

"I told you to stay in the wheelhouse." Samuel's voice was thick with emotion. "If something happens to—and where'd you get that blackjack?"

Filipe glanced at Chavez and hung his head, while Chavez suddenly took a great interest in the shadowed shoreline.

Samuel glared at Chavez. "You should have *mas* sense. What if he'd killed somebody? This isn't Nicaragua; they've lawmen here."

Behind Filipe, Padraig turned away to hide his smile, and that infuriated Samuel even more.

"From now on, the boy carries no weapons," he declared. "Not even a fork. Do you hear me, Chavez? You too, Padraig."

"Fair enough," Padraig said. "You're right, the little bugger could be deadly—even with a fork."

CHAPTER SEVEN

"When Brogan told me that you were honorable and a man of action, Captain Kingston, he failed to mention you were ruthless, too." Cornelius Vanderbilt's smile reached all the way to his eyes as he waved Samuel and Padraig toward the easy chairs by the large fireplace.

Samuel unbuttoned his frock coat and took a seat. "Now you know we mean business."

Vanderbilt took a cigar from a box in the single drawer of his long desk, clipped off the end, and lit it before padding to the fireplace, where he eased into a chair and crossed his legs, inclining back on a cloud of smoke. The sweet scent reminded Samuel of Father and home.

The Commodore blew another spiral at the corniced ceiling. "So how is my business any of yours, young man?"

"I know of your vendetta with William Walker, and I don't blame you." Samuel took out his snuffbox and offered it to Padraig.

"He shouldn't have taken over the Nicaraguan Transit Route." Padraig took a pinch of snuff. "You pioneered it."

Vanderbilt frowned at the snuffbox and puffed on his cigar.

"You stole Live Oak George's rifles from under his nose," "He's not going to like that."

"When we were unable to come to an agreement on working together a month ago, I took the guns to prove to you how useful I can be."

The shipping magnate shrugged. "How does this help me?"

"William Walker is now short two thousand guns," Padraig stood and approached the model steamers on the mantlepiece. He was interested in any kind of boat.

Samuel flexed his fingers. "And if you buy the guns from us, you can supply them to any of the allies fighting Walker—the Costa Ricans, the Guatemalans, the Salvadorians, the Hondurans, whomever you please. These rifles can't be traced back to you."

Vanderbilt tipped ash from his cigar, and his eyebrows furrowed as Padraig poked at one of the model ships. "I could buy them, yes. But I couldn't deliver them while keeping my name out of the transaction."

Samuel raked his fingers through his hair. Vanderbilt was angling for something. "I don't know how I can help you with that."

"I'll tell you what," Vanderbilt said. "I'll buy the rifles and provide you with funds to charter a boat. You'll deliver the rifles. I know Lieutenant Kerr here is a sailor. I only hope he doesn't sail my model of the *Prometheus* off the mantel there."

And just like that, they were going back to Central America. Samuel shifted uncomfortably, and his chair creaked.

Vanderbilt blew gently on tip of his cigar and watched it glow.

If Samuel refused Vanderbilt again, all was lost: Springbough Manor estate, the house he was building, and his family's future. But to return to Central America . . . the memories, the fiascos, the place where he'd failed to save his own father . . . He'd sworn to return for Father's body someday, but he wasn't ready.

Vanderbilt tapped his foot and glanced at the crystal clock on the mantel.

Samuel ran his palms down his trousers. "Fine. I'll do it."

Vanderbilt nodded curtly and stroked his pork chop whiskers. "You can charter a brig. A sailing ship will draw less attention from the authorities here and from the British and American navies."

"Less attention?" Padraig glanced at Samuel for reassurance. "That sounds like quite a bit of attention, actually."

"I've pressed both governments to prevent arms and recruits from reaching Walker," Vanderbilt said. "We don't want them sweeping you up. If that happens, you're on your own. I can't be involved."

Padraig sat and folded his arms over his chest.

"So where are the rifles headed?" Samuel asked.

"Costa Rica," Vanderbilt replied without hesitation. "General Mora's shown his commitment to removing Walker."

Padraig sat forward. "Well, he hasn't done a good job so far. If he—"

"Mora thrashed Walker in Rivas and would have finished it if cholera hadn't wiped out his army," Vanderbilt said. "It was a mistake to bring infected men back to Costa Rica. The cholera killed ten thousand people there."

"That's huge for a tiny nation," Samuel said.

"One tenth of Costa Rica's population. Mora won't make that mistake again. He's the best option to remove that pirate and those crooks, Morgan and Garrison." Vanderbilt smiled and rose from his chair. "And that's where you come in, soldier boys. Don't screw it up."

The exotic aromas of coffee and spices shielded Samuel's nose from the stench of the industrial detritus and human waste in the sluggish Hudson River as his chartered brig, *Spartacus,*

drifted past wharfs clustered with sailing craft and steamers—coasters as well as seagoing and inland vessels. It had been a scramble to secure a brig on short notice, but finally, after a frantic six days, they'd secured the right ship. Padraig and Brogan had thoroughly checked over the three-masted square-rigger and declared her fit for the voyage. All that remained was to load the weapons and set sail in the morning.

The deck rocked in the stern wave of a passing steamer, and he adjusted his balance as the other boat whistled contemptuously. It was becoming a hostile world for sailing vessels. The faint breeze tickled the sweat soaking his armpits and dribbling down his back. Beyond the sandstone walls of the Emigrant Landing Depot at Castle Clinton, a battered three-master schooner was disgorging a throng of shabby and bewildered Irish emigrants. Samuel's stomach hollowed at the thought of home. He'd been such an ass the past few months, withdrawn and brooding. It was a gift that his wife had put up with him, for he could scarcely recall the last time they'd been intimate. He shouldn't have parted from Sofia so coldly. He should've held his son longer, got to know him better before dashing away to America. He sighed and looked back at the schooner's cluttered deck. This mission would help him regain their financial security, to protect his wife and family.

Padraig and Filipe threaded their way between the barefooted sailors toiling on deck and joined him at the starboard gunwale. Samuel shot a glance at Filipe. The boy had disappeared at dinner time the night before; he'd better not have been up to mischief.

"Where've you been?" Samuel asked. "I've not seen you since yesterday afternoon."

Filipe avoided his gaze. "*Que?* What do you mean?"

"You never showed up for dinner. That was downright rude."

Filipe pawed a hand through his wavy hair. "I'm fifteen, not five. I don't have to report to you. You're not my father."

Samuel cracked his fingers. "But I am your caretaker. While

we're on this mission, you'll go nowhere without my permission, or I'll ship you back to Ireland."

"That's most unfair." Filipe's eyes flashed, and he stalked forward to the bow.

Samuel kicked the guardrail and glared at the passing ships. He couldn't send Filipe back to Nicaragua, where Colonel Valle's blind allegiance to Walker had already landed his son in danger, and Sofia didn't need Filipe complicating her life at home, either. Samuel was stuck with him.

Padraig placed a hand on his shoulder. "He's a good lad, merely confused as to where his allegiance should lie. Walker has him and his father hoodwinked."

Samuel shuddered at the thought of the rows Filipe would have started with his sister if they'd left him at home with Sofia. It boggled the imagination.

A quarter of an hour later, the crew slipped the sheets and clawed up the luffing sails as they coasted alongside a weather-beaten pier on the Jersey City side of the river.

Even before sailors had leaped ashore with mooring lines, Chavez ran from the warehouse, waving his arms wildly. Something was wrong. Four horsemen burst from the dray-wide warehouse doors in a clatter of hoofbeats and pistol fire. Chavez toppled forward, and lead balls thumped into *Spartacus*'s wooden hull.

Samuel drew his Colt and fired three times at the riders. Padraig's revolver barked at his side. The long-faced, bearded rider in front wheeled his mount and led the others back into the warehouse.

Samuel cocked the Colt and rushed for the pier. "Come on, they didn't expect anyone to have revolvers. Get to Chavez."

Filipe seized Samuel's arm. "Samuel, I can—"

"Stay here."

Samuel snapped a fourth shot at the shadowed warehouse. The last horseman jerked and toppled from his horse as Samuel landed on the quay.

Chavez had rolled onto his back and was clutching a wound in his shoulder with bloody fingers. "*Estoy bien*. After them! They've taken the rifles."

Samuel crossed the worn timber pier in four strides. The riders poured out of the warehouse through the front doors, galloped up Hudson Street, and disappeared into a side road. He shuddered to a halt with a curse.

Padraig grabbed his wrist. "That's the churl who raided the manor. I'd swear it."

Samuel whirled around, his skin tingling. "What?"

"I told you I'd know him." Padraig holstered his Colt. "The rifles?"

Samuel's body felt heavy. "If they took the rifles, we're done for."

The warehouse was empty. All that remained was the dusty outline of crates on the earthen floor.

"Oh, Lord, this can't be. How the hell did they know? Who could they—" He remembered Chavez and gestured toward the fallen rider. "Watch this bastard, would you?"

He hurried back to the yard, where Filipe knelt beside Chavez, staunching the wound with a bloodstained handkerchief.

Filipe looked up with bulging eyes. "First mate's coming. They said he's got medical skills."

Sweat beaded Chavez's bruised face. His skin was pale, but his peering eyes were alert, and when he spoke his voice was shaky. "Must have been eight or nine of them. They surprised me about four hours ago and tied me up."

"They wanted the rifles?"

Chavez nodded. "They loaded them onto four wagons, then worked me over. They demanded to know when you'd return, but I pretended I knew no *inglés*. The bearded bastard went crazy and punched me until I passed out." He coughed and groaned. "They must've waited to ambush you. When I woke, I worked on the ropes they'd tied me with, then took a chance and ran out to warn you."

Samuel squeezed Chavez's forearm lightly. "You saved our lives, Emanuel. Thank you."

The first mate scurried up from the wharf, trailed by a barefooted boy lugging a leather satchel. The mate, a dumpy man with a waxed mustache and a well-fed paunch, flopped down beside Chavez. "I've treated many wounds, but never a gunshot. Jesus."

That singsong accent sounded European, Italian, maybe. The mate ripped Chavez's sleeve down, and Samuel leaned forward expectantly.

He'd seen wounds on the battlefield, and this one wasn't bad. "Check the other side. Perhaps it went clean through."

Holding a white rag to the wound, the mate helped him sit up and cut away more bloody cloth. Chavez inhaled sharply as the mate poked at the wound, and Samuel resisted the temptation to crane over the mate's shoulder.

Eventually, the mate sat back on his haunches and scratched his ample belly. "You're a lucky man. Ball went right through all that muscle there. All we need do is disinfect it and bind it. But you must rest."

Samuel laughed shakily. "If a thousand *Legitimistas* failed to kill you, what hope had that bearded wretch?"

Two men ran down the gangplank with a canvas stretcher.

The mate uncorked a dark brown bottle. "Take a swig of this. Morphine. It'll take the pain away. You'll love it."

Chavez grunted his thanks and settled back as the morphine washed through him. Samuel strode to where Padraig stood over the wounded rider, a middle-aged man with a weathered face and web of red veins on his bulbous nose.

"The bullet hit him in the small of his back," Padraig said. "No exit wound."

The man lifted his head. "Mercy's sake . . . A doctor. I need a doctor. I'm dying."

Fat chance of mercy, Samuel thought. This man had tried to kill him. "Who are you? Why did you attack us?"

"Go to hell. He'd kill me."

"Suit yourself." Samuel turned away.

The rider groaned. "W-wait." He flicked his eyes toward the first mate. "He's a doctor?"

"Ex-navy surgeon." Samuel had no compunction about lying to this criminal. "Best there is for gunshot wounds."

"All right. We're led by Colonel Benjamin Fry, William Walker's man. Hired us to get his rifles back."

"Fry? He's the bearded one?"

The raider looked away and groaned.

Padraig poked him with his boot. "Man asked you a question."

The raider's chin trembled.

"The tall bearded one with a long face?" Padraig asked.

"Yes."

Padraig nodded to Samuel. "The louse who attacked us at the manor."

"More than that," Samuel said bleakly, catching Padraig's elbow and drawing him into the warehouse out of earshot.

"What do you mean?"

"He went after Baltimore's papers," Samuel said. "Why would Fry steal Baltimore's papers, unless—"

"—unless they're working together." Padraig looked around as if they were being watched then and there. "Fry and Lucan, Lawrence too, and the devil knows who else."

"This has been a long time coming."

"But how did they know we were here?" Padraig asked. "That the rifles were here?"

"One of Brogan's crew must have talked," Samuel said.

They blinked at each other for long moments. The wind gusted through the empty warehouse, stirring dust, suddenly chilling cold in the height of summer, icy fingers rippling over Samuel's spine. In this land, it seemed they could trust very few.

Samuel straightened. From now on, we share our plans with nobody. Fry must still have the Baltimore papers with him. We must catch him the next time." Those papers were Samuel's shield against Lawrence and the Anglo-Irish consortium. "Come on."

"Where?"

"First, we face the music and convince Vanderbilt to give us another chance."

"Aw, Samuel, why would the man—"

"Then we talk to Brogan, try to find out who betrayed us," Samuel finished grimly. "Perhaps that will lead to Fry. And the papers." He caught Padraig's arm. "But don't tell Filipe they're trying to murder us. It'll only frighten him."

Cornelius Vanderbilt's rage passed as quickly as a summer squall. As the commodore paced the office, Samuel ran his sweaty palms down the thighs of his trousers as he waited for the shipping magnate to pronounce judgment. He caught Padraig's eye, and Padraig shrugged.

Vanderbilt stopped in a wide stance before Samuel. "I should run you clowns out of New York, but first you're going to fix this."

"Of course," Samuel said. "That's why we're here, sir."

"Especially considering you now have as much skin in the game as I have. A personal interest, shall we say?"

Samuel's eyes widened. He hadn't breathed a word about Fry or Lucan. There was no need to reveal his private affairs to this man, but apparently Vanderbilt hadn't left any stone unturned. "What do you mean?"

"Passengers traveling to Nicaragua are of special interest to me," Vanderbilt said.

Fry? Already? Samuel and Padraig exchanged a glance.

"Yesterday, one Sofia Kingston-Valle sailed on the *Southern Star* for Nicaragua with her infant son."

Samuel drew his head back. That was impossible. Sofia and John were safe in Clonakilty. "That's ridiculous, sir. Someone's feeding you bad information."

Vanderbilt crossed his arms and tilted his head. "It's a fact. And if you're the kind of man I think you are, you'll be desperate to follow her."

Padraig's nostrils flared. "You smug bastard. All the money in the world won't buy you decency." He rose halfway from his chair.

Samuel's head was reeling, but he raised an arm to stop Padraig. It couldn't be true . . . but if it was . . .

"Why would she do that?" he asked. "There's a war. There's disease in Nicaragua—all through Central America right now."

"Beats me how the female mind works." Vanderbilt rolled his eyes. "I once locked my wife in a mental institution until she came to her senses. Literally. The woman was talking to the whole of New York City society, telling them . . ."

This changed everything. Samuel couldn't stay here in New York City, puttering about on behalf of Vanderbilt, if his wife and child were sailing into danger. But why, oh why, would Sofia do something so damnably foolish? This was moving way too fast. He ran a hand through his hair. Dear God, if Walker captured Sofia down there, he was vengeful enough to shoot her for helping him steal Walker's gold.

". . . so here's what I propose," Vanderbilt was saying, moving back to his desk, "because it's urgent the allies get weapons as soon as possible." Samuel snapped back into the office with ships lining the walls.

The weapons. Samuel dragged his mind back to the matter at hand.

"I've stockpiled more rifles, almost two thousand rifles and two cannons. You'll load them onto *Spartacus* and deliver them to Costa Rica."

Padraig sputtered. “Costa Rica? And what are we supposed to do once we’re in bloody Costa Rica?”

Vanderbilt shrugged. “I don’t give a damn what you do. But if I were you, I’d catch a boat up the coast and chase my wife.”

Samuel scraped his chair back. “Damn you and your guns. We’re going straight to Greytown after her.”

“Suit yourself.” Vanderbilt opened the drawer of his desk. “The next passenger steamer sails in twenty-nine days.”

Twenty-nine days. That was far too long. Samuel’s chest caved. He’d no choice but to sail on *Spartacus* now.

CHAPTER EIGHT

Ropes stretched everywhere, strung into bewildering lines, ratlines, and knots, and the smell of paint, turpentine, and tar bittered the sea air. Taut shrouds and stays angled around Samuel, and running rigging fell to the gunwales like a net cast from the tangerine sky. Another crate swung over from the pier with a creaking groan on the stork-like derrick, and sweating sailors guided it into the hold.

On the deck, Padraig was pointing to the main mast soaring above them and lecturing Filipe. Samuel smiled. Of course that tangle of cables excited Padraig; he loved the sea and could handle a sailboat as well as he helmed his steamboat.

Captain Keller coughed politely. In his late forties, Keller's face was leathered from years at sea. His ready smile feathered crow's feet at the corners of his green eyes. "That's the last of the, ah, small supplies. Shall we load the large crates?"

There was still a risk the illegal artillery would be spotted. Samuel pitched his voice low. "We'll wait until nightfall."

They couldn't risk languishing in jail for breaching the Neutrality Act, even under the pressure of such separation from Sofia and little John. Worse, Walker could execute Sofia down there, if he laid hands on her. And yet he'd seemingly lost them all the same. He should've been a better husband. Twilight faded to night as he reviewed the countless times he'd wallowed in self-recrimination over losing Father instead of spending time in the present with his wife.

The peal of a distant church bell roused him. It was dark enough.

He caught Keller's anxious eye. "Load them, please?"

The derrick creaked and the block chirped as it took up the slack, and a large wooden crate swayed from a wagon and over the ship.

". . . but that French twelve-pounder can fire shells, shot, or canisters," Padraig was telling Filipe as they arrived at Samuel's side.

Filipe stepped to port for a better view. "I'd like to see that. Have you ever fired a cannon?"

"Several times in India," Padraig said. "A long story for another day. Look, here comes a second crate. I dare say it's a gun carriage."

"What time is high tide, Captain?" Samuel asked.

"About an hour and a half. Nine thirty-five."

"Can't come soon enough," Padraig said, turning to Samuel. "So tell me straight. Do you believe Brogan?"

"He's always been honest with us," Samuel said with a shrug. "If he trusts that his men didn't betray us, I believe him. Maybe we weren't discreet enough. Hell, it could have been the warehouse manager, or even someone from the *Spartacus*. We must proceed with more care from now on." He turned away and pulled out his snuffbox as the last crate disappeared into the hold.

"Are we doing the right thing?" Padraig asked in a low voice.

Samuel took a pinch of snuff. "What choice do we have? The next steamer to Nicaragua doesn't leave for a month. Costa Rica's right next door to Nicaragua. This takes us closer to Sofia."

"And the long-faced bastard who stole the Baltimore papers," Padraig said. "Walker's man."

Samuel nodded. "He'll have to deliver the rifles to Walker, and where he goes, my papers will go."

"You're gambling a lot on this hunch of yours."

They draped themselves over the rail and idly surveyed the yard below.

Padraig pointed to three men arguing with the warehouse manager. "What's going on over there?"

That didn't look good. Samuel strode over to Captain Keller. "How soon can we sail?"

Skirting the rules of strong nations and tin pot dictators was all in a day's work for Keller, who'd worked the Caribbean for fifteen years. He knew the penalties for smuggling contraband. "Five minutes if need be, sir."

"Thank you, Captain. Please get ready. And may I suggest you retrieve the mooring lines now, with the exception of one? Leave the gangplank, as well. Filipe—"

Filipe grimaced. "*Yo sé*, I'm to stay here."

"And don't move. Padraig, let's deal with our visitors."

They met the strangers fifty yards back from the pier. Behind them, Keller's sailors slinked about the ship and took to the ratlines, climbing casually.

"Gentlemen," Samuel called. "What's your purpose here?"

A tubby man with bulldog jowls and sporting a derby at a jaunty angle stopped at Samuel and Padraig's approach. "Peter Tingle, federal attorney for the Southern District of New York. This is Deputy US Marshal Raine." He pointed to a grizzled man in a tweed suit who was scratching a bushy mustache then pointed to the swarthy pinch-faced individual beside Raine. "And Deputy US Marshal Stone."

"We're departing shortly," Samuel said. "Is there some matter at hand we should be concerned with?"

Tingle dangled an official-looking document from his manicured hand. "The State Department of the United States of America has ordered us to prevent the departure of the *Spartacus*, to seize any weapons and ammunition bound for Central America in contravention of the Neutrality Act, and to question one Samuel Kingston."

Samuel snorted. "Ridiculous. I've a contract to deliver industrial machinery to Costa Rica. If the *Spartacus* doesn't sail at her appointed hour, we risk breaching that contract. Will your State Department pay my forfeiture fees?" He raised his eyebrows and made eye contact with each man. Hopefully they wouldn't notice the increased activity by the water's edge.

Raine tucked a thumb in his belt. "Not my problem. I've a legal warrant here. You're Kingston?"

"I'm Kingston." Samuel took the letter and glanced at it. "I can't read this. Can we move into the warehouse? There's more light."

"Anything to convince you that this boat is going nowhere," Raine said.

Samuel switched to Spanish. "Padraig, have the captain raise the gangplank and slip the last hawser."

"What about you? We—"

"Do it. *Ahora*."

Inside the warehouse, the officials fidgeted while Samuel read through the writ, tracing the words with his finger as if struggling to read them. He dropped the document, and it drifted to the ground. In the split second the officers' eyes followed it, he dashed for the boat.

Jibs full and pulling, *Spartacus* was already off the pier, and the crew was dropping some of her square sails. They'd moved too soon; he wouldn't make the ship.

The marshals bellowed. He dug deep and pushed faster. Boots crunched the loose cinders behind him. He'd hit the pier at full tilt, determined to jump no matter the outcome. A halyard dangling from the mizzen mast was unfurling from the pier. *Very clever, Captain.*

He leaped for the halyard. His fingers closed on the prickly hemp, and the halyard whipped him over the foul-smelling water like a fish hooked on a rod. He soared out over the water and crashed into the gunwale, smacking his knuckles against the weathered timber. His frock coat split up the back as Padraig and Filipe grabbed it and hauled him inboard.

Raine roared on the wharf, and there was the sound of a splash. Samuel pulled himself up to peer over the rail. Raine was thrashing in the water below.

Padraig pumped his fist in the air. "Have a nice swim, Marshal."

Samuel flopped back onto the deck, wheezing, his lungs burning. By the time he recovered and stood, Tingle and Stone were fishing Raine from the harbor. Above Samuel, sails flapped, and the rigging shivered as the *Spartacus* piled on the canvas. The brig settled on a tight reach south, aided by the ebbing Hudson River.

Filipe whooped and hugged Samuel. "That was fantastic. You showed them."

Samuel sagged against the gunwale and nodded his thanks to the captain. He squinted at the shore. It was hard to tell in the gloom, but the pier and yard seemed empty. "Nice work. I was terrified I wouldn't make it. Who left the halyard out?"

"The captain," Padraig said. "I suspect this isn't the old bugger's first escape."

"We picked the right chap, then. He's no bumbling aristocrat."

Twenty minutes later, the *Spartacus* was nearly abeam of Castle Clinton on the southern tip of Manhattan Island when a revenue cutter emerged from the crowded wharfs.

"Jaysus, a cutter; she'll have the legs on us." Padraig undid the top button of his white shirt.

Samuel rubbed his eyelids and sighed. They were getting no breaks this night. "Let's talk to Keller."

Hands coaxing the wheel with tiny adjustments, Captain Keller was dividing his attention between the outer roads ahead and the cutter astern. His pursed lips and furrowed eyebrows held little encouragement.

"Can we beat them?" Samuel asked quietly.

"Not likely," the captain replied. "But if we can make it to Gravesend Bay, we might find rollers big enough to slow that smaller craft."

"How far is that?"

"Best part of nine miles."

Samuel darted a glance at the ocean. His luck had run out. Sofia and baby John were en route to a war-torn, disease-ridden destination, and he was powerless to halt them. He sagged against the coaming. The brisk breeze suited the *Spartacus,* and she plowed ahead gamely with the wind strumming her taut rigging, but the revenue cutter was skimming over the waves like the Jesus lizards he'd seen in Nicaragua. The moonlight danced on the two six-pounders forward of her single mast.

He accepted a cigarette from Padraig with a shaky hand. "They're catching us."

Padraig lit a lucifer in his cupped hands. "What then? Fight? I wish we'd kept those French twelve-pounders on deck."

"Are you out of your mind? We've no choice but surrender." Samuel turned his back to the wind and lit his cigarette.

Sailors on the cutter ran forward and clustered around the portside cannon.

Padraig dragged on his cigarette. "I'm not going to jail in this place."

"Brace back that forecourse," Captain Keller called, his eyes glued to the sails. "Haul on the spanker sail."

The cutter's cannon vomited an orange tongue of flame and smoke and boomed a second later. The warning shot gouged a fountain of water fifty yards astern of the *Spartacus*.

Samuel's limbs tingled. Things were happening too quickly, and he was powerless. "You're the sailor, Padraig. Is there anything more the captain can do to move us faster?"

Padraig shook his head. "That cutter's too quick and beats far higher. She'll get the weather gauge on us."

Fifty yards to windward, the cutter drew abeam of *Spartacus*'s transom, and the cannon thundered again. This time, the shot soared over *Spartacus*'s bow and splashed into the moon-silvered water in a fountain of spray.

Keller sighed dejectedly and released the helm, avoiding Samuel's eyes. The *Spartacus*'s bow swung into the wind, she lost way and wallowed in the troughs with her mizzen top scribing circles in the starlit sky.

A whip-thin lieutenant on the cutter raised a bullhorn and shouted over the clatter of yards and the boom of sails. "Bring her about and return to the North River. Drop anchor off pier number five."

Samuel covered his face with his hands. He'd failed Sofia and John. Who knew how long he'd be in prison while they faced grave danger in Nicaragua? He hadn't moved from the rail by the time the *Spartacus* glided to a halt a hundred yards from the pier, some half an hour later, and her anchor chain rattled out between the catheads.

Padraig threw up his hands. "That's it, then? We give up?"

Samuel spoke through his teeth with forced restraint. "What else can we do? Winch out those French cannons and battle them?"

A V-shaped wave creamed from the cutter's bow as she surged close and spilled the wind from her sails.

The young commander across the way was so close he no longer needed his bullhorn. "You'll remain here until morning, when we can make room for you at our dock. Don't try any funny stuff. We're dropping a hook right beside you, and our guns will cover you all night."

Sailors climbed up the ratlines and fanned out on the

yardarms. As the *Spartacus* tugged on her anchor chain and swung to face the ebbing tide, a depressing silence cloaked the ship.

Samuel touched the captain's elbow. "Thank you, Captain. Nobody could have done more."

Keller spat downwind. "That cutter's just too nimble."

On the revenue cutter anchored thirty yards away, sailors lowered the gaff-rigged mainsail and tied off the helm. Samuel stepped to the gunwale for a closer look. The cutter was such a nimble little thing . . . but what if she couldn't steer? She'd be hard-pressed to chase them then.

Samuel's belly roiled, and he turned back to Keller. "I don't fancy spending two or three years in a New York prison. How about you?"

The captain's eyebrows wormed together and snapped back. "Hell, no. Why?"

"Because if I get my way, we'll be sailing on the morning tide and those revenue boys won't be able to follow us. Are you with me?"

~

Conscious of the onlooking crew's reaction to the livid scars on his shoulder and thigh, mementos of the Crimean War, Samuel stripped to his drawers and belted on Captain Keller's serrated knife. The night breeze tickled his back, but that wasn't why he shivered. His liberty—the entire crew's liberty—and his young family's lives depended on him now.

Padraig checked his pocket watch and looked at the starlit sky. "Five o'clock, and still too much moonlight."

"We can't wait any longer. It'll be dawn soon." Samuel rolled his shoulders and swung his arms in his customary precombat ritual.

"I hope they don't see you. Why won't you let me come?"

Samuel tried to sound more confident than he was. "Because

you're the sailor, and I'm the swimmer. I've always been better than you in the water. I got us into this mess, so I must extract us."

Padraig gave a reluctant nod.

"Make sure the crew prepares quietly. We don't want to tip them off." He nodded to Keller and stepped through the entry port.

The wooden rungs swayed under his weight, and the foul stench of the Hudson River assaulted his nose. Though accustomed to swimming in the Celtic Sea, he still shuddered as he slid into the river's cold embrace. Salt water stung his eyes as he struck out for the cutter.

He paused under the cutter's entry port to listen, rising and falling with the lapping waves. The continuous *whoosh* in his damaged left ear made it hard to hear—not a sound, only the creak of the rigging and the groan of the swaying hull. A surge knocked him against the copper bottom, and razor-sharp barnacles grazed his knees. His hands slipped in the algae sliming the bottom rungs as he scrambled up the chine.

He glanced around the deck. The coast was clear. He crept aft on his hands and knees. Jesus, his scratched knees were leaving telltale blood stains on the deck. His heart was racing by the time he reached the shadows of the stern and drew his knife. Following Padraig's instructions, he pried off the hatch to the steering cables with trembling hands and sawed the first line until only a few strands remained. Not so bad. He started on the second line.

Someone coughed in the bow. A watchman! A shadow rose on the foredeck and drifted to the port gunwale. Samuel held perfectly still. A second later, he heard urine tinkling into the sea. The watchman sighed deeply, hacked up phlegm, and spat.

Bare feet padded down the deck toward Samuel. The watchman was coming aft; he'd better not notice the blood on the deck. The hair lifted on the nape of Samuel's neck, and he pressed back farther into the shadows. There was nowhere else to hide.

Seconds dragged as the watchman drew closer and his outline took definition beneath the waxing moon: a pin-headed man with sideburns sprouting like jibs in the wind. He halted midship, facing the *Spartacus*, and lit a pipe. Samuel caught the sweet scent of tobacco smoke as the watchman's face colored and waned in the pulsing glow from the bowl of his pipe. He clenched his teeth at the cramps in his hands from sawing the ropes. *Jesus, please move back.*

Finally, the watchman tapped his pipe on the gunwale and dawdled back to the bow. Samuel sank on the deck. Ignoring his cramping hands, he finished paring the second rope down to a few strands. There. Now to make his escape.

The watchman was still on the bow. Samuel could hazard sneaking down the boarding ladder, or he could risk making a splash by dropping over the transom into the sea. The watchman wheezed again, giving Samuel his answer. He confirmed the main sheet was securely cleated, waited endless seconds for the watchman to wheeze again, and immediately dropped the bitter end over the transom.

In a flash, he slipped overboard and lowered himself to the river. He managed to enter the water almost soundlessly despite the shocking cold that stung his skin. Nobody above him stirred; the only sounds were the gentle clinking of hardware and the creak of taut rigging as the cutter rocked on the Hudson.

His mouth was parched despite all the water surrounding him as he kicked off toward the *Spartacus*. Now they had a chance.

High tide just before dawn found Samuel blinking his gritty eyes in *Spartacus*'s cockpit, watching the sailors silently coil down braces and belay them at their marks set for release. Others hung from the yards, fingering the gaskets, and several more manned the capstan, ready to raise the anchor.

Nearby, where he watched the cutter with Padraig, Filipe was as taut as the rigging.

With his crew in position, Keller stepped to the helm and sniffed the wind. He tugged the sleeves of his reefer, gave Samuel a crisp nod, and waved his hand. "Fore-topsail . . . single jib . . . main topsail . . . mizzen topsail . . . and spanker, Mr. Ricardelli."

Canvas unfurled, cascading down, and sailors walked the capstan aided by the ebbing tide. Left to fly in the morning breeze, the sails boomed until the crew hauled in the sheets and braces, and *Spartacus* glided slowly forward. The sailors bent their backs to the capstan and it groaned, winding the slackening anchor line.

Samuel's left cheek quivered as he darted glances from the revenue cutter to the sails above him. Any second now, they would notice.

And there it was: A shout erupted from the cutter, loud across the open water. Men rushed from her companionway, and gunners sprang to their feet in the bow.

"They'll be underway in a jiffy—she only has a few sails," Keller said. "And then soon enough, we'll know."

Weariness washed over Samuel. He'd lain awake, tossing and turning, questioning every move he'd made last night. Failure promised only prison and strife. Now he'd know, indeed.

The cutter hauled her jibs and main gaff in an instant. The sails flogged, then hardened when the crew braced them back.

"Belay that maneuver, *Spartacus.*" The cutter commander's shout was angry and tinny through his bullhorn. "No more warnings. My first shot is aimed amidships."

As if in reply, *Spartacus's* anchor broke the surface of the river and crashed home in the cathead, and she fell off to port.

Keller's leathered face swiveled between the sails and the outer roads ahead. "Trim the jib."

Wind filled the triangular sail up forward, helping the bow fall off until wind filled the square sails.

"Haul on the spanker."

The irregular-shaped sail with four sides tautened amidships above the captain's head, and he crouched for a better view. "Brace round forward."

The crew hauled on the braces to swing round the foremast yards, and the *Spartacus* picked up speed.

Samuel hastened to the port gunwale. It was cold to the touch as he spread his hands on it. The cutter was underway now as well, and it was moving faster than the behemoth *Spartacus*. As Samuel watched, a gunner dropped a charge into the barrel of his six-pounder, and his comrade rammed it home.

"Damn that cutter's steering fine, full and by. She's going to catch us." Keller sighed heavily.

Samuel squeezed the rail until his hands ached and held back a bellow of rage.

The cutter pulled abeam some thirty feet off, and the gunner sighted his cannon. Samuel could see the lieutenant clearly, watching *Spartacus* with his neck corded and his jaw set and a hard face that promised no quarter. The gunner raised his sights and prepared to fire.

Samuel unconsciously pressed his elbows into his sides. There was no escape.

Beside him, Padraig pushed Filipe to the deck. "This is going to hurt. Down, boy."

A loud *crack* sounded from the cutter's stern, and she jounced and spun into the wind, sails flogging. Her crew roared, cursing as she shuddered in irons and fell back.

The *Spartacus* surged ahead.

Samuel sagged against the rail, his eyes gummed to the stricken cutter. It had worked.

Keller glanced aft with a tremulous laugh. "We'll be over the horizon before they can jury-rig another system."

The crew cheered and slapped each other's backs as the *Spar-*

tacus glided toward Upper Bay on the ebbing tide. Several men climbed the rigging to set the topsails.

They were headed for the deep green waters of the Atlantic.

The cool caress of the breeze and the soothing motion of the deck refreshed Samuel's spirit as *Spartacus* bore steady on, chasing the lean shadows of her masts. A soldier's wind had whisked the brig down the East Coast and through the Florida straits, placing them east of Cuba in just over eleven days. The bowsprit bracing the triangular jibs swirled like a stylus scribbling on the distant horizon. Underfoot, the *Spartacus* rocked and swayed merrily, tossing foaming waves to both sides of her bucking bow.

Flexing his muscles, Samuel savored the satisfying ache of regular saber drills with Padraig, Filipe, and Chavez. They'd sparred two hours a day on the rolling deck, missing only a single day during an early summer gale ahead of hurricane season.

In the waist, Filipe was prancing around the brass cannon the crew had hauled on deck. The boy was a pest, albeit a capable one. Drilling had improved his swordsmanship and added muscle to his lean frame. Still, there was something about him . . . Samuel had warmed to him during their close confinement, but he couldn't shake a suspicion that the boy was holding back, hiding something—a thought Padraig had dismissed out of hand when he raised it. Samuel wasn't persuaded, but damn, it was like catching snowflakes.

He shrugged and returned his attention to the cannon crouching on deck like a predator. Filipe had been pestering them for days about firing the cannon, and with nothing better to do at that point, Captain Keller had finally agreed to sway one of the French guns on deck and have the carpenter lay blocks to stop the carriage from rolling. The Costa Ricans wouldn't miss a couple of balls and a few grains of powder.

Padraig's sunburned face was alight as he led Filipe and Chavez through the steps for loading the cannon. Padraig shoved a black powder charge down the barrel and stepped aside so Chavez could tamp it in. Filipe loaded a round shot and moved back with a grin so Chavez could ram it home.

With an entire ocean as his target, Padraig wasted little time on sighting. He nodded to Filipe. The youth bounced on his toes as he waved at the grinning sailors, then yanked the lanyard. The gun roared, belching flame and smoke, propelling the ball low across the spray-flecked green waves. Saltpeter stung Samuel's nose as the round hit the sea one thousand yards away, fifteen points off the port bow. It skipped once and plunged deep.

The crew let out a cheer, while Filipe was already begging for another shot.

After a dozen more balls had pounded the innocent waves without forcing their submission, Samuel called a halt to the exercise and ordered Filipe to polish the cannon. Sweat plastered the boy's powder-stained white shirt, and his hands grew black. Padraig's clothing was in a similar state. Soon, the brass gleamed like gold in the morning sun.

Padraig left Filipe buffing a final time and joined Samuel aft. "A productive project after all, eh?"

Samuel scratched his itchy head. Somehow the water in half of the barrels had spoiled, and there was no longer enough water to wash his hair. "Perhaps he merely needs focus. He's still just a boy."

"Something's been bothering me since we sailed," Padraig said.

"You too, now? I've always felt that Filipe seemed a little—"

"No, not the lad." Padraig swatted at the air dismissively. "How the hell did those government marshals know we were smuggling weapons?"

Another frustration. "I don't know. It doesn't add up. That wretch, Fry, perhaps?"

"And how'd they know when we were sailing?" Padraig scrubbed his powder-blackened face with his handkerchief.

Samuel peered more closely at his friend. "Are you saying you think there's a spy on board?"

Padraig waved his approval at Filipe, who'd finished polishing the cannon and whose face now shone as brightly as the gleaming brass. "Why would anybody on this boat betray us?"

Samuel shrugged and rolled his shoulders in a vain attempt to release the tension creeping across his frame. Nobody on this ship knew any part of his business beyond their destination, and he got the sense that the crew either didn't know or didn't care about their cargo.

He'd have to keep an eye on everyone all the same and hold his cards closer to his chest.

CHAPTER NINE

A day later, the crew were gathered in a knot near the catheads when Samuel climbed on deck, shading their eyes and pointing west. He joined Keller in the cockpit. "What's all the excitement, Captain?"

Keller snapped his brass spyglass shut. "Land ahead. We've sailed over two thousand miles since leaving New York seventeen days ago. If my sightings and calculations are right—but we need a landmark to be sure. I'll take us in for a closer look." He turned to his first mate, the affable Italian who'd patched up Chavez. "Mr. Ricardelli, kindly lay us onto a port tack. Let's see how well we've navigated."

"Yes, sir." Ricardelli cupped his hands around his mouth. "All hands! All hands to reduce sail!"

Men repeated the call throughout the ship. The sight of land excited every sailor, and for once the watch belowdecks did not complain as they surfaced, squinting in the harsh equatorial sun. Bare feet beat the deck as they hastened to their places and readied to release or sheet home. Top men leaped into the rigging like monkeys.

Samuel's pulse quickened. He was so close now. Sofia was somewhere over there, perhaps in trouble. What had led her to make such a perilous journey with baby John? He closed his eyes. He'd been such an idiot, wallowing in remorse and ignoring his wife. He'd find her and make things right. War-torn Nicaragua was no place for a woman and child, even a woman as capable as Sofia.

A drop of melted tar fell from the standing rigging onto his hand, hot and sticky. He couldn't see land in the gray haze where the blue sky met the distant horizon, but the *Spartacus*'s motion changed as the helmsman eased her off the wind.

Keller touched the helmsman's shoulder. "Hold her there full and by, Clarke. Mr. Worthy, prepare to come about."

Boson Worthy, a small man with thinning gray hair badly cut in a short fringe, snarled and growled at the sailors as they coiled down the braces on the leeward deck and belayed them at their marks set to be released. *Those missing teeth, pale skin, and the way the old goat is constantly complaining of aching joints are all signs of scurvy*, Padraig had said days ago. Samuel smiled; a voracious reader, Padraig was seldom wrong.

Tacking a square-rigger was tricky even in fair winds, but Keller knew his business, and the *Spartacus* came about without a hitch. Even when she settled onto her new tack, the land was not visible to Samuel. He snapped his spyglass shut with a huff.

Keller lifted his nose from the Admiralty chart and eyed Samuel with a wry smile. "Takes a practiced eye to spot land from this far out. Give it some time." He turned to his first mate. "Mr. Ricardelli, send young Barclay aloft to watch for keys and shallows, if you please."

"Aye-aye, sir, aloft it is." Ricardelli beckoned the skinny boy who'd helped when Chavez was shot and sent him scampering up the rigging.

Time dragged, and the forging *Spartacus* seemed fixed in place. The horizon drew no closer, no matter how Samuel paced the deck. Finally, the long gray line firmed until Samuel could make out clusters of palm trees feathering the lowlands.

Beside him, Keller glassed the coast. "Right on the money.

Gracias a Dios ahead—and no better name for it. The headland marks the Nicaraguan frontier."

"Thank God, all right," Samuel said with a smile. "Perfect name for a perfect waypoint. How far is it to Limón?"

"Three hundred miles. We'll dock there in two days, if the wind holds."

Not a moment too soon. Then he could offload the cursed rifles and get on with finding Sofia. Samuel lifted his spyglass again.

On the deck below them, the sailors were stirring in the waist and gathering around Padraig and Filipe.

"What the devil's going on down there?" Keller asked.

Padraig waved at Samuel and raised a round green soda bottle. "Ready for a bang?"

Samuel's eyebrows shot up in alarm. "Hold on." He turned to the captain and rolled his eyes. "Apparently the boy's training has progressed to grenades. Do you mind?"

"Grenades?"

"Remember the discussion at dinner about the grenades we used in Crimea?"

"Mm?"

"Padraig's made some to show Filipe. Now he's hoping to try them out."

The captain considered. "Is that safe?"

Samuel made a calming gesture to Padraig, who was impatiently gesticulating at Samuel as the sailors pressed around to see. "Perfectly. Padraig knows what he's doing. He'll use a lanyard to sling it far from the boat."

"Better be," Keller said in a gruff voice. "How will he light it?"

"He's rolled a slow-burning fuse in dampened gunpowder and dried it. The fuse sits through a hole drilled in the wooden plug that stoppers the bottle. I assure you, it's quite safe in the right hands. Do we have your permission to use it?"

The captain reluctantly shrugged. "I suppose it would break the monotony."

Samuel smiled his thanks and waved back to Padraig. "Go ahead—but be careful."

Padraig leaned in and said something emphatic to Filipe, who lifted a smoking pail of burning charcoal. Padraig straightened the fuse in the soda bottle and lit it. The sailors shrunk back as everyone watched it burn. Then Padraig whirled the bottle by the lanyard tied to its neck and launched it high over the rolling waves.

The grenade exploded with a loud bang, and a cloud of metal balls showered the green water. The crew cheered, and Filipe danced on deck.

"Deck there, sail ho!" Barclay's squeaky voice rang loud and clear over the celebration below.

Ricardelli cupped his chafed hands to shout aloft. "Watch her, boy, and let us know which way she's headed."

"Another merchantman, I dare say," Keller said to Samuel. "If she's coming this way, we'll close with her. It's always useful to receive news of the ports ahead. Best your boys cease their carrying on, lest our friend over there think we're pirates—or worse."

Samuel perked up. Maybe the ship out there had news of Sofia. He frowned at himself; what a ridiculous idea. In his guilt, he was grasping at straws.

"Padraig!" He waved to catch his friend's attention as they prepared the next grenade. He sliced a hand across his neck. "Wait. Time to shut down for now."

"Wait? Wait for what?" Filipe wailed.

Samuel pivoted back to the sea. Padraig could deal with it. He raised his spyglass, but the rolling deck made it difficult to find the spot of white and impossible to contain it within the circular lens. He snapped the spyglass shut. He too would have to wait.

Padraig and Filipe blustered aft in high spirits. It was

surprising how even a distant sign of humanity stirred the blood after almost three weeks at sea.

"Where's this ship, then?" Padraig asked.

Samuel pointed to the speck of white off the port bow. "There. It's hard to make her out."

"May I borrow your spyglass?" Filipe held out a sooty hand. He smelled of brimstone and sweat.

Samuel handed the glass over and turned to Padraig. "If she's headed this way, we might get news."

"News of what?"

Keller cut in. "Depends where she's coming from—but yes, we're looking for news. We don't want to sail into a yellow fever port or one of the wars these tin pot tyrants in Central America provoke all the time."

"I thought that's exactly what we're doing," Padraig grumbled.

From the masthead, Barclay's breaking voice was shrill. "She's altering course to intercept us, sir."

Keller squinted at the white speck with renewed interest. "Seems our new friend's as hungry for news as we are."

Accepting his glass back from Filipe, Samuel scanned the brilliant blue sea in the white dot's direction but still failed to pin it in his lens.

"Deck there. She's a square-rigged brig, on the starboard tack with no top gallants," Barclay hollered from the mast top.

"Appears I was right. Another merchantman." Keller smoothed his worn reefer. "Up a point, Clarke."

"I've got her in my lens now, sir," Ricardelli said.

Samuel followed Ricardelli's finger. Two minuscule white squares, golden in the sun, lifted from the blue sea.

Keller's head swiveled back. "Top gallants! I thought the boy said she was sailing easy."

Ricardelli blinked furiously. "He did, sir."

"Then he's added sail," the captain said. "Must be in a damned hurry to meet us."

By the time Samuel, Padraig, and Filipe had finished a quick meal of hard biscuit and dried fish, they could make out swollen pyramids of canvas and the spray creaming from the other ship's bow. Several minutes later, the four black eyes of cannons materialized from the haze.

Samuel turned to Keller in alarm. "She's armed. Is she a navy boat?"

"What navy?" Padraig asked. "American? British?"

"Neither of them." Keller began packing his pipe. "They use steam frigates now. Could be the Hondurans. We'll know soon enough."

Samuel glanced back at the brig. "Should that ship concern us?"

"Can't see why. Nobody knew we were coming." Keller stooped out of the wind and struck a lucifer.

Through Samuel's spyglass, a flag unfurled from brig's shrouds: five horizontal blue stripes on a white background with a single five-pointed red star in the center.

A sudden cold expanded from Samuel's core, and his mouth fell open. "Christ, that's Walker's flag."

Keller dropped his pipe.

Padraig, eyes bulging, made a grab for Samuel's spyglass. "Here, let me see."

Samuel pulled back. "Wait." He scanned the frigate's deck. A score of riflemen in blue tunics lined the brig's gunwales. "Get us out of here, Captain. Quickly."

Padraig snatched the glass. "Bloody Walker's got the buggers fancy uniforms now and all. Cheap bastard never even gave us shirts."

Filipe jostled Padraig's elbow for the glass. "Let me see."

"You're right, it's Walker's flag," Keller said. "She's fast, maybe faster than us. Lighter, as well. Not carrying cargo." The captain's body odor was suddenly strong and bitter in the cockpit.

"No cargo," Padraig said. "Just a hundred bloody riflemen."

Samuel's answer was low and tight. "We've no choice but to try, Captain. Best get a move on. Filipe, fetch our rifles and revolvers from the cabin."

"Ready to go about, Mr. Ricardelli," Keller said. "This one must be perfect."

Despite their efficient tack, they lost ground. By the time the sails filled and drew, with *Spartacus* on a parallel course to the filibuster brig, Walker's ship had gained a hundred yards. Close-hauled on the wind, the *Spartacus* canted steeply, bucking over the waves with the wind harping in the rigging, forcing Samuel to wrap a leg around a shroud to hold his balance.

Keller propped a knee against the leeward gunwale to observe the other vessel. "She's badly sailed. Mr. Ricardelli, ship's log, if you please. I'd like to know our speed."

"I bloody hope we're faster," Padraig said. "The way she's sailing, she'll have weather gauge advantage when we fight."

"What do you mean?" Samuel asked.

"I mean, I'd give an arm for a steam engine right now," Padraig finished. "I love sailing ships, but not when they're sinking."

At Ricardelli's command, Worthy produced a wooden wedge tied to a neat coil of thin rope. He thrust it to a weathered sailor and shoved the man toward the mizzen chains. "Throw it on my mark, Jackson." Brushing back a gray strand that had escaped his skull-squeezing ponytail, he flipped an hourglass over. "Now."

Jackson tossed the log into the foaming wake astern and counted the knots off as the logline slipped through his fingers. When the last grain of sand fell twenty-eight seconds later, he stopped the log line's run and searched for the next tail of knotted string seized to the log line. "Just shy of four knots, Captain."

Eyebrows drawn in tense bars of concentration, Keller glassed the frigate. "I'd swear she's gaining."

Samuel couldn't see the difference. The distance between the boats looked the same, but Keller was the sailor, not he. "How long have we got?"

"At this rate, four hours. Maybe."

"Maybe's not good enough." Samuel scanned the *Spartacus* frantically. The yards at the very top of her masts were bare. He rounded on Keller. "I see some space at the tops of the masts. What sails go there?"

"Royals," Padraig offered. "But they're for lighter weather than this. They're usually used off the wind."

"Well, get them up, Captain. Hang every sail you have, and your shirts too, if—"

Padraig grabbed Samuel's elbow. "Adding more sail will add no speed upwind. Ship's already heeling too far."

Samuel massaged his temples. He couldn't let Walker delay him from going after Sofia. "We must stay ahead of her until dark. Perhaps we can slip away then." He checked his pocket watch. "Almost an hour before noon. What time's sunset?"

"Six ten or thereabouts—too late, I'm afraid." Keller used the binnacle to pull himself amidships, where he balanced on the canted deck to take measure of his ship's trim. "Let me take the helm and work her on the wind, see if I can buy us some time."

Samuel pounded his fist on the coaming and gazed back at the receding coastline. They were racing into the Atlantic away from his precious family, and the emerald coastline of Honduras was disappearing behind them into the brilliant blue sea.

The *Spartacus* was making four and half knots when Worthy read the log line again. Samuel's hopes inflated. They appeared to be holding the enemy at bay. If they could hold that till nightfall, they had a chance—and nightfall came early in the tropics.

Keller glanced back at the filibuster craft. "Damn it, they're closing. They're beating higher than us."

Samuel had ducked down to roll a cigarette, determined to

appear calm in front of the others, even if he churned inside. He stood. "Can we outrun them downwind?"

"No chance," Keller said. "She's a faster ship. They should've had us by now, but they're poor sailors. Any landlubber can steer downwind. But in a faster ship, they'll catch us, eventually."

The brig closing the gap behind them was a sobering sight. Carving through the water, her black hull heeled to show a weed-free bottom on the weather side. A clean bottom—that explained her fine turn of speed. Samuel glowered at the bowed masts towering into the azure-blue sky, with flattened sails packed on the yards and William Walker's odious single star—a symbol of his oppression—flapping from the masthead.

"We need more sail," he growled.

Keller scratched the gray stubble on his chin. "Too much canvas. We could lose a mast."

"Aye, but we've no choice," Samuel said. "If they catch us . . ."

Keller looked aloft, considering.

Calculating.

"You're right," he finally replied. "We might get away with it." He cupped his hands around his mouth. "Mr. Ricardelli! Top gallants, if you please."

The tightly wound crew made it so in no time, and it was a wild ride once the top gallants were on. The *Spartacus* bucked through the waves, heeled so far over that waves lapped over the gunwales.

A rogue wave doused Padraig, and he clawed his way higher on the canted deck. "Were you holding out on me, Samuel? I thought you knew nothing about sailing."

Samuel looked back. The frigate was definitely falling behind. He gave Padraig a knowing grin. "I'm a fast learner."

"Now all we need do is hold them off for a few more hours," Padraig said.

Samuel nodded grimly. "Until dark."

The *Spartacus* plowed on, her hull pounding the waves, every patch of canvas straining and her rigging groaning and creaking.

Keller's face was pale and tight as he wrestled the helm along with Bosun Worthy.

The filibuster frigate was flagging in *Spartacus*'s curving wake when two monstrous waves slammed together under *Spartacus*, tossing her high on the swell. Samuel dug his nails into the hardwood coaming as she bottomed out with a shuddering crash. Above them, the mizzen shroud parted with a whiplike *crack*. The royal sail luffed, and *Spartacus* fell off the wind.

"We're going to lose the mizzen." Keller pushed Worthy off the wheel and let *Spartacus* spin up into the wind.

Sails flapped, blocks slapped, and yardarms clattered in a cacophony of doom.

"Get the sails off the mizzen, Mr. Ricardelli," Keller roared. "I'll have those topgallants off, too. Lively now, and we may save the mast."

Worthy and Ricardelli staggered across the deck, bellowing and pushing sailors toward the rigging. Men swarmed up the shivering ratlines, shirts flapping in the breeze.

Padraig craned around to watch the frigate plowing closer. "A right proper louse up. They have us now for sure."

"We can save the mizzen." Keller's calm, even gaze was glued aloft. "We can keep going with the sails off the mizzen while Bosun reeves a new shroud. But we'll be much slower. They'll catch us before twilight, for—"

"Can you sail downwind?" Samuel asked.

All eyes turned to Samuel.

"Well, yes," Keller replied. "But like I said, they'll catch us even quicker than—"

"How *long* will it take them to catch us downwind?"

Keller considered the frigate, slicing through the waves behind them. "An hour at most."

Samuel pushed off the coaming. "Then here's what we'll do."

Nearly an hour later, Padraig returned from the bow with sweat streaming down his grimy face and his sooty shirt glued to his chest. "Ready. It's a bloody mad plan, but we're ready."

Samuel watched the brig careening downwind as it chased the *Spartacus* into the Atlantic. "It's our only chance."

"This is most irregular," Keller said. "Are you certain?"

"Do you have a better strategy to save your ship, Captain?" If Samuel could commit to this madcap plan, so could the captain. He'd learned the loneliness of command a long time ago, and everything depended on their decisive leadership.

The captain cast his eyes up at the sails and gave a taut nod.

Filipe approached with a sparkle in his eye. He touched the two pistols in his belt. "What's my station for the fight?"

As if Samuel hadn't enough to worry about already. "Go below to your cabin and remain there until this is over. I don't want anything to happen to—"

"Ah, come on. Father let me fight in Santa Rosa." Filipe's voice was strained, almost whiny.

Samuel glanced at the filibuster brig surging closer. He didn't have time for this. "Get below. You're not too big to start with a rope end, and I'll do it here in front of the entire crew."

Filipe scowled and slunk away. Samuel immediately regretted his sharpness, but he'd much on his mind.

Two hundred yards behind them, a puff of smoke erupted from the filibuster ship. The cannon's roar reached them a second later, as a six-pound ball skipped on the surface of the sapphire sea in a geyser of water fifty yards astern.

"They've turned a forward gun." Samuel whirled and picked out the officer standing behind the offending gun.

Before he could lift his rifle, Padraig's barked. The breech-loaded Sharps had a rifled barrel and an effective range of three hundred yards, making this an easy shot for an expert marksman like Padraig, even from a pitching deck. The wind snatched the pungent smoke clear of Padraig's weapon as an officer toppled in the frigate's bow.

"Bring it on, you spalpeens." Padraig plucked another cartridge from his box and yanked down the lever. "The more, the merrier."

Samuel aimed along the ladder sights and selected an officer with the light dancing on the brass buttons of his frock coat. He waited for the roll of the ship and squeezed the trigger. The butt kicked against his shoulder, and the officer spun and collapsed.

Spurts of smoke puffed along the brig's gunwale, and bullets buzzed the humid air around them. More rapped against the *Spartacus*'s transom like a flock of woodpeckers and punched holes in the billowing sails. The thumps and patter of lead lifted the hair on the back of Samuel's neck, but he resisted the primal urge to duck; he had, after all, been a British officer. The crew scattered for cover on the afterdeck.

He pulled a cartridge from his pouch and reloaded his Sharps with clammy hands. This time his shot was one with Padraig's, and two more filibusters fell to the deck. By the time he had reloaded, the gunwale of the chasing brig was deserted. The filibusters were hiding below the gunwales, content to let the cannons do their dirty work.

Padraig fired again, punishing a filibuster for peeping over the gunwale. The round hit the man in the head.

Samuel snapped a shot at the cockpit to make the helmsman nervous. "Bring her on the wind, Captain, if you please."

"Slack all sails." Ashen-faced, Keller turned the wheel to starboard.

The sails flogged in the wind as the *Spartacus* lost way, rocking on the waves. Samuel braced himself against the coaming. The filibusters would believe Keller had panicked.

The enemy ship held the weather gauge now, and she was sailing faster than the *Spartacus.* She drew abeam of their stern quarter, and several rifles flashed from the cover of the coach roof.

The black maws of four nine-pounder cannons winked at

Samuel across the blue water, vomiting tongues of orange-yellow flame and disappearing into a curtain of smoke—a ragged broadside. Two balls splashed into the water, launching geysers ten yards off the *Spartacus.* Another shattered the gaff, and Samuel ducked as the spanker fell, billowing over the binnacle like a tent. He wrinkled his nose at the tang of salty mildew and tore at the stiff canvas. If he didn't give his order now, they were finished.

The hull shuddered, and the sound of smashing wood came from the port side.

"Clear this sail," Keller bellowed. "I can't see a damned thing."

The ship shook and wallowed, and sailors roared and jostled on the other side of Samuel's canvas shroud. His breath turned to desperate panting. A fingernail ripped to the quick as he clawed at the canvas.

And then the sail whipped free, grazing his face, and he sucked fresh air in the welcome daylight. The enemy's bow was still abeam of *Spartacus*'s stern quarter, and filibusters were popping from the cover of the gunwales, raising their rifles as the gunners reloaded the cannons.

Samuel caught Chavez's eye next to a tarp-covered object. "Ready?"

"*Listo*, Capitán." Chavez whipped away the tarp, and the brass cannon tilted up on *Spartacus*'s deck glinted gold in the sunlight.

"Fire!" Samuel shouted.

Chavez yanked the lanyard. The deck jounced as the twelve-pounder spewed flame and smoke. Samuel winced at the resounding boom.

Musket balls hacked splinters from the enemy's gunwales, ripping through the filibusters and hurling bodies across the deck of the enemy ship, shredding limbs, torsos, and heads. Samuel sagged against the gunwale, cold to the core, fixated by the reeling brig and the blood spilling across her deck. The acrid stench of sulfur filled his nose. Jesus, he hadn't expected such slaughter.

Mercifully, a veil of cannon smoke drifted across to obscure the horror.

"Holy Mother of God." Padraig made the sign of the cross.

Samuel rubbed at his twitching cheek, his mind reeling. "Get her moving, Captain."

Stirring from his daze, Keller thumped the wheel. "Set the mainsail. Trim those jibs. Mr. Ricardelli, have the topmen aloft to finish securing the mizzen."

The hull throbbed as the carpenter's mate pounded in a wooden plug to seal the hole in it. Sailors scrambled to clear the tangle of canvas and cordage as the *Spartacus* drifted away from the stricken brig, but they couldn't escape the screams of the wounded and dying filibusters. Sweat streaming down his back and armpits, Samuel lowered his eyes. It was the hollowest of victories.

Padraig touched his elbow. "There was no other way. It was them or us."

Samuel gave him a vacant-eyed stare.

"We already let Walker take two thousand rifles. We couldn't gift him two thousand more."

Without a word, Samuel headed for his cabin to brood, ignoring Filipe bounding up from his confinement below decks.

CHAPTER TEN

Silence pulsed once the anchor chain ceased rattling overboard. The headland of the bay, a hundred miles south of Cabo Gracias a Dios, provided some shelter to the wounded *Spartacus.* Lazy waves foamed, creamy white, onto the endless strip of gray sand.

Slumping against the cockpit coaming, Samuel pressed his palms to his eyes. Captain Keller and his crew had patched the hole just above the waterline and nursed *Spartacus* inshore with her mizzen bare of sails.

"How long will it take the carpenter to repair the damage?" he asked.

Keller glared at the offending mast. "Four or five hours, with any luck. Time enough to send a water party ashore. With all the rain that falls around here, should be water about. Look how green the hills are."

Samuel swatted at a mosquito and tried to hide his nerves.

"Would you mind leading the water party?" Keller continued. "I need Mr. Ricardelli to oversee the repairs."

"Not at all." It would do him good to stretch his legs after three weeks at sea. Maybe he'd work off some of this anxiety as well. "But that filibuster boat—are you certain they're immobilized?"

Keller lit his pipe in a swirl of comforting, sweet tobacco smoke. "Can't say for certain. But you left them a mess of bodies to sort. Your grapeshot wouldn't have damaged her hull, not four inches of oak. Regardless, they were dead in the water when they dropped hull down on the horizon."

"You think they're in real trouble?" All that blood . . . All those bodies . . ."

"They'll take a while to get going," Keller said, "and longer still to search the coast from Cabo Gracias a Dios to here, if they're so inclined. Personally, I think they'll limp home to lick their wounds."

"Nevertheless, we should make haste. I'll take my three men. Who can you send?"

"Bosun Worthy and three or four more. That'll be plenty."

Samuel nodded.

"I'll have them lower the long boat," Keller said.

Samuel headed to the cabin. With filibusters about, he wasn't going ashore empty-handed. By the time he retrieved his guns and cartridge box and returned with Filipe and Padraig, Worthy had the boat in the water, and Chavez was helping sailors load it with empty wooden casks. Despite his constant irritability, the old bosun knew his trade. Padraig had said a bad temper was another symptom of scurvy.

Keller poked a finger toward the four sailors stowing barrels and casks. "Thin fellow there with the hawk nose is Grimsby. The darkie is Smith; picked him up in Trinidad. Beefy fellow with wild curls is O'Brien—a countryman of yours, if I'm not mistaken. The squeaker is Barclay. Solid lads, they'll give you no trouble." He smoothed the front of his tar-stained shirt. "All my crew are good men. Nineteen men and five boys—too many boys, but I couldn't refuse them. They were all I could find. Everyone wants to crew on those infernal steam machines."

Damn right. Samuel dragged on his cigarette. He'd have preferred a steamer, too. They'd be in Costa Rica already and might've avoided yesterday's confrontation altogether. But he knew better than to bring it up with the old salt.

The tapping of mallets and whir of a brace and bit filled the furnace-hot air. At least spars and rigging were easier to repair than mechanical bits and bobs; he thanked God for that small mercy.

Keller stepped aside from the entry port and motioned to the worn ladder. "Down you pop. Mind, don't step on the gunwales or you might capsize the longboat."

Samuel glimpsed a pair of pistols tucked into Filipe's belt as the boy pushed past him. What other weapons had the little pest hidden under his billowing shirt? There was no point in scolding him—a brace of pistols was a fine idea this day.

"Easy, Filipe," he noted mildly. "Where are your manners?"

Filipe's head was already disappearing over the side. "*Perdón*, can't wait to be home again."

Glancing at the empty cove and the dense jungle spreading to the blue horizon, Samuel remembered Colonel Valle's vast estate with its bronze fountains, marble columns, shaded arcades, and acres of manicured gardens. If Filipe thought the jungle onshore would be like the overripe beauty of his home, he was in for a surprise.

At a bark from Bosun Worthy at the tiller beside Padraig, one sailor gaffed off the bow and joined the others, bending their tanned backs on the oars. Squeezed on a thwart beside Chavez and Filipe, Samuel trailed a hand in the glittering water. It was nice and warm. Perhaps he'd have a swim once they were resupplied with water. After three weeks of washing from a bucket, he smelled as ripe as a lancer's horse.

The longboat crunched onto sands the color of porridge, and a grunt from Worthy launched the sailors over the side to run the boat onto the virgin sand. The heat on the *Spartacus* had been oppressive, but here it combined with high humidity to make sweat stream. Yes, they were most certainly back in the tropics. Samuel vainly slapped at the mosquitoes buzzing around his head.

"Look about and give us a shout when you find a stream," he told Chavez. The Nicaraguan was jungle-born; he'd find water in a heartbeat.

Chavez loped off toward the forest with one of Vanderbilt's rifles. Samuel grinned. The Costa Ricans wouldn't miss one or two out of thousands. He scanned the tightly knit foliage of the jungle. It seemed peaceful enough. "The rest of you, get the casks ashore and ready for his return."

Twenty minutes later, two green macaws soared upward on blue-tipped wings, hurling their boisterous calls into the cloud-strewn cornflower sky, as Jimenez stepped from the trees. Even from this distance, Samuel could see the oily sheen of sweat on his dark face.

His returning footprints left a second trail on the hot sand as he trotted up to report. "Found water, *Capitán*, not a muddy river but a fresh rainwater stream. Maybe a half-a-mile back. The *jungla* is thick. It'll be hard going."

"Beg pardon, sir, but that's why the lads brought cutlasses," Worthy said, "to hack into the forest and all."

"Most thoughtful of you, Bosun," Samuel said. "Lead on, Chavez, if you please."

Except for Worthy, who would remain with the boat, they picked up the empty casks and followed Chavez. Even Samuel swaggered across the sand in the wide stance and rolling gait of men who lived on the ocean waves. Barclay staggered under the girth of his cask; poor lad, he couldn't have been over thirteen.

The jungle was more alien than any jungle Samuel had seen in Nicaragua. Chavez hacked furiously with his borrowed blade, widening an animal trail through the tangled undergrowth between knuckled boles wound with creepers that twisted up into the frond-filtered sunlight. Ignoring the dozen strange insects that had joined the mosquitoes' feast was difficult, but at least Samuel had sturdy boots, unlike the sailors who cursed and complained as jungle thorns pierced the hardened soles of their feet. The greenery shivered overhead, and several monkeys popped their white faces through, lips and noses almost human, tracking the invaders with big black eyes. Samuel's skin crawled, and his sweat-soaked shirt clung to his frame.

Padraig whipped off his damp hat and scrubbed his shirt sleeve across his face. "The devil can take this place, bugs and beasts and all. Give me cold Ireland any time. Monkeys can keep Nicaragua. Walker can have it too, for all I care."

His remark must have plucked a patriotic string in Filipe. "*El país de dios*. This is God's country, and that's why I'm willing to die for it."

Padraig grinned and nudged him ahead. "Better get a move on, then, or you won't need to. Sure, I'll kill you myself."

The sound of falling water was as unexpected as it was welcome. Moments later, the jungle opened onto a rocky chimney cascading water to a pistachio-green pool twenty feet below. The small clearing reeked of animal scat and rotting fruit.

The sailors dropped their casks and splashed into the rocky pool, squealing like children.

Conscious of being in unknown territory, Samuel caught Filipe's elbow. "If you're a soldier, you must stand guard with us."

Filipe pulled a face but stood his watch while the crew enjoyed the fresh water. Five minutes later, Samuel had the sailors fill the casks while he and the others bathed. The cold water was refreshing and caressed his skin like silk. He rinsed his hair and scrubbed his body while Filipe and Padraig frolicked in the crystal water. It would've been better if he'd remembered to bring soap.

They lugged the casks back along Chavez's freshly cut trail and poured the water into the barrels in the longboat before returning to the waterfall for more. Samuel grimaced at the stifling heat. He'd need another bath by the time they finished.

It was three hours before the barrels in the longboat were almost full, and the sun had sunk over the jungle. Worthy puffed on his corn pipe and called for one last trip to fill the casks. Samuel's legs were jelly; a few hours a day wielding his saber on deck had been ill preparation for their present toil.

The last cask reminded him of the straw that broke the camel's back as he labored with its weight on his shoulder on the return journey. It would be delicious to splash in the sea when he lay his burden down, but he wouldn't complain, considering that young Barclay was stumbling ahead of him without a cheep. The sailors were cursing up a storm, but like soldiers, sailors were only happy when complaining.

An arrow thumped into the trunk of a tree inches from his face. Samuel flinched, dropped his cask, and whirled about. Grimsby screamed as a long shaft pierced his breast and hurled him into the undergrowth. The sailors' casks thumped to the ground as they shoved past Chavez, racing down his leafy tunnel.

"Find cover and return fire!" Samuel barked. "Don't make targets of yourselves."

He crouched behind the knobby bole of a kapok tree, drew his Colt, and sought the others. Chavez was down on one knee scanning the jungle, and Padraig sheltered behind a leaning tree with Filipe beside him. Musket balls whipped the leaves overhead. The ambushers were aiming too high—a common error. Samuel snapped off two blind shots toward the sound and jinked over to join Padraig.

The stench of bitter sweat washed over Samuel as Chavez crashed down beside them a moment later. "*Indios, Capitán*. Never figured they'd be this far over."

Samuel peered anxiously into the wall of leaves around him. Indians had captured a filibuster north of Rivas the previous year. They'd stripped the young American, lashed him five hundred times, then killed him slowly, agonizingly, by cutting him in pieces. "Where are the sailors?"

Another burst of musketry, and the foliage rustled around them.

Padraig fired two rounds, blindly. "At least six muskets. Thank God, they're firing high."

Chavez flinched when an arrow twanged into a tree three feet from his face. "The sailors ran for the boat like scalded panthers."

"Good." Samuel reached for his cartridge box. "We've got to get back to them. They're defenseless."

Padraig reloaded. "The ambushers won't expect six-shooters."

Revolvers were still rare in the world, but thank God they had two, "When you're ready, we'll lay down covering fire and run for it," Samuel said. "Filipe, are you all right?"

Filipe nodded with bulging eyes and hefted his pistols. Despite his shaking hands, if he saw a target, he'd hit it. Samuel reloaded his spent chambers with practiced ease, rolling his shoulders to calm his nerves.

Padraig fiddled his last cap onto the nipple. "Ready."

Cocking the hammer of his revolver, Samuel scanned the green curtain. Nothing. "Shoot down the trail and to the right. I'll shoot to the left and behind us. Filipe, save your charges, just in case. On three."

Time stood still.

"*Un, dos, tres.*"

They fired into the jungle.

Samuel cocked the trigger and fired again. "Run, Filipe, run!"

Filipe's collar ripped as Chavez yanked him down the trail after Padraig. Samuel fired again and followed, snapping another shot over his shoulder, lifting his feet high with every step. This was not the time to trip.

Muskets crackled in the jungle and bullets plucked the surrounding air, but miraculously, none struck them. The buggers had as much difficulty sighting a target through the trees as he did.

Lungs heaving and legs burning, he burst into sunlight onto the pliant sand, which was roasting hot, and disinclined to let them pass easily. Worthy stood rigidly by the longboat, cutlass at the ready.

Alone.

"Jesus, what happened to the sailors?" Samuel squatted to reload. "Padraig, take Filipe to the ship. I'll search for them."

Chavez touched Samuel's shoulder. "*Capitán*, I was born in a place like this. I can move undetected."

"Chavez, I can't ask you to—"

"Return to the *Spartacus*, sir," he said. "I'll stay behind and hide in the jungle. They won't know I'm here. I'll find where they took the *marineros* and meet you back here at midnight. We'll mount a rescue . . . as long as they're still alive."

Samuel glanced at the jungle and then at the *Spartacus* rocking at anchor. The Indians were hanging back somewhere in the trees. They'd never seen six-shooters and must fear the Colts as they fired an endless barrage of bullets. And Chavez was the best man to reconnoiter the enemy camp. He nodded curtly. "Midnight, then. Three flashes of the dark lantern before we come ashore. Be careful. Filipe, tell the bosun we're pushing off. Let's get their heads down, Padraig."

He and his friend turned as one. The Irishmen blasted their Colts into the jungle, their balls whipping the foliage as Chavez melted into the trees and Filipe raced down the sand to warn the bosun.

Cracking the dark lantern three times, Samuel moved to the boarding ladder, taking care not to tangle his saber as he climbed down to the longboat. Padraig moved two rifles aside to make room, and Samuel stepped onto the thwart amidships so as not to rock the boat. The sight of Filipe, face blackened with boot polish, fidgeting with his pistols made him shake his head, but he needed the boy. While the four sailors who'd volunteered as rowers had fired muskets before, they were no fighters, unlike

Filipe, who could shoot straight and more than hold his own with a saber. Samuel had agonized all evening, sweltering in the humid, musty staleness of the cabin, puzzling how to rescue the sailors without bringing Filipe—knowing his presence would rile Sofia—but he'd failed to devise a rescue requiring fewer than four shooters. The thought of savages torturing the sailors, especially young Barclay, who hadn't even begun to shave, had horrified him into his hard choice.

Worthy put the tiller to starboard. "Cast her off, me lads, and may God be with us."

With the thole pins well-greased, the muffled oars dipped soundlessly into the water, flexed, and lifted, dripping water like a shower of diamonds in the moonlight. Each sailor had two loaded minié rifles, compliments of Vanderbilt and the Costa Rican army. They would remain on the beach to cover the escape. Knowing the names of every man who followed him into battle had always been important to Samuel, and this time was no exception. The red-faced fellow with a bulbous nose and gray tobacco-stained beard was Flynn. Whip-thin with sunken cheeks, Macy was from Kentucky and claimed that everyone from there could shoot the eye out of a "coon" at one hundred paces. Jenkins, once a runaway slave, was tall like Samuel, clean-shaven with a ready smile. The last sailor, Gambino, was thin and lithe; he was from the Five Points in New York City, and surviving that place was ample reference for his fighting ability.

They rowed carefully round the headland, and the low waves moderated as they came under its lee. Watchmen on the boat had spotted no guards on the beach in the daylight hours, but Samuel took all precautions, keeping the boat inconspicuous and the rowing silent. Better to act like a granny than add more names to his conscience.

Twitching in the darkness on the silent longboat, bile bubbling his belly, Samuel drummed his fingers on the hilt of his saber and loosened the Colt in his holster. He'd no right to risk Padraig's or Filipe's life, and it wasn't too late to turn back. But those sailors and the child, Barclay, would suffer a hideous death if he deserted them. He couldn't live with that either.

The moon was rising from behind the hill—a waxing moon, almost full, with a silver light that would soon illuminate the bay. The cove had enough sand at low tide that they could bypass the rocky outcrop and skirt the jungle to rendezvous with Chavez, if he was there. His shoulders curled forward at the possibility of Chavez being captured.

The rustle of wavelets foaming onto sand sounded ahead.

Worthy spat his spent wad over the side. "Stretch out now, my beauties, and drive her up on the beach."

The sand grated the underside of the longboat like chalk on a board as she scraped onto the beach, rocking Samuel forward. He forced himself to wait until the sailors jumped out and hauled the boat higher. Padraig and Filipe passed them their rifles and stepped out. Samuel followed, passed the dark lantern to Padraig, and led them north around the headland, boots sinking in the wet sand.

The susurration of crickets at the edge of the jungle made it difficult to hear anything else, especially over the insistent ringing in his shattered eardrum. He rolled his shoulders and peered into the blotchy, shifting darkness. *Dear God, if they've a watchman, don't let him see us.*

At the jungle's edge, he slumped against the prickly bole of a tree. The air smelled like a greenhouse, sodden and moldy. A whippoorwill trilled its soulful nocturnal opera. Padraig and Filipe dropped next to the tree beside him, the whites of their eyes enormous in the darkness. Drawn by the sweat covering their bodies, a cloud of mosquitoes droned in, buzzing and biting.

"What now?" Padraig asked.

Leaves rustled. An overpowering acrid body odor wrinkled his nose, and a smoky figure touched Samuel from the shadows.

He jumped and whirled, hand flying to his Colt.

"It's me, *Capitán*," Chavez whispered. "Found them. They're in a stockade a mile from here, locked in a hut. It's not much, bamboo walls we can cut through, but there are a lot of Indians. Maybe twenty. Too many for us to take on."

"Never," Padraig said. "More to slay, that's all."

"Any guards on the beach?" Samuel asked.

"I killed both of them." Chavez's big teeth flashed like a half moon. "I found their main path through the jungle. It'll get us there *rapido*."

"How's the stockade laid out? How many weapons have they got?"

"Nine huts clustered around one large hut in the center where the single men sleep. Twenty men in total. The sailors are imprisoned in one of the smaller huts."

"How do you know?" Samuel asked.

"I counted the bastards while they whipped the sailors with bamboos. Thank God we're getting them out tonight. *Ellos no durarán otro día*."

If they got them out. Three men and one youth against twenty—Samuel lacked Chavez's confidence. "Weapons?"

"Most have old muskets, the rest have bows and arrows. Every bugger has a machete, long as a cutlass."

"Guards?"

"One on the gate."

There wasn't time to go for more men from the *Spartacus*; it would be daylight before they landed a large party, and more men would make too much noise, in any case. If the Indians were warned, they'd use the hostages as shields.

Samuel gulped down excess spittle. "We have to attack now."

An eight-foot palisade surrounded the stockade, and though it sat in a clearing, its residents had not cleared the surrounding vegetation.

Samuel ducked back into the jungle and joined the others

crouching there. "It's exactly as Chavez called it. We can work our way up to the gate with little fear of detection." A deep-throated roar made him jump, and his heart skipped a beat. Idiot—it was only a howler monkey. He'd seen and heard them on the San Juan River last year. "Padraig and Filipe will wait outside the gate. Chavez and I will go in. Everyone clear on what they must do?"

The others nodded.

"Let's go, then."

He crouched and sprinted through the undergrowth, Chavez pattering softly behind him. He halted at the palisades and listened. The crickets were screeching like a million kettles boiling in the jungle, but he heard nothing else. Chavez leaned against the palisade and cupped his hands together. Grabbing his sweaty shoulder, Samuel stepped up and reached high. He could feel the top, but his fingers couldn't hold on.

He lost his balance and toppled sideways with a thud. Even on soggy ground, the noise seemed loud enough to wake the bay. Breath bursting in and out, he lay still, cursing his clumsiness. The only sounds were the chirping of the crickets and the warbling of the night birds. He took Chavez's hand and pulled himself to his feet.

"I'll go, *sí*?" Chavez nudged him against the wall. "I grew up in a village like this."

The coarse poles scratched Samuel through his sweat-soaked shirt as he leaned against the wall. Nimble as the howler monkeys growling in the jungle, Chavez placed a muddy boot in Samuel's cupped hands, rose with the boost, stepped on Samuel's left shoulder, and launched over the top of the palisade. For a stocky man, he was graceful.

Samuel sprinted for the gate where Padraig waited with Filipe in the welcoming shadows. Padraig squeezed his shoulder in greeting and held up one finger.

One sentry. Chavez had been right again—and now, it was up to Chavez.

Time dragged, and Samuel blinked furiously as he strained to hear any sound. Chavez had better hurry; every second increased the chance of discovery.

Someone coughed and hacked on the other side of the gate. The sentry was alert. If he spotted Chavez, they were finished.

Samuel's skin itched from mosquito bites as the tiny pests buzzed and bit. Spotting a chink between two posts, he peeped through. Nothing stirred in the compound, but when he looked harder, he noticed a figure creeping through the moonlight, slinking from shadow to shadow. Then Chavez passed out of his narrow view, and Samuel moved to the gate.

A grunt, a long wheeze of expelled air, and a soft bump issued from inside. The gate lifted two inches then creaked open to reveal Chavez's tense face. They slipped inside and crouched to reconnoiter. Black in the night, blood pooled around the guard sprawled on the trampled earth.

Chavez pointed to the right. "They're in the second hut."

Filipe, pale but determined, drew his pistols and stood back to guard the gate. As Samuel and Padraig scurried toward the communal hut, Samuel skirted a cooking fire with smoking embers. The compound stank of rotting waste, burned wood, and piss.

Samuel halted at an open window cut in the bamboo walls of the communal hut. This would suit his purpose nicely. The squat bottle he drew from his satchel was as round as a small cannonball and surprisingly heavy. Padraig placed the dark lantern on the ground and cracked it enough to light a fuse. The gunpowder-coated cord glowed and spluttered. Samuel hesitated; he didn't want to kill men in their sleep, but it was the only way.

Padraig straightened at the next opening as the fuse of the second grenade sizzled, fully lit, and they tossed their grenades inside. They sprinted for the hut with the prisoners.

White light exploded behind them, illuminating the compound, and a blast of hot air hurled Samuel to the ground. Over his shoulder, the walls of the hut exploded, and a second later, piercing screams erupted. Visions of Crimea—cannons roaring, detonations everywhere, dirt, shrapnel, the shrieks of the stricken—flashed through his mind. He clambered to his feet.

The tendons in his neck corded as he drew his Colt and hurried to the prison hut. He recoiled at the wave of sweat and blood that rushed out when he unbarred the door—the stench of fear. The naked sailors struggled to sit up, hands and feet bound, the whites of their eyes huge. Barclay, his pale flesh scarred and bloody, whimpered when Samuel stooped to cut him free.

The bastards. With any luck, Padraig's grenades had killed them all.

"Let's go lads, we're taking you back to the ship." He lifted Barclay to his feet. "Can you walk?"

Three gunshots sounded in the compound.

"No . . . No more, p-please." Barclay's squeaky whisper made Samuel's nostrils flare. Only monsters would beat a child like that.

"Shush, now, lad, we're taking you home. Can you hold on a second?" Without waiting for an answer, Samuel cut Smith free.

Smith massaged his chafed wrists. "Thank God, I thought we were dead men."

"We're not clear yet." Samuel cut the rough twine binding O'Brien.

The hefty Irishman rolled to his knees and used the wall to pull himself upright. "Never thought a Brit would rescue me."

"I'm as Irish as you are. Can you walk?"

More musketry sounded out in the compound.

"Yes. Young Barclay's in terrible shape, though."

"We'll carry him." Samuel helped Smith to his feet.

"Me and O'Brien will take the boy," Smith said.

"Good. Let's go."

It had been ten years since Jerry Kerr trained him to shoot with either hand, and Samuel had honed that skill further in the

Seventeenth Lancers. He switched his Colt to his left hand, drew his saber, and stepped from the shack, squinting against the flames twisting around the other hut.

A snarling Indian swiveled a musket his way. Samuel snapped off a shot and hit him between the eyes. Blood and brains sprayed the air, and the Indian crumpled ten feet away. A tongue of flame licked from the darkness beside the gate, another a second later. It sounded like Padraig; he carried the only other revolver.

Barclay cried out in pain as the sailors carried him behind Samuel.

Two men in tattered trousers charged from the smoke, firelight dancing on the blades of their machetes. Samuel opened the first man's belly before the man could begin his downstroke and gagged at the stench of intestines spilling out. The second man's dark eyes bulged, and he spun on his bare heels to run. Samuel swung again with a grunt and opened the man's back to the spine. The man's screech cut off as he toppled.

Fanned by the sea breeze, the flames from the burning hut had ignited two more huts, and women and children ran screaming toward the palisades. Samuel choked on the pungent fumes as he willed the sailors to reach the gate. Another pistol shot cracked in the haze, and Chavez burst from the smoke like a black wraith.

"Everyone's here," Padraig's breathless voice called from the gate. "Let's go."

Samuel loped after Chavez, flicking glances over his shoulder until they reached the jungle. The humid air there was refreshing after the smoke and stench of the compound.

Samuel's lungs were burning. "The others?"

"I sent them ahead," Padraig said. "We should reload."

Filipe was already ramming a ball home in his pistol.

"No," Samuel said. "Keep moving. After that thrashing, they'll lie low—and anyway, I've another few rounds. Back to the boat." He mussed Filipe's sweaty locks. "You all right?"

"Fine." Filipe stowed his ramrod and padded up the path.

Samuel's eyebrows curled together. No one got used to the horror of killing close up. Filipe may have seen a shot or two fired in the Battle of Santa Rosa, but this was the first time he'd been in the thick of it.

They scrambled down the narrow path in silence with the jungle wrapped around them, picking their way in the moonlight dripping through the green canopy. They had succeeded without losing a man.

Moonlight glittered on the water and haloed the longboat floating off the strip of silvered sand.

The oarsmen stood guard while Bosun Worthy helped O'Brien aboard and Smith cradled Barclay in the bow.

O'Brien bent over the side and spat. "Christ, I thought I was done for. Saved by a Brit, of all people."

"Brit, me arse." Padraig grabbed the longboat's gunwale. "He's as Irish as you are. Better, in fact, because he's from Cork, you jackeen."

O'Brien guffawed, and the others joined in. It was the first time Samuel had seen the cantankerous boson show the gaps between his rotten teeth in a smile, and he stank of stale rum and cheap tobacco when he turned and surprised Samuel with a hug.

"God bless you, sir," Worthy croaked. "You've worked a miracle."

~

Pinpoints of light winked on the dark waters of the sluggish San Juan River sweeping through Greytown, and the reflections reminded Benjamin Fry of Willy's excitement when they'd passed through here on the way to join Walker's filibuster army. This land had thrilled Willy. *It's just as I imagined it would be*, he'd said, his brown eyes sparkling as he inhaled the alien scents of moisture, soil, and decaying vegetation. *The smell of life*. They'd planned to build a new home here together, away from the tedious grind of West Virginia . . .

And now Willy was dead.

The cramped dining room was full of passengers recently disembarked from the SS *Orion*, waiting to catch the steamer upriver to Lake Nicaragua. They were mainly prospectors and settlers headed for California, but there were also a dozen volunteers for Walker's filibuster army, wild young men eager for adventure.

Fry stared over the river, his vision blurring and his heart aching. He should never have returned to Nicaragua. This had been Willy's dream. He thrust out his chin. That's exactly why he *should* be back, because it was all that remained of Willy—this dream and vengeance.

His stomach rumbled, but he couldn't eat. The simple dinner of pork rinds, beans, and rice tasted like dust. He shoved the plate away with a sigh. Every meal since Willy died—no, was murdered—had been dreadful, even the fine steak in New York.

Samuel Kingston had proven a challenge; he'd escaped in Ireland and again in New York. He shouldn't have bungled that second chance to kill Kingston, but the bastard wouldn't get away again. Frank Anderson was searching for him in the Caribbean, and with any luck, he'd caught him already.

Willy's death was all Kingston's fault. If he hadn't stolen Walker's gold, the filibusters would have received the men and arms they needed to defeat the allies. By now, Willy would've been safe on the farm Walker had promised them; instead, he moldered in some unmarked grave.

Damn those Irish bastards for not killing Kingston on the road. *My dear colonel*, Lucan had said. These *cavalry veterans are the best money can buy. They'll take care of Kingston. You focus on returning those stolen papers to me.* He should've ambushed Kingston himself. Well, to hell with his lordship. Lucan would have to pay a pretty bounty to get his precious papers back now.

Fry cracked his knuckles and looked over the bamboos

thrusting up like a forest of spears on the other side of the night-blackened river. Captain Anderson's frigate would catch Kingston on his way down. He took another swig of whiskey and coughed when it stung his throat. Bloody rotgut.

The dining room hushed as a shapely young woman entered, cradling an infant in her slender arms, her fashionable, green dress sweeping the dusty floorboards. Fry shot her a bored glance and then looked again, whiskey glass frozen inches from his lips—that was Sofia Kingston. He'd seen her when he reconnoitered the Kingston manor in Clonakilty.

If she was here, was Kingston here too? But Kingston would never dare return to Nicaragua; Walker would have him shot on sight for treason.

Casually, Fry turned in his chair and checked the street. Nobody. How daring of the bitch to travel alone—and how opportune.

He threw back his whiskey and hurried to the reception desk.

Nancy Blake, the Greytown Inn's owner from Tennessee, was working the desk herself. She was lean, and the unkempt, gray hair framing her narrow face made her look like a whiskey bottle wearing a wig. She wiped the sheen of sweat from her wrinkled brow with the back of her sleeve. "Evening, Colonel. Everything satisfactory?"

"Fine, Mrs. Blake." He nodded back at the Kingston woman as she sat in the dining room. "That lady—the lady . . ."

". . . in the green dress." Nancy rolled her eyes.

"Ah, yes." Let her think he was smitten like all the other fool diners.

"Mrs. Kingston from Ireland, she said she is," Nancy said. "But she's as Nicaraguan as the waitress there. Wonder where she got those airs and graces from?"

"Is she traveling alone?"

Nancy nodded disapprovingly. "Young women today . . ."

Fry placed a cheroot between his lips and picked up the box

of matches on the reception desk. Kingston's bitch was bouncing his spawn on her knee as she ordered from the waitress. His body heated. Here was a way to repay Kingston in spades. If he could take her hostage, Kingston would come running and . . .

He averted his gaze. Jesus, what was he thinking? Willy would be disgusted. And if Colonel Valle discovered he'd harmed his daughter, he'd want revenge. Besides, he'd two thousand rifles to deliver to Walker.

He replaced the matchbox and turned it over and over on the scarred counter. His breath hitched. But Kingston *had* caused Willy's death. A dull ache started beneath his right temple as he glared at the Kingston bitch.

"Oh, what on earth is that girl doing? How many times have I told her to serve diners from the left side?" Nancy clucked and bustled into the dining room.

Fry glanced about, spun the dog-eared register around, and ran his finger down the page. What room was she in?

CHAPTER ELEVEN

"Puerto Limón," Padraig said as *Spartacus* tugged in her anchor line in the turquoise waters of the Caribbean. "Columbus was the first European to set foot here. It was his last voyage to the New World in 1502. When he saw the Carib Indians wearing gold jewelry, he named it Costa Rica—rich coast."

Samuel stirred from watching the ramshackle town and the jagged mountains behind. "I'll bet there's gold here. Look at all the gold and silver mines they have in Nicaragua."

"Why are we stuck here waiting for Keller?" Padraig asked. "I need to stretch my legs. He can keep his blooming sailing ship; it takes too long to go anywhere."

"There's no wharf," Samuel said, "so we must remain here until Keller returns with permission to land. He should've been back by now. It's well past noon."

Padraig swatted a mosquito feeding on his neck. "Bloody mosquitoes. You think it was wise to let Filipe go ashore with him? Lad can be impetuous." Padraig's face was peeling again; his fair skin was ill-suited to the tropical sun.

Samuel drank warm water from his canteen and pulled a face at the metallic taste. "He pestered me more than your mosquitoes. He'll be fine. They'll think he's a Costa. Anyway, Keller says they're not concerned about Central Americans—they don't consider them foreigners. Even so, I stopped him from taking his pistols ashore."

"And that little knife of his?" Padraig wiggled his eyebrows. "How about the blackjack Chavez gifted him? Half of Limón could be dead by now."

Samuel pushed off the guardrail and pulled down the brim of his hat against the blinding sun. "Enough. How the hell did I get stuck with the little bugger?"

"You should've left him back in Ireland. Dad would've hammered some sense into him."

Samuel wrinkled his nose at his frock coat. "This coat stinks." *Spartacus* was a damp ship. The bunks in the tiny cabin he shared with Filipe and Padraig were never quite dry, and the bedding was musty. Their clothes had soured with mold.

From around the headland came a teak twenty-footer swept along by eight oarsmen. Two black-uniformed officers wearing wide-brimmed Spanish hats sat by the mast, but it was the ten soldiers crammed amidships, muskets upright, that quickened Samuel's pulse.

"Bloody hell, what's going on?" he barked. "Where's Keller?"

"Not there, that's for sure," Padraig said. "This doesn't look good. What shall we do?"

"Nothing. Stay calm and see what they want."

The Costa Rican boat bumped alongside minutes later, and Samuel and Padraig met the officers at the entry port. A young lieutenant with white blotches discoloring his skin boarded first and squinted at Samuel and Padraig with narrowing eyes. The soldiers climbed clumsily up the ladder and promptly pointed their muskets at Samuel.

A stout captain boarded last. He plopped a dated cocked hat on his head before looking down his nose at them, quite a challenge considering that he was much shorter than they were. "Samuel Kingston, Padraig Kerr?"

Samuel's limbs tingled. "I'm Kingston, and my friend here is Padraig Kerr. How can I help you?"

The captain clapped his hands. "Seize them."

The stench of stale sweat and musty serge was overpowering as soldiers grabbed Samuel by the arms. Chains rattled, and a boatman passed manacles up to a soldier at the entry port.

The captain twisted the waxed mustache on his wizened face. "I am *Capitán* David Maduro of the Costa Rican Army. I'm arresting you as *enimigos* of the Republic."

Samuel pulled back his wrists, resisting the soldiers. "What do you mean? We're delivering rifles for your petty war. You've no right to do this. I'll have you know we're British citizens."

Maduro's head flinched back slightly. "You're *español*? I was told you were British, but you speak *castilliano*.

How did this captain know anything about them? Samuel jerked his head back. "What's the meaning of this? Enemies of the state?"

The soldiers grabbed his arms, pinning him where he stood.

Maduro snorted. "You deny you're a captain in William Walker's filibuster army?"

They knew everything about him. "That was a year ago. Now we're mortal enemies."

"I'm sure you are." Maduro snorted. "And that's why you're bringing rifles to arm the enemies of our beloved President Mora."

"This is bloody ridiculous." Padraig twisted so hard he shook free from the guards.

A soldier clubbed him in the gut with the butt of his musket. Padraig doubled over, and they toppled him to the deck.

Another blow knocked Samuel to his knees beside Padraig, and pain speared his back. Rough hands snapped manacles on his wrists with a cruel pinch, reminding him of the dungeon of the condemned in London's Newgate Prison. A dark time in his life, indeed.

He flushed. "Now look here, Cap—"

"Get them in the boat." Maduro jabbed a finger toward the tender, then swept his hand around the deck. "Search the vessel and mount a guard. We don't want her disappearing tonight."

Ruthless hands forced Samuel to the entry port and spun him around, and he had no choice but to climb down into the boat. The boat rocked as he stepped aboard into a tang of teak and resin.

A soldier shoved him over a thwart, and he fell to the floorboards on his back. The soldier poked him with the muzzle of his musket. "Don't move."

For someone to tip them off to the Costa Ricans was the last thing he expected. It must've been Fry. He or one of his cronies could've arrived here by steamship long before their sluggish sailing vessel. This was serious. The Costa Ricans had executed every filibuster they'd captured, and Samuel had no proof he brought the guns they carried for the Costa Ricans, not even a letter. Vanderbilt had insisted on anonymity; the sly old goat didn't want anyone to discover his vanity-fueled feud with Walker.

So now they were dead men. He'd never catch up with Sofia and John.

The boat tilted, and Padraig crashed on top of Samuel with a grunt.

"Bastards." Padraig squirmed and rolled onto the damp floorboards. "When I get out of these chains, I'll bust your bloody heads."

More soldiers stepped on board, rocking the boat, and water sloshed in the shallow bilge.

Samuel twisted toward Padraig. "Have you seen Filipe? The captain?"

"I hope Filipe hasn't done something dumb." Padraig shook his head. "Why don't you ask the fellow in the stupid Napoleon hat there?"

A bare foot stomped on Padraig's belly, and he doubled over. "Shut up, *yanqui*."

“Don’t provoke them,” Samuel whispered. “Bide your time until we sort this out.”

Samuel’s cramped muscles ached by the time the harbor boat bumped against the wharf. He winced as soldiers snatched them to their feet and manhandled them ashore.

Maduro started toward the town without looking back. “Bring them to the harbor office. If they cause trouble, shoot them.”

The handful of storehouses and palm-thatched shacks along the beach barely qualified Limón as a town, which as Samuel soon discovered had no jail either. Instead, the soldiers shoved them into a narrow adobe building with a mud floor and two tiny windows high in its west-facing wall. The airless heat hit Samuel like a furnace fire.

A manacled Filipe met them inside the door. “What’s going on? The *stupidos* Costas grabbed me and locked me up. You’d think they’d be glad we brought them weapons.” There was a bruise under his left eye, and his clothes were covered in mud.

“At least you’re unharmed.” Samuel touched Filipe’s shoulder. “Where’s Captain Keller?”

Filipe showed the palms of his hands and shrugged. “I waited outside the port commander’s office while he reported. Ten minutes later, two peasant soldiers came out and grabbed me. Me! They put their sullied, cane-cutting paws on me, and they locked me up.”

“And the captain?” Samuel stood on his toes to look out the small window.

Filipe shrugged. “Never saw him.”

“Lout sold us out.” His chains rattled as Padraig pounded his fist into his palm. “I’ll break his bloody neck.”

“Hold on, we don’t know that.” A ball of cold apprehension was forming in Samuel’s gut. “Filipe, *Que dijiste?*”

"I told that pig of a captain I was Colonel Valle's son," Filipe shouted, "and if he didn't release me, my father would rain hell on his horrible little country."

"Filipe!" Padraig roared.

Samuel covered his face with his hands. "Lord, help us. That was stupid."

"What else would I have said? That rube can't just—"

"You just tied us to Walker." Samuel sank against the wall and covered his face. "You handed them all the proof they need."

"Proof they need for what?"

"To hang us."

Through the small windows, the rain spilled from the morning sky in silky sheets, pounding the earth, streaming down ruts in the muddy road, flowing under the door to flood their cell. Too exhausted to stand, Samuel slumped beside the others on the muddy floor. The rain had fallen for three days, streaming through a dozen holes in the moldy thatch.

The nights were the hardest, when his mind spun in meaningless circles. He fought to stay awake, dreading the nightmares fueled by the scalding temperatures and relentless humidity, regretting his neglect of Sofia and hating himself for dragging his companions into danger, knowing the next day promised more of the same.

The others were streaked with mud and sweat. Angry red bites pocked Padraig's peeling face, and he had dark circles under his eyes. Nobody could sleep in the stifling heat. Samuel's feet were bite-free in his soaked boots, but they suffered their own plague—rot setting in. Only Chavez seemed immune to the bugs, and he slept soundly in the corner.

Samuel squirmed to relieve the ache in the leg he'd broken off the coast of Crimea in what the British papers had called the Storm of the Century. "Three days and no news. Where the hell are they? What are they doing?" His voice was croaky, his mouth as dry as sand.

Padraig opened his eyes. "Don't ask me . . . I'm bloody starving, All we've eaten is a spoon of rice each day. They think I'm a Chinaman or what? I'd give my nuts for some spuds right now."

"That would relieve many a mother back home." Samuel smiled weakly.

"What do you mean?"

"To know you couldn't chase their daughters anymore."

"Wait." Filipe sat up. "Have you got nuts?"

Padraig chuckled. "Not the kind nuts you eat. He meant . . ." He sighed and shook his head. "Forget it."

Samuel's eyebrows drew together. Filipe sounded weaker. He didn't have red welts from mosquito bites, but there many ways men died in such harsh conditions: malaria, cholera, yellow fever . . . Yellow fever plagued the Caribbean Coast.

The door creaked open, and a sergeant poked his pock-marked face inside the door. A cluster of bedraggled soldiers cradled muskets behind him.

The sergeant prodded Samuel with his musket. "On your feet, *yanquis*. They've decided your fate."

Their *fate*. Samuel's skin shivered. Soldiers with muskets meant a firing squad.

Outside, the muggy air and driving rain was refreshing after the steamy confines of their cell. A soldier jabbed Samuel in the back, and he stumbled toward the port commander's office. The tic under his eye quivered as they sloshed through the mud. Down here, nobody even offered a mockery of a trial. It was straight to death—and too often, a gruesome one. Now nobody would save Sofia and baby John.

The sergeant stepped aside and motioned them to enter the port commander's office. Samuel took in the two men seated inside. The stout Caucasian with close-cropped hair across from Captain Maduro looked familiar. Where had he seen that bullet-like head before?

"Nice to see you again, Mr. Kingston, although I wish it were under better circumstances," the man said. "Clifford Webster. We met in New York, with Sylvanus Spencer and Frank Brogan."

Samuel exhaled. "The Englishman from Granada." This was fortunate. Surely Webster would help them.

"Smuggling weapons into Costa Rica is a crime punishable by death," Webster continued.

"President Mora wants to stand you in front of a firing squad."

Samuel's hearing had muffled. So it was the end, then. A firing squad. Several heartbeats pulsed before he could think again. But a firing squad made little sense, as little sense as Webster's presence.

"Unlikely," he replied, gathering what little authority he had in this situation. "Our deaths could spark an international incident. What's your business here?"

Webster huffed. "My business? I'm trying to save your life."

Samuel held his gaze without dignifying the response.

"You're an unpopular man down here, Mr. Kingston," Webster said. "If it hadn't been for you and your native troops, Walker would have been finished already. By helping Walker to victory in Rivas last year, you handed him the presidency of Nicaragua and put Costa Rica in peril."

"I'm no ally of Walker's," Samuel snapped.

Webster held up his hands. "Yet now you appear with a boatload of arms and the son of Walker's ally. It certainly looks as though you're here to start some mischief, and Juanito Mora is not happy about that." He made a show of brushing dried mud from his sleeve before gesturing to two wooden chairs.

Samuel straightened. "I'll stand. Cornelius Vanderbilt hired me to deliver those guns to Mora. And Filipe is just a boy. He has nothing to do with the war."

"Oh, I know you work for the Commodore, Mr. Kingston, but the Costa Ricans will never hear it. You see, I'm working for Mr. Vanderbilt as well, although he himself would deny it. A businessman of his caliber can't be seen in breach of the Neutrality Act."

Samuel folded his arms. "Enough! What exactly do you want?"

A flush crept across Webster's jowly face. "Sylvanus and I presented your idea of capturing the San Juan River to Mr. Vanderbilt, and he liked it. He liked it a lot. He'll reward us handsomely if we convince President Mora to act on it. It would be an easier endeavor if you joined us."

Heat flared in Samuel's cheeks. "I don't have time to—"

"I know you trained a crack native company in Nicaragua last year." Webster dabbed his brow with a handkerchief. "I need you to do the same here."

"To hell with you," Samuel said. "I delivered the rifles for Vanderbilt. The Costa Ricans can't hold me here."

"Yes, they can, and they can shoot you. You see, President Mora and I have come to an agreement. He'll make an example of the foreigners who tried to foment treason among the peasants he disenfranchised. This country's a tinderbox, and you've brought the match."

"You filthy *Sasanach*. Nobody can trust an Englishman." Padraig lunged forward, but the sergeant jabbed him in the back with his musket, and he buckled to his knees inches from Webster.

Webster calmly moved his foot aside. "You'll be in no position to dispute the charges, because Captain Maduro intends to execute you this morning—unless you agree to help me capture the San Juan River."

Padraig rocked back, spluttering.

Samuel dropped a hand onto his shoulder and spoke in a low tone. "Not now, Padraig. We can't win." He glared at Webster. "What do you want from us?"

Webster crossed his arms. "I'm not a military man, so I need you to convince President Mora that your plan to capture the river will work and then make it happen."

"Oh, is that all?" Padraig snarled as he climbed to his feet.

"I'll reward you handsomely, of course," Webster said. "Otherwise, you're dead men."

A thousand calculations raced through Samuel's mind, but what kept coming back to him were the faces that stayed in the forefront of his every waking moment: his wife and son. Every moment he spent dealing with the quagmire William Walker had made of this region was a moment he wasn't saving his family.

"Impossible," he said. "Only trained troops would have the discipline to sneak through the jungle and capture those forts. If Mora had such men before, they're all dead now. Cholera wiped out his army on the march back from Nicaragua."

Webster waved a hand in dismissal. "Not a problem for the man who trained a crack company of natives up in Nicaragua. You did it there, you can do it here."

"Listen, Webster, I don't have time to train soldiers," Samuel said. "My wife and child are traveling to Chinandega or León. They're in danger. I intend to cross the frontier at Los Chiles."

Webster sneered. "Mora's brother has sealed off the frontier. You'll never get through."

He locked eyes with Padraig. What choice did they have?

Webster produced a banana and peeled it fastidiously. "If you wish to save your family, I advise you to begin training the Costas immediately. If the good captain here executes you, you'll be of no use to your loved ones. And look at it this way: If you help me take the San Juan River, you'll be halfway to León."

Webster had him in a bind. Samuel rubbed the back of his neck. It would take too long to train raw Costa Rican recruits, but the Euronicas were already in Costa Rica. Perhaps they could help.

Samuel addressed Chavez in Spanish. "Chavez, can you find the Euronicas down here?"

"*Sí, Capitán. Estan en San José.*"

"Will they help us with this attack?"

"They're eager to go back and stop Walker." Chavez's voice was steady and low-pitched. "I believe they will."

He meant what he said, Samuel was certain. But even if they captured the river for Mora and he emerged unscathed, Samuel couldn't reach Nicaragua from there. No Costa Rican boat would sail to Greytown. Perhaps he could find a coaster or a fishing boat on the Pacific side, but there was no guarantee of that.

Samuel lifted his chin. "Do I have your word we're free to leave once you capture the river?"

Webster tipped his head lazily. "Of course."

The man's attitude was infuriating. "Then listen to me, because this is what's necessary."

"I hardly think you're in a position to dictate terms, Mr. Kingston."

"Oh, I think I am. You can't succeed with a bunch of Costa Rican farm boys, and neither can I. I'm sure Vanderbilt is paying you well for this, and I need seasoned veterans . . . the Euronicas . . . and you must pay them. Without them, we'll all die before we reach the river." He thrust out his chin. "And if that's the case, you may as well have us shot right here."

"Speak for yourself." Chains rattled as Padraig stepped closer to Samuel. "Nobody's shooting me anywhere."

Webster stared into the distance, wiping his forehead with his sweat-soaked handkerchief. "Very well, gentlemen. Ten thousand dollars when you complete the job."

Padraig rolled his eyes. "I'll bet Vanderbilt is paying you ten times that."

"That covers the men." Samuel cocked his head. "What about Padraig and me?"

"You get to live." Webster reached inside his rumpled shirt and scratched his belly. "But if that's not enough, I'll pay you each ten thousand when you complete the mission."

Ten thousand dollars was plenty for the Euronicas, and Samuel would wring their own share from Webster when the time was right. But at that moment, his priorities were to survive, to secure their freedom, to find Sofia and little John, and to recover the Baltimore papers. If capturing the river was his only way, he'd do it.

"We must be ready to march north within three weeks." Even that was too long. Anything could happen to Sofia and John in three weeks.

Webster stared at him incredulously, then shrugged. "Ambitious. But it's your mission." He nodded to Captain Maduro, who beckoned the sergeant.

When their manacles clanged to the floor, Samuel massaged his chafed wrists. "Where's Captain Keller?" He had a few choice words for that traitor.

"Oh, don't worry about him—or the rifles," Webster finished the banana and tossed the peel on the earthen floor. "He offloaded the rifles and sailed. Now then, clean up, and I'll fill you in. Keller left your trunks there, in the corner. We'll keep your weapons, however—for your protection, of course. Make yourselves look respectable; we're going to meet President Mora in the capital."

Towering trees blanketed the mountains, their canopies cradling the sullen mists in their boughs and surrounding Samuel with their musty, green-leaf smell as they rode up the high mountains on the way to Cartago. The temperature was still falling as the horses plodded up the wheel-rutted road winding around the rim of the mountain. If he failed to convince the president his plan to attack the river forts would work, they might still face a firing squad. He scrubbed a cold hand across his face and looked back at the cart trundling through the mud. His oilskin coat was in one trunk beneath the canvas cover, along with a sampling of the rifles. Their weapons were there also, guarded by Webster and two American thugs, their rifles resting on their saddles with muzzles aimed at Samuel and his companions. A wiry Carib Indian corporal and another soldier provided by Captain Maduro rounded out the escort.

One of the two bullocks bellowed as the *boyeo* whipped it with a bamboo cane. Samuel ground his teeth. He hated senseless cruelty, and the herder had no reason to prod the plodding beast.

Padraig's breath turned to smoke in the air. "It's just like Ireland up here. The trees look the same, the bushes, even the wildlife."

"Just as cold, too." Samuel blew on his hands and called ahead. "How much farther, Corporal?"

The corporal wrapped the colorful blanket tighter over his soiled white shirt. "Maybe thirty miles. It will warm up once we descend to the Central Valley. But . . . before that . . ." He shrugged.

"Bloody hell, so long as we get there today," Padraig said. "I don't fancy another night freezing in a cowshed."

Samuel glanced back, and Webster met his eyes. Did the bastard ever relax?

"Really?" he replied to Padraig. "And when you were nice and warm at the beach, all you did was complain about the heat and the mosquitoes."

The mist condensed as they labored uphill until they couldn't see ten feet on either side and had to trust the horses not to stumble off the road. Behind them, the *boyeo* cursed and cracked his whip as the wide-horned buffalos lowed mournfully. Samuel twisted in the saddle. The two-wheeled cart was stuck in the mud again. Triangular pieces of wood filled the metal hoops binding the wheels, like enormous pieces of pie, to ease the passage through mud. A hybrid of the disks used by the Aztec and the Spanish spoked wheel, the cartwheels were ideal for transporting coffee beans across muddy mountain trails and beaches, but sometimes even they got stuck.

Webster waved the barrel of his rifle. "Right there, Kingston.

Since you're in a hurry to go north, you and your mates should give that cart a heave."

Padraig's nostrils flared. "Someday, I'm going to cut the head off that English bastard."

"Do as he says." Samuel took his mud-caked boot out of the stirrup wearily. "We've no choice for now."

This was the fifth time he'd put his shoulder to the rough-hewn boards of the cart, and his feet groped for traction as the others grunted and cursed. Filipe slipped and fell.

A rifle crashed out nearby, the sound echoing around the valleys, and a bullet splintered the board where Filipe had stood a second earlier. Samuel gasped and whirled, his face heating. Which one of their escort was daft enough to—

His heart skipped a beat. Webster and the others stood gaping at the trees. None of them had discharged a weapon.

Ambush!

Tongues of flames lashed from the mist-shrouded forest. Corporal Diaz pitched out of his saddle. Another ball struck a soldier's mare, and she bolted into the fog. Seconds later, a high-pitched scream sounded from below as horse and rider plunged into the ravine.

Webster and the two Americans swung down from their saddles. Muskets barked behind them, and one American toppled as his boot touched the ground. Webster and the other crouched into a cluster of green umbrella plants and fired blindly into the forest.

The raw scent of freshly picked coffee was sharp as Samuel threw back the canvas cover and reached into the cart.

"Quick, our guns!" He tossed Padraig's holstered Colt and cartridge box to him and threw his Sharps and ammunition to Chavez before clawing up his Colt and ducking under the cart as lead splattered the mud close by.

His hands shook as he poured powder down a cylinder while counting musket shots. It sounded like five, maybe six attackers, moving closer.

Chavez fired first; the Sharps was quick to load through its breech. Filipe popped up beside Samuel and reached into the cart.

Samuel jabbed him in the side. "Stay down. Under the wagon." He rammed a ball home in the chamber and spun the cylinder.

"Let me get a rifle. I can help." Filipe's voice was shrill.

The last American pitched out of the broad-leaved bushes with a bloody hole in his chest.

The hair lifted on the back of Samuel's neck. "Stay *down*."

They were sitting ducks. He dropped a lead ball into the final cylinder and rotated it under the ramrod. The mist cleared for a second, and orange flames licked out from the foliage to his left.

He placed the last cap and shook the gun to clear the lead shavings. "Ready, Padraig? Chavez?"

Padraig finished loading a second later.

Chavez's mahogany face was ashen. He dragged a shaky hand across his forehead. "Ready."

Samuel pointed to the jungle on his left. "Filipe, stay behind me. On my word, Padraig, fire a shot and run for those trees there. You too, Chavez. That'll put us in front of those bastards."

The hidden enemy fired again—tongues of flame belching from the left, but closer.

"Now!" Samuel fired into the forest and leaped to his feet.

His legs wobbled like India rubber as he skated across the mud. Hypersensitive, he quailed as the wind of a slug zipped past his neck. Three jolting steps, and wet leaves flogged him as he plunged into the undergrowth. The bushes and ferns rustled as Padraig, Filipe, and Chavez crowded in behind him. Thank God, they were unharmed.

His heaving lungs burned as he scanned the swirling fog. Nothing stirred. The ambushers were reloading—or creeping closer.

Padraig pushed over beside him. "How many?"

"Not sure. Five, six muskets, maybe."

"Kingston! Where are you?" Webster's high-pitched voice warbled from the other side of the trail. "There are too many. For God's sake, save me. We must turn back before they attack."

Turning back *was* a wise choice. Samuel squinted into the fog. They courted death by pushing on, but if he turned back, it would be a month before he reached Greytown, and who knows what terrible harm could befall Sofia and John by then. The rain began again, first light drops pattering on the broad leaves, then heavy drops as fat as raisins.

Padraig rubbed his hand down his breeches. "They triggered their ambush too soon. Lucky for us."

Flames flickered in the rain, and musketry rattled, echoing through the mountains.

Samuel cocked his head to favor his good ear. Nothing but the patter of rain on the trees. The enemy was no longer advancing; the unexpected resistance had cooled their courage. Energy pumped through him. Maybe this was an opportunity, then. They had recovered their weapons, and their guards were dead except Webster. Perhaps this was a chance to head directly to Nicaragua, and to hell with attacking the river.

"They haven't moved. Probably afraid to. But we must winkle them out if we want to continue." He twisted to face the others. "Chavez, go right and work your way forward along the ravine. Kill anyone who moves. Padraig and I will approach from the other side, along the edge of the forest. Filipe, stay right here and don't move."

Chavez loosened the knife in his scabbard and melted into the mist.

Padraig tapped Samuel's shoulder and motioned with his head. "Lead on."

The rain stopped again, and the forest fell silent, no crickets whispering, no cicadas whirring. Samuel dodged under the wet branches, picking his steps across the slick ground. Flames flashed again, and muskets crackled. His nerves flared. The enemy was much closer now, to his right.

A high-pitched scream broke from the mist and cut off abruptly. He crept another twenty yards. Ramrods rasped in musket barrels directly ahead. He ducked into a cluster of umbrella leaves and shuddered as chilled water spilled down his back.

Muskets crashed in a ragged volley that gave him his chance. As the attackers reloaded, he shouldered through the foliage. Three men looked up from pouring powder down the barrels of their muskets and cursed.

Samuel pointed his revolver like a finger and fired, hitting one in the torso. The man screamed and toppled into the bushes with a snap of breaking branches. Samuel cocked again and pulled the trigger, and this slug hurled a second man into the undergrowth. The third ambusher raised a pistol, and Samuel shot him three times as the bark of Padraig's Colt sounded from his left. The first man clambered to his feet, leveling a pistol and yelling. Samuel took a step closer and shot him again. The man shrieked and pitched backward into the rain-drenched trees.

The Colt was empty, and Samuel crouched behind a rock. He'd been stupid to leave his cartridge box beside the cart. The distinctive sound of a Colt spat to his left, and then the forest fell silent. Samuel blinked rapidly. How many bandits remained? He'd wait thirty seconds.

Padraig whistled and called out. "Think that's all. Anyone hurt? Samuel? Chavez?"

"All clear," Chavez yelled from the forest.

"I'm all right. Let me see who they are." Samuel looked back. "Filipe, stay there. Don't move."

His feet sank in rotting leaves as he wriggled through the bushes, ignoring the scratches. Ten yards downhill, two bodies sprawled in the undergrowth, slightly built men with unkempt black hair and dark complexions paled in death. He rolled one over, fighting the urge to vomit at the stench of blood and shit. He never got used to that.

He searched the body and took two heavy coins from the dead man's jacket. "Golden eagles. American coins."

"Same here." Padraig rolled the other body over. "Nothing else on him. Let's find the others."

Four more bodies lay in the forest. Samuel's arms prickled when they found a gold coin on each corpse.

Leaves rustled gently, and Padraig flinched as Chavez appeared. "Jaysus, don't sneak up like that. You want to get shot? What happened over there?"

Chavez's dark face broke into a wintry smile. "Killed two over there. Nothing on them but these." He displayed two gold eagles in his blood-streaked hand.

Padraig whistled. "This is a fortune."

"They were paid to ambush us," Samuel said.

"But who knew we were coming?" Padraig asked.

"I don't know. I just don't know." Samuel needed a smoke, but it was impossible to roll a cigarette in this rain. "This is the third time someone's moved to stop us."

"Hey, w-what's going on?" Filipe called in a trembling voice. "Is everything all right? Will they attack again?"

"It's safe now. We're coming back to you." Samuel pocketed the coins. "For expenses. Chavez, keep yours. You earned them. We must get going now. It gets dark early at the equator, and we need to round up the soldiers' horses so we can bring their bodies in."

Padraig poked the corpse with his toe. "And these fellows?"

"Leave them," Samuel said. "Has anybody heard from that wretch Webster?"

"Not in a while." Padraig spun the cylinder of his Colt, and it clicked. "No ammo? Here, use mine."

They reloaded and edged back to the road, where they found Webster lying behind the cart, his lifeless eyes staring at the forest canopy. Samuel quietly exhaled. There was no longer any reason to visit San José. He was on his way now to Sofia and John.

He'd need Webster's map to find a route to the Pacific Coast. He searched Webster's body, wrinkling his nose at the metallic smell of the blood covering the neck wound. The map was in Webster's breast pocket.

He stood and opened it. "Chavez, it's your lucky day. Take his revolver. He won't be needing it where he's going."

"Hell." Padraig spat into the undergrowth. "I hope he's going to hell."

"Chavez, take Filipe and round up the horses. Find as many of them as you can, so we can carry our baggage on the spare mounts." He studied the creased map. "We must be close to the top of this mountain range. That puts us around here, in the Dulce Nombre de Jesús district—Christ, you Catholics love these names. Look, it's about eighty miles to the coast. With spare mounts, we can reach Puntarenas in twelve hours. We should be able to find a boat there to carry us to San Juan del Sur."

Padraig's eyes widened. "You're not helping capture the river, then? And getting another crack at Walker?"

"As much as I'd like to, especially if Vanderbilt pays me for it, I only care about finding Sofia."

"Right, then," Padraig said, closing the matter. "So how can we waltz into San Juan del Sur without Walker's men spotting us?"

He hadn't thought of that. The others stared at him until he shook loose the only available alternative. He folded the map. "You're right. We'll sail past it to Chinandega. If Sofia doesn't go to León, she'll go to her father's hacienda in Chinandega."

CHAPTER TWELVE

Dawn pinked the rolling landscape and coaxed verdant hues from the shadowed forest east of Puntarenas, Costa Rica's Pacific port, fifty miles west of San Jose, and some three hundred miles south of Chinandega, Nicaragua. Samuel twitched awake in the saddle and forced his gummy eyelids apart. The long night ride had drained them; nobody had said a word for hours.

Padraig's teeth chattered, and he moaned. Samuel twisted in the saddle to look at him. His friend's face was swollen and red, his green eyes dull and bloodshot.

"Christ Almighty! What's wrong with you?"

Padraig toppled slowly from the saddle and thumped onto the muddy road. Samuel's mare tossed her head and skittered sideways.

He reined in and dismounted. "Chavez, get his horse."

Padraig's forehead was burning hot, and sweat streamed over his body. "S-sorry, I thought it would p-p-pass. Should have told you." His teeth clattered.

Filipe climbed down from his saddle and stooped beside them in the mud. "What happened to him?"

Samuel opened Padraig's shirt to search for any marks or bites. A rash of angry red dots covered his chest; any closer together and he'd have been red all over. The spots covered his face, too, beneath his peeling, sunburned skin.

"My muscles are aching all over," Padraig whispered, "as if they're ripping apart." He vomited, and Samuel rolled him onto his side.

There were so many tropical diseases in Central America that would never be found back in Clonakilty. Samuel peered at the others' concerned faces. "You know what he has? I've never seen the like before. Was he bitten by something back in the forest?"

Filipe shook his head. "Don't know."

"He's shivering," Samuel said. "Get our coats from the bags. Water, too. Make haste."

Even wrapped in two frock coats, Padraig was still shivering violently when the rain began fifteen minutes later. "We must keep him dry. Get the oilskins, Filipe. Chavez, we need a doctor. You think Puntarenas is the closest place?"

Chavez stared down at his hands. "I've never been this way before."

The rain pelted down like a salvo of grapeshot, drumming the oilskin over Padraig's quaking body and pocking the mud. The map was a limp mess by the time Samuel unfolded it, the surface peeling off in soggy pellets. He hastily shoved it back into his coat.

"We're six miles from Puntarenas," he said. "Not too far. Help me get him on the horse. Padraig? Padraig, listen to me. I need you to hold on. Remember when you charged with the Light Brigade? Can't be worse than that. All right?"

Padraig nodded feebly.

"Good man. I'll be right beside you." Samuel slid an arm under him. "Help him up."

Padraig's skin was burning as they forced his limp arms into his oilskin and heaved him into his saddle. Chavez and Filipe steadied him as Samuel mounted and rode alongside to hold him up.

"I've got you," Samuel said. "Chavez, ride ahead and see if you can find us shelter."

Only a cavalryman raised around horses could have held his seat in Padraig's condition, and Samuel marveled at Padraig's tenacity and skill as they rode boot to boot. He ground his teeth so hard they ached. The rain was pounding a million tiny craters in the mud, streaming down the horses' flanks and lashing Samuel's eyes. Thunder rumbled overhead. Lightning flashed across the sullen sky, and Samuel's horse flung up its head, skittering sideways. He calmed it with a hand on its wet neck.

It seemed they'd been riding forever when Samuel heard the roar of a river above the drumming rain. A minute later, hooves sounded ahead, and Chavez trotted out of the gloom.

"I found no place to shelter, and the river has swamped the bridge," he said. "We can't cross over. But I came across a fisherman with a boat."

Samuel spat gummy saliva. "A boat! But if the river's flooding . . . He thinks he can make it?"

"For that piece of gold that I offered him, he's willing to try."

Samuel touched Padraig's swollen forehead. He was burning up and needed a doctor. "Take us to him."

"I'm w-with you," Padraig mumbled and clung to his reins.

Tears blistered the corners of Samuel's eyes. Padraig had saved his life so often.

By the time they halted at the racing river, Samuel ached all over from leaning out of the saddle to prop up Padraig. The air smelled of wet earth, grass, and algae. The fisherman was throwing paddles into a bungo sitting on a grassy bank by the roaring water. His weathered face was as craggy as the shell of his dugout boat. He was at least fifty years old, possibly more, but muscles corded his wiry arms, and his body was etched like that of an ancient gladiator. Here was a man who'd worked for a living.

Engorged by the heavy rain, the frothing brown river roared past, bending reeds and crumbling the clay bank, sweeping debris, driftwood, and enormous trees to spew them into the distant ocean. The fisherman looked capable, but even a steamboat would struggle in this current.

Samuel approached the man. "What's your *nombre, amigo?*"

The fisherman's lips peeled back in a toothless smile. "*Pablo, señor.*"

Samuel swept a hand toward the river as Filipe ran around to support Padraig so Samuel could dismount. "Look at this, Pablo. How can you possibly carry us across this maelstrom?" He swung down from the mare as Chavez and Filipe lifted Padraig from his saddle.

Pablo pointed south to a bend in the river. "If we launch here and paddle hard, we'll ride the current diagonally and land on the far bank at that turn in the river."

Samuel tugged at his oilskin. "Have you crossed when the river was this fast before?"

Pablo looked away. "I've crossed the flooding river before . . . but it was never this bad."

Samuel's stomach squirted bile. They couldn't carry their trunks or their weapons on the bungo, but they couldn't leave them behind.

Padraig groaned weakly where he lay on the wild grass, and Samuel stooped to put a reassuring hand on his breast. Padraig was trembling like a rush, and his breathing was shallow.

"Filipe, stay here with the horses," Samuel said. "Bring them across later when the river comes down."

Filipe's dark eyes widened, but he nodded.

"Chavez, help me put him into the boat." He tucked his hands under Padraig's armpits.

Chavez lifted Padraig's feet, and they carried him to the riverbank. Padraig was broad, tall, and heavy, and Samuel's weary feet had sunk ankle deep in the mud by the time they lowered him into the boat. The odor of wet moss, mud, and salt was strong at the river.

Pablo pointed to paddles in the curved bottom of the rough-hewn boat. "You're going to have to paddle, too. Do this when I say 'paddle.'" He drew an imaginary paddle toward himself. "Do this when I say 'backwater.'" His chiseled muscles rippled as he swept his imaginary paddle away from his body.

Filipe gathered the horses as the others heaved the bungo into the swirling water.

Pablo pinned the boat to the bank. "Hold it while I prepare."

Samuel gripped the worn gunwale with both hands as Pablo boarded. The buck of the hull quickened his pulse. Chavez climbed in next, as Pablo scribed a sign of the cross in the stern.

Pablo picked up his paddle. "Get in."

Samuel's boots were stuck in the mud, and he eased them free before he jumped into the boat.

As the thundering river whipped them away, Pablo dug his paddle deep by the stern, and his face contorted as he guided them clear of the bank. "Christ's sake, start paddling. Hurry—left side first, both of you."

Samuel sat on his heels on the bottom of the careening boat as they hurtled toward a whirlpool and the cluster of rocks that caused it. If they hit either, they would capsize or the debris behind the rocks would trap them. He plunged his paddle into the water. It clattered clumsily against Chavez's paddle.

"Together, damn you, *juntos*," Pablo cried. "Do you want to drown us?"

Samuel timed his next stroke with Chavez, and the gunwale dipped so precariously that water spilled in. The little craft righted again as they finished their stroke, and the bow swerved to the right.

"Again!" the fisherman yelled, straining on the paddle he held over the stern. "God's sake, again."

Samuel dipped and pulled, and the eddying water tore at his paddle. He dipped and pulled over and over until his arms ached. The boat plowed toward the floating trees and debris trapped behind the cluster of rocks. The bow oscillated with each stroke as the dugout clawed through the mayhem toward the center of the storming river. Rain cascaded from the sagging brim of Samuel's slouch hat, blinding him. The hull jarred against a rock, scraped along it, and plunged into the whirlpool beyond.

Water poured into the boat and washed over Padraig, choking him on the boat's bottom. He lifted his head feebly, spluttering and coughing. Samuel's vision blurred as the river spun them in a full circle and spat them toward the other bank.

"One must paddle on the other side," the fisherman roared. "Quickly."

Samuel swung his paddle to the right gunwale and paddled with all his might. His shoulder clicked alarmingly, and his muscles screamed at the strain. They were racing helter-skelter at right angles, creeping closer to the far bank. Samuel nibbled his lip. They were going to make it.

"Paddle! Paddle, God damn you!" the fisherman exhorted.

The boat crashed into a rock, dangled for a split second, flicked around, and plunged onward. Samuel was thrown forward. He seized the gunwale as the boat rolled, and he grabbed Padraig's coat with his free hand.

The world went dark as the boat capsized and trapped them underneath. Muddy water shot down his throat and hit his lungs, choking him, making him cough uncontrollably. Adrenaline coursed through his veins, and he clawed at the bottom of the boat above him. He was drowning. Spots of white light swirled in the darkness.

Padraig's coat slipped from his fingers.

Pressure spurted through his head as he flailed in the dark for any sign of Padraig. His fingers caught cloth, and Samuel drew his friend closer in their watery tomb.

Samuel felt almost peaceful, as if he were drifting through the eye of a hurricane. Then something bashed his foot, and pain lanced up his leg. His feet struck another rock, and he drew his knees up to his chest. He might have felt peaceful inside, but they must still be hurtling downriver beneath the capsized boat. It was only a matter of time before they smashed against the rocks.

His lungs burned, and he was dizzy from whirling in that wet, dark womb. His feet hit another rock. He made the surface and gasped in a deep breath, then another. He twisted his fist more firmly in Padraig's coat, caught the submerged gunwale, and forced both of them underwater until he shoved Padraig's head under the side of the boat. As Padraig popped clear, Samuel jackknifed under the gunwale after him. He kicked his feet and propelled Padraig to the surface. Spent air exploded from his lips.

Gasping, coughing, he clawed at the smooth hull, breaking his nails, but lost his grip and the boat slipped away. Padraig's limp body spun him around as the river tried to part them. He squeezed his fingers tighter and opened his eyes. The muddy riverbank was flying by, not far away.

He wrapped an arm around Padraig's neck, turned on his side, and swam. Incredibly, an entire tree surfed in the swell behind him, its thick gray roots rising six feet above the water, then rolling under, only to resurrect again like death's claws. Silty water stung Samuel's eyes. Every muscle ached, and his tired brain screamed. The water washed over him and shot down his throat, tasting like mud and rotten vegetables. Retching, hovering on the edge of panic, he heaved for air and swam on.

His feet touched bottom—mud—and his heart soared. They were going to make it.

The spinning tree swept up from behind, and one long branch hooked his oilskin and snatched him off his feet. It lifted him like a turning screw, and then Padraig, carrying them high over the water before plunging them under.

Pain sparked all over as the tree scraped Samuel across the muddy riverbed, and the impact drove the air from his lungs in an eruption of bubbles. Sofia holding their baby, Father, exploding cannons, and battlefields flashed in the sparks before his eyes. He wriggled and fought to free himself.

Miraculously, his feet touched the bottom again. He flung himself toward the shore and vomited mud, puke, and bile between gagging gasps. Finally, he stopped choking and drew a decent breath. Padraig lay face down in the mud and water nearby, lifeless.

Samuel scrambled for traction. It took the last of his strength to drag Padraig out of the shallows and heave him onto the grassy bank where he clung to the reeds, wheezing, before finding the reserve to mount the muddy bank beside Padraig.

His friend was deathly pale. His lips were blue, and he wasn't breathing. Samuel straddled him and pumped his thorax with both hands as he'd seen medics do in the battlefield. Padraig remained waxen, motionless. On the third pump, Padraig coughed, then vomited acrid water and gagged. Samuel rolled him on his side until he stopped retching. Despite his time in the river, his pal was burning up. Samuel peered around in the driving rain for any sign of the others. He shrugged off his oilskin, covered Padraig, and stood.

Chavez and Pablo were staggering toward him from the west, with Pablo's arm draped around Chavez's shoulder. Samuel beckoned them and hunkered down beside Padraig.

Padraig's face and neck were swollen and crimson bright. He coughed violently, and his eyelids blinked open. A second later, his lips moved.

Samuel put his good ear close to him.

"M-my muscles feel like they're tearing off the bones," Padraig mumbled. "Can't stand it."

Feet sloshed in the mud, and Chavez lowered Pablo onto the grass. "Thank God. I fell clear of the boat and the current swept me downriver. I found Pablo as I searched for you."

"Ask him where we can find shelter," Samuel said. "And a doctor. Padraig is much worse. He says his muscles are ripping from his bones."

Chavez closed his eyes with a grimace. "I've seen this before. It's breakbone fever. We need a doctor now."

The fisherman's legs creaked as he rose. "Hernan Nuñez has a small cabin nearby. We can take him there, and one of you can run to town for the doctor."

A silver crown bought them access to Nuñez's wooden shack a quarter mile along the river. He was an old man, with sharp eyes and a scanty gray beard on his time-chiseled face. The shack smelled of ashes and mildew.

In the space Nuñez cleared for them, Samuel peeled off Padraig's clothes. Samuel nearly wept at the fiery rash that covered his body, as if he were bleeding inside. He patted Padraig's clammy skin with a damp cloth and covered him with a moth-eaten blanket. With nothing else to do, he borrowed a rag and oil from Nuñez and set about cleaning their revolvers.

Chavez barged in about half an hour later with a lean, clean-shaven young man. "Dr. Ramirez reckons it's breakbone fever, too. There he is, Doctor. Take a look."

Dr. Ramirez blinked furiously and knelt beside Padraig without a word. He touched Padraig's forehead and peeled back the blanket, then tutted in dismay. "You're right. It's breakbone fever."

"What's that?" Samuel asked.

The doctor covered Padraig with the blanket. "We get outbreaks here all the time. In your part of the world, they call it dengue. They say it's caused by the bad jungle air. Where exactly are you from?"

"Ireland."

"You'd never find it there. Too cold."

"It may be foul air," Chavez said. "But I've observed it more where mosquitoes swarm."

Samuel's eyebrows furrowed and released as he glanced at Chavez. He was a deep one, that was for sure. "Will it—will he recover?"

The doctor avoided Samuel's eyes and fussed with his leather bag. "Hard to say. Some patients recover in a week, but others die from internal bleeding or simply waste away. This man is strong. Maybe . . ."

Samuel fixed him with a pleading look.

"All you can do is give him water and use a damp cloth to keep him cool. You can't move him. Any bump or knock might make him bleed. Those scars on his face, his hand . . . He's a soldier?"

"Used to be," Samuel fished out a silver coin. "Any medicine we can give him?"

"Only water." The doctor pocketed the coin. "My thanks. Send for me if he worsens. Though I must confess, there's little I can do anymore. He's in God's hands now."

The rain stopped as the doctor departed. The sky cleared with tropical abruptness, and the sun blasted away the clouds.

Samuel slumped beside Padraig in the small cabin and picked up the damp cloth. Reeking sweat lathered Padraig, and his breathing was shallow, but he could do nothing but watch him shiver and moan. He hurled down the cloth. *Oh God, rescue Padraig from this crucible, and I'll do anything.*

Hope swayed into favor. Padraig was strong. He'd pull through—he had to. If Webster had known they were in Costa Rica, then others might know too. They might be hunting them right now. And the ambush . . . Somebody wanted them dead.

Samuel looked up at Chavez. The burly Nicaraguan's face was drawn, and purple circles ringed his eyes. "Return to town and find us a boat going north. Tell them we'll pay in gold."

They were running through the gold they'd taken from the bandits, but there was no other option. They would leave when Padraig was well enough to travel. The breath caught in his throat—*if* Padraig was well enough to travel. If he survived.

He stood to relieve his restless legs and carried Padraig's wet clothes outside to dry in the sun. He stripped to his thigh-length underdrawers, hung up his own clothes, and laid out their soaked boots in the sun.

Inside, Nuñez handed him a trencher with a corn tortilla and an egg. "You look starved."

"Gracias." Samuel took the wooden plate and stumbled back to where Padraig lay shivering in the corner, his face ballooned and scarlet. He sat and stared at the egg. He had no appetite, despite the growl in his stomach. He forced himself to eat and placed the trencher on the earth floor. Despite the open door and the shutters swung wide on the hole that served as a window, the heat had built to a swelter in the hut, and the stench of Padraig's sweat tainted the dripping air. He went to the door and looked toward the river. Where was Filipe? How long would the river take to recede? Pablo had promised to go back for the boy.

Feeling faint and drained he returned to sit beside Padraig.

A voice woke Samuel in darkness, and he recoiled, reaching for his gun before remembering it was empty.

"*Capitán*, I'm back and I found Don Filipe." Chavez plonked two bags on the floor. "*El teniente?*"

Samuel cringed. He should have been caring for Padraig, who was still asleep, quivering under the blanket, candlelight dancing on the sweaty sheen covering his forehead. Samuel touched him. "He's still burning up." He saw Filipe and brightened. "You're all right?"

Filipe slumped down beside Padraig. "The fisherman directed me here. Will Padraig recover?"

Samuel gasped and hugged Filipe. "You're safe. I was—"

Chavez reached for a drink of water. "I found a boat. A coaster, but it departs tomorrow. *Será el ultimo, Capitán*. The Costas are bringing in a second schooner to tighten the blockade, and not even a bungo will get through to Nicaragua after that."

"The last boat leaves m*añana*?" Samuel grabbed a fistful of hair and groaned. If they didn't get out the next day, who knew when he'd catch up with Sofia? But Padraig could die if they moved him now. He numbed inside. Perhaps he should leave Padraig behind with Chavez.

Lord, no! Padraig would never desert him. And should Padraig die, God forbid, he would need a friend in those last moments.

Samuel reached for the damp cloth to cool Padraig's steaming brow. "We'll find another way. By land, across the frontier."

"That'll be hard," Chavez said. "The Costas have checkpoints on the border."

"I said we'll find a way." Samuel immediately regretted the hard edge on his voice. Chavez was only trying to help.

If only someone could help them now.

CHAPTER THIRTEEN

"Stop mollycoddling me, I'm fine." Padraig threw off the tattered blanket and struggled to his feet. "I've been sitting on me arse for four days. It's time to get going. Filipe, bring my bloody clothes, will you?"

Samuel laid down his sharpening stone and saber and rose from the homemade stool. "Are you certain?"

Padraig's eyes were still sunken, and he looked spent, but he had no fever. "Of course I am. We've wasted enough time. It'll take us days to ride north, and then we must sneak past the Costa patrols and checkpoints."

Samuel glanced at Chavez's his dark eyes before going to the open doorway. The morning sun was already blistering hot, steaming the night's rain from the wild grass into a shimmering haze. The river whispered tranquilly to the sea in the distance, as if the storm had never happened, and the air was fresh with wild blossoms. It was a good day to move on, but . . .

"We'll wait another day." He returned to his stool. "I don't need you getting sick again."

Filipe dashed inside with his arms full of stiff clothes. "Riders. Six of them. Heading here." He dropped Padraig's clothes and returned to the doorway.

Samuel's skin prickled. He snatched up his Colt and pushed Filipe back. "Arm yourselves. Chavez, Padraig, outside quickly. Take cover at each end of the cottage. Filipe—"

"I know. Stay here, out of sight," Filipe moaned but reached for his pistols anyway.

Hoofbeats drummed the earth as the riders drew closer, sunlight flashing on whetted lances, black uniforms coated with dust—Costa Rican lancers and one civilian. Samuel squinted into the hammering sun. He recognized the civilian: Sylvanus Spencer, the late Clifford Webster's partner.

Samuel spat across the threshold but failed to expel the sour taste in his mouth. "We're outnumbered, boys, and there's no doubt what's coming. May as well gather your things and prepare to move. They're going to drag us back to the capital."

President Juan Mora's drawing room was handsomely furnished with brightly patterned muslin draped over the mantel and the gilded frame of the wall mirror. Oil paintings of self-important folk in old-fashioned finery lined the wine-red walls, and coil-spring chairs were carefully arranged around the Persian carpet. The coffee trade must be lucrative, Samuel mused as he sat beside Sylvanus Spencer in front of the Costa Rica president's massive hardwood desk, waiting for him to decide their fate. Whatever it would be, Samuel was glad he was at least freshly shaven and bathed for the first time in weeks.

Mora fixed him with dark close-set eyes. "How do you propose . . . I trust you, given that you double-crossed . . . your last commander, William Walker?" Mora asked in halting English.

Samuel stilled his fidgeting fingers and answered in Spanish. "I told you, sir, they forced me to fight for Walker. His accomplice would have murdered my father. But when I learned that

Walker planned to bring back slavery, I couldn't continue to fight for him."

"And why might that be? *Cuando*?" Mora asked?

Mora was a cautious man; Samuel would have to remain patient if he wanted to convince him. "I can't abide men who take the liberties of others; I had enough of that in Ireland. Every peasant should have the same civil rights as his landlord, and no man should be the property of—"

"Are you insinuating I am an unjust man, sir?" Mora's gaze raked Samuel. "Judging me, perhaps? Men must earn the privilege of citizenship in Costa Rica. The penniless contribute nothing, so I changed the law to require a higher yearly income for the right to vote or run for office. Are you objecting to that?"

Samuel twisted the wedding ring on his finger. He'd blundered into a thorny issue. This man was yet another dictator extorting the common people, as bad as the gentry back home if not as deplorable as Walker. He tried to ensure his lack of response did not appear disrespectful.

Mora glowered anyway. "I should make an *ejemplo* of you and your thugs by executing you for supporting William Walker."

Heat climbed above Samuel's color. "Shooting us would be a mistake. You would risk an international incident. The British press would disgrace you for murdering a man whose only crime was trying to save his family. And for what? Hoping to bend me to your will?"

"Noted." Mora folded his hands on his desk. "And Mr. Spencer needs you for his mission."

Like his last time in Central America, Samuel was left with no good choices: hand the keys to Nicaragua to unscrupulous men with self-serving goals or face a firing squad. Meanwhile, Sofia and John would be lost in Nicaragua—not that this man either knew or cared.

But there was another way.

He scooted forward in the chair. "Look, I need to go after my wife and child, who are headed into potentially dangerous territory at this very moment. I realize that your plans are larger in scope, and who am I to impede a president? So let's make a deal."

President Mora exchanged glances with Spencer. Mora nodded at Samuel to continue.

"I'll convince my veterans to help train your army, and I'll draw up a plan to capture the San Juan River forts. In exchange, you'll discharge our obligation once the expeditionary force is ready to march and grant us safe passage across your frontier."

Mora steepled his fingers and tapped the tips, looking again at Spencer.

"Without our help," Samuel added, "you'll never find the Euronicas. And they won't fight for your cause."

Spencer slowly inclined his head. "I can work with that."

Bastard wanted all the glory. Well, it wouldn't be as easy as Spencer thought. The jungle was a treacherous place.

"But can we?" Mora asked. "What makes you think your plan will work, Mr. Kingston, when one of my finest generals failed to capture the San Juan River with three hundred men?"

Samuel leaned forward. "With all due respect, sir, General Alfaro took so long to hack his way through the jungle—a month—that many of his men died of fever. Walker's men at Hipp's Point heard them coming twenty miles away and had plenty of time to arrange an ambush. My proposal is different."

Mora glanced at his pocket watch, levered his frame out of the chair, and moved to the window. He was short in statue compared to his portrait on the wall and slightly overweight. His hands curled into fists and relaxed. "What about the old Spanish fortress at El Castillo? You've no chance of capturing a stone fort like that, especially with the garrison alerted and entrenched."

"I broke into that fortress to rescue Lieutenant Kerr last year." It was a risky admission, but Samuel had to convince the president; his family's safety might depend on it. There had already been too many delays. If Walker caught Sofia, he'd murder her for her role in stealing his gold.

Spencer half rose from his chair. "I don't think tales of ill-conceived, treacherous—"

President Mora silenced him with a finger and considered Samuel for several long, uncomfortable moments. "*Muy bien, te permitiré continuar.*"

Samuel nodded once. "Thank you, sir. I'll—"

"But if I perceive that the men aren't ready when the time comes, you will join the expedition. If you refuse these terms, I'll have you shot."

What a self-serving cur. All that mattered to Mora was access to the blasted Transit Road. The only difference between this president and the British aristocracy was geographic; they were rich, privileged men who preyed upon those they ruled.

He pursed his lips and gave the president a curt nod.

Mora returned to his desk and picked up a letter. "Mr. Spencer, a word in private."

Samuel slipped out silently, pulling the massive wooden door closed behind him with a discreet *snick*.

Padraig met him in the hall. "How bad is it?"

"Just as we suspected," Samuel said. "Mora wanted us to join the river expedition, but I persuaded him to let us leave once we train his soldiers."

"It'll take months to train raw recruits," Padraig said dejectedly, "and it's almost October already. It'll be November before we can march."

"And we have to get him the Euronica Company," Samuel added.

"Think they'll join us?"

"Spencer's willing to pay them a lot of money. I can't see them turning it down. And they want a crack at Walker."

"Mr. Kingston, may I have a word, please?" A Royal Navy captain in dress uniform stood at the end of the hallway.

Samuel stopped in midstride. What was the Royal Navy doing here? "Of course, Captain."

The captain clutched Samuel's arm and drew him toward the

entrance hall. "Captain Peter Simpson, a longtime friend of Sofia."

Samuel's heart surged. "She's mentioned your wife. You've heard from her? When?"

"Oh, dear," Simpson said, his long face tilting down. "You don't know. This is what I feared."

"Good God, Captain, do you know where she is?"

"I met your wife when she stayed with my family during her studies in Bluefields. Lovely young lady; we were all taken with her."

"Captain, please . . ."

"Yes, yes, so sorry. We were surprised when she contacted us recently out of the blue, given the unrest in the area, and I confess I'm worried sick about her." He stepped closer. "I believe Sofia and the baby are missing."

"Missing?" Samuel's forehead pulsed. "What do you mean?"

"Four weeks ago, my wife received an invitation from Sofia to meet her in Greytown. Her note advised that she and the baby were overnighting there before catching the steamboat upriver. We were surprised, as we believed she settled in Ireland with you." Captain Simpson raked a hand through his close-cropped gray hair. "But when Carol arrived, Sofia wasn't at the hotel. She had checked in, all right, but she was nowhere to be found. I had the HMS *Orion* send longboats to search for ten miles upriver. Nothing."

A chill like icy fingers ran down Samuel's spine. She had not even made it to her father's hacienda—but it made no sense. Greytown was a civilized place, secured by the Royal Navy.

"Are you certain of the timing? Show me the note."

Captain Simpson released a hard sigh. "I'm sure of it. The owner of the hotel confirmed her presence, but nobody has seen her since."

That couldn't be right; there had to be a reasonable explanation. "Nonsense. Nobody just disappears."

"Greytown is a British port. My men have searched everywhere." Simpson dabbed at one eye. He seemed to have aged ten years relaying his bad news. "She's nowhere in Greytown. I've sent a messenger to her father's home in Chinandega, but it'll be weeks before we hear news."

Samuel's legs weakened. His worst fear had come true: They were lost in the jungle or drowned in the river.

Padraig appeared at his elbow, his face tight with concern. "Samuel?"

No, he'd never accept this. "Perhaps she took passage on a fishing boat or continued on to Panama intending to cross their isthmus," he said in a rush. "Yes, that's probably it. It would be safer than bumping into one of Walker's patrols."

Padraig put a hand on Samuel's shoulder. "Yes, that must be it. She might even have taken passage on a coastal trader up the Pacific coast to El Realejo. She could've bypassed San Juan del Sur altogether."

Samuel's head was pounding. She should never have gone to Nicaragua. "The Costas have sealed the border and blockaded the ports. Captain, how did your messenger get by?"

"That's Miskito territory up there," Simpson said, "and my contact is one of them. The Indians use jungle paths no white foot ever touched. Don't worry, Mr. Kingston. I'm confident I'll have my news."

Yes, but would it be good news?

Samuel stared at the captain. "And you? How will you return to Greytown?"

"I'll be here for nine weeks as an observer. Then a Royal Navy frigate will collect me."

Far too late. He'd get there quicker if his stuck to his original plan and completed President Mora's assignment, earning a pass through the frontier.

"I can't believe this. What made her do something so . . . so stupid?" Samuel grabbed Simpson's arm. Perhaps the captain could get more than messages to Nicaragua. "Please advise me when your Indian returns. Do you think he would take me back to Nicaragua, back through the jungle? I'll pay handsomely."

Simpson's features softened. "I'll ask him, but I can't see why not."

Samuel turned to Padraig. "We must be ready to leave as soon as this guide arrives. The thought of Walker getting his hands on my—"

His throat closed around the rest of the words. Padraig slid his hand around Samuel's shoulders in a rough embrace.

Simpson patted Samuel's forearm. "Chin up, old boy. We'll do all we can."

CHAPTER FOURTEEN

The temporary training camp was in the mountains outside Cartago, some fifteen miles east of San Jose, where the cool climate was a pleasant change from the blistering heat of the Pacific Coast. Twenty-two Nicaraguans of Samuel's old Euronica Company sat around three campfires, eating breakfast with Samuel and Padraig, chatting and joking with the ease of men who'd survived battle together.

It seemed to rain all the time in these mountains—mostly a steady patter like back home in Ireland, but sometimes it was a deluge as if Noah was launching another arc. Fortunately, it was only a drizzle for the company's reunion this September morning, with mist resting on the verdant canopies of the million trees stretching for the sky. Samuel had called, and his old crew had come. Bright and melodious bird calls, the chatter of brazen monkeys, and the whirr of crickets filled the forest. The smell of vegetation, wood smoke, and roasting iguana laced the cool air.

Samuel avoided the stomach-churning sight of reptiles crackling over the fires and drew in a deep breath as he studied the Nicaraguans' faces. Pedro Cortez caught his eye and flashed a wide white grin. The youth looked African, but he was a Caribbean Creole from Bluefields, where the Royal Navy had their base, and spoke English with a Caribbean lilt. Chavez, beside him, was the only Euronica besides Cortez who understood English, but Chavez was an enigma for a conscript—he could read and write; and Samuel still puzzled how. Eighteen months before, Cortez and Chavez had helped Samuel unravel the intrigue surrounding Louis Greenfell, the Earl of Baltimore, when Greenfell had plotted Samuel's demise.

Samuel nodded to Cortez and let his gaze wander to the next man. Like many Nicaraguans, Gustavo Arguello was a small man. In his mid-twenties, Arguello was spare as a chicken bone, with full colorless lips. Loyal and steady, he'd never said a word to Samuel except for "*Sí señor. No señor.*" Sergeant Zamora reckoned Samuel's gentleman bearing intimidated Arguello, who'd never seen a foreigner before Walker arrived with his filibuster army almost two years ago. The Euronicas were peasants the Democrat army had conscripted and armed with ancient muskets, rusty bayonets, and no ammunition to fight the Legitimist army. When Samuel had informed them of Walker's plan to bring back slavery, to a man, the Euronicas had deserted to Costa Rica rather than support Walker. Samuel had sent them some of his stolen gold to tide them over. After Samuel's return to Ireland, William Walker had hijacked the civil war to feed his ambition to rule a Central American empire. Now Walker was the President of Nicaragua. That was Samuel's fault; after choosing to stop Walker before rescuing Father, he'd failed to do both. Chilly fingers glided over the skin of his back. His faith and Walker's seemed intertwined and drew them relentlessly toward a collision that neither might survive.

Oscar Vargas was also a head shorter than Samuel but big of heart, with a smile as wide as a slice of watermelon. He reminded Samuel of Jamie Begley, who'd served with him in the Seventeenth Lancers at the beginning of the Crimean War—a pointless conflict that still thundered on. Both soldiers had a remarkable way with animals; it had taken the threat of a hiding before Sergeant Zamora had persuaded Vargas to leave his white-faced monkey back in San Jose.

Samuel remembered the expedition commander, Colonel Brailier, was arriving this morning and startled. He fished out his watch. Six fifty; plenty of time yet. He settled back against the rough bark of the tree and wondered how Jamie Begley was faring in Crimea. The lad had survived the Charge of the Light Brigade—surely things could never get worse than that.

". . . *Capitán*, didn't we?" Mario Rubio's nasally voice pulled Samuel back to his damp seat on the wild grass.

"What, Rubio? I was five thousand miles away."

"Jimenez said that Butcher Guardiola is now the President of Honduras, *Capitán*," Rubio said with a smile showing a mouthful of crooked teeth. "And I said, we should march up there and take over. We're more than his match; we beat him in Rivas last year."

So, General Guardiola, the old butcher, now ruled Nicaragua's northern neighbor. Samuel smiled bitterly. Central America traded tinpot tyrants like Europe had back in the Middle Ages.

"Well then, Rubio, we better not wander over into Honduras's frontier or he'll butcher us," Padraig said, pouring coffee for wiry Jimenez, the ex-thief who was another of Samuel's favorites. "To be sure, he's not forgotten how the Euronicas turned the Battle of Rivas into his own personal Waterloo."

Rubio's black eyebrows shot up his low forehead. "Waterloo? *Teniente?*"

Samuel chuckled and climbed to his feet. "I'll leave you to explain that, Padraig, since you raised it. I'm going to the house to wait for the new commander."

It was almost nine when a captain and two black-uniformed lancers escorted Colonel Pedro Brailier into the camp. Brailier was in his fifties with deep-set hooded eyes and a pale complexion. Even the rain failed to dull the shiny brass buttons and gold braid on the colonel's black uniform and the bright blue sash tied around his ample gut.

The sight of Brailier's cocked hat made Samuel look down to hide his smirk—Padraig had mentioned Waterloo, and here was Wellington himself. Times might be hard in Central America, but Brailier wasn't going hungry. Samuel snapped off a smart salute and caught the bridle of the colonel's horse. "Colonel Brailier, it's a pleasure to meet you. I look forward to working with you."

"Working *for* me, *Capitán* Kingston?" Brailier snapped. "I'll remind you that I command this expedition." His saddle groaned as he shifted his bulk to dismount, and his stallion side-stepped with a whinny.

What a peevish churl. Samuel bit his lip and brushed the stallion's silky nose with his fingers. "There, boy. Easy now. You're a fine fellow, aren't you?"

The velvet nostrils flared, and warm misty breath puffed over Samuel. It was a fine thoroughbred, not black, but a deep dark brown in color. It was seventeen hands high, from its iron shoes to its withers, smooth and balanced with its shining coat unblemished. The bristly fur tickled the pads of Samuel's palm and fingers as he stroked the stallion's neck, and it whickered as Brailier dismounted with a grunt.

Thwack!

The stallion screamed, heaving up its regal head, and would have reared if Samuel hadn't gripped the bridle.

"Damned *mula*," Brailier shouted and raised his riding crop again. "You'll stand while I dismount."

"No." Samuel seized Brailier's meaty wrist. "That's no way to treat a horse . . . Colonel. You'll ruin him."

"Unhand me, *señor*, or I'll have you up on charges." Brailier drew his arm back, but Samuel had it pinned.

The captain danced in between them. "Colonel, the men are watching. Perhaps we should speak in the house?"

Samuel released Brallier's wrist, and the colonel planted his legs wide, breathing heavily as he glared around at the men observing them from their cooking fires.

Dark eyes bulging, Brallier flexed his fingers for seconds that dragged on forever.

Damn it, Samuel cursed himself. When would he learn to curb his impulses? "I'm sorry, Colonel, I was out of order."

Brailier inhaled and blew out a long breath. "Very well, *Capitán Blanco*, lead the way."

Inside the room the army had commandeered in the blacksmith's house, Brailier rounded on Samuel. "How dare you strike a superior officer? I'll—"

"Colonel," Captain Blanco said calmly. "*Capitán* Kingston is not in our army, he's here as an advisor." He held up both hands. "Now, why don't we begin afresh? Perhaps, as a cavalryman, the *capitán* is sensitive about the treatment of horses. Eh, *Capitán*?" Blanco raised his black eyebrows. He, at least, looked like a real soldier, of average height, lean, with black hair swept back like wings and a waxed mustache and goatee.

Brailier reminded Samuel of arrogant lords, like the Earls of Lucan and Sligo, and that had boiled his blood. He knew better, he should have controlled himself. He needed Brailier if he were to get to Nicaragua and find Sofia. He faked a smile. "My sincerest apologies, Colonel. I was out of line. *Capitán Blanco* was correct, we cavalrymen have a close bond to the animals we ride into battle. Perhaps I can make amends by schooling your horse while we're in camp?"

Brailier scowled for seconds and then uncurled his fists. "Very well, *Capitán*, we'll say no more of this matter. However, I need *Rey* to ride back and forth from my hotel, but thank you for your offer, all the same."

That the colonel didn't bivouac with his troops spoke volumes to his ineptitude. Samuel broke eye contact with Brailier and fought the urge to shake his head. This mission was getting harder by the minute. God, he needed to get after Sofia, but how? "Thank you, Colonel. I appreciate your understanding."

The colonel nodded briskly. "I called this meeting to discuss the expedition. Now that I'm here, I'd like to get things rolling; Costa Rica depends on me to protect it, Nicaragua depends on me to liberate it, and all of Central America expects me to lead them."

What a pompous ass. Brailier was a perfect candidate for Lord Raglan's idiotic staff in Crimea. Samuel's heart shrank. If he didn't watch out, the colonel would be the death of the Euronicas.

Don't tell me Brailier will command the expedition, Jimenez had complained about the colonel when he arrived two days ago with the Euronicas, *he's a wealthy coffee baron, but the bastard's never been in a war . . . he wouldn't know a bayonet from a butter knife.*

"I've reviewed the plan you left with President Mora," Brailier said, stroking that odd square beard that sprouted into a goatee and hid his double chin. "It won't work . . . not at all. We're the Costa Rican army, the largest army in Central America, we're not sneaking around in the jungle like a frightened animal; I need to bring my cannons to level Walker's forts." He moved uncomfortably close, and his breath stank of cigars and meat. "We'll carve a road through the jungle for my cannons. When Walker sees our artillery, he'll tremble and turn tail."

Samuel's mouth slackened. This man hadn't a clue. "But General Alfaro tried that in the spring, cutting a road through the rainforest to the Sarapiquí River. Many of his men died of disease en route, and the filibusters ambushed the rest; it was a disaster. It took far too long and left the filibusters all the time in the world to prepare for them. It'll never—"

"I'm not Florentino Alfaro. I've read volumes on military strategy and history, and I know how to do this right. Now, there'll be no further argument." Brailier crossed his arms. "Train my men as pathfinders—scouts who sneak around in the jungle like frightened mice? Never! Report with your company of

Nicaraguan savages to the parade ground immediately, and we'll teach them how to march. Discipline, *Capitán*. Discipline wins battles."

Sweat trickled down Samuel's spine, and his face flushed. He wouldn't take the bait. If he'd learned anything serving in the British army, it was not to challenge an imperious ass who was his superior. He turned his gaze through the mud-smeared window toward the men at the campfires who depended on him. "Very well, Colonel, as you command."

Brailier nodded crisply. "Thank you, *Capitán*. I heard you were a smart man . . . I knew you'd see reason. I bid you good day."

Captain Blanco swallowed and moved closer to Samuel. "I'll see you out, *Capitán*." Outside, he continued in a soothing voice. "I'm sorry about that. I know he's wrong. It's a problem with our culture down here . . . men promoted for their position, their connections, and not for their abilities. I don't know what to do."

Sofia and John were all who mattered, and Samuel was going to get to them if he had to ride over Brailier. His brain was already spinning. "Incompetent leadership is not exclusive to Costa Rica, Captain. We have it in the British army as well. We'll just have to manage, despite the good colonel. I'll see you on parade." He poured sarcasm into his last word.

"Until then, *Capitán*." Blanco grinned and returned to the house.

Oh, the Euronicas would play Brailier's marching games all right, but at nightfall he'd sneak them into the rainforest for the real training. And when the time was right, they'd teach Brailier the error of his strategy. Samuel forced his tensing muscles to relax and hastened over to bring his men up to date.

~

Samuel could barely make out Emanuel Chavez's shaved head beside him. It was the only sign of the Euronicas hiding in the dense rainforest. A knowing grin crept across his face. They hadn't forgotten their training; they could blend into the jungle more seamlessly than the humble iguana.

Three hundred yards ahead, trees rustled, branches groaned, and machetes thumped trees as Colonel Brailier and his Costa Rican expeditionary force blundered through the undergrowth. Officers barked commands, cajoling two hundred men to hold formation—an impossible task, given the denseness of the undergrowth.

Brailier had tortured everyone with outdated drills for four weeks. But finally, Samuel had convinced him to play a war game. Hopefully, this exercise would show Brailier the futility of forging a path through bamboo, thick vegetation, and marshland for the sake of holding a battle formation. In today's exercise, Brailier's objective was to capture a banner guarded by Samuel's little company. Judging by the racket his force was making, the colonel was confident his superior numbers and firepower would defeat Samuel in jig time.

He checked his watch. Four twenty-five. He nudged Padraig crouching beside him. "Off you go. Make a racket and draw away as many of them as you can."

Padraig led his ten men off to circle behind the Costas, and their green shirts and blackened faces quickly blended into the undergrowth.

Samuel beckoned the rest of the company and crawled toward the enemy. The marshy ground stank of vegetation, mildew, and mud. He moved silently by resting the rifle barrel on his forearm to keep the muzzle from tangling in roots, pushing his arms ahead through the undergrowth. Soon his hands and forearms were cut and scratched, as if he'd been flung into a briar patch, and his skin stung from insect bites. The Euronicas followed him using the same technique, barely rustling the leaves or disturbing any branches. It would be worth it to teach the overbearing Brailier a lesson. Perhaps they could convince him not to make the same mistakes as the last commander who'd failed to oust Walker from the San Juan River.

A patch of white flickered in the trees fifty yards ahead, and Samuel focused on a spot slightly to the right of his sighting, a technique a Burmese scout had shown him to better spot targets. More glimpses of white and the sound of voices reached him. The thud of machetes grew louder. Christ Almighty, they couldn't make more noise if they were building a damned road.

He pulled out his watch again. Five thirty-five. Padraig would be in position, concealed in the waning daylight. It was time. He waved his hand, aimed his Sharps high, and fired with a grim smile—some reality for this exercise.

The bark of his men's rifles behind him sent monkeys screeching through the trees. He leaped up and pushed through the dangling creepers and hooking branches, confident that his men followed. More shots crashed out, this time from behind the Costa Ricans—Padraig adding his rifles to stir the pot.

Samuel spotted Brailier by the gold braid dangling from his frock coat, like a popinjay on a parade square. Brailier was yelling at poor Captain Blanco, blaming him because his large force of conscripts had fled screaming. Thorns clawed Samuel, and branches hooked his shirt as he broke through to the freshly cut trail, shouldered two soldiers aside, and tipped off Brailier's ridiculous cocked hat with the barrel of his rifle.

"Yield or die, Colonel," Samuel announced. "I think this wins us the day."

Brailier flinched and stumbled into the bushes, where he became fouled up like the screw of a steamboat in seaweed.

Three feet away, Blanco's jaw dropped as Vargas appeared from nowhere, his wide mouth split in a grin, and pressed a musket to his ribs.

"You bastard, Kingston," Brailier sputtered. "Get me out of this tangle."

Samuel exchanged a knowing glance with Blanco and

suppressed another smile. He didn't need to anger the commander further. "Cortez, your machete."

Cortez turned away briefly to hide his grin and drew his long blade. Samuel was going to smack him if he didn't wipe that smirk off his face.

Cortez chopped Brailier free and Samuel helped him to his feet. Brailier's jowly face was flushed and sweaty as he pawed the mud on his trousers.

"How dare you, Kingston?" Brailier tore at the cobwebs and debris stuck in his iron-gray sideburns as he spluttered. "*Absurdo*. This isn't war, it's trickery and deceit. You must meet us line to line in the battlefield, like real men."

"I don't know, sir, but I think he caught us fair," Blanco said. "I didn't even see his boys until this one poked me."

"Rubbish, *Capitán*," Brailier snapped. "*Trucos* and games like this won't work in the battlefield. I've had enough. Kingston will do it my way, or by God, I'll slap him in irons and send him back to Cartago."

Samuel had served under many pompous commanders like Colonel Brailier, all British aristocrats. He drew the colonel aside. "Colonel, sir, this isn't a battlefield with ranks of men blasting at each other in a long, bloody line. I experienced enough of that in Crimea. This is jungle warfare, and if a handful of men can cut you and your senior officer off from two hundred men, imagine the slaughter if you blundered into Walker's army. You need to color your men's shirts and find more suitable attire for yourself."

"I'll be damned if I'll waste money dyeing clothing green to sneak around in the jungle," Brailier said. "With a bayonet charge, I'm more than a match for this so-called General Walker."

Blanco stepped over from the gathering gloom. "I'm afraid not, sir. Kingston had us cold." He picked a bug from his waxed mustache and looked at Samuel. "I see what you mean about invisible iguanas; I'd no idea you were there. And we never knew Lieutenant Kerr's platoon was about until it hit our flank."

Samuel took a wide stance. It was time to put the pressure on. "Colonel, I planned this operation. This is the only way to survive out here. The British won in the jungles of Burma by swapping their red coats for green jackets. To capture the San Juan River, you must do likewise."

"You arrogant pup!"

Samuel shrugged. "It's all the same to me. I'm putting in my time and heading west into Nicaragua. You're the one who'll be leading these men through the jungle to the river."

"I have Walker's measure," Brailier said. "I beat him in Santa Rosa, and I'll beat him again."

Brailier had won a skirmish in Santa Rosa when the odds were ten to one in his favor. He was no match for the seasoned adventurers who'd flocked to Walker's flag. But Captain Simpson had heard nothing more from his Miskito Indian courier, so it looked as though Samuel was stuck with Brailier until the pompous ass marched into the jungle. Only then would President Mora allow him to leave.

Samuel headed back to the campsite.

With the ruckus over, the cicadas resumed their insistent high-pitched whine and the first night birds sang. Deep roars issued from the trees: panthers hunting in the dense undergrowth, or howler monkeys cradled in the lofty branches. Samuel couldn't tell their sounds apart.

He'd told Brailier he didn't care what happened, but he did. He'd dragged his Nicaraguan men into this. True, the Euronicas would collect payment from Vanderbilt, but they were doing this for Samuel. He lashed out at a tree stump.

Padraig caught his shoulder. "You need to hold on to your horses. Don't anger that turd yet. We're not in the clear until we cross the border into Nicaragua."

"You're right. But Brailier reminds me of Lucan and Lawrence—another wealthy man playing at soldiering who doesn't give a damn about his men. Worse, he'll get our boys killed, and I'm the one who recruited them." He couldn't join the river mission; he had to get to Greytown to search for Sofia and John. He'd had barely spent a week with little John before he'd left Ireland; he wouldn't recognize his own child if he passed him in the street.

"Blanco seems reasonable," Padraig said. "Maybe he'll talk some sense into the colonel."

Samuel scrubbed a muddy hand across his face. "Where's Filipe? I told him not to wander off. That boy is more trouble than he's worth."

Padraig's teeth flashed in the darkness. "Reminds me of you in the old days."

Samuel stalked through the camp, peering about for his young charge. Filipe was nowhere in sight, and one horse was missing from the paddock at the edge of the encampment.

He caught Padraig's arm. "The bay is missing. Ask the blacksmith if he's seen Filipe while I check our quarters."

Samuel hastened to the blacksmith's outhouse, where he bivouacked with Filipe and Padraig. Where could the boy be? The young idiot might have fallen off his horse. Perhaps bandits had attacked him.

Samuel flung the door open. The moonlight pressed back the darkness to show an empty room, and the stuffy air told of rust and sweat. The room was so cramped, Filipe slept beneath a heavy workbench in the back corner. Samuel strode over and peered into the shadows under the bench. Nothing. Filipe had disappeared. He hammered the solid oak worktop. Damn that boy; he was nothing but a nuisance.

Padraig's silhouette blocked the silver light. "The blacksmith saw him ride out two hours ago toward Cartago."

"Cartago? Why the hell would he go to Cartago?"

"Beats me," Padraig said. "But if he went in that direction, where else would he go? Maybe he went to get laid."

"Don't be stupid," Samuel snapped. "He's not a dog like you."

He drew his Colt and clicked the cylinder around. One could never be sure with all the rain, but the powder looked dry. "Let's get the horses."

"Aw, Samuel," Padraig said with a moan. "I'm starving."

"We'll find food in town."

"I'm going to kick the little bugger's arse when we find him," Padraig growled.

Samuel hurried to the barn to collect his tack. It was rare that it hadn't rained that night, leaving the road dry for a change. At least they would make good time.

An hour later, the twinkling lights of Cartago appeared as they crested the final hill. In the distance, the wooden spire of the basilica pointed the faithful toward the star-seeded heavens against a backdrop of jagged mountains lit by the waxing moon.

Padraig removed his slouch hat and ran his fingers through his thatch of damp hair. "Bloody hell, town's not as small as I thought. How will we find him?"

"We'll ride around and look for the bay." Samuel heeled his horse.

Cartago was still busy. The plaza was alive with chattering vendors breaking down the lean-tos used to shelter their produce. Women swayed along with baskets on their heads or dragged weary mules draped with enormous wicker hampers. Bullocks hauled carts loaded with coffee or fruit or timber between the terraced houses, the plodding beasts braying their objections. The pong of cooking fires and animal dung lingered in the steamy air. A woman in a shabby hooped skirt shook a fist at a driver after the wheels of his wagon splashed mud onto her whitewashed walls.

Samuel stood in the stirrups and craned around. "Must be market day. It'll take ages to get through here. Let's cut through that ally."

Padraig reined in. "There's no place on this road the little bugger would stop, anyway."

Samuel pointed to several taverns scattered along the west side of the plaza. "Let's try over there."

There was no sign of the bay horse at the hitching rails, and a vein throbbed in Samuel's head. "It's impossible to ride here with all these carts. Let's stable the horses and search on foot. It'll be faster if we split up. You take the west side, and I'll take the east. Meet back at the stable in thirty minutes."

"Fair enough." Padraig twitched his bridle. "And then we eat."

They made better progress on foot. Samuel was steaming. He hadn't time to waste on Filipe's games; the boy's antics were a distraction. From now on, he'd make Filipe stay with the Euronicas. It would do the little snob no harm to train like a real soldier. He turned left where several carts lumbered down the street, and a faded shingle swaying in the wind halfway along the street caught his attention. He would check that tavern out.

The tavern's shutters were wide open, and Samuel could see the patrons inside as he approached. And there he was: Filipe was leaning across a table, his head close to a young man with the dark complexion of a Nicaraguan. Samuel frowned. He hadn't known Filipe had acquaintances in Costa Rica.

A thud on his shoulder knocked him sideways just before the tip of a horn flashed past his head. Pain lanced through his shoulder, and Samuel landed in the mud.

"Watch where you're going, idiot *yanqui*."

Harnesses jingled, and a bullock bellowed as the cart jolted to a halt. Samuel rolled to his knees, fingers spread in the warm gooey mud, and pushed to his feet.

The wizened *boyeo* tipped back his battered straw hat. "Are you loco? You could have been killed."

"*Si, si*, I'm all right," he replied, shaken. "Sorry about that. I was distracted." He glanced in the tavern window, but the table was now empty.

The bullocks were moving again, ambling in front of

him, and he caught the whiff of green coffee as he dashed behind the cart and across the road. When he reached the far side, a shadow disappeared into the darkness in the street ahead.

When Filipe stepped from the tavern, his glance met Samuel's eyes, and he blanched.

"Filipe!" Samuel barked. "What is going on? Who was that man?"

A vein pulsed beneath the skin of Filipe's neck and his lips trembled, but he didn't speak for seconds. When he did, his voice was shrill. "*Por favor*, Samuel, I meant no harm. I swear to you. I only—"

"You only what?" He grabbed Filipe's silk shirt and drove him against the wall. "You could be killed out here. Who was that man? Why did you sneak away?"

Blinking rapidly, Filipe pulled a *jicara* from his coat pocket and waved the clay jar in Samuel's face. "I was buying *guaro* from him."

Samuel released Filipe and swallowed hard. The cheap alcohol made from sugarcane was popular among the natives but known to blind men or even drive them mad. "Why would you buy that cheap crap? It can kill you, you know."

"Y-your men . . . the Euronicas said *guaro* makes you feel great. It blows your head off. I'm stuck at the camp all day on my own, bored to death, so I came into town to buy some."

Samuel rubbed his temple. "The man with you, the dark fellow. Why did he run away?"

"He sold me the liquor."

Samuel's head tilted to one side. "How did you meet him?"

"I . . . The taverns refused to serve me, and he approached me offering to help."

Samuel pushed Filipe down the street. "You haven't—"

A pistol barked, and a bullet chipped the adobe wall a foot from Samuel's head. He threw himself on Filipe, barreling him to the ground, before rolling to his knees and drawing his Colt.

There was no sign of a gunman in the gloom, but someone had tried to kill him. Or Filipe.

Hoofbeats drew nearer, and three riders cantered from the gloom. Samuel cocked the Colt and aimed at the leader.

"Hold your fire," one rider called out. "It's *Capitán Blanco*."

Samuel took no chances; he kept the revolver on Blanco until the captain pulled his horse to a skidding halt a yard away.

Blanco dismounted with a pistol in his fist. "*Que pasó*? We heard a shot."

"Don't know. Someone fired at us outside the tavern." He pointed to the west end of the street. "From down there."

Blanco waved a hand. "Find him."

The two troopers galloped up the street.

"Tell me exactly what happened. Why are you and the boy here in town?"

Samuel told what little details existed.

"Sounds like a crackpot fanatic," Blanco said. "Plenty of people here have reason to hate *yanquis*. They invaded our country with Walker, and thousands of Costa Ricans have died from the cholera brought from abroad."

Samuel holstered his Colt. The explanation made little sense beyond its surface. Nobody could have known he would be here, and no random Costa Rican would try to murder them.

The troopers trotted back around the corner and reined in close to Captain Blanco.

One shook his head. "*Lo siento, señor*, no sign of the assailant. We searched the roads nearby, but he could have dodged up any alley. He got away."

Captain Blanco answered with a small nod and moved to his horse. "It's best you stay close to camp from now on, *Capitán* Kingston." He swung into the saddle and drew his shoulders back. "Which brings me to the reason I came to find you. Colonel Brailier invites you to dine with him tonight."

A sour taste rose in Samuel's mouth. He didn't want to have dinner with the pompous Brailier, and he had much to think about. Nothing added up—Filipe sneaking off to town, the attack . . . He was missing something. "Another night would be better, Captain. We've endured much excitement already."

Captain Blanco nudged his horse a step closer to Samuel. "I'm afraid that wasn't a request, *Capitán.*"

Samuel sucked in his cheeks. Things were going from bad to worse. If this wasn't a request, Brailier was about to rain more mischief on them. "Very well, *Capitán.* If you'll let us pass? Our horses are at the stables."

Padraig met them in the plaza and addressed Samuel in English. "What happened? I heard a pistol shot." He frowned at the mounted Costa Ricans. "Why are they here?"

"Someone fired on me and Filipe."

Padraig switched to Spanish. "*Gracias, caballeros*, for your timely help." He turned back to Samuel. "Blessed Virgin in heaven, are you all right?"

"We're fine. Let's fetch the horses. Colonel Brailier wants to see us."

Padraig scowled and dropped back into English. "Does he, now? Wants you to embarrass him again, does he? I hope you told him we were busy."

Captain Blanco coughed and tugged at the collar of his dusty uniform.

"Apparently it's not a request." Samuel looked at Captain Blanco. "Where shall we appear for our . . . ah . . . invitation?"

"The Grano de Oro Hotel." Captain Blanco flicked a thumb over his shoulder. "Other side of town."

"Can your men escort this young fellow back to camp?" He put his hand on Filipe's chest before the boy could voice a protest.

"I think that's wise," Blanco said. "Your ward seems to have flair for getting into mischief."

"Flair!" Padraig muttered in English. "He's a bloody nightmare."

The bullock carts and their *boyeos* had disappeared from the streets by the time they rode across the plaza, and only a handful of pedestrians strolled in the cool night air. Samuel shivered in his sweat-stained shirt. Costa Rica's climate was so varied, sweltering hot in the lowlands and chilly, even freezing in the hills and mountains. Cartago was a considerable height above sea level.

The brightly lit Grano de Oro restaurant, gleaming like a pearl in the sand, was the last thing Samuel expected to see in a farm town like Cartago. He let out a low whistle.

Captain Blanco flashed a knowing grin. "Something else, eh? The coffee barons needed a comfortable place to stop over on their journeys from coast to coast. Grano de Oro refers to a coffee bean—a grain of gold. The stable boys will take care of the horses. Let's go in."

Gaslight from burnished brass lamps highlighted burgundy swirls in the rosewood panels dressing the walls, and the scent of wood polish mingled with the aroma of rich food.

"Colonel Brailier has a suite here for the duration of the training exercises," Captain Blanco said as he led them through the white marble-tiled lobby.

Samuel's lip curled. "That might explain his discomfort in the jungle. Perhaps if William Walker lived in a marble palace, the colonel would be more of a match for him."

The corners of Blanco's mouth twitched. "Perhaps."

Colonel Brailier slid a silver candelabra down the table and rapped his knuckles on the wood surface with a flourish at Samuel's approach. The gall of this churl, living like a lord while his men slept rough in the rainforest. He was as bad as Lord Cardigan, who'd slept on his luxury yacht in Balaklava Harbor while the brigade slept in the freezing Crimean valley. Cardigan's incompetence had contributed to the death of hundreds of men at the Charge of the Light Brigade. Hopefully, Brailier's river campaign wouldn't end so tragically.

"*Ron-ron.*" Colonel Brailier's lumpy face broke into a smile.

"I beg your pardon, Colonel?" Samuel said.

"Double rum?" Padraig quipped. "I don't mind if I do."

Brailier stroked the polished table with his soft hands. "*Ron-ron—goncalo alves* to the more erudite. It's the magnificent wood in this table. It comes from the rainforest."

Samuel squinted at Brailier. What a jackass. It wasn't the wood in the rainforest Brailier should worry about, it was Walker's cutthroats. He should never have dragged the Euronicas into this affair. Brailier would get them all killed.

"But where are my manners?" Brailier waved a hand. "Take a seat, please. You're going to love the food here."

Samuel had lost his appetite despite the pang in his stomach. "Thank you, Colonel. We were heading back to camp. But seeing that you insist—"

"I do." Brailier uncrossed his knees and sat back. "May I recommend the pork? It's splendid here."

The food and wine *were* excellent, and despite his misgivings, Samuel cleared his plate. The juicy pork melted in his mouth, a pleasant change from the beans, rice, and plantains served at camp. He didn't fancy the chocolate dessert, so he discreetly slipped Padraig his portion. He couldn't help tapping his feet under the magnificent table. When would Brailier get to the point?

While the white-uniformed waiter poured coffee, Colonel Brailier reached into his jacket. "*Cigarro, señores?* I've some fine Cubans here."

Samuel shook his head.

"No thanks, Colonel. I'll roll a real smoke." Padraig fished in a pocket for his tobacco tin.

The colonel quenched his lucifer and blew a spiral of blue smoke into the cool air. "General Cañas crossed into Nicaragua two days ago, with orders to seize control of the Transit Road.

It's the first phase of President Mora's plan to annex Southern Nicaragua. If investors build a canal, Costa Rica will control it." The colonel puffed his chest out.

"Mora, the fox, is turning this into a two-pronged attack," Padraig observed.

Samuel twisted the napkin in his lap. Mora's policies were almost as bad as slavery. He caught the comment before it tumbled from his lips, but he couldn't change that he was helping yet another bully capture Nicaragua. He was counting the days until Brailier released him to ride for the frontier.

"I see you doubt us, *Capitán* Kingston, but it's the truth." Brailier steepled his fingers and rested his chin against them. "And that's where you come in. You see, I'm a big enough man to admit when I'm wrong—and you were right. There are only a handful of veterans in my army, and I need every edge if I'm going to capture that river. I need you on my expedition. Therefore—"

"*Impossible.*" If Brailier forced him to join their march on the river, only God knew when he'd be free to search for Sofia and John. "We never agreed that. I must find my wife and child more urgently now than ever, now that General Cañas has begun another offensive."

"Now, *Capitán* Kingston—"

"I won't do this."

Padraig's eyes darted from face to face during the tense silence around the big table.

"If you don't, we'll execute you and your companions as filibusters, and that includes the boy." Colonel Brailier tipped ash into the ashtray and squinted at Samuel with a hard smile. "Don't think you can run. General Cañas has the border tightly buttoned, and our navy is more than adequate to stop renegade boats from sneaking up the coast."

Padraig slammed his glass on the table. "You double-dealing churl, Brailier, you can't do this."

Samuel drew himself up in his chair. The popinjay colonel in his ridiculous uniform was bluffing. “This isn’t your decision. I made my deal with President Mora.”

Colonel Brailier waved a hand dismissively. “Indeed you did. I’ll tell you what, you can take it up with him. He’ll be here in two days. But I assure you he sees things my way. Until then, I suggest you continue training the men, because I’ve pushed our departure date forward seven days. Now, we march for the San Carlos River on December second.”

The words hung heavily between them, and it took all of Samuel’s willpower to stop from slumping in his seat. He was caught.

He pushed back from the table with an incoherent murmur and stalked away. He’d be damned if he’d let Brailier see the tears welling in his eyes.

CHAPTER FIFTEEN

On the ride back to the training camp, the rain drummed relentlessly on the leafy forest canopy, louder than the waterfalls cascading down the mountainsides. It streamed from the brim of Samuel's hat, poured inside the collar of his coat to soak his shirt, seeped into his boots, and drowned his sinking spirits. Other than cursing President Mora roundly, he hadn't spoken a word since storming from their meeting with Colonel Brailier. They had trapped him, and he'd find no more justice in Central America than he'd found in Ireland. He worked the problem over and over in his mind, but he always reached the same conclusion: It was William Walker's fault that he had to fight Mora's war rather than hasten north to find Sofia and John.

"Snap out of it," Padraig finally said. "It could be worse. At least he didn't shoot us. Few men vex not one but two presidents." When Samuel didn't chuckle, he pressed on. "With Brailier moving his plans forward, we've shaved a week off. Maybe we can sneak away to find Sofia once we reach the San Juan River and leave Brailier to fight his war."

Samuel stared numbly at the mountains blanketed in a million subtle greens. He shouldn't have dragged the Euronicas into this. That had been shortsighted and selfish. "We can't desert and leave the men to Brailier. He'll get them killed."

"But Sofia and—"

"I know," Samuel snapped. "Either way, somebody gets hurt. We have to believe Sofia and John have reached her father's hacienda by now, and that's far north of the fighting." If they weren't dead along the river. But to say that aloud might have made it real.

Padraig looked into the rainforest and said nothing.

"Mora only wants the southern end of Nicaragua," Samuel said. "He wants the Transit Road and the river, on the chance that he makes a deal with someone like Vanderbilt to build a canal someday. What if—"

An unearthly shockwave shuddered through the trees, and the horses threw up their heads. Samuel flinched and laid a hand on his mare's neck. The ground was moving—impossible, but it crawled. Thunder rumbled from the belly of the mountain, and the earth juddered violently underfoot. The horses reared, screaming, eyes rolling. Samuel hauled the reins and clamped on with his calves as he floated out of the saddle. He teetered a second, then crashed back in his seat as the mare alighted on her forelegs.

"Jaysus, Mary, and Joseph," Padraig shouted as his mare bucked again. "It's Judgment Day."

The dirt road parted with a lingering *creak*, and a crack ten feet long ripped open in front of them. A prolonged squeak came from behind them, and Samuel twisted in the saddle just as a tree toppled—branches cracking, leaves rustling—with a thump across the road.

His mare bolted, and he whipped around in time to guide her away from the long wound in the road. He hauled the left rein until her muzzle almost touched her lathered neck, and she finally halted.

The mountain groaned and quaked. The road quavered again and stilled after a final jolt.

"Earthquake. That was an earthquake." Samuel's heart pounded faster.

Padraig coaxed his mount down on four legs. "What do we do?"

More thuds shook the rainforest. Trees were toppling as if slashed by a giant saber.

Above that, a sound like a large boat grinding over rocks began on the far side of the mountain.

Padraig laid a calming hand on his mare's neck as she cavorted sideways. "Do you hear that?"

"The camp. That's coming from the camp. Ride!" Samuel dug his heels into his trembling mare, but she didn't move as Padraig started up the hill. Samuel lashed her rump with the reins. It was hateful to treat her like that, but there was danger all around. And the camp . . . God only knew what was happening there.

Blinking against the driving rain, he guided the flighty mare around fallen trees and the earthy scars in the road, following Padraig to the crest of the ravaged mountain. His jaw drooped when he saw the valley below. A wall of mud taller than a house and one hundred feet wide gushed down a fresh gash in the mountain like molten lava, distending the river below with trees, broken branches, and debris. Swollen with mud, the river had swamped its banks and was roaring through the valley, obliterating everything in its path to the camp where the army bivouacked.

Samuel's hands shook. Filipe was down there. The Euronica Company was down there . . . the Expeditionary Force, too.

Samuel nudged the frenzied mare down the broken trail. With the road crumbling, littered with toppled trunks and stricken trees wavering above them, it was too dangerous to ride faster. A black jaguar streaked across the road, lithe muscles rippling, and his mare shied with a whinny. He hauled her head back to the broken road, and two white-tailed deer broke cover behind the jaguar—the wildcat less threatening than the cataclysm behind them.

The river of muddy soup roiled trees, branches, and kindling toward the village. The thunder of artillery cannon and explosions in Crimea's Valley of Death had been nothing compared to the roar of this churning wall of mud and debris. The mountain would swallow everything.

The mare halted abruptly, almost pitching him from the saddle. She stood unsteadily, legs splayed, sweat lathering her flanks and neck, and would budge no further. He dismounted and left her in the rain, boots slithering on the muddy road as he jumped fresh fissures. Padraig swung down from his saddle and followed, twenty yards behind him.

The growl of the vomiting mountain grew ever louder as they staggered downhill with their feet sinking into a trail turned to mush. The ground jolted again, and the jungle lurched. A loud *crack* like a pistol shot sounded behind them, and Samuel looked back. A Guanacaste tree was toppling, falling with majestic slowness amid the chaos. As Samuel watched, its leafy canopy crashed down in an explosion of branches and leaves, burying Padraig from sight.

Samuel lost his footing and pitched forward, rolling head over heel down the muddy trail. He skidded to a stop, his mind reeling, coated in mud. Padraig! Padraig was crushed beneath a tree.

He forced himself to his feet and slithered back through the mud, coldness expanding in his core. Padraig was dead. Nobody could have survived that.

The tree sprawled across the road with twisted limbs thrusting skyward, and no sign of his friend.

"*Padraig*!" He screamed into the curtain of rain, staggering from branch to branch, peering into the caverns beneath them.

There.

He glimpsed a white face in the depths and plunged between the branches. They snagged and scratched him cruelly, poking him and tearing his clothing while rainwater cascaded over him, but he managed to touch Padraig's bloody face. "Padraig. Speak to me."

Nothing.

He wriggled deeper and placed a hand on Padraig's neck. The pulse was steady, and Samuel bit his lip. He tugged Padraig's arm, but his lifelong friend was stuck.

The grind of sliding mud and debris continued in the distance, drowning out the drumming of the rain. The avalanche would bury the entire camp alive. Samuel jerked away. He couldn't think of that now.

He grabbed Padraig's chin and rocked his head from side to side. "Padraig, wake up." He slapped Padraig's face. "Wake up. For God's sake, speak to me."

Padraig groaned.

"Yes," Samuel rasped. "Yes. Tell me you're all right."

"Wh-what happened?" Padraig moved his arm. "Christ, I'm trapped. Where am I?"

He squeezed Padraig's arm. "A tree fell on you. Anything hurt?"

"Ugh, every bloody thing. What do you think? A tree fell on me. Get me out of here." Branches crackled as Padraig wriggled again. "I'm not hurt. I ache all over, but everything seems to function. Now get me out of this hole."

Samuel clasped his arm again. "Can you move toward me?"

Leaves rustled. "My right foot is caught. It won't budge."

The earth quaked again, and the tree rocked. The ominous roar of the mudslide persisted in the distance. Samuel flinched as the canopy shivered overhead. Trees creaked, but nothing else fell.

"God, get me out of here." Padraig's voice broke.

"Let me." Samuel squeezed farther in toward Padraig's feet and slid his hand down Padraig's leg to his ankle. There was the problem. "You're caught in a forked branch. Slide toward me and push your leg forward." Planting an elbow and his toes in the ground, he arched his body to take his weight off the boughs pressing on Padraig.

Padraig grunted and slid his body down an inch, but his ankle remained stuck tight in the fork.

Samuel flexed his muscles and clasped Padraig's right shin with his free hand. "Again. Scoot lower and stretch out your leg."

Padraig wriggled once more, and Samuel heaved. The ankle slid down an inch, then another fraction, and Samuel yanked it free of the bark-covered jaw. "Got it."

"You did. Now get off me, for heaven's sake."

Samuel rolled clear and reached back to help Padraig crawl out. Padraig's face and neck were covered in blood.

Samuel knelt over him, shivering. "You're injured. Here, let me see your head."

"I don't feel anything," Padraig said as he bent his neck.

"That's because you're thick." Samuel picked through the tangled locks. "Not bad. The rain spreads the blood, making it look worse. May need a few stitches. Can you walk?"

"Mm-hmm. What about the horses?"

"They won't go down any further." Samuel yanked Padraig to his feet and gave a shaky laugh. "Not sure if I want to, either."

They slogged down the rest of the way to the bottom as quickly as they could. Three feet of clay, boulders, and branches buried part of the camp. Half-naked men covered in mud and blood staggered about like drunks. Others dug frantically with shovels, bayonets, pieces of wood, or their bare hands.

The blacksmith's house had disappeared. Samuel numbed inside as he clutched Padraig's arm. "Filipe!"

His eyes skittered to the outhouse, covered by a three-foot mound of mud and debris, with its back wall listing at forty-five degrees. The soggy air stank like the fresh-turned earth of a grave. Soldiers scrabbled in the dirt like chocolate-covered demons. Samuel couldn't tell them apart, couldn't tell who was groping at the mass of mud piled on the outhouse, but if they were digging, someone was buried in there.

He stumbled forward. “Filipe!”

He recognized the burly shape of Chavez clawing a boulder out of the mud. He seized Chavez’s arm. “Filipe! Is he—”

“He’s here, Capitán. But we’ll dig him out.” Chavez’s eyes were white and weary in his mud-caked face.

Samuel hurled himself at the mound and tore into it with his bare hands. He should have left Filipe in Ireland. Now his death was on Samuel’s hands, just like Father’s. Stones grazed his fingertips and grit slipped through his fingers as he clawed back fistful after fistful of ravaged earth. Within twenty minutes, his nails and the pads of his hands were cracked and bleeding, and he was getting nowhere. This was too slow; he needed a shovel, a piece of wood, something. He wrenched a forked tree limb from the slime. This would do. He plunged his crude spade into the wall of mud.

They toiled through the night, and Samuel barely noticed when the rain ceased with monsoon suddenness some time before midnight. His breath whistled in his ears, and his muscles ached. He attacked the earth, hating it as if it were a living thing.

Slowly, he recognized the surrounding men by their speech, their mannerisms. Dumpy Rubio was easy to spot, as was stick-thin Quintero, and Vargas with his broad smile among them, raking back mud with weary arms.

It was taking too long; nobody could survive this. Filipe’s lifeless body was buried in there. Samuel attacked the mud with renewed fury.

“Samuel.” Padraig’s shout recalled him from his trance to find Padraig and Zamora beside him. “It’s after two. We’re changing teams; we’re all shagged. Sergeant Zamora has a rested team ready to relieve you.”

Samuel’s objection died in his gullet. Padraig was right. He was exhausted; his hands blistered and bloody from wielding the rough branch.

Chavez approached, caked in mud. Only his hands were clean, cradling his battered Bible. “*Capitán*, the men and I, *señor*. . . We're sorry for your plight. I was wondering if you'd like to join us in a prayer?"

Gratitude flooded Samuel. These men, they were family to him too. "Thank you, Chavez, I will."

The Euronicas linked hands like a line of wobbly gingerbread men and raised their streaked faces to the starlit heavens, where God seemed to have turned a blind eye.

Chavez bowed his head. "Our Father, who art in heaven . . ."

These Catholics were as close to God as any Protestant. Samuel squirmed as he recalled his spats over John's baptism with Sofia. He'd been such an ass. It didn't matter if a man believed that bread and wine turned into the body of Christ or if they only represented Christ. It was closeness to God and fidelity that made a man a true Christian. He should have dropped his archaic bigotries and let Sofia christen John. Now it was too late. He'd made—

Padraig's muddy hand touched his shoulder. The prayer had ended. "Captain Blanco has brought more men and shovels from the town. Zamora and the boys will power through the mud now."

Fixated on digging for Filipe, he'd never checked how many men had survived. He turned to Zamora. "The men. How many did we lose?"

Padraig's grin was white against his mud-caked face as he answered first. "None. The Costas gave our boys the worst campsite, furthest from the river on that knoll. The mudslide never reached them."

"And the Costa Ricans? How many—"

"At least fifty so far." Padraig pointed to a line of corpses on high ground, far from the river. "Twenty-one still missing."

"Colonel Brailier?"

Padraig spat in the mud. "Strutted back to town. He's not the type to get his hands dirty. But Captain Blanco is amazing. He's digging alongside his men and organizing deliveries of more tools." Padraig let out a sigh and closed his eyes for a second. "Do you think he's still alive?"

Samuel fought the heavy numbness creeping over him. Sofia would be overcome with grief if Filipe perished. "We must believe it and trust in God. That's all we have to cling to."

"Captain—you must eat, sir." Cortez offered Samuel a *jicara* and two maize tortillas. He spoke English, and he liked to show it off.

"Thank you, Pedro." Samuel smiled warmly and clutched Cortez's shoulder. "How are you holding up? And the rest of the boys?"

"Don't worry about us, sir. We're used to hard work. We're gonna get that boy out. You rest."

When Samuel woke, it was daylight and hot and airless on the knoll, even in the shade, but it was better than the furnace below where the men toiled. The perfumed scent of wild blooms was a welcome change after the stink of earth and death. The irregular thump of tools and urgent calls assured him the rescue progressed as the Euronicas fought to save a boy they hardly knew. That was the caliber of these men.

He watched them scratching at the earth below the knoll. Not that long ago he'd scorned the working class, puffed up by prejudices drilled into him by the arrogant ruling class. But he'd learned that the Euronicas, like his friend Padraig, were loyal. They were here to support him and to bring justice to William Walker, and he wouldn't let them down. He would lead them to success on this river expedition.

"*Está vivo!*" He's alive!

The cry from the outhouse made his belly clench. He staggered to his feet as cheering men hauled a muddy form from the shambles.

Padraig ran to meet Samuel. "He's alive, shook, but fine. Thank God, they build everything with heavy wood around here. He heard the mudslide coming and sheltered under the workbench."

Samuel's weariness floated away. "That workbench—it took two of us to shift it an inch."

Filipe looked like a ball of mud where he sat against a tree, drinking greedily from a jicara. He stank of urine and grave. He coughed and hacked, then spit out a muddy gob and poured the rest of the water over his head.

Samuel knelt and grabbed Filipe's shoulders. "You all right?"

Filipe rubbed his forehead. "Buried alive . . . I thought I was dead." He dissolved into tears and clung to Samuel.

Samuel lifted him. "Come along. Let's get you cleaned up." He hadn't realized how much he cared for the boy until he'd almost lost him. He sagged against Filipe as tension drained from his body. "Thank you, Lord."

The river was a seething muddy soup, so Samuel and Filipe rode a mile uphill to a mountain stream, where they stripped and washed the mud from their bodies before rinsing off their clothes.

Filipe was subdued as he knelt by the babbling stream, wearing only his drawers as he rinsed out his shirt. "When your father was taken, you'd have done anything to save him, Samuel, right? I mean anything?"

That was a strange question. But for the last year, Samuel had wondered the same himself. Could he have done more to save Father? He stopped hanging his wet trousers on a branch and observed Filipe. "Certainly."

"Even . . . even if you knew it was wrong?"

He'd faced that very dilemma a year before, on his last trip to Nicaragua, and had made the gut-wrenching choice to oppose Walker when he heard Walker planned to bring back slavery even if he sacrificed Father. "No. I couldn't live with myself if I did something dishonorable, something that led to evil." But he wasn't easy in himself. If he'd found Father earlier and rescued him, perhaps Father wouldn't have caught cholera.

Filipe's shoulders dragged low, and he stopped kneading his shirt in the water; his hands losing all tension. "I see. It's just that . . ."

Was something upsetting Filipe? Something bad he'd done in the past. Samuel took a small step toward the boy. "Is anything bothering you?"

Filipe's mouth opened, but no words came out. Then he rubbed his shirt on a stone furiously. "No, nothing. I was just thinking about your father . . . That must have been hard on you."

"Yes, it was." Samuel blinked. "You know you can talk to me about anything, right?"

"Yes." Filipe pinched his lips together and attacked the shirt again, saying nothing more.

CHAPTER SIXTEEN

The stone walls of the cell-like chamber made Benjamin Fry restless; he'd never get used to the stench of wet stone and damp earth. Even the acrid smell of the camphene lamp failed to cover it. It must be far more uncomfortable below in the dungeon. Perhaps he should move the woman and child upstairs where it was cooler? He squirmed and muttered. "Too hell with that. Willy's dead because of her husband. They can rot down there, for all I care."

There was a rap on the rickety door.

He took a swig from the green bottle on the table, and the whiskey warmed his insides. The El Castillo Hotel down the hill was a shithole, but Hollenbeck kept some passable whiskey behind the bar. "What is it?"

Shane Dawson popped his head around the door. "Time for a word, Colonel?"

"Captain Dawson." It was good to see Dawson had survived the bitter fighting in Granada. The bed creaked as Fry rose. "How goes the campaign? Tell me General Henningsen has whipped those greasers back to Honduras or Guatemala, or wherever they came from. Here, have a whiskey. It's the good stuff from the hotel."

Dawson flopped his heavy frame into the rough-hewn chair. "I'm afraid the news could be better, Colonel. Looks like we're losing Granada. General Walker only left Henningsen five hundred men when he sailed off to attack Rivas, and the allied army launched three simultaneous assaults soon after the general left the city. That damned place is full of spies." He accepted the glass with a grateful nod. "I needed this. Henningsen's lost too many men. He retreated to Guadalupe Church, burning every building east of there to slow the enemy down, but he ain't getting no further. Enemy has them surrounded."

Fry went cold despite the heat. "Where's General Walker? He can't let that happen."

"He's standing offshore in the lake on a large riverboat with most of the army, waiting for a chance to rescue them. But the enemy has thousands of men in the city. They're thick as fleas on a swamp hound. Walker sent me for more men. How many can you spare? I want—"

"God damn it, man, is General Walker crazy? This river is his lifeblood. If he loses it, there'll be no more recruits, no more arms or supplies." Fry rested his face in his hands. "Sorry, Shane. It's not your fault. But he only left me a hundred men to hold the fort. Not enough."

They stared at each other glumly.

Fry brightened. "Look, the *Tennessee* should have arrived in Greytown this morning, and she'll have hundreds of volunteers from New Orleans. With any luck, a riverboat will land them here tonight. Can you wait until morning?"

Dawson shook his head. "Walker needs us back now, in case he mounts a counterattack."

A rap came at the door, and Sergeant Wulchak entered without waiting for permission. "Colonel, there's a greaser here, name of Calero. Says you know him."

Fry's pulse quickened. Calero wouldn't have risked crossing the border unless there was important news. "Send him in."

Tall and wiry, Calero had light skin for a Nicaraguan Indian, making it easy to pose as a Costa Rican when he sneaked back and forth across the border on William Walker's business. The acrid bite of ripe sweat followed him in. "Colonel, our contact warns me that Kingston is still free. The Costas didn't buy the tip he was running guns for a revolution. They've recruited him to help them now."

Aching compression built in Fry's head. Bloody Kingston had nine lives. "Damn it, can't they do anything right? First, Anderson misses him off the coast and gets ten good men killed. And now this."

"I know what Kingston's plans are, sir," Calero said. "He's leading the Costa Ricans through the rainforest to capture the river forts."

Kingston couldn't be that stupid. Calero had it wrong. "The Costa Ricans tried that already. They got their asses whooped."

"This time, Kingston's going to float an army down the San Carlos River. On rafts."

"Rafts!" Fry scratched his unkempt beard. He hadn't known such a thing was possible. If it was, the Costa Ricans would arrive soon, well rested, and the forts wouldn't even hear them coming. "How many men does Kingston have?"

"Your man reported two, three hundred."

"Three hundred bloody conscripts—ten of them ain't worth one of us." He moved to the map on the table. "The San Carlos River, eh?" There it was, east of Hipp's Point. He bounced on his toes and swatted Dawson's arm. "We'll nip this in the bud, ambush them on the Costa Rican side before the San Carlos river joins the San Juan. The river's narrow there, and they'll never expect it."

Dawson's eyes widened. "You can't leave the fort. Walker would never condone it."

"I can't, but you can," Fry said.

"I won't. General Walker—"

Fry grabbed Dawson's arm. "Walker would support this plan. If Kingston and the Costa Ricans take the river, we're finished."

Dawson blinked at him dubiously.

"You'll have three hundred volunteers here on the riverboat from Greytown tomorrow, all armed with rifles, many of them veterans of the Mexican-American War." Fry took a drink of whiskey and sat back. "And you'll have Theo Dennison's men."

Dawson recoiled and put his hands up. "Deserters. Dennison's nothing more than a brigand. He ran out on us."

"That's what Walker wanted the world to believe." Fry unrolled a map of the frontier on the table. "He sent Dennison into Costa Rica to seize those gold mines *because* he's a deserter. We needed that gold to finance the war. We couldn't take it legally. But Dennison's a deserter. He can do as he pleases."

"He never really deserted?"

"Walker sent him away." Fry smirked. That surprised Dawson. He jabbed the map with a long finger. "And right here, that's where Dennison and sixty of our rangers are cleaning out the gold fields. With those veterans plus three hundred new volunteers, you'll be more than a match for the Costa Ricans."

Both men straightened from the map.

Fry swallowed his whiskey in one slug and gasped at its smokey sting. "Do this, and Walker will make you a major."

Dawson eyes sparkled. "You're right. We'll take a riverboat and disembark at the junction with the San Carlos river."

"Dennison should know the area." Fry reached for the whiskey bottle. "He'll pick the best place to stop the Costas. Don't worry about—"

The door flew open and Sergeant Wulchak rushed in. "Colonel, the woman's gone."

The world dropped out from beneath Fry's feet. "Gone! What do you mean, gone?"

Wulchak ran a hand through his lank hair. "I went down to feed her, and the cell door was open. The woman and child—they're gone."

Fry slammed both hands onto the table. "How? The door was bolted."

Wulchak recoiled. "I know, sir. Somebody let them out."

"Lock down the fort and search it." He pushed past Wulchak and Dawson. Walker wanted to use the woman to lure Kingston to Nicaragua; he'd be furious if she escaped. "I'll check the village. We're surrounded by jungle; they can't leave until the next boat comes through. I'm going to hang the man who helped her."

He took the steps down to the courtyard two at a time. The square bristled with armed Americans in black shirts and more in the new blue shirts of Walker's army.

He clapped to get their attention. "Men, a spy has escaped with valuable intelligence, and you must apprehend her." He steadied his voice and lowered the pitch. "Don't let her mother-and-child act fool you—this woman is dangerous. That said, I want her captured unharmed. Captain Dawson can help. We'll check the riverboat docked upstream of the rapids. I don't want it returning to the lake until we find her. Shane, take four men to guard the boat once we've searched it and four more to look upriver from there. Sergeant Wulchak will take three men and hunt for them downriver. The rest of you, comb the village."

The men shuffled and exchanged reluctant glances.

"Ten dollars for the soldier who brings her back."

The men formed groups quickly, and he led Dawson's small detachment through the battered gates guarding the fort's only entrance and down the steep hill. The thunder of whitecaps surging over rocks on the river grew louder as he turned onto the river path, where the *Santa Maria* rocked at the wooden jetty upstream of the village. Soon that river steamer would return across the lake. If she brought news that the woman had escaped, Walker wouldn't be pleased.

They stopped at the gangplank. "You four, guard the road and let nobody past. The rest of you search the boat."

Boots rapped the gangplank behind him as he boarded and

climbed the stairs to the upper deck. It didn't take long to inspect both decks and the engine room below. Nothing.

He halted under the canvas awning to catch his breath, where the captain, a nervous young man with thinning hair and an acne-scarred face, shifted from foot to foot. "Can I help, sir?"

"You're not hiding a woman or child on here, are you, sonny?"

The captain's eyes flicked to the gangplank. "I seen a woman with a baby running up the path toward the hotel about an hour ago with one of your native soldiers. Woman was a native, too."

She couldn't have gone far yet. "I reckon it's her."

He whirled and headed for the entry port. The bitch was going to regret causing this trouble. The village was only a score of wooden shacks that any stiff wind would blow over, clustered around the crappy hotel owned by that young fellow Hollenbeck. Likely she was hiding there.

He called for the men. "Right, boys, to the village. You lot, start at the far end. We'll take this side, and we'll meet up at the hotel."

By the time he'd searched all nine meager shanties and rejoined his men outside the hotel, Fry was boiling, and his sweat-stained shirt clung to his back. The infernal woman was nowhere in sight.

He kicked open the front door of the hotel and stalked inside.

Hollenbeck, a fat, clean-shaven man in his twenties, bobbed his head like a nervous bird at the intrusion. "Colonel. Is . . . is something the matter? You can't just kick in my door like that." His eyes flicked to the wood stairway beside the reception desk.

Sure as shooting, the bastard was hiding something. "I run this town, Hollenbeck, and I'll do as I please. We're looking for two fugitives and a baby—a man, a woman. Seen them?"

"N-no. I've been working on my accounts here. Nobody's come in. The hotel is empty until the next riverboat comes through."

He was lying. Fry scanned the dining room and bar. "Search the place. I'll look upstairs."

The whiff of roasting pork from the dining room made his mouth water as he clumped up the worn stairs and turned right along the wood-paneled hallway. The bronze knob on the first door turned with a squeak. The room was empty save for the motes of dust floating in the sunlight lancing through the shutters. He stepped inside and ripped back a musty curtain to find the closet empty.

Outside, the floor creaked and boots rapped the planks as his men searched the other rooms.

"Colonel! Down here." The shout made his fingertips tingle.

"Out of the way, God damn it." He pushed through his men crowding the narrow hallway.

Gibson, a wiry wharf rat from New Orleans, appeared in one doorway. "Got them, sir. This way."

A baby wailed.

Five strides took him there, and he looked inside. The Kingston bitch crouched against the window, clutching the squirming baby to her bosom.

"Don't you dare touch me," she snarled, "or my father will have you skinned."

Her nursing breasts rose and fell as she panted, and his loins tingled. The bitch was beautiful. He'd have his way with her before this was over. "Nobody will harm you, Mrs. Kingston. We're here for your protection. It's what your father would want."

Private Alvarez stepped from the shadows with trembling lips. "Colonel Valle will be furious when he hears how you've treated his daughter. You must let me return her to him."

So here was the traitor. "Take this snake to the upriver dock."

He stepped into the room and approached the Kingston woman.

"You're not protecting me. You kidnapped me, and you've kept me prisoner for months." She pressed back against the wall.

Oh, what a beauty. What spirit. He was going to enjoy breaking her when the time came. He raised his hands, palms out. "Now, Mrs. Kingston, there's no need for this. I assure you I'm only acting on your father's orders. Don't worry. He forgives you for running away with that traitor and stealing the country's gold. He only wants to see you home and safe. He understands you were besotted when you eloped with him."

"Liar!" A knife blade flashed in her free hand. "Papa would never condone this. He'll kill you."

"Shush, you're confused." He opened his arms wider and took a step closer. He nodded toward the screaming baby. "Think of your child."

She looked down at the baby, and he slapped her across the face, knocking her sideways onto the bed. She yelped, and the mattress creaked as she landed on her back.

Alvarez surged forward. Fry punched him, and pain crackled his knuckles. Jesus, that felt good. He grabbed a fistful of Alvarez's hair and drove his head to meet his rising knee. Alvarez's jaw fractured, and he crumpled.

"Take this deserter to the dock," he snapped. "Do it now. I'll deal with him there."

The Kingston woman was curled around her screeching brat on the bed, sobbing.

"Shut your pup up, woman. What were you thinking? That you could escape through the bloody jungle?" He had no time for this bitch's antics. "On your feet. We're going outside, and if you cause any more trouble, I'll feed your brat to the crocodiles." He grabbed her arm and yanked her off the bed.

Threatening her brat brought her in line, and she tottered meekly down to the lobby.

Hollenbeck, his face ashen, jammed his hands into his armpits. "I . . . I . . . can't allow you to take this woman."

Fry's cheeks burned. The swine had been hiding her. He shoved the Kingston woman at one of his soldiers. "Hold her."

He grabbed Hollenbeck's shirt and dragged the fat bugger's

face close to his. "You're lucky I don't hang you. If you try a trick like this again, I'll burn your hotel to the ground. Understand?"

Hollenbeck nodded vigorously. "No sir—I mean yes sir, I understand. And no sir, I won't."

The stupid pig. Fry released him, snatched the stone paperweight from the desk and hurled it through the window for good measure. Glass exploded onto the walkway, and the woman let out a little scream.

Fry smoothed his shirt and pushed her out the door. "Let's go reward Alvarez for helping you, shall we?"

He hustled her down the narrow road along the river to where Dawson stood on the dock beside the riverboat, speaking with the two riflemen who held Alvarez between them.

"Colonel, I had to save her," Alvarez began as soon as he saw Fry. "I was born on the Valle hacienda. I couldn't bear to see them suffer."

Fry stamped onto the dock, dragging Kingston's woman with him. This was a lesson she'd remember. He drew his revolver and pointed it at Alvarez. "You forgot you're under my command now. That makes your action treason, and the sentence is death."

The gun kicked in his hand, and the barrel spit smoke. Alvarez cried out, clutched his chest, and toppled backward into the murky river.

The Kingston woman crumpled to her knees with a moan.

Fry blew on the barrel of his handgun. "Would you look . . . at . . . that. Enough blood to create a good scent, and still conscious for his last supper."

The whitecaps whisked Alvarez downriver, bouncing and churning him across the rocks, before spitting him into the calmer waters downstream. Along the riverbank, long muddy shapes sprang to life. Tails lashed the dull, brown waters as the crocodiles flashed after Alvarez. His screams were louder than the roar of the rapids, and they tore him to pieces in a bloody frenzy.

The Kingston woman sobbed and speared him with a venomous glare. "You'll pay for that, you monster."

Fry chuckled unpleasantly and holstered his gun with a flourish. He didn't think so. In fact, he was fairly certain she had it backward. He'd be well rewarded for his foresight and results. And enjoy it, he would.

CHAPTER SEVENTEEN

"Hard work" didn't describe squeezing through the vines that snaked down the black-trunked trees with water dripping down the bark. Samuel's skin crawled and itched from insect bites and scratches, and his eyes were gritty from marching through the hostile jungle. The soupy air was thick with the sweet, acrid scent of rotting vegetation, body odor, and animal musk. Carving a path ahead, Jimenez and Cortez were shadows in their faded green shirts, almost invisible. What remained of those who survived the mudslide followed, grunting, cursing, and making a hell of a racket. No wonder Walker's men had heard the previous army's approach.

"I don't think we've enough men," Padraig panted behind him. "Barely two hundred. Sure, it's not enough at all."

Samuel ground his teeth. Padraig was right, but he didn't have to rattle on about it. "What did you expect me to do? Sixty-nine dead or injured, and a dozen men down with fever. It's not enough, I know, but we couldn't wait for reinforcements. And I need to get this over with."

"I'm only saying. Walker will have hundreds—"

"Shut up. It was hard enough to persuade that nincompoop

Brailier to proceed in the first place." Samuel wrenched another vine out of his way. "Do you want him turning back?"

"No, no. You're right."

"Every . . . damned . . . delay keeps me from Sofia and John."

"Sorry." Padraig removed his sweat-stained hat and wiped his sleeve across his forehead. "Jaysus, I'd kill for a smoke."

A flock of blue and green birds exploded from the trees above, and Samuel's hand flew to his Colt. Christ, he was jumpy.

"It's nothing, only parrots." Padraig crammed on his hat and waved Samuel onward. "We must be close to the San Carlos river by now."

The Nicaraguan frontier was miles away, and the forts farther still. Samuel fished out his compass and peered through the steamed-up glass. Still heading north. "Soon. I reckon we're on the right course."

"I hate damned Costa Rica," Cortez moaned up ahead. "There are too many *insectos*."

"It's only you, Cortez," Jimenez cackled. "They smell a tasty Carib from Nicaragua and want to eat some new meat."

The thud of their machetes decreased.

"Jimenez! Keep chopping or we'll never get out of here," Padraig bellowed. "Three days in this stinking botanical garden, and the undergrowth thickens with every bloody step. I've had enough, so chop with your machete, not your jaw."

The march was taking too long. Tempers were getting frayed. Samuel glanced at Padraig's peeling pink face. If easygoing Padraig was irritable, the rest of the men must have been at their wits' end. At least that peacock Brailier was suffering alongside them, far from the luxury of the Grano de Oro hotel. Samuel smiled bitterly.

The pounding of machetes ahead stopped altogether. "I'm exhausted, Teniente. How much longer before it's time for the next two to take over?"

"Soon, Jimenez, soon." Padraig looked at Samuel and shrugged. "Who's counting?"

"I am." Samuel moved forward, calling ahead. "Another fifteen minutes. Keep it up, lads."

The volume of grumbling increased behind them, and Samuel craned around.

Colonel Brailier, hatless and disheveled, pushed through the Euronicas. "*Capitán* Kingston, I thought you said we were close to the river?"

"We are."

The colonel adjusted the dusty cocked hat tucked under his arm. "How close, exactly? Because as commander of the expedition, I ought to lead us to it."

Did the idiot think he was a conquistador? Samuel bit back the retort and took an exaggerated step sideways into the undergrowth. "By all means, Colonel. You can see if the filibusters are lying in wait for us, as they did for the last expedition. Lead on."

Brailier peered up the rough trail. "Not now, *hombre*. When we see the river. I don't—"

"What's the holdup?" Sylvanus Spencer's thin voice was barely audible far back in the line of weary men.

Brailier brushed at the leaves clinging to his uniform and took a slight step back. "Just checking we're going the right way. Carry on, Kingston. As we're close, I'm going to rest my men; they look done in."

Blasted coward.

Samuel ducked through the trees and winced as a wet spider web tickled his skin. That could've been poisonous. He drew his elbows in and moved with more caution.

Padraig spat behind him. "His men are done in—yeah, right. It's Brailier who can't keep up. The fool's afraid of walking into an ambush."

Sergeant Zamora and Quintero moved to the front to spell the others, and the blows of their machetes rang through the wet trees as the party crept forward. Samuel tried to ignore the scratches, the bites, and the throb of his blistered feet. Everything was taking too long; it had been weeks since Sofia disappeared.

He let out a weary sigh. "We'll never find them at this rate. We need to move faster."

"Sofia's resourceful," Padraig said, catching the shift of subject. "I'm sure they're fine. She'll have found another way to reach her father. Don't fret yourself. Once we're on the rafts, we'll shoot down the river in no time." He wiped the sweat from his face with a grimy handkerchief. "At least we've left that whining louse Brailier behind. The cheek of him, pretending his men were weary."

"Padraig," Samuel said.

"Since when did that arrogant bastard ever care about his men?" Padraig continued. "Shit-scared of bumping into the filibusters he is, that's all."

"Padraig," Samuel repeated. "Look. The ground's marshier, and the trees are thinning out."

"The river," Sergeant Zamora called from ahead.

They'd made it; the hard part was over.

Samuel moved briskly now, ignoring the grasping thorns and slap of wet leaves. The whisper of the river buoyed his spirit as he broke into leaf-dappled sunlight and spotted the muddy water. The air carried a tale of animal droppings, wet grass, and wildflowers. Frogs croaked their protest from the swaying reeds as the men poured from the brush, chattering and bouncing like children on a picnic.

Padraig rested on a lightning-blackened trunk and began to roll a smoke. "This is an awful place to build rafts. Too marshy."

"I know," Samuel said, looking downriver. "We'll follow the water until we reach higher ground. Come on. We've wasted too much time already."

"What about the colonel and Spencer?"

Samuel shrugged to ease the ache in his shoulders. "They can catch up."

Half a mile downriver, they found a plateau where the land

rose gently three feet above the slugish water. Samuel ordered six men to clear a workspace, while he led the others into the forest with axes and machetes. Those tall trees as slim as the pines back home looked easy to cut, strip, and move.

Quintero tugged at his muddy shirt and shook his head. "No, Capitán. Those don't float."

Jimenez swung his axe at the tree, and the thud startled a flock of brown birds into flight. "Wood that don't float. What do you know? You're a damned fisherman."

"Exactly." Quintero sucked in his cheeks and squinted at Jimenez. "If a *pescador* doesn't know what floats, who does?"

Padraig chortled. "He has you there, Jimenez."

"Right." Cortez flashed a grin. "If we wanted to steal a raft, we'd take your advice, Jimenez."

Trees that didn't float—Samuel had never seen that in Ireland. He looked around and pointed to a stand of trees with buttercup-yellow flowers. "How about those, Quintero? Some must be a hundred feet high."

Quintero's face brightened. "Ah, the Gallinazo. Yes, that will work. And that"—he pointed to a triangular trunk tapering into the azure sky, devoid of branches save for a dense green plumes on top—"the *jícaro* there would be perfect for a dugout canoe."

"Like we've time for that," Padraig said. "We don't have a bloody shipyard here. The yellow tree it is."

Once the first tree toppled, Samuel borrowed a machete and began hacking off the branches. He worked relentlessly, ignoring the weariness in every limb, until his hands were blistered and chafed. The sooner they launched the rafts, the sooner he could move against the forts. The sooner he could move against the forts, the sooner he could be back with his wife and son.

Forty minutes later, Captain Blanco arrived with some Costa Ricans and joined in. The captain was a stark contrast to Brailier, always willing and unafraid of getting his hands dirty.

By the time the colonel struggled up the muddy slope, the Euronicas had felled and stripped three trees. Mud splattered

Brailier's once immaculate uniform, and its gold fringes and epaulets were tattered. He wiped the grime from his flushed face and frowned. "I told you I must lead us to the river."

Samuel's nostrils flared, and he bent forward to hack another branch from the tree. He hadn't time for this pettiness. "Colonel, if you don't start acting like a leader, I'm taking my men and moving on without you, and you can explain what happened to President Mora." He glared at Spencer and switched to English. "Get him under control, or I'll take the San Juan with my men and claim the entire payment from Vanderbilt."

Spencer's thin face crinkled. "You wouldn't dare."

"Try me." Samuel spat on his blistered hands and scythed off another branch.

A chilling scream from the jungle made him miss his next stroke, and the axe blade struck the trunk, sending a shock up his arms. At the edge of the trees, a Euronica writhed on the ground, and sunlight flashed on Jimenez's machete as he swung it down again.

A pressure wave surged through Samuel's body. He dropped his machete and raced across the trampled undergrowth.

"Jaysus wept, he's not murdering him, is he?" Padraig's voice shook as he pounded after Samuel.

Jimenez threw down his machete with a curse and dropped to his knees where Gustavo Arguello lay coiled in the fetal position, clutching his leg and whimpering.

"*Barba amarilla.*" Jimenez pointed to the broad, flattened head of a snake where it lay severed from the six-foot body.

Chavez reached them a second later. "A pit adder." He too knelt beside Arguello.

"It was hiding in the grass." Jimenez's face was ashen. "We never saw it until it attacked."

Samuel couldn't tear his eyes away from the thick brown and yellow coil covered with black V patterns, still squirming in the grass. "Where did it bite him?"

Chavez's lips trembled as he examined Arguello's leg with a gentleness uncustomary for a man of his strength. "On his calf."

"Will he be all right?"

"The spearhead, they call this *bastardo*," Chavez said.

Jimenez curled his lip as he lifted the snake by its tail.

"Its bite causes anything from blindness to rotting flesh and death," Chavez continued. "We need to get the venom out." He drew his knife while the others gathered around. "Lay him on his belly over that log there and—no, no, keep his wound lower than his heart. Now hold him still." He looked up at a pimply young soldier gawking at the scene. "Perez, fetch a foot of rope quick."

Jimenez tossed the snake aside. "We'll eat that murderer tonight."

Without hesitation, Chavez cut the skin open at the bite and sucked on the wound. He spat blood out and sucked on the wound again. When he'd removed more blood, he took the rope from Perez and tied it around the leg. "We need to loosen that every ten minutes."

Samuel's belly roiled. Perez had been with him for the La Virgen campaign a year ago. "Would a doctor help?"

Chavez shrugged. "I'm not sure what more he could do. It's in God's hands now. Pray for him. Let's carry him back to the river and make him comfortable in the shade."

Colonel Brailier arrived, wheezing for breath, and took a cursory glance. "He's a dead man. You should put him out of his misery."

The cold comment boiled Samuel's blood. "Never." He turned his back on Brailier and grabbed Chavez's arm. "But seriously, what if we could get him to a doctor? Is there any chance?"

Chavez thumbed his ear and avoided Samuel's glare. "It's possible . . ."

"The Royal Navy kept at least one frigate in Greytown." Samuel knelt and touched Perez's forehead tenderly. "Their surgeons might help."

"We have to get past Walker's forts first." Padraig poured

water from a *jicara* onto his handkerchief and patted Arguello's sweating forehead with the damp cloth.

Samuel stood and shoved his hands into his pockets. "We need to finish those rafts."

The soldier's dark eyes were sunken, seeming to implore Samuel for salvation. He beckoned Samuel down. "Don't let me die, *Capitán*."

Samuel knelt and squeezed Perez's clammy hand. "*No te preocupes*, Gustavo. I've got you, and I'll see you through this."

The riverbanks quickly echoed with the renewed thud of axes, the clatter of machetes, and the rasp of saws as one hundred and fifty Costa Ricans and the Euronicas chopped trees, stripped their trunks, and hauled them to the water's edge.

Padraig pointed with his machete toward where Brailier was directing the two men building a lean-to. "Would you look at that? His lordship needs a castle. Will he ever catch himself on?"

"Don't mind him." Samuel looked at Quintero. "Can we use bamboo for the floor? It'll be easy to tie together."

The wiry fisherman looked up from binding the frame of the first raft together with rope using clove hitch knots. "*Si, Capitán*. The hollow stems of bamboo trap air, and they float well. But they're tough as hardwood, and it's difficult to cut them down."

Samuel sighed. Another monumental task.

"But if we burn them at the bottom," Quintero finished, "they'll fall over."

"What a man." Padraig grinned. "I'm taking him back to Ireland to crew my boat."

Samuel stuck the tip of his machete in the earth and stretched. "Show Sergeant Zamora and four men what to do and tell them to fell plenty. The Costa Ricans will need bamboo too. I hope we brought enough rope."

Padraig gave a disgusted snort. "Why the hell would you want to help Brailier?"

Samuel pinched the bridge of his nose and squeezed his eyes tight to fight his exhaustion. Sometimes Padraig could be so childish. "You know as well as I do that we can't capture the river on our own, despite what I said to that ass. We're in this together, and we'll keep building until we've enough rafts. We can rest later, on the river."

"No rest?" Padraig's voice rose in pitch. "We've been fighting the jungle forever. The men are wrecked."

"Look," Samuel said. "Arguello's getting worse. We need to get him to a doctor." He snagged Padraig's sleeve and pulled him closer. "And another thing: Fry and Walker have been ahead of us every step of the way. We may have a traitor among us, and every minute we delay increases the risk that the enemy gets word we're coming."

"Who?" Padraig flicked his head back. "One of us? A spy?"

Samuel's conscience twanged, and he looked from Filipe, hacking branches for a felled tree, to Chavez, who was praying over Arguello. When Padraig said it, it sounded ridiculous. "That's stupid, isn't it? But it could be one of the Costa Ricans. Regardless, we can't take chances. We need to get downriver fast."

Padraig nodded toward Colonel Brailier, who was lounging in the shade as he talked to Spencer. "And what about his nibs?"

Samuel spat into the brush. "He wants the glory of leading the river assault. He'll make sure his men finish ahead of us. So let's push them."

CHAPTER EIGHTEEN

The raft drifted through the muddy water, skimming over dead bugs, leaves, and branches. It didn't even rock when Samuel moved to the edge to urinate; Quintero's fifteen-foot creations worked well. Eighteen rafts floated low in the water, ten men sprawled on each bamboo deck and most of them were dozing. Spots flashed before Samuel's eyes, and his weary limbs sagged. Lucky buggers were sleeping like babies. If only he could slow down his mind and rest.

But he couldn't stop thinking about Sofia and John.

And yet here he was. At this point, the San Carlos River was no wider than the River Bandon back home, murky and ponderous, winding past the twisted creepers dangling from gnarled trees like a curtain of serpents. Clouds of buzzing gnats hovered in sweltering air that reeked of briny algae, methane gas, and sweat; their filthy touch on his lips made Samuel splutter and bat at them in vain. On the right bank, three crocodiles slipped into the water with hooded eyes fixed on their flotilla. He drew his rifle to him. If they came close, he'd have to shoot, and the sound would travel far downriver.

Clack! Clack! The squawk came from the other side of the raft. Rubio's shirt rippled, and the young soldier's face flushed.

"What have you there, Rubio?" Padraig demanded.

Filipe paused from sharpening his saber. "Rubio rescued a toucan with a broken wing. Isn't that grand?"

"Just until he recovers his strength, *Capitán*." Rubio opened his shirt to show them the fat yellow bill. "I'll let him go when he heals."

The bird would have been safer back in the rainforest than with the command of Colonel Brailier, but he would not say that. Samuel shrugged. "Poor bird might regret it."

"We all might," Padraig quipped in English.

The lead raft carrying Colonel Brailier and Sylvanus Spencer disappeared around the bend, and four red-breasted macaws exploded into the air, their raucous calls drowning the chatter of cicadas and crickets as they flapped their yellow and blue wings over the trees.

Padraig snorted. "Even the birds can't stand the bastard. Don't let your toucan see him, Rubio. Why did the Costa Ricans have to take the lead, anyway? It's your plan, and you navigated us here."

It wasn't worth an answer. Padraig was never happy unless he was grumbling. Samuel looked back at the last raft, and Sergeant Zamora lifted his steering paddle to wave. He was keeping the flock together.

"Brailier wants the glory of leading this so-called invasion." Samuel shook his head. "To be fair, even he couldn't get lost now. The river only flows one way."

He touched Arguello's brow. The unconscious soldier was burning up. Samuel dipped his neckerchief in the warm river and draped it across Arguello's face. It comforted little, but it was all he could do. "He's getting worse. He can't last much longer."

"Let me see." Chavez shut his tattered Bible and lowered his ear close to Arguello's face. He closed his eyes. "His breathing is so shallow, I fear you're right, sir." He pulled a wooden cross from under his shirt and blessed himself. "*In nomine Patris et Filii et Spiritus Sancti . . .*"

Samuel's eyes widened, and Padraig outright gasped. They'd trained with Chavez, fought with him, and shared victory with him—but apparently, they hardly knew the man. No simple conscript knew the last rites in Latin. Samuel had been right all along: There was far more to Chavez than he let on.

Chavez finished, touched the cross to his lips, and opened his eyes, finally noticing Samuel watching him. "*Que?*"

"How do you speak Latin?" Samuel asked. "For that matter, where did you learn to speak English? Those are rare accomplishments for a peasant."

A flush crept across Chavez's dark face, and he glanced around the raft. The rest of the men lay around with their eyes closed, seemingly asleep. Nevertheless, he switched to his rocky English. "I've never told the boys this. It's . . . it's . . ." He rubbed the sweating dome of his bald head. "This is personal. But I give you explanation."

Samuel softened his features to encourage him.

Chavez fingered the chipped crucifix at his neck. "Before you came to Chinandega last year, I was accused of being with a . . . How say you? A woman of God."

"A nun?" Samuel asked, trying not to look aghast.

"A nun. They give me choice, ten years in jail or join *Democráticos* army."

"A nun! You dirty hound." Padraig scooted closer.

Samuel's nostrils flared. "Shut up, Padraig." He offered Chavez a small smile and touched his arm. "Carry on, Emanuel."

"I chose the army," he said, "but I was mad with grief. I wanted to die in war. I had—you see, I was a priest in her parish, and we worked together at the small hospital. We became good friends . . . then more than friends."

The others fell silent around them.

Chavez laid a hand against his breastbone. "I sinned. Fell in love, and so did she. I could see it in her eyes, the way she looked at me. I'm certain she see same in me." He switched back to Spanish. "It's too hard to say all this in *inglés*, I don't have the words . . . We stayed true to our vows and never acted on our desires, but we spent too much time together."

Filipe leaned forward. "So then how did—"

Samuel silenced him with a glare.

"Eventually someone accused us of lying together." Chavez squirmed and stared down at his meaty hands. "The sanctimonious bishops who led the Catholic church in Nicaragua have a lot of power and no mercy. They defrocked me and brought me up on charges."

Even Samuel's mixed marriage wasn't as complicated as this relationship. He looked away into the jungle, where green iguanas as big as cats scanned the passing rafts from the trees with beady black eyes. "I can't imagine how you felt at that point. And your—this nun, what happened to her?"

Chavez's face went slack, and he wrung the tail of his green shirt. "I never heard from Teresa while we served in Chinandega. When we escaped to Costa Rica after we helped you take Walker's gold, I wrote letters to friends, to anybody who might have news of her. One of the few people who stood by us, Padre Francisco, sent word that she had left the order and moved to New York." He wiped a tear from his eye. "That's why I went there. To find her."

"And did you?" Padraig asked.

Chavez's crushed expression told all. "I tracked her as far as a Protestant missionary society, but the people there wouldn't even meet me. They said I wasn't of her family." He stared upriver with dull eyes. "That's when you found me in *Nueva York*. I was out of money, out of options, I'd all but given up. So I joined you. If I couldn't save my love, perhaps I could save yours." His voice broke. "I don't know where she is, and I can only pray she returns to Nicaragua."

Samuel rested his hand on Chavez's shoulder. "I know it's selfish, but I'm glad you came. You've been invaluable. Thank you."

"Look, when this is all over, we'll return to *Nueva York* with you and find Teresa," Padraig said.

"You will?" Chavez raised his eyebrows and offered Samuel a questioning gaze.

Samuel squeezed Chavez's shoulder gently.

Chavez thumped his barrel chest with a fist. "Thank you, *Capitán* Kingston. God bless you." He bent over Arguello again. "He's fading fast. I'll pray a rosary for him. The Blessed Virgin will ask God to make room in heaven for his soul."

Samuel watched as if from a thousand miles away. Sofia was heaven for *his* soul. He prayed that he might be reunited with her before it was too late.

The others lost interest, but the sight of Chavez's ministrations to the stricken soldier hypnotized Samuel. Emanuel Chavez was a Catholic priest, he mused, educated in ecclesiastical doctrine; perhaps he could help with the religious wedge that was splitting him and Sofia apart.

He waited until Chavez was done. "Emanuel, may I ask you a question?"

"Of course, *Capitán*."

"In my religion, we see Catholics as idolaters. Their worship of Mary, the Mother of God, is a sin."

Chavez stared at him incredulously. "That's not true. Ever since the Reformation, Catholics and Protestants have been at war, and cruel practices like the Inquisition compounded the rift. Too many shepherds on both sides have taken church teachings out of context in their zeal to keep their flock in line and find more converts." He thought a moment. "You honor your mother, don't you?"

Samuel cocked his head. "I never knew my mother, but I would. Of course I would."

Chavez nodded. "See? And that's what God wants for his mother too. Our devotion to her."

That made more sense than Reverend Welby's intolerant

words. "Why would our reverend back home say those things about Catholics? Even our pastors in school spoke ill of them."

"It's always been them against us, especially in Great Britain, where enmity between the faiths runs deep." Chavez dipped Samuel's handkerchief in the river and laid it back on Arguello's forehead. "Each religion preaches that those of other faiths are going to hell."

"And what do you believe?"

"I don't believe that. God loves us too much, and any man who lives a righteous life is going to heaven, regardless of his religion."

Samuel looked away to the swaying reeds on the riverbank where frogs croaked and a woodpecker drummed staccato on a tree. Once again, he'd been an idiot. He'd argued with Sofia about John's baptism when it simply didn't matter in God's scheme of things. She'd gone off on her own because he'd been thinking of nothing but his own selfish desires. He would make things right when he found her. If he found her. Cold crackled through his body despite the jungle heat. His wife and son could be anywhere: lost along the river, prisoners, dead.

Dear God, let them be safe at Colonel Valle's hacienda.

"Thank you for your insights, Emanuel," he whispered. "You can't imagine how much you've helped me. Please remember me in your prayers. I'll do the same for you and Teresa."

Chavez smiled wanly, laid a hand over Arguello's heart, and prayed.

Samuel inclined back on his elbows as the raft drifted down the sunlit river. A harlequin green Jesus lizard broke from the reeds. Samuel watched its webbed feet beat the murky surface of the river furiously as it sped across, walking on water. He tracked its progress with widening eyes. If he was a superstitious man, he might have considered that to be a sign that God didn't mind if they raised John as a Catholic so long as they raised him with strong Christian values.

Filipe stirred on the far side of the raft and stretched. "How long have we been on this hellish river? The bugs are eating me alive. Will we reach the San Juan soon?"

Samuel pulled out his pocket watch and tapped it to shake the condensation from the glass. "One twenty. We've been floating for six hours already."

The sound of axes cracked the air. As the men sat up and looked around, timber creaked and two trees fell toward the river.

Samuel flinched. "Another earthquake?"

A tree crashed down upon one raft ahead, and the Costa Ricans on board screamed as it exploded into kindling. Men and supplies spilled into the water. Immediately, tongues of flame flickered in the undergrowth along the river and rifles barked.

Axes thumped again, preceding more creaking and groaning. Samuel flinched, but it was too late. Another tree toppled with a tremendous *splash*, capsizing the raft just ahead of them.

An ambush.

Rubio grunted, clutched his bleeding neck, and toppled off the raft.

The raft rocked as two men reached over the side for Rubio, but the murky water closed over him, leaving only a red stain. Samuel lifted his rifle and scanned the jungle, but there was no sign of the enemy. Bullets thumped into the raft like the woodpecker drilling its holes by the riverbank. There were a hundred enemy rifles out there.

He grabbed the rough plank he was using for a paddle. "Head for the left bank. Go, go! Paddle for your lives." He frantically beckoned Sergeant Zamora in the last raft. "Left bank, follow us."

The water churned as they paddled while men screamed in

the river. He could do nothing for them until he was on the bank.

"Help!" Rubio had surfaced and was thrashing in the turbulence. "Can't swim . . . *Ayuda me*!"

"I'll get him." Padraig blessed himself and put his Colt on the bamboo deck.

"No! Stay—"

The raft dipped as Padraig dived into the water.

Damn it. There were crocodiles in the river.

More rifles flashed in the trees, and splinters flew from the raft. Miraculously, the bullets struck nobody on Samuel's raft. He didn't dare check the others behind. Instead, he paddled harder, ignoring the pain as the rough edges of the makeshift paddle cut into his hands. The raft sank into the muddy embankment and tilted precariously as men scrambled off. Fifteen feet away, Padraig was drawing closer to Rubio, but Rubio let out one more cry and sank under the rolling water.

A bullet shattered a bamboo crosspiece as Samuel stuffed Padraig's Colt into his belt and twisted away. The men in the water were sitting ducks. He slung his Sharps rifle over his shoulder and reached for the unconscious Arguello. "Chavez, help me get him ashore. Sanchez, secure the raft. We can't lose the supplies. Filipe, stay here."

Chavez took most of Arguello's weight as they dragged him onto the muddy bank, and Samuel's feet promptly sank into the mud. He unslung his rifle and cocked it. "Into the trees, boys. We'll flank them."

He plunged into the undergrowth. Branches scratched and tore at him as he squeezed through. The faint odor of gun smoke mingled with the musk of greenery and animal scat, and he glimpsed muzzle flashes ahead that could only be Walker's filibusters. Leaves rustled as some Euronicas fanned out beside him, nearly invisible in their muddied shirts. The undergrowth closed in on him, vicious with thorns, but he plowed ahead. The

Euronicas were experts in this environment and could fire and reload as fast as any British regiment.

"Ready." He aimed at a patch of black. "*Fuego!*"

Twenty rifles blazed a ragged volley, and leaves shivered as slugs lashed the brush. Several enemies cried out ahead, and energy surged from Samuel's chest. They'd hurt the bastards.

He slung his rifle, palmed his Colt, and aimed where the leaves flickered ahead. He tightened his trigger finger. "Ready. Fire!"

Another crash of rifles. Bullets whistled through the trees, and men cursed or cried out in pain. Branches whipped, and undergrowth shivered. Samuel cocked and fired, again and again, drawing courage from the kick of the Colt against his wrist and the zing of sulfur piquing his nose.

The hammer fell with a mechanical click. Empty. He holstered the hot revolver and drew Padraig's.

"They're behind us," an American bellowed ahead.

More shouts issued from where the undergrowth swished and moved. Samuel's heart drummed. The enemy was retreating from the Euronicas' heavy pressure, his men were firing as rapidly as they could reload.

He aimed at a wisp of dark cloth. "They're on the run. Keep shooting."

Shots rang out in a ragged rhythm all around them. The undergrowth shivered ahead, and men screamed.

Samuel's veins pulsed. The filibusters were indeed falling back. "Prepare to advance . . .are you with me? Ready . . . Now. Push them hard." He hurled himself through the brush.

Their jungle training paid off. He and his men slid through the trees like green wraiths. Wild eyes dancing, a jowly face materialized from behind a tree and a rifle blazed. The breeze of the bullet tickled Samuel's cheek, and he shot the man in the face. Smoke puffed from the barrel of his Colt, and the man crashed back into brushwood.

A flash of blue in the green vegetation. Samuel snapped off a shot. Someone yelped, and the shadow disappeared within the curtain of lush vegetation.

Gunshots and shouts echoed through the forest, and wounded men shrieked in the trees. It was too confusing out there; they could shoot their own as easily as the enemy. Samuel pulled out the whistle hanging from his neck and blew a long blast. "Regroup! Back to the river."

Someone clattered through the undergrowth nearby, and Roy Perez emerged from the broad-leafed umbrella leaves, his shirt ripped, his pimples raw and bleeding. "*Capitán*?"

"Fall back to the river. Pass the word." Samuel's damp hair fell into his eyes, and he pawed it away.

"But *Capitán*, the *yanquis* are running from us."

He didn't know where the Americans were, and there were far too many of them. Samuel swept his arm in the air. "Fall back *now*!"

Perez's face blanked, and he darted back toward the river.

"Chavez, Lopez," Samuel shouted. "Pass it on. Fall back to the river. *Al río*." He blew his whistle again. It vibrated between his lips, and the blast pierced the jungle.

Where was Padraig? He should have caught up by now. The mesh of brambles and tangled trees grew so thick Samuel couldn't pass. He backtracked and found another path, spurred by the blood-chilling screams from the river. Behind him, the gunfire dwindled, but the sound of crackling branches and leaves followed him—his men.

The ground softened underfoot. The river was close. He pumped his legs and pushed through the tangled foliage. A thorn ripped into his forehead just above his eye. Through the undergrowth, sunlight sparkled on water. The river—almost there.

He sloshed onto the riverbank and slumped to his knees, coughing and spluttering.

Crocodiles reared and whirled in the river, churning the

bloodstained brown water. Ten feet from the bank, a fifteen-foot crocodile spun on its axis, shaking a soldier in its jaws like a terrier rattles a rat. It dragged the body under the scummy water. Another crocodile sprawled dead beside Juan Delgado, who knelt in a puddle of blood alongside Rubio. Only a thread of tendon held the bloody bone and gristle that had been Rubio's right leg to his body.

Samuel staggered over to Delgado, trying not to look at Rubio. He'd never seen such a cruel wound. "Where's the lieutenant?"

Delgado's bloodshot eyes were glazed over, and his mouth moved, but no words came out.

Samuel lowered his eyes. So many dead and dying. *Dear God, don't let Padraig be one of the torn bodies floating downriver*.

He shook Delgado gently. "Where is he?"

"They're dead."

"God damn you, man. Where's Lieutenant Kerr?" He was shaking Delgado hard now, rattling him senseless, and he couldn't stop. He could smell the blood, the shit, and the fear.

"*Muerto*. They're all dead." Delgado's thin frame heaved, and he puked green, slickened chunks on the trampled reeds.

Samuel dropped Delgado's shirt and whirled about. "He can't be dead. He can't be dead. He's a swimmer, a swimmer."

He splashed into the river, searching the silty water, and faltered. Padraig wasn't here. He wheeled and dashed past Delgado, pounding along the bank upstream.

Crocodiles glided through the water, snaking from side to side as they crisscrossed the river. More gunshots boomed in the jungle, and men shouted. Bodies trapped in drowned branches bobbed in the river, painting the water red. Filipe! Filipe was missing also. His head reeled and he staggered back a step. He'd told Filipe to wait by the river. He clawed at the tree roots on the muddy bank and pulled himself from the water, his breath shallow and raspy.

There was no sign of Filipe. Samuel scanned the undergrowth

in the forest, The young fool must have followed him when he charged. His chest caved. Filipe too? Gone? Lost in the forest, dead, or captured. *Dear God, no.*

There was nothing he could do for Filipe now, and nothing he could do for Padraig anymore. He must save the rest of his men, and then he'd search for the boy.

"*Capitán, Capitán!*" Rough hands spun him around. Chavez's eyes were bulging, and his voice was shaky. "*Capitán*, the enemy has gone. What do you want us to do now?"

He panted through parched lips. "Where's Padraig? *Teniente* Kerr?"

Chavez gripped his rifle so tight his knuckles were white. "I don't know—but the men, *señor*. What shall we do?"

With Padraig gone, he was all they had left. He looked around, willing himself to calm down, clenching and unclenching his hands. Perez and Florez slouched behind Chavez, their faces ashen. David Rivera had survived, too; he slumped with an arm around Delgado by the water's edge. "They're all who survived?"

Chavez deflated with a nod.

"*Colonel Brailier? Capitán Blanco?*"

"Dead," Chavez said. "Or they floated on without us."

"Take Rivera and Perez and stand guard at the edge of the jungle." Samuel waved his hand. "The rest of you, help me search downstream. Where's Arguello? I dropped him on the bank by the river."

"I'm sorry, *Capitán*, he's gone." Chavez looked down at his battered boots.

The crocodiles must have got poor Arguello. It was a complete disaster. "All right. Spread out to the forest's edge and keep watch. A few of you can follow me. I'll continue to search for *Teniente* Kerr."

Fifty yards upstream, Samuel spotted Padraig's gray hat dangling on the limb of a gnarled tree stretching into the river.

That was it; Padraig was gone. He'd never hear his clownish

jokes or ride stirrup to stirrup with him again. He should never have dragged his loyal friend to this hell. He'd caused Padraig's death as surely as he'd left Father to die. A bundle of black and red feathers floated by, twisting on the bloodied river, and Samuel glimpsed the yellow beak. Rubio's toucan was dead too.

Dazed, he plodded through the mud toward the water's edge, his eyes fixed on the hat. And Filipe—

"That's far enough, partner." The drawl from the undergrowth made Samuel freeze. "Twenty rifles covering you. Hands above your head, or you're all dead. Tell your greasers. We've taken your sentries already. Don't go expecting them to save you."

Samuel saw nothing out of place in the forest. The enemy could be anywhere, and he couldn't fight what he couldn't see. His will to fight seeped into the mire, and he lifted his hands, squinting into the forest. "Boys, don't fight them. Lay down your rifles." He unslung his Sharps and placed it on the ground.

"Waist guns too," the disembodied voice commanded. "Then bunch up with the greasers."

Samuel unbuckled his belt, laid it with both Colts on the ground, and plodded back to Jimenez.

A dozen unkempt Americans stepped from the jungle with rifles raised, eyes shadowed beneath wide-brimmed hats. By the state of their tattered clothing, they'd been living rough for a long time.

A stocky man in a faded black shirt spat in the mud and grinned. "Now look here what the river's drug up. Looks like them crocs ain't getting no more supper."

"Let me go, you peasant, or I'll cut your throat the next time." Filipe squirmed between two filibusters as they dragged him from the undergrowth. One man had a bloody slash across his face.

Samuel gasped and covered his mouth with his hand. Filipe! Thank God, at least he was alive.

"Little bastard cut me," the wounded man growled. "Shot Brixton dead back in the jungle too. Let me kill him, Absum."

"Damn your hide," the stocky man said. "Serves you right if you can't fend off a child. I need all the healthy bodies I can muster. Put him with the others."

CHAPTER NINETEEN

"They tell me you like gold, Kingston." The stocky man's chin disappeared into his rolls of fat as he looked down at Samuel. "Stole all Walker's gold, didn't you? Well, now you can dig him some more."

Samuel's limbs tingled with fatigue where he sat in a trampled clearing surrounded by bamboo-walled shanties. His shoulders ached as he draped his hands around his knees. It seemed like they had marched forever through the jungle, but it was probably only half an hour. Just before the attack, Quintero had estimated they were five hours from the confluence of the San Carlos and San Juan rivers.

Filipe was alive, thank God, but only Chavez, Perez, Rivera, and Florez survived from the Euronicas. Of the twenty-five he'd led into the jungle, they alone remained. His head pounded, and tears blurred his vision. He'd led them to their deaths. And Padraig . . . He shook his head to clear the white spots dancing before his eyes.

". . . it. No, Absum, you can't use him," said another American. So the man who'd captured them was called Absum. "Dawson said Fry wants Kingston dead."

Absum's thin lips curled back. "Forget it, McCann. Look at

the shoulders on him. I'll be damned if I'm shooting that work-horse. Useless natives don't last longer than a candle down in the mine. Now Kingston here . . . I reckon he'll dig a pile of gold before he keels over. Walker won't know the difference." He gestured to the three guards standing in the shade with rifles trained on Samuel and his men. "Put them in the pit."

A thin man with a tangled red beard prodded Samuel with his rifle. "On yer feet."

Samuel's chest twinged as he rose and moved toward Filipe. He'd dragged Filipe into this mess, too. He moved closer and murmured quietly. "Don't worry, Filipe. You and your sister are both strong. She'll make it, and so will you."

A bark of laughter erupted in his ear as a hand spun him around, and he recoiled from Absum's rancid breath. "Were you lookin' fer your piece of greaser ass?"

"What?" Samuel twisted the chains in his hands. "Do you mean my wife?"

Absum chuckled nastily and shoved him ahead. "Wife, whore —who gives a damn?"

"Here? Sofia is here?"

"Fry has her in El Castillo, deep in the dungeon." Absum grinned. "When the garrison tires of playing with her, he'll throw her and yer pup to the crocs."

Samuel's stomach turned to stone. Absum was bluffing—but no, he clearly knew about John, too. His head sank. Christ! They had her. One guard hit him with the butt of a rifle, driving him forward. He barely registered the pain, and his moan was for Sofia and John.

Absum kicked him. "Keep moving, or I'll throw you in the hole and save you the bother of climbing down."

Samuel's feet dragged as the guards herded them between bamboo-walled shacks. The spice of wood smoke and burning meat drifted across the compound, and two native women laboring over a cooking fire flicked him hooded glances. They passed an open shed where two cadavers in loincloths were cutting a log with a pit saw; their blotchy skin was stretched over prominent ribs like a hide on a drum. Slaves.

Samuel staggered ahead in a daze. He never should have come on this expedition. He should have run from Mora's men and tried crossing the frontier. His head ached as he reviewed the map he'd burned in his memory. Five . . . fifteen miles to the San Juan river junction, and less than forty upriver to the fort at El Castillo where Sofia and John were prisoners. They were so close, but they might as well be a thousand miles away now that he was going deep underground in this hole that Absum called a gold mine. Tears welled behind his eyelids. They languished in the same dank fortress that had imprisoned Padraig a year ago. Even if he escaped from the mine, he'd never capture that stone fortress. Not without an army.

"Turn here," the man with the red beard growled.

The path led through the waning light in the forest to a clearing, where a crude timber tripod rested beside a hole some four feet wide. A rope tied to the harness of a donkey dangled into the pit. The odor of paraffin pushed back the peaty forest scents.

Absum lit a torch from the barrel beside the tripod and dropped it down the hole. "Home sweet home. You're going to love it here. Down the ladder."

"I can't." Filipe's plea was a high-pitched squeak as he cringed from the black maw. "Please."

"You can climb down or I'll throw you down, boy." Absum kicked Filipe in the leg. "Move it, greaser."

Samuel pulled Filipe back. "It'll be all right. I'll go first."

He stooped and gripped the ladder, seeing nothing but the torch flickering far below. The ladder swayed and bowed as he climbed down, and an abysmal stench floated up to greet him.

He couldn't name it: rotten flesh, but a living rot, hovering in the stale air.

His boot sank into mud at the bottom, and someone clawed his arm.

His heart jolted, and he yelped, lashing out at the beast attacking him, hitting bone. "Uff!"

The body flew back, light as a feather, and hit the earthen wall. A woman's small scream made his skin crawl. A woman. What had he done?

"*Perdón, Perdón, lo siento*." The woman struggled to her feet. "I didn't mean to frighten you. We're prisoners, too—slaves more like it." Her Spanish sounded cultured.

In the miserly torchlight, the white orbs of a dozen pairs of eyes winked in the darkness like moths in a tomb. The heavy air reeked of earth, body odor, and human waste, making Samuel's eyes water. The ladder trembled beside him; someone else was descending. His eyes darted to the gray opening far above. Christ, he was dizzy. He squeezed his eyes shut and tried to slow his heaving breath.

". . . from?" The woman spoke in accented English.

He focused on her through the gloom. A filthy smock reaching below her knees covered her emaciated body, clinging to her like a second skin. Her face was so grimy, he couldn't guess her age.

Mud squelched as someone stepped off the ladder with a whimper: Filipe. Samuel drew the quaking boy close, but he had no words to console him.

"I can't stand it here . . . We'll die." Filipe lunged for the ladder.

Samuel held him back. "They'll shoot you. Take a deep breath and let it out slowly." He turned back to the woman. "How many of you are down here?"

"Eleven. There used to be more, but they're all dead now. Where did you come from? You're a *yanqui*."

Another slim figure descended into the parsimonious light of the torch—Perez, by the shape of him. The slaves muttered and shuffled back to make room as more Euronicas stepped off the ladder. Chavez was the last to climb down, the rungs creaking under his weight.

The woman gasped and lunged past Samuel. "Emanuel! Holy Mary, Mother of God . . . Emanuel, is that you?" She asked in Spanish.

"*Teresa!*" Chavez cried. "*Teresa, mi querida Teresa.*"

Samuel's head snapped back. Teresa? That name . . .

Chavez wrapped his arms around her with a small moan. "It's you, truly you."

This must be Chavez's nun. Samuel stared at her in the faint light. She was emaciated, not much shorter than Chavez, who was less than average in height.

"I thought you were dead." She clung to him. "I heard you died in the war."

At that moment, the torch spluttered out, and darkness blanketed them like a shroud. Only the faintest hint of starlight seeped down from the opening above.

A shadow folded over the circle of light, and Absum cackled. "Sleep well. Your new friends will show you the tools in the morning. Remember: no gold, no food."

The ladder shook and slid upward, showering them with clay. Another burst of laughter, the faint scraping of boots, and they were alone in the malodorous hell.

"Come with me." Teresa brushed past Samuel, drawing the bulk of Chavez after her. "We'll have more privacy back here."

"It's her, *Capitán*." Chavez trembled with elation as he squeezed past Samuel. "It's Teresa."

Then they were lost in the darkness.

Filipe shifted beside Samuel. "We're going to die down here. I can't stand it."

A sudden heaviness inside pulled Samuel down, and he closed his eyes. He didn't even have a false hope for the boy. He slid down the clay wall, folding his knees in front of him as his body sagged. Padraig was dead—most of his men were dead—and Fry held Sofia and baby John, apparently with plans to use her and murder them both.

Samuel slumped forward, draping his hands over his mud-spattered knees. He'd never escape this tomb to rescue them.

They were gone.

Time crawled. Somewhere on the fringe of Samuel's nightmare, prisoners talked urgently in frightened voices, while others groaned and cursed. Sometime later, Filipe sobbed beside him, his shoulders shaking. But amid them all, Samuel was alone. Sofia was gone, John was gone, and Padraig was gone. His head whirled, and he couldn't form a sensible thought. He sat numb, until for the first time in almost two full days, he collapsed into a fitful sleep.

It must have been a restless prisoner moving who woke him. He scrubbed his eyes with grimy hands and prized them open. They were trapped in a mine with no hope of escape, all doomed, already buried, just waiting to die. He flopped his head forward on his folded knees, smelling clay and urine as he grabbed a lock of greasy hair.

"*Capitán,*" came a voice, oddly energized in this pit. "*Es Chavez. Esta es Teresa*. Remember?"

He blinked at Chavez.

"I told you about her."

Samuel didn't know what Chavez wanted him to say.

"You won't believe this, *Capitán*, but she met your father once. In San Juan del Sur."

All sound around him muffled. Father? She knew Father. How could this woman know Father?

"*Como?*" he croaked. "When?"

Slender hands cupped his face, tender despite the calluses and dirt. "You poor man, you've suffered so much." Her voice was soft and kind, almost saintly in the darkness. "*Es verdad.* I met your father, John Kingston."

"John Kingston. Yes, yes, that's him!"

"What a wonderful man."

"But how?"

"When the scandal broke"—she gave a hasty glance at Chavez—"my order moved me to their clinic in San Juan del Sur. *Una noche*, masked strangers broke in, blindfolded me, and took me away to treat a sick man in a distant hacienda." She sighed heavily, and her hands fell from Samuel's face. "I wanted to tell someone, but they threatened to slaughter everyone in the hospital if I talked."

"And this was my *padre*?"

A radiant smile spread across her face. "The man told me his name was John Kingston. I'll never forget his kind eyes. He was a perfect gentleman."

"Christ, you found him!" Samuel's hands curled inward as reality hit. "You found him, and I failed to. If I'd searched harder, he'd still be alive."

She placed a hand on his shoulder. "It wouldn't have mattered."

Samuel shook his head. "It would've changed everything."

"*No, Señor*. Even then, your father was dying."

Samuel sat upright. "Those bastards. He was an old man, a gentleman. You said so yourself. How could they have—"

"*No, no, Capitán*, it wasn't his captors. You see, his heart was failing. Not even the finest surgeon could have saved him."

"It was cholera." He dropped his head into his hands. "It's my fault they brought him to Nicaragua, and my fault cholera struck him, and my fault—"

Teresa stroked his face. "It wasn't cholera that killed your father. Your father's heart was weak. There was nothing you could have done. I knew he would die within days, and he knew too. We prayed the rosary together. It comforted him."

"The rosary?" He grasped for understanding. "But Father was a Protestant."

"We talked quite a while. I explained that the Blessed Virgin had always been good to me, and as the Lord's mother, she had his ear." She let out a peaceful sigh. Her breath smelled like sour milk. "I hope it's not my *vanidad*, but I believe our prayers put him at ease."

"At ease," he repeated.

He hadn't failed Father; it was his heart. He would've died even if he'd been at home. There was nothing Samuel could have done.

Samuel rubbed his moistening eyes. Greenfell had lied when he said Father died of cholera. It was just like Greenfell to drive in such a barb. Samuel remembered bringing his saber down on Greenfell's head, the fountain of blood that sprayed from his forehead before the last Earl of Baltimore collapsed at his feet.

May he rot in hell.

She squeezed his shoulder. "He was enormously proud of you, you know."

Goose bumps prickled down his back.

"He was certain you were out there searching," she said. "That gave him comfort, knowing you cared enough to hunt for him. I'm glad to see he was right."

Despite being trapped in the bowels of the earth, a weight tumbled from Samuel's shoulders. He hadn't failed Father, and he wouldn't fail Filipe and his men.

He took Teresa's bony hand in both of his. "Thank you, Sister. You'll never know how much this means to me."

"I'm not a sister anymore, not after—" She bit her lip and threw Chavez a wry smile. "Well, I'm just a humble servant now."

Samuel smiled too. "Now tell me about this place and how you got here."

"*Mala suerte*, I suppose," Teresa answered in a monotone voice. "Or the good Lord punishing my sins."

"Never that." Chavez took her hand from Samuel and smiled.

She returned Chavez's tender gaze in the weak starlight trickling down. "Grief overcame me after I lost Emanuel. Eventually, I found the self-righteous scorn of my peers intolerable and left the order. But I still wanted to serve those less fortunate than myself, so I joined a Protestant missionary society in New York. They financed my mission to help the indigenous people here in the rainforests."

"Even as I searched for you," Chavez murmured.

"These deserters swept me up when they kidnapped my flock as slaves for this gold mine."

Samuel lifted his head. "And when was that?"

"Some two months ago, *creo*," she said. "There were thirty-one of us back then. Now, we're only nine."

Samuel replied in a steady voice. "I'm going to get us out of here, I promise. Help me understand the challenges. What's further back along this tunnel? Where does it lead?"

"A maze of digs in several directions," she said. "We only follow the one we're digging, and we use a ball of string to guide us back."

"How do you see?" Samuel asked. "Candles? Why don't you light them now?"

"They only supply enough for our fourteen-hour work shifts," Tereasa said.

Samuel gasped. "Fourteen hours."

She chuckled. "*Exactamente*. And the days we fail to send up enough ore, we go hungry."

He frowned. Every passing day would weaken them further. "What about the ladder? How—"

Rifles barked on the surface, and men yelled. The prisoners squirmed as the sounds of fighting filtered down to their pit. The skirmish was over within minutes, and a deafening silence filled the mine, as if the prison held its breath.

Boots thumped dully overhead. Their captors were returning.

CHAPTER TWENTY

Samuel's stomach knotted as he peered up at the circle of starlight. A shadow blocked the night sky.

"Samuel," called a familiar voice. "You down there?"

Padraig!

Samuel raised both arms in exultation. "I'm here! My God, Padraig, I thought you were dead."

A snort. "You know what Mam always says . . ."

"'You can't kill a bad weed,'" Samuel finished along with him.

Padraig's laugh energized him. Samuel grinned at the others gathering around him beneath the opening.

"Shift your arse," Padraig said. "I'm lowering the ladder."

"There are about a dozen other prisoners here," Samuel said. "I'm sending up the weakest first."

He backed against the press of jostling bodies. Everyone was talking at once, some laughing, others crying. "Patience, and we'll get you out. Send the feeblest forward first."

Clay and pebbles rained on their heads as the ladder slid down, and the prisoners flinched as they waited breathlessly for it to land. Samuel was beaming. Padraig had survived in the river—and some others, too, it seemed.

He shot a conspiratorial grin at Teresa and Chavez beside him. *Thank you Blessed Virgin, indeed.*

The ladder plonked into the mud as he set the legs, fighting the urge to scramble up first. He couldn't wait to hear what had happened, how Padraig had come through again.

Samuel could feel the bones beneath their skin as the prisoners brushed past him. Time dragged as each one inched unsteadily up the ladder. He sent Filipe up next, and then his men. When it came his turn, he wanted to spider up like a sailor in the rigging—he was bursting to discover what had happened—but his weary body was incapable. It took ages to slog to the top.

The scent of vegetation, fruit, and wood smoke invigorated him after the stench below. He grabbed Padraig's hand as he breached the hole, and Padraig hefted him into a sweaty embrace. A mob of Euronicas crowded in, patting his back and shoulders.

"Back off, boys, give him room to breathe." Despite his words, Padraig squeezed him even tighter before releasing him. "Thank God. We couldn't get here sooner because we had to clean the weapons and round up the rafts and supplies."

Samuel scanned the dark, smiling faces around him. "How many of you made it?"

Padraig's smile disappeared. "We lost Arguello, Rubio, and Vargas." He examined the men who had climbed from the hole, ticking off their names. "Chavez, Delgado, Perez, Rivera, and Florez . . . Welcome back, boys. The rest are with me."

"Only three gone, then," Samuel said.

Padraig frowned. "May they rest in peace. I left Rubio on the riverbank to join the skirmish, and a crocodile ripped his leg off. I should have—"

Samuel knew better than to take this road. "No, you had to fight. It was your duty. The rest are all here?"

Padraig nodded. "Poor Arguello. We couldn't find him, but the unlucky bugger was dead anyway from that snake bite."

"A crocodile must have dragged him into the river too. Poor fellow was unconscious, defenseless." Samuel took an unsteady step forward. "I thought we'd lost all of them. The damned crocodiles were tearing men apart in the river."

"Those were the Costa Rican troops." Padraig passed Samuel a canteen. "The enemy capsized four of their rafts by dropping trees, and the crocodiles tore the men to pieces."

"Where are the Costa Ricans now? And Colonel Brailier?" Samuel gulped the water down. It was warm and tasted like metal.

"No sign. I think those who survived carried on downriver."

Samuel looked at the trail toward the shacks and sawmill. "We should go back to the camp. I want to find my weapons."

Padraig lowered his head. "I lost my Colt."

"With any luck, it's in the camp. I took it off the raft."

"Ace. So what happens now? This changes everything. The swine knew we were coming. Someone must've tipped them off."

Samuel pushed back a clump of filthy hair and regarded the night sky. "This place is as corrupt with traitors as Ireland. It has to be one of the Costa Ricans. I trust our men."

"Well, if it is, the Costas have abandoned us now, spy and all." Padraig snapped up the lever on his rifle and reached into his cartridge box for a cap. He did it unconsciously, the action as natural as breathing. "Unless the spy was among those who fell in the river; then he's crocodile food."

"We'll continue upriver and find the Costa Ricans. The attack must go on." Samuel halted and caught Padraig's elbow. "Fry has Sofia and John."

"*What*? How do you know?"

"Deserters from Walker's army took over the mine," Samuel said. "Their leader told me Fry has Sofia and John locked up at El Castillo, where the *Legitimistas* held you last year."

Padraig's mouth hung slack as he absorbed the news.

Samuel hurried onward. "Make haste; Fry intends to harm them. We must rescue them as soon as possible, and for that we need the Costa Ricans. We're too few to capture that fortress on our own."

"Jaysus, Mary, and Joseph. Even with them, we're too few." Padraig hurried after him.

A handful of deserters sat cross-legged in the clearing with their hands on their heads, under the guns of Jimenez and three Euronicas.

Padraig pointed at the deserters. "How do you know these bastards are deserters?"

"Remember Chavez's nun, Teresa?" Samuel said. "She told me."

"Where under the heavens did—"

"Jimenez, take some men and find our *armas*." Samuel pointed to the bamboo huts. "Check in there."

Padraig grabbed his hand. "This Teresa. What do you—"

Samuel motioned behind them at the slaves clustered around Chavez. "She's there with Chavez. We don't have time for this now. I'll tell you the entire story once we're on the river."

Padraig waved and grinned at Chavez over the heads of the others. Chavez beamed in return.

"How many rafts did you find?" Samuel stopped at a bucket and splashed water on his face. "Do we still have supplies? Ammunition?"

"Damn it, I'm always the last to know." Padraig hailed Sergeant Zamora. "Sergeant, how many rafts did you find?"

Zamora trotted across. "Three, sir."

Twenty-four Euronicas, Padraig, Filipe, himself, and the slaves. That made thirty-six. "Not enough. We need four rafts."

"What do you mean?" Zamora asked. "Three are plenty."

Jimenez strode from a shack with an armful of rifles.

Samuel gratefully accepted his Colt and gun belt. "Thanks. We're taking Teresa and her people, too. We can't leave them here. Padraig, there's your Colt. Zamora, there's plenty of timber in the sawmill. Take some to the river and build another raft. The people here can help you. Have the slaves bathe in the river afterward. Poor things could use a bath. And load the deserters' weapons and ammunition on the rafts too."

"*Si, Capitán.*"

"What exactly is the plan?" Padraig picked up a wide-brimmed felt hat lying beside the body of a deserter. "If Walker's men already knew we were on the river, they'll be waiting for us, and there'll be hell to pay when we reach the forts." He beat the hat against his thigh and placed it on his head. "Fits well enough."

"As far as Fry knows, we're dead." Samuel spun the Colt's chamber. "If we find the Costa Ricans and hurry, we may reach the fort before news of the deserters' defeat here reaches Fry. The ones who escaped into the jungle are on foot. It will take them forever to reach the San Carlos River."

"What about them?"

"We'll take their boots and leave them here unarmed. They'll be too scared to leave the compound."

"It's a win for the Euronicas too." Padraig grinned. "Soon all of them will have boots."

Samuel tapped his finger on the stock of his rifle as the raft swept past walls of reeds, bamboo, and trees stretching for the kiss of the blazing sun. The journey was taking too long, even paddling in shifts. They had to link up with the Costa Ricans before the defenders at El Castillo got word that Samuel had survived the ambush and returned to finish them or, worse, harmed Sofia and John.

He tugged at his shirt and scratched the mosquito bites on his chest. He only had twenty-six fighting men, including Padraig and himself, and his plan would fail without the Costa Ricans. Two thousand British soldiers and blue jackets had failed to capture the fortress at El Castillo a hundred years earlier, even when Horatio Nelson bombarded it with naval artillery—and that was when Nelson still had two arms and two eyes.

Samuel sighed. “El Castillo will be a hard nut to crack.”

“You’re thinking about that too?” Padraig reeled in the twine fishing line trailing the raft. He’d scrounged a hook from Quintero and was determined to catch a fish. “What if we attack from the land side? From the north?”

“We’d have to cross a ravine and charge up that steep hill, under fire all the way.” Samuel spread a cigarette paper on his thigh. “No, a frontal assault is impossible. But perhaps I could sneak over the wall at night, as I did when I rescued you. I could open the gate and let our men in.”

Padraig set another worm on his hook and cast. “I wonder how many men Fry has there? There were around forty Legitimists when I was a prisoner, but Fry could have doubled the garrison.”

“Unless General Cañas’s attack on the Transit Road forced Walker to pull reinforcements back to Granada.” Samuel licked the cigarette paper, sealed the crumpled cigarette, and watched the rafts drifting behind them in the leaf-dappled sunlight. It was another blistering day, and the jungle panted, desperate for a drink of rain. He grimaced. Whatever the odds, he was breaking into that fort to save his family. “Sorry I was snappy back there.”

Padraig shrugged.

“You asked about the deserters,” Samuel said.

“Aye.”

“Apparently, they were Mounted Rangers who deserted Walker, seized the gold mine, and raided the local villages for slaves to dig out the ore.” Samuel passed the cigarette to Padraig and began to roll another. “The twist is that they’re still loyal to Walker.”

“What?”

“They’re sending the gold back to him to fund his war.”

“So Walker brought in slavery.” A flat brown fish splashed in the water twenty feet from the raft, and Padraig reeled his line around the stick in his hand. "There you are, my beauty. Step over this way and take this juicy worm from Uncle Padraig."

"I guess so." Samuel lit his cigarette; the smoke eased his tension. "I'm sure he doesn't want the world to know about it though, not unless he wants to curry favor from the southern United States."

Padraig chuckled. "I'm sure Teresa will tell the world when we get her out of here."

Samuel nodded. "Remarkable lady."

Padraig grinned. "I have to hand it to Chavez. If—"

Padraig's hand jerked, and his eyes lit up. "Got one, and it's a monster."

Samuel smiled. He was such a clown.

Padraig whirled his wrist, winding in the twine as fast as he could. A shadow flashed in the brown water, and the fish broke the surface, gamely fighting the hook. It looked like a brown trout from back home.

Elongated jaws with jagged yellow teeth flashed from the depths, opened with a throaty snarl, and snatched the fish and hook away.

Padraig yelped and jerked back. "Jaysus, a bloody crocodile, and the bastard nearly took my hand clean off. Did you see the size of it? It was fifteen feet long."

Samuel exchanged a knowing look with Filipe and chuckled. "More like three feet. A baby, nothing more."

"You're blind." Padraig stared into the water. "It was a bloody monster."

Filipe grinned. "That was a caiman. They're much smaller than *cocodrilos*, though they can grow up to eight feet."

"Eight feet? Well, this monster was an exception." Padraig gesticulated at Filipe. "And who do you think you are, Charles Darwin? You should pay attention to that revolver, mister. Ram that ball down like a man, not some old lady poking her husband with her finger. Where did you get that, anyway?"

"That fat fellow you killed." Filipe pushed the ball down and rotated the cylinder.

A faint tapping rang in the distance downriver.

Samuel held up his hand for silence and tilted his head to favor his good ear. He looked at the others—nothing. He might have imagined it. But then it began again.

"Did you hear that?" he cried. "Stop paddling, men."

The splashing petered out, and when those on the following rafts also stopped paddling, the only sounds were the chuckle of the raft on the water, the whir of insects, and birdcalls from the jungle.

The distinct rapping of shovels or picks striking earth drifted from the river bend. Somebody shouted in the distance, and Samuel's hand flew to his rifle. That couldn't be the Costa Ricans making such racket; they should be advancing against the river forts, if they were still alive.

He gestured to the riverbank. "Take us ashore."

Once they had secured the rafts, Padraig and Jimenez joined him in the reeds and bamboos by the water's edge. The warm breeze tickled the sweat streaming down his torso, and Samuel's skin prickled. This could be another trap. He blinked his gritty eyes and fought the fatigue stiffening his limbs and dulling his senses. An ambush made no sense; the filibusters didn't know they were back on the river.

The only way to find out was to go and see.

Beyond the sweeping bend where the San Carlos eddied into the wide San Juan, a crowd of men in green shirts were piling earth on a cleared knoll at the junction of the rivers.

"Well, I'll be damned . . . the Costas. Come on." Samuel loped ahead, kicking up red clay and splashing through deep puddles.

"What are they doing?" Padraig gasped as he hurried after him.

"Don't know. But we'll find out." Samuel jumped over a fallen tree.

There were no sentries out, and the Costa Ricans were so engrossed in their construction that nobody noticed them until Samuel was just yards from the lean-to shelter where Colonel Brailier lounged in the shade. Samuel squinted at the refuge and snorted. Far more elaborate than his last one; Brailier liked his comfort.

The fat commander struggled to his feet. "Kingston! How the devil did you get here?" His dress uniform was ripped, and the three remaining brass buttons were tarnished.

Samuel offered a fake smile. "It wasn't easy. Especially when you disappeared downriver in the middle of the ambush."

Brailier glanced toward the trench where Captain Blanco and Sylvanus Spencer were scurrying out with their sleeves rolled up. "We'd no choice. There were too many of them. The current was too strong, and we couldn't paddle back."

True, they couldn't have paddled back. But they could have pulled off the river and marched back. Still, Samuel didn't want a confrontation with the colonel, not when he needed his men. He gestured to the earthworks. "Why build a fort? I thought you'd have moved upriver against El Castillo."

Captain Blanco arrived, breathless, and extended a grubby hand. "*Capitán* Kingston. Thank God you're alive. I was worried about you." At least he seemed pleased to see Samuel.

"Likewise, *Capitán*." Samuel shook hands and nodded at the construction site. "What's going on here?"

Blanco slanted away from Samuel. "Well, we . . . we . . ."

"We're building a defensive position." Brailier crossed his arms. "We couldn't take that fort with less than one hundred men, so I sent ten men back to San José for reinforcements. We're digging in here should the enemy come back."

"Oh, they'll be back, all right." Samuel snorted and pointed to the San Juan River sweeping past the construction. "And the cannons on their steamers will turn your toy fort into a sand pile. We must press on and attack while we still have surprise on our side."

"We no longer have the men to assault the fort." Brailier clutched his ridiculous cocked hat to his chest like a shield.

"Yes, yes," Samuel continued with annoyance. "Not a frontal assault. I'll climb the walls and open the gate for you."

"*Absurdo*."

"All you need do is march in and—"

"We won't be part of such nonsense."

Heat flooded Samuel's face. "We can't sit here and do nothing. That's tantamount to—"

"How dare you, Kingston? I command this expedition. You're nothing but a gun for hire." Brailier thrust out his chest. "I lost forty men back on that cursed river, shot by those cowardly filibusters and ripped asunder by *cocodrilos*. We're staying here, and I won't hear another word on the matter."

Blanco shoved his hands into his pockets and stared north at the San Juan sweeping past the point.

Samuel clasped his wrists behind his back. He should have expected nothing else from this swaggerer. "You, *señor*, are no leader. Men like you are the reason Walker will rule Central America: pompous, wealthy men playing at war. You're not a soldier, you're a coffee farmer, and if you don't find the courage to fight today, Walker will attack Costa Rica again and—"

"*Capitán* Blanco, arrest this man for insubordination." Brailier's hand flew to the pistol in his belt.

Blanco flinched and stared from Brailier to Samuel.

"Fat chance of that," Samuel said with a sneer. "I'm going into El Castillo, with or without you. My family is imprisoned there, and nobody can stop me from saving them. If you won't help, you and your ragtag army had best get out of the way."

Blanco glanced around uneasily, reluctant to intervene—perhaps because the Euronicas had fanned out behind Samuel, grim-faced, porting their rifles. "Are you certain we still have that option? Do you truly believe we've enough men?"

Samuel tightened his hands into fists and loosened them. The Costa Ricans' heavy losses made any attack difficult, and perhaps he was letting his fear for Sofia cloud his judgment. He avoided the captain's intent gaze. "It's possible."

Brailier sniffed and brushed the mud on his sleeve. "As I told you . . ."

Was he leading more men into a plan too hastily conceived? Samuel fiddled with the gold signet ring on his finger, remembering Father, and his scalp tingled as he saw things clearly. Father hadn't died last year because of Samuel's bad choices. He'd done everything right, and this was an excellent decision too. He studied the San Juan River. There might be another way —if they went in the opposite direction.

". . . let me command my expedition," Brailier blustered. "And so I—"

"We need not attack the fort at El Castillo." Samuel stepped forward, cutting Brailier off. "We'll go east to Greytown, hijack a riverboat, and use it to sail in under their guns. They'll think it's new volunteers if we fly Walker's flag."

"You dog!" Padraig rubbed his hands together with delight.

"Greytown's a British port." Filipe looked around the circle of men with animation. "Walker has no men there. No authority there."

"And the river steamers are anchored off Punta de Castilla." Padraig continued rubbing his hands together. "Ripe for the plucking."

Samuel thrust out his chin and glared at Brailier. He'd better not get in Samuel's way. "We capture one riverboat and take it brazenly to the fort flying Walker's Nicaraguan flag. They'll welcome us in."

"What about the fort at Hipp's Point?" Spencer dragged a hand through his hair. "It's impossible to pass that fort unseen."

"We storm it." Samuel crossed his arms. "It's a redoubt, little more, and the garrison there can't comprise over thirty or forty men."

Blanco plucked at his pointed beard as he listened.

Spencer nodded. "You're right. It only has mud walls." He pointed to the fort under construction. "Rather like this one."

Samuel squinted at Spencer. Perhaps he'd underestimated him. The man had done his homework.

Brailier sucked his cheeks in. "I'm not risking any more of my men on foolish plots. We'll wait for reinforcements."

That would take two weeks or more—too long. Samuel locked his eyes on Blanco. Blanco had suffered under leaders like Brailier, whose indecision had paralyzed his forces, but Blanco might step up and show he's made of sterner stuff. "*Capitán*? You're not going to let this chance slip away?"

"I think the plan has merit." Blanco moved closer to the colonel. "Colonel, if you'll let me take just fifteen men. With *Capitán* Kingston's Nicaraguans, it should be enough."

Samuel pitched his voice low and even, forcing himself to sound more confident than he felt. "It will be." Come what may, he wasn't turning back. He'd risk everything for Sofia and John.

Brailier twisted a frayed gold rope dangling from his chest and looked away.

"Think of the glory, *señor*," Blanco said. "You'll go down in history as the man who stopped William Walker."

Brailier pressed his lips together before replying. "All right. Fifteen men. I'll need the rest here to protect your rear."

Samuel didn't care how the colonel justified himself. "Thank you, *señor*." He held out his hand. The colonel had better not feel it tremble.

Filipe hooted and bounced from foot to foot as a smile slowly spread across the others' faces.

They were going to war.

CHAPTER TWENTY-ONE

The afternoon heat shimmered around the four rafts drifting silently on the pistachio-green river, and only the footprints of their makeshift oars reassured Samuel that they moved at all. Melodious bird calls, the whirr of insects, and the chatter of white-faced monkeys scolding them from the trees filled the air.

"But Colonel Brailier's afraid of Samuel!" Filipe said earnestly in English. "That's why he agreed to let us go."

Padraig huffed. "No, Filipe, Samuel didn't intimidate Colonel Brailier. What you witnessed back there was Irish diplomacy."

"Irish diplomacy? What's that?"

Padraig puffed out a cloud of cigarette smoke. "Sure, isn't it the ability to tell a man to go to hell in a way that makes him look forward to the trip?"

Filipe squinted at Padraig and shrugged.

"See? Nobody gets your stupid jokes." Samuel grinned as a butterfly floated onto the map spread across his knee, flapped its iridescent blue wings, and drifted over the sun-kissed river. He drew his eyes back to the blue line marking the river on the tattered parchment. Earlier, he'd seen few homesteads along the river, but there were more signs of humanity now, humble shacks nestled in undulating fields hacked from the surrounding rainforest. They were drifting close to the Sarapiquí River junction.

Spencer tapped the map. "Building the fort at Hipp's Point paid off for Walker back in February. Tom Green ambushed General Alfaro's expedition from there."

Padraig swatted at the mosquito feeding on his neck. "Little buggers, they're biting me all over." He glanced at Spencer. "So that's why Walker built the fort—to guard against a Costa Rican sally down the Sarapiquí."

"And they'll see us coming, too," Spencer said.

Samuel reached for his canteen. "It's hard to stay alert in the loneliest place in Costa Rica, day after day in the heat and humidity. But if they are, they'll only be watching the river and the Costa Rican frontier. Not this way."

"You're thinking we'll float right up to it, then?" Spencer squirmed and scratched his arm. "Wretched bugs."

"We can't take that chance. We'll pull in soon and march the rest of the way."

"Not too soon, though." Padraig dunked his blue handkerchief in the water and draped it around his sweating neck. "It'll murder us to slog through the bloody marsh for hours, and I don't want to catch that break bone disease again. Chavez said you catch it easier in the jungle."

"Nobody knows that for sure. It's probably an old wives' tale." Samuel folded the map carefully. It was the only one he had, and it was dissolving. "Another mile, and we'll pull out so I can scout ahead. That way, if my navigation is wrong, I'll be the one hoofing it and not the chaps. I need to count the garrison, anyway."

"I'm coming with you," Padraig said. "You can't have all the fun."

Filipe stirred where he lay sprawled on the other side of the raft. "Me too."

Samuel held his hand up, palm out. "No, you're not; I've no time to babysit you."

The men shifted when the raft bumped into the soft riverbank, and when Cortez leaped ashore with a rope, his boots sank to his ankles in the marshy ooze. "Damnation, my new boots." He was proud of his first boots ever; taken from a dead filibuster back at the gold mine.

Samuel's own boots were finally dry, and he didn't want them wet again. He stretched out his leg as far as possible and found a firmer ground. "Cortez, post guards. Nobody strays from the rafts until we return. Check your weapons—bayonets, too. We may have to charge the enemy."

The blue sky was clear overhead, the sun bright and piercing, and the river threw off sheets of light. Bushes and trees covered the hills like earthbound clouds of juniper, fern, and basil green. Three palm-thatched shacks sprawled along the water's edge among feathering palms, but there was no sign of inhabitants. The redolence of manure and fish hung in the air as Samuel led the way along the ribbon of mud, cradling his Sharps. His grimy britches chafed his thighs with every step he took. It seemed a lifetime since he'd enjoyed a proper bath.

They crested the first hill and dipped into another shallow valley before rising again to see no sign of a fort.

Padraig stuck a hand inside his sweat-soaked shirt and scratched his chest. "Bloody mosquitoes. Bloody heat. What I wouldn't give for a pint of ale, even if there's a Queen's shilling in it."

Samuel ignored him. They had to be close; he'd followed their progress on the map carefully. He approached a cluster of yellow elders crowning the second hill and parted the branches.

There it was. Hipp's Point.

The earthen redoubt commanded the knoll on the Costa Rican side of the river, west of the confluence where the narrower Sarapiquí River flowed into the San Juan. Constructed with dirt excavated from trenches and piled into a steep embankment, the fort was small but solid.

Samuel lifted his battered brass spyglass. Two men wearing

blue tunics with white numbers or letters on the front were eating at a rough-hewn table outside a log building. He couldn't make out the faces shadowed beneath their black felt hats, but the flag with the single star of William Walker's new republic hanging limply from a pole in the center of the compound confirmed they were filibusters.

"Fancy new uniforms," he murmured. "Walker's got a proper army now. No more black-dyed shirts."

Leaves rustled as Padraig changed position beside him. "Only two? There's got to be more."

Samuel swiveled the spyglass from left to right. Clothing hung from a line strung across the compound, and rifles stood in neat stacks around the post. He squinted and counted the weapons as best he could; at that distance, it was like tallying matches. "Forty rifles, give or take."

"We can manage that." Padraig rubbed his hands together. "Sentries?"

Samuel wiped the sweat from his eyes and lifted the spyglass again. The sun was behind him, and there was little chance of a reflection to alert the men below. "Nobody in sight. We've caught them off guard." He smiled in grim satisfaction. About equal numbers, and he had the element of surprise. He snapped the spyglass shut and checked his fogged-up watch. "Four thirteen. Sun sets around six. We'll attack after dark. Bring the men ashore but keep them quiet. I'll stand watch should something change."

Not long after Padraig left, the wind picked up, and while it wasn't very cool, the breeze refreshed him. The filibusters below finished their meal, had a smoke, and disappeared into the shack. Samuel settled down to wait.

A dugout boat drifted around the bend far to the east. Damn it, that could be a problem. He lifted his spyglass. Two fishermen in straw hats paddled slowly against the current, their skin burned to the color of toast by the tropical sun. The San Juan was wide where the Sarapiquí joined it, and as calm as a lake, but the bungo's slow progress attested to the river's relentless push to Greytown on the Caribbean Coast, thirty miles away.

Samuel nibbled his lip. They'd find the river steamers at anchor in Greytown, and once he'd commandeered one, all he had to do was steam back upriver some seventy-five miles, bluff his way into El Castillo, and hope for a miracle.

The bungo crawled up the Nicaraguan side of the river like a water bug on a moss-colored lake. His scalp prickled. They weren't halting at the fort; they seemed to be headed upriver. If they spotted the men and rafts, they might give the game away.

He backed through the elm trees on hands and knees, rose to his feet, and hurried down the hill. By the time he crossed the second hillock and was close to the rafts, he was wheezing for breath.

Blanco and Padraig met him ten yards out.

"What's the matter?" Blanco tugged at his collar.

"Were you spotted?" Padraig asked. "What is it?"

Samuel raised his hand. Jesus, wouldn't they give him a second to catch his breath? "Fishermen. A boat, coming upriver. Conceal the rafts. Cut some branches, bushes, anything to disguise them. We'll hide in the trees. Cortez . . ." He looked around as the men drew machetes and headed for the abundant trees. "Where's Cortez?"

"*Aquí, Capitán.*"

Cortez was a man Samuel could rely on. "Take a soldier east to the top of the second hillock. You'll see the enemy redoubt from there. Hunker down out of sight and watch it. There were no sentries when I left, but send word if anything changes. The rest of us will be along at dusk, and we'll attack after nightfall. Stay off the skyline."

Cortez swung into motion with a quick nod.

Samuel approached the water's edge, rubbing his neck with exhaustion, and peered downriver. The wind was blowing west. The fishermen wouldn't hear the thuds as his men hacked down bushes and branches to disguise the rafts. He gratefully accepted a tortilla and some dried fish from Quintero and hunkered down to eat. The tortilla was as tough as tree bark and the fish was far too fishy but he needed the fuel.

Soon the rafts blended into the riverbank undergrowth, and Samuel relaxed as the men shouldered their supplies and lugged them into the trees.

The *bungo* materialized as the last light seeped from the evening sky, and the fishermen's voices floated up the river. Would they ever hurry? Beside him, the click of a Colt cylinder told him that Padraig was checking his loads. He'd be better off doing something useful like that, too. It was preferable to fretting over things beyond his control.

After many painful minutes, the fishermen passed without incident and disappeared around the next bend.

Samuel smiled at Padraig and checked his watch. "We'll move out in forty-five minutes."

An hour later, Samuel led the attack party uphill, as the sun sank in crimson glory, and stars slowly punctured the sky. There had been no word from Cortez, but that had to be good news. He led half the Euronicas, and Padraig led the remainder. Captain Blanco had split the Costa Ricans between himself and Lieutenant Guzman, a short, taciturn man who'd never spoken a word to Samuel. Each party carried a six-foot ladder made from trees cut down by the river.

A bird called, the sound sweet and tuneful, reminding Samuel of the song thrushes back home in Clonakilty.

Filipe loosened the revolver in its holster for the umpteenth time. "The plan seems too simple. We climb over two walls and attack. Why don't we attack all four sides at once?"

"And slaughter each other in the dark?" Samuel snorted. "Stop fiddling with that revolver. You'll shoot yourself in the foot. Remember, you're only the lookout. I don't want you near the fort until we've captured it."

"Ah, come on, Samuel, I'm not a *niño*. I fought in—"

"I know, I know, you fought in the Battle of Santa Rosa. Well, you're not fighting here. Sofia will kill me if something happens to you."

They reached the tree line, and Cortez beckoned from the undergrowth.

Samuel dropped to his knees and crawled alongside Cortez. "Anything happening?"

"A couple of them came out for a leak. *Nada mas*."

"Won't be long now." Samuel rolled his shoulders, beginning his customary pre-battle ritual. He freed the flap of his holster and loosened the Colt. He slid his saber six inches out of the scabbard and dropped it back in; like Padraig, he preferred a saber to a rifle with bayonet fixed. He smiled wryly. "Once a cavalryman, always a cavalryman."

Cortez turned his head. "What did you say, señor?"

"*Nada*."

He crept forward to survey the earthen fort. The whine of a cicada rang in his ear, and the piercing pitch rose and fell to call others into the choir. Soon the hissing was louder than a thousand whistles. Samuel relaxed. The noise would cover his men's approach.

A million stars brightened as the loom of a quarter moon peeked above the horizon. Samuel massaged his temples. Once it rose much farther, it would bathe the hillside in light—too much light. They were out of time.

He nudged Cortez. "We go in three minutes. Pass it along."

The undergrowth crackled and birthed shifting shadows as men climbed to their feet. Filipe rose to follow him, and Samuel turned to scold him. Filipe recoiled, stumbled backward three steps into a bush, and hit the ground with a grunt.

His revolver barked. The orange flash momentarily blinded

Samuel as the sound bounced across the river and echoed through the valley.

Samuel dropped to cover the boy, and fear gripped his belly as he realized Filipe wasn't moving. He jerked Filipe's head up. Filipe's chest was still; no breath passed in and out of his nostrils.

Then Filipe opened his eyes and wheezed. "I'm all right, I'm all right."

"Bloody hell?" Samuel hissed, rolling off him.

"I tripped, and my gun went off."

"I told you to stay put." That had torn it; the shot would have alerted the enemy. He scrambled back to his feet. "Attack now—at them, boys. Cross the rampart before they've time to organize."

He whipped around one last time. "And Filipe, don't move from here."

Although they caught the filibusters by surprise, Filipe's shot had given the enemy some warning, and they tumbled from the shack in underwear or in shirt sleeves, snatching rifles from the stacks and bellowing their alarm.

Resisting the urge to rush, Samuel sidestepped down the hill and jumped three feet into the trench. Mud squelched as men thumped down beside him. Jimenez swung a ladder up, and loose soil rattled down the embankment.

"I'll go first." Samuel grabbed the rough wood. Five steps and he'd reached the clay bank on top.

He drew his saber as his men joined him on the rampart, bayonets fixed, and leaped in. He landed with a jolt, and pain lanced up his leg. There was a piercing cry and shouting as more men ran from the building, tumbling over one another in their haste to snatch up the stacked rifles.

He limped two steps to meet a young filibuster with terror twisting his face. The filibuster raised his rifle as Samuel hit him in the shoulder, driving him down into the mud. Someone was bellowing for the enemy to form up, but it was much too late. Samuel kicked the youngster's rifle clear just as blood sprayed the air—Jimenez's savage bayonet had sliced the fallen fighter's throat.

"God damn it, Jimenez," Samuel snarled, "he was a helpless boy."

But Jimenez's blood was up and he kept running, hamstringing a gaunt man who was shouting at Quintero. The man screeched as Quintero stabbed him in the gut.

An American's rifle blazed. The shot was deafening in the tight space, and the ball gouged the clay wall only a foot from Samuel's head. He ducked involuntarily, in time to spot starlight glittering on a bayonet lancing toward his midriff. He hacked the rifle aside and swung his saber back to slice the filibuster's throat. The man's roar cut off abruptly, and he collapsed, burping a last breath through the bloody gash in his neck. Warm blood spurted onto Samuel's face, the taste of copper-salted death.

Samuel drew his Colt with his left hand and searched for another opponent. Gunshots, the clash of metal, and screams filled the fortress. Men battled hand to hand.

A pudgy officer bulging out of a frayed US Army uniform raced around the corner and swung his sword. "So you want a fight then, greaser?"

This fellow had no sword craft, but few Americans did. Samuel stomped his right foot forward, knees flexed, and met the man with his saber. The American chopped at Samuel's head. Steel rang on steel, and the shock jolted up Samuel's arm. He struck. The saber was death in his hand as its glittering blade, sharp as a razor, flicked out like a hummingbird's tongue to pierce the officer's chest.

The rancid breath in the officer's last scream made Samuel recoil, and he yanked back his blade. "Sorry, you gave me no option."

Two bedraggled filibusters burst from the gloom, screaming at the top of their lungs. Samuel could smell shit and blood all around him now, the stench of battle, and embraced it. He'd kill these men so his family could live.

Time seemed to skew in his favor. He fired the Colt, the kick reassuring in his fist. The back of one man's head exploded, spewing brains and blood across the embankment. Lift. Cock. He fired again. The shot hurled the second filibuster back.

He whirled and scanned the gloomy fort for another opponent, but the fighting was over. One minute, the filibusters had been clawing and hammering in do-or-die resistance; the next, they were dead or throwing down their weapons.

He dragged the back of his hand across his sweating forehead. Only Sanchez was wounded; blood ran between the fingers he pressed to his side.

Jimenez was dancing from foot to foot as he taunted three prisoners. "Now call us greasers, you *yanqui* pieces of shit."

Samuel gave Jimenez a shove. "Cut that out. You should know better, and I doubt they understand Spanish, anyway. Secure them and treat the wounded."

He pushed past his cheering men, stepping over bloody bodies and wrinkling his nose at the stench of death. He needed to check on Padraig and the rest.

Padraig was around the corner, detailing guards to watch a handful of prisoners. He waved his bloody saber. "Just like the old days, eh?"

What old days? The old days had been bad days—any killing day was a bad day. He swallowed to ease the pain in his throat. These filibusters weren't warriors, and the skirmish had been too easy, almost murder. "Where's Blanco?"

Padraig shrugged. "Haven't seen him. Try over there."

A gun fired on the river side of the fort. His heart skipped a beat, and he raced around the corner in time to see a filibuster hit the ground. The Costa Rican standing over him waved his smoking rifle in the air with a howl as his comrades cheered.

Heat flashed through Samuel, and he strode over to Blanco. "Your men are murdering those prisoners."

Blanco's nostrils flared. "These *bastardos* invaded our country. They want to enslave our people. They deserve to die."

"Not while I'm guiding the mission, *Capitán*." Samuel stepped close to Blanco.

"The president ordered us to execute any filibuster caught with a rifle."

Samuel drew himself up. "Unless you give your word this won't happen again, I'm going on without you and your men."

"You can't tell me what to do," Blanco bellowed. "This is my country. I—"

"The moment we push off onto the river, *Capitán*, we'll be in Nicaragua," Samuel turned his back on Blanco and returned to Padraig, who was reloading his Colt on the south side. "We're going on to Greytown alone."

"What?"

"And we're taking the prisoners."

Padraig studied Samuel's expression. "The Costa Ricans were shooting them?"

Samuel nodded. "Can't leave them with these butchers."

"We don't have enough men on our own." Padraig ran a hand through his matted blond hair.

"We'll manage." Samuel looked at his bloody saber and wrinkled his nose. He couldn't sheath it like that. "We'll put the prisoners on the Costa Ricans' rafts; they won't need them anymore. Send some men to fetch them." He beckoned to Sergeant Zamora. "*Sargento*, bind the prisoners and move them down to the water's edge. And bring me that filibuster flag. We're leaving."

"*Si, señor*." Zamora saluted and headed for the prisoners slumped along the bamboo wall of the shack.

Samuel pinched his lips together. It hadn't been that long ago that the Euronicas would have slaughtered their prisoners too; it was how wars were fought in Central America, as bad as Burma. He headed to a water cask to wash off the blood drying like rust on his blade.

"*Capitán*." Captain Blanco's ears were red as he approached. "I have considered our exchange, and I agree to your terms.

We'll harm no more prisoners. I implore you to let us accompany you. The success of this mission is important for Costa Rica. We must stop William Walker."

Samuel gave him a hard look. He'd hoped Blanco would come around. "Very well, *Capitán*. In that case, leave two men here to guard the prisoners, and we'll pick them up when we complete the mission."

"Understood. Thank you, *Capitán*."

Samuel consulted his watch. "Six forty-five. By my calculations, it's twenty-eight miles downriver to Greytown. It'll be tight, but we've the current with us. If we cut more paddles and row like the devil is after us, we can make it before dawn."

"Why so quickly?" Blanco asked.

"It's best we capture a steamer as soon as possible. If we wait another day, we risk Fry discovering that we're loose on the river and turning the fort's cannons on us."

Blanco nodded. "*De acuerdo*."

The fort smelled of death when they left it, muddy and metallic, with the flies thick on the corpses like patches of black fur, a stark reminder of what lay ahead for this handful of exhausted men advancing against an army with modern weapons and veteran officers. Samuel's vision narrowed as he gazed upriver. Sofia and John were up there, and he'd march through hell and Satan's legions to rescue them.

CHAPTER TWENTY-TWO

Luis peris, luis peris. The bird call woke Samuel, and he forced his eyes open to see a yellowthroat perched on a tree branch. The bird sang again—*luis peris, luis peris*—and launched into the brightening sky.

Samuel's hands flew to the bamboo deck of the raft he lay on. "Christ, it's dawn." He glared at Padraig, who was kneeling beside him. "Why didn't you wake me?"

Padraig's sunburned face was more flushed than usual. "I was about to. We've just passed Greytown."

"You should've roused me earlier."

"You needed the rest. You paddled like a madman for four solid hours."

Samuel bolted upright in frustration. "But we're too late to approach the steamers. It's daylight already. They'll see us coming."

Padraig nodded once. "It's just after five. The boat crew will still be ashore. It was my watch, and I know my business. The entire town is dreaming. Look!" He thrust Samuel's brass spyglass into his hand.

Nestled behind them in stands of palms with fan-like leaves, Greytown was a rickety colony of shacks with thatched roofs and bamboo walls. Knots of evergreen trees and luxuriant bushes colored the landscape. Cornelius Vanderbilt had breathed new life into the town when he pioneered a route from the East Coast of the United States to San Francisco via the San Juan River and Lake Nicaragua, ten years ago, almost to the day, back in the year eighteen fifty. But William Walker had stolen that route from Vanderbilt and handed it to his comeptitors.

Vanderbilt's retribution was now drifting in on four humble rafts.

Samuel focused on the walled wooden hotel that sat close to the riverbank. Sofia and John had been there. It was their last known location, reportedly where that bastard Fry had captured them. He turned the spyglass east. He was going to pile pain on Walker and Fry. He would destroy them—or die in the effort.

A girdle of light from the rising sun lit the ocean, and beyond the headland, an enormous screw-driven steamship lay at anchor. He centered his lens on her. "That's a warship!"

Padraig craned his neck. "British or American?"

"Does it matter? Either one's a problem." Samuel glassed the long black hull slowly. Enormous guns prickled her decks, so many they were almost impossible to count. There were fifty on each side, and the Union Jack filled the canton of the white ensign fluttering from her flagstaff. He lowered the glass. "Royal Navy. Paddle close to the headland. We're low in the water, and they might not see us."

Five minutes later, the warship's name came into focus.

"HMS *Orion*." Samuel scanned the empty deck. "Wasn't that the ship Lord Paget had waiting here for us last year?"

Padraig nodded as he continued paddling. "Paget was a fool to think we would hand the gold over to him."

They rounded the headland on the south side of the bay, and the old stone castle at Punta de Castilla came into view. Beneath it lay the yard of the Accessory Transit Company, glistening with piles of shiny-black coal and four river steamers idling at anchor twenty yards offshore.

There was their prize.

Samuel bit his lip. "Ah, look at that. We've a fleet to choose from."

Padraig grinned. "Put your back into it, boys."

Samuel plunged the piece of timber he was using as a paddle into the water. Every muscle ached as he scooped with all his might, blisters popping on the pads of his hands. He'd forgotten how far and hard he'd rowed during the night.

He flicked a glance at the man-o-war. Nothing stirred; they hadn't been spotted. In the raft behind them, someone let out a low whoop when they came around the corner. Samuel frowned. The idiot would give them away.

One of the four river steamers, the *Sir Henry Bulwer*, was a stern-wheeler; the *Clayton*, the *Temple*, and the *Machuca* were all side-wheelers. Samuel had escaped across Lake Nicaragua on *Temple* the previous year, and he knew her well. But Spencer had captained *Machuca* before Walker had stolen the steamers from Cornelius Vanderbilt, so she was the boat they'd take.

The lone house in the Accessory Transit Company yard with whitewashed walls and rolled, manicured lawns, belonged to Morgan and Garrison's manager. What was the chap's name? Something Scott—ah, Captain Joseph Scott. Samuel let out a gratified sigh and waved to Blanco and Zamora in the rafts behind him. They would secure the yard and house while he helped Spencer prepare the steamer for departure.

The raft bumped against the *Machuca*'s hull, and Samuel grabbed the entry port ladder. The lower rungs were slippery with weed, and the boat as silent as a grave. The only sound was the wavelets lapping against the hull. He scrambled up the side and stepped onto the sun-bleached deck.

Across at the Accessory Transit Company yard, the rafts had already pulled up alongside the narrow dock, and Blanco was leading Zamora and twenty riflemen ashore. The sound of their feet padding the timbers reached across the silent water. They split into two teams to capture the house and the yard.

Spencer slapped his neck and missed a mosquito. "Let me see the state of the engine."

The skin beneath Samuel's left eye began to tic as Spencer and several of the others went below. This engine had to work; they'd no time to try another boat. He clawed a hand through his sweaty hair and peered at the warship. Her decks seemed deserted.

"Quintero," he said. "Where's Quintero?"

"*Aqui, Capitán.*" Quintero popped his head out of the companionway. "Just looking at the engine. She's a wonder, isn't she?"

"You're the fisherman. Take three men and show them how to cast off the boat. We may have to leave here in a devil of a hurry."

Samuel tapped his finger on the guardrail while he waited for Spencer to report, dividing his attention between the Accessory Transit Company yard and the British frigate.

Sweat streamed down Spencer's oil-streaked face and his hands were black when he reappeared. "As I expected—I had to light the fire. Now we must wait until the boiler heats and makes steam. It'll be a few hours before we've enough pressure to sail."

"Hours?" Samuel's eyes skittered to the warship. She was an unwelcome surprise indeed. "If we have a few hours."

"And we need fuel. Someone must bring wood aboard." Spencer scratched his neck, streaking it with oil. "There'll be wood in the yard."

"Christ Almighty, anything else? Fine. I'll have Quintero take some lads ashore in the tender to collect it."

Their abandoned rafts had drifted five hundred yards out to sea by the time Samuel finished his tour of the boat. That was good; they wouldn't draw the *Orion*'s attention. There were sailors moving about the warship now, attending to their daily duties, but his men were keeping out of sight. So far, nobody from the Royal Navy seemed interested in the *Machuca*. Gray light flooded the eastern the sky and edged the mare's tail clouds with a silvery glow. Gulls wheeled overhead and cried out to their mates, rafting on the long, lazy swells.

Samuel whipped out his soiled handkerchief and wiped the sweat from his forehead. The old wounds in his leg were aching, reminding him of moments like this in Crimea, but he didn't have time to dwell on the past when the future was equally daunting. He fiddled with his wedding ring, picturing Sofia, and watched Quintero's crew push off from the jetty. Now it was up to Spencer; he'd better not take much longer.

A whiff of tobacco smoke told him Padraig was at his side. "I've stationed the men along the gunwales. Don't know why, because there's no way we're fighting that." Padraig pointed to the *Orion*.

Across the water, somebody shouted from the Accessory Transit Company yard. A horseman galloped from behind the manager's house, pursued by three of Blanco's men.

Samuel pounded the guardrail. "Not now!"

The rider's coattails flapped as the horse raced toward the sleepy town. It was a disaster. He would raise the alarm. Samuel craned around and looked at the companionway, but there was no sign of Spencer.

"Bloody hell, that's all we needed." Padraig flicked his smoking stub overboard. "I guess we might rattle sabers with the Royal Navy after all."

Samuel checked the funnel: only the faintest wisp of smoke. Spencer needed to fire up the boiler faster. He reached for his watch but stopped. It didn't matter what time it was; he needed steam.

Quintero's team was finishing loading the fuel logs when a rowboat launched from the beach toward the *Orion*. The burly man seated aft was the rider who'd escaped from the house.

The jig would soon be up.

Samuel's eyes flicked from the rowboat to Blanco's men gathered on the jetty. He beckoned to Quintero. "Ferry Captain Blanco and the rest of the men back to the steamer. Padraig, keep an eye on the man-o-war."

Without waiting for an answer, he hurried to the engine room. The heat below made the hot morning seem cool. Florez and Rivera had stripped off their shirts, and their lean backs glistened with sweat as they watched the flames through the open door of the firebox with Spencer.

Samuel undid another button on his shirt. "The navy will soon know we're hijacking the boat. How much longer?"

"God damn it." Spencer kicked the firebox door. "An hour . . . hour and a half . . ."

"Too long. They'll board us before then."

"It takes what it takes; it's physics." Spencer spat on the deck, and spittle sizzled on the hot plates. "Can you stall them?"

"Stall them? How the hell will I do that?" Samuel snorted and stalked to the stairs. A distant alarm bell clanged before he reached the deck.

The HMS *Orion*!

Five hundred yards across the tranquil green ocean, men scurried about the behemoth *Orion*'s decks and indistinct commands drifted across the water.

Captain Blanco was standing with Padraig. He looked away when their eyes met and pulled down his peaked cap. "One of them gave us the slip. Sorry about that."

"Captain Scott?"

"Mm-hmm."

Padraig kicked the bulkhead. "And the Royal Navy's going to stop us."

Grating, grinding sounds came from the warship, and two of her enormous guns stirred. A jolly boat shot out from under her stern.

Padraig slumped against the guardrail. "And I thought the Don Cossack artillery in Crimea was bad."

Samuel recalled the papers he'd seen in *Temple*'s chart table the year before, and he rubbed his hands together. "Padraig, come with me. I've an idea."

They pelted across the deck and took the steps to the upper deck two at a time up to the pilothouse. Out the window, the *Orion*'s jolly boat was only fifty yards away now. Her guns rotated. Samuel rummaged in the chart table—he'd seen them there only last year.

There!

He yanked the notepaper from beneath the dog-eared log. "Here it is."

"Letterhead?" Padraig pointed at the paper with his index finger. "A bit late to write home, isn't it? And us about to be hanged for piracy."

"Hush and let me think straight." He looked to port. Quintero was bringing the last of the shore party alongside. "Line the men along the guardrail. Don't let the navy aboard."

"What about them?" Padraig gestured to the *Orion*'s cannons, pointed their way.

"You've ridden against more guns than that." He took an inkpot and pen from the chart table.

Padraig stood there, chewing his lip.

"Do it."

By the time Samuel returned to the entry port, the jolly boat was tethered to the ladder and a Royal Navy captain, a marine lieutenant, ten marines, eight sailors, and one civilian—presumably Scott, manager of the Accessory Transit Company—were glaring up at him.

The Royal Navy captain removed his bicorn hat and dabbed the sweat from his pale pate. "Are you the leader of these pirates, sir?"

"I'm the man acting on behalf of the Accessory Transit Company's legitimate owner." Samuel squared his shoulders. "And who, pray tell, are you?"

"Captain James Erskin of Her Majesty's Ship *Orion*."

"Would you care to come aboard, Captain?"

Scott moved forward alongside Captain Erskin.

Samuel wagged his finger. "Uh-uh. Only you, Captain Erskin."

The captain and Scott exchanged glances. "I will—but should you try any antics, the *Orion* will blow you out of the water." He climbed the ladder as nimbly as a man twenty years his junior. "We're here to protect the Morgan and Garrison's manager and his family from Costa Rican aggression and forcibly restore control of this steamer to him."

Erskin sounded like a typical arrogant Briton, and that type of leader—well, Samuel had their measure.

He placed his hands loosely behind his back. "I assure you that we have no intention of harming Captain Scott or his family. As for this American vessel, the rightful owner, the Accessory Transit Company, authorized me to recover their property." He passed the letter in his hand to Captain Erskin. "This is from Cornelius Vanderbilt, lawful owner of the company, authorizing me to act on his behalf. You'll note that it's signed and validated with his seal."

He sneaked a glance at Padraig, who was studiously looking out to sea.

Erskin pursed his lips as he read and wrinkled his Roman nose. His blue eyes bounced between the page and Samuel as Spencer arrived on deck, smudged with grease and soot. Erskin tugged his left ear and settled his eyes on Samuel. "You're not American. You're British."

"Irish." In the last year, Samuel had gained clarity about where his true allegiance lay.

"May I see your papers?"

Samuel produced them from his breast pocket.

The captain looked up sharply. "Lieutenant Samuel Kingston, formerly of the Seventeenth Lancers? You're the man I waited for right here last year. You never showed up."

"My apologies if I inconvenienced you, Captain. I was diverted."

Erskin lowered his voice. "Is this operation related to General Paget?"

Samuel was hyperaware that Padraig, Spencer, and Blanco were staring at him. Bollocks—George Paget *was* affiliated with Lord Lucan and the other aristocrats whose skullduggery had landed him in this mess. He leaned forward. "It is, Captain, but let's keep that between us." He touched his nose.

Captain Erskin nodded and handed back the letter. "Your papers seem in order, including an official seal. I can't stop you from doing your job. The steamers are yours—all of them—but . . ." His shaggy gray brows furrowed as he fixed his gaze on Captain Blanco. "Britain and the United States both consider Punta de Castillo to be Nicaraguan territory. I must insist that the Costa Rican army cease their occupation forthwith."

The flush of victory radiated through Samuel's body. He would deprive Walker of not one, but all four riverboats. "Thank you, Captain. The Costa Ricans will help me move Mr. Vanderbilt's steamers to Costa Rican waters immediately. I bid you good day, sir."

As the jolly boat pulled away across the water, a powerful hand grabbed Samuel's arm from behind.

Padraig spun him around. "You tricky dog! You faked that letter and Vanderbilt's signature—but Vanderbilt's seal? How did you do that?"

"I used candle wax and this." Samuel held up Father's signet ring with a grin. Flakes of wax clung to the etching of a rampant lion beneath a knight's helmet. "I figured it unlikely that the good captain could tell the Kingston family crest from Cornelius Vanderbilt's personal seal."

CHAPTER TWENTY-THREE

Every revolution of the *Machuca*'s paddles propelled Samuel farther upriver and closer to his imprisoned family. His mouth gummy, he watched the wake ripple and eddy against the riverbanks. The muggy air on board was thick with body odor, hot grease, and wood smoke. He twisted his wedding ring on his finger. They'd been steaming for twenty hours, but he'd slept only fitfully, tossing and turning with Sofia and John on his mind . . . and Father.

He'd already captured one fort and all of William Walker's riverboats. Now he would do whatever it took to rescue Sofia and John. He'd save them both, slamming William Walker's back door and destroying him. He'd capture this river.

Another farm materialized on the edge of the rainforest; they were drawing close to El Castillo. He could almost hear their bones creak as a peasant and his wife straightened to watch them pass, their faces leathered beneath straw hats. The rest of the family clustered around a buffalo at the water's edge, a young boy and a woman in a faded yellow dress with a baby at her breast. The boy gave a hesitant wave until his mother hurried him away from these intruders in their land.

The *Machuca* had already collected Colonel Brailier and most of the Costa Ricans from Hipp's Point. Samuel now had one hundred and twenty men on board to capture two forts, but he was under no illusion that it would be easy. He shoved his hands into his pockets as he gazed over the luxuriant foliage bourgeoning in the tropical humidity. If they lost the element of surprise, they'd pay a high price. He glanced at the lone red star between the blue bars on the flag waving overhead. Would the filibusters fall for his *ruse de guerre*, or would the fort's cannons sink *Machuca*?

At least Colonel Brailier had capitulated and let him command.

On the second deck below, Filipe trudged to the forward rail, kneading his chest with the palm of his hand, peering upriver. Samuel's eyebrows drew together. The boy had been far from his chirpy self since leaving the training camp outside Cartago—darting strange glances at Samuel and Padraig, withdrawn, and no longer joining in when the men joked around. He should talk to him.

He turned to Spencer helming in the tiny wheelhouse. "How much longer before we reach El Castillo?"

"Not long. Thirty minutes."

"All right. I'll get the lads ready."

He descended the narrow stairs, slipped through the soldiers lounging on the upper deck, and eddied to Filipe. "You ready for this?"

"Ugh." Filipe startled, and his head flicked around. "You scared me. Yes. Yes, I am."

"I want you to stay at the back when we rush the gates."

"*Yo sé*. Always behind."

Samuel tilted his head and stared at him. "Everything all right? You all right?"

Filipe's face scrunched up and relaxed. "Yes, of course I am."

"You sure? You've been silent lately."

Filipe turned his head to stare upriver and said nothing.

"You haven't even tried to stab anybody recently." Samuel forced a laugh at his poor joke.

"Are you worried about Sofia? We're going to get her back, you know. John too."

Drawing his knife from nowhere it seemed, Filipe began fidgeting with it. The boy had fast hands. "I know. I hope so."

"Is it your father? He's a brave man, you need not worry about him." Samuel cupped a hand around Filipe's shoulder.

"He was wrong to support Walker." Filipe squirmed free. "I was wrong; Walker's an evil man." His words were full of venom.

"El Castillo," someone shouted, and the men surged forward, crowding around Samuel and Filipe at the rail.

It was time.

Ahead, tiny ripples stirred the muddy green water, a preamble to the turbulent rapids beyond. The men chatted excitedly, and Samuel's skin prickled. He'd have to press Filipe more after they assaulted the fort; something was bothering the boy. He rolled his shoulders and drew his Colt. The cylinder clicked mechanically as he checked the charges. His saber rasped against the scabbard as he drew it six inches and dropped it back; the greasy leather wrapping the hilt was smooth, familiar, and reassuring to his touch.

He looked at Padraig's sunburned face where he chatted with Captain Blanco, and the weight on his shoulders lightened. With men like Padraig and the Euronicas, he wouldn't fail, no matter what the odds.

Padraig raised his eyebrows. "Time?"

"Yes." Samuel was much less confident than he tried to appear. "Colonel Brailier will take the village, and we'll attack the fort. It's imperative we reach the gates before they close them. Otherwise, it's a standoff. We can scale the curtain wall tonight, but they'll be alert, so there's no guarantee we'll succeed."

He saw the three-story barbican first, then the rest of the one-story stone fort on a steep, grassy knoll when they rounded the bend. El Castillo de la Inmaculada Concepción was almost two hundred years old, and though time had degraded it, it still looked impregnable. The six cannons crouching in the crenels gave it sharp teeth.

"Everybody out of sight." Samuel moved to the entry port.

Sergeant Zamora and the Euronicas squatted low on the deck, and the lighter-skinned Costa Ricans disappeared below.

In front of the fort, two Americans dressed in the blue tunics, canvas leggings, and black felt hats of Walker's Army of the Republic of Nicaragua lounged on the timber jetty with their rifles leaning on the railing beside them. A handful of civilians, mostly porters, milled around the dock.

"Two ARN riflemen." Samuel spoke to his prone men from the corner of his mouth. "They don't appear to suspect anything."

Cortez, Jimenez, and Quintero had stripped off their shirts and stood by the starboard gunwales to handle the mooring lines. Spencer nudged the *Machuca* alongside the dock, and the three men leaped ashore.

Cortez and Jimenez lunged at the guards, whisking knives to their throats. The guards surrendered their rifles without a sound.

Samuel drew his Colt and bolted up the steep steps leading to the fort. He took them two at a time, boots pounding the stone slabs, the Euronicas' bare feet beating the ground behind him. The stairs seemed endless, and his springing steps turned to labored thuds by the time he hustled around the weathered stone wall at the top.

The iron gates were open. The black-bearded guard's eyes bulged as he cursed and fumbled to raise his rifle. Samuel shot him in the sternum, and the guard tumbled down the stone ramp.

The dungeon was downstairs. He knew that from the time he rescued Padraig. He hustled along the musty corridor and stormed toward the river-facing scarp, with the shouts of his men echoing through the fort behind.

Thump. He crashed into a redheaded filibuster and bowled him over a six-pounder cannon.

"I'll get him," Padraig called from behind.

A Colt barked, and the redhead screamed. Samuel blustered down the stairs to the dungeon, into the reek of damp limestone and paraffin. Almost there.

He hesitated at the bottom.

Padraig's breath was hot on his neck. "It's as black as the devil's boot down here."

A match spluttered. Its weak light flickered in the open doorway: empty.

They were gone.

Padraig dropped the match with a curse, leaving them in darkness. Samuel's heart plunged along with the light. He was too late; he'd failed them.

Another match stuttered alight, and the faint flare illuminated footprints and scuff marks in the dust around the single cot.

A piece of cloth lay under the cot.

"Bloody hell!" Padraig dropped the spent match.

That rag or cloth . . . It might be a clue. "Another match, quickly."

A flame flared, and the acrid bite of sulfur tingled Samuel's nose. He picked up the damp cloth and sniffed.

Urine.

"A nappy." He dropped the cloth. "They were here, all right. Hurry, back upstairs."

Sunlight stung Samuel's eyes when they burst outside. He closed them briefly and opened them to find Captain Blanco bouncing from foot to foot.

"They surrendered without a fight," Blanco said. "We have the fort. The prisoners are over there."

Samuel clutched Blanco's elbow. "Did you see my wife? My child?"

Blanco's face slackened. "I'm sorry."

Some forty prisoners huddled inside the gate, pinned under the rifles of Blanco's Costa Ricans and the Euronicas. Samuel stormed over to them. Walker could dress his filibusters in blue uniforms and call them Army of the Republic of Nicaragua, but they were still little more than pirates. If they had harmed Sofia and John, he would shoot them like dogs.

Samuel pointed his rifle at a gaunt lieutenant with sunken cheeks dressed in an old US Army uniform. "Where are the woman and baby? I know they were here."

The man paled. "We had nothing to do with that. I don't hold with locking up women or kids."

Samuel clenched his teeth. "Where . . . are . . . they?"

"They were here, but now they're gone. General Walker ordered Colonel Fry to take command of the fort at San Carlos, and the colonel took the woman and child with him."

Samuel deflated. The fort at San Carlos would be a tough prospect to crack, high on the hill with solid walls. "How many men are over there?"

The lieutenant threw up his hands weakly. "Don't rightly know, but he took fifty riflemen from here."

"Watch them," Samuel said to Blanco. "I'm going to San Carlos."

Blanco shook his head. "I'll see this through with you." He turned to his lieutenant. "*Teniente Muñoz*, hand these men over to Colonel Brailier and join us on the steamer. We're going to San Carlos with *Capitán* Kingston."

Samuel realized he was tapping his foot as he gazed upriver and stilled his fidgeting. His eyes stung, heavy in their sockets, after six hours of steaming on the endless river in the hammering heat, fear gnawing at his insides. The day had cheated him, and now he relived every choice, reviewed every moment.

Fry would never take her across the lake; he couldn't risk

Colonel Valle's discovering that he'd imprisoned her. Sofia's father was still Walker's trusted ally, though Samuel couldn't fathom why.

The *Machuca* swept around another bend, and Lake Nicaragua appeared as a polished bronze sheet. High on the hilltop, the stone walls of Fort San Carlos gleamed tangerine in the last rays of the sun. Eight cannons thrust from its crenellated walls to cover the river, and the harbor hunkered far below. Even if they managed to land there, it would be impossible to reach the fort before its imposing gates slammed shut.

Padraig rested his rifle against the guardrail. "Bloody formidable, isn't it?"

Samuel stared at it glumly.

"I wish Colonel Brailier hadn't kept fifty men back to garrison El Castillo."

"Seventy soldiers or seven hundred—we can't capture this place by force." Samuel rested his elbows on the guardrail and formed his hands into a steeple, gazing at the lone red star fluttering over the pilot house. Guile was his only hope. "We must trick them. Better get the men below deck. We should go too, in case somebody recognizes us from the old days."

He waved up to Spencer in the pilothouse and hastened to the lower deck. The Euronicas and the Costa Ricans were mixing now, in bonds forged through action and a common cause: ridding Central America of the tyrant, William Walker, and his slavery laws.

Samuel found Captain Blanco on the lower deck. "It's time. Please be so kind as to order your men below. Cortez, Jimenez, and Quintero will remain on deck as crew."

Below deck was sweltering, and the dense odor of dripping oil, wood smoke, and sweat made Samuel queasy. The growl of the engine and the hiss of steam almost drowned out the gurgle of water rushing along the hull and the creak of timbers. The open firebox flickered grotesque shadows across the logs stacked against the hull. He rubbed his clammy hands down his breeches. If the fort caught on to his ruse, they would be dead men down here. The cannons would blow the hull asunder and send them to the bottom before they ever reached the ladder.

The telegraph rang, and the shirtless fireman reduced the engine speed. They must be approaching the jetty . . . now the guns couldn't shoot low enough to strike them. The line shaft stopped clanking, and the hull shuddered as the boat bumped against the jetty.

Now it was up to Spencer.

Ten minutes later, Spencer's head appeared at the top of the steps. "They sent for Fry. The guards didn't board, didn't even look around. It's safe to come up."

Samuel hastened to the companionway.

Benjamin Fry had a bounce in his step as he hurried toward the dock with a sergeant in tow. He was taller than Samuel had expected, with a bushy beard covering his long face. The bastard was excited, but what commander wouldn't be after receiving an eyes-only message from President Walker himself.

Samuel drew Padraig into the shadows as Fry approached the gangplank.

"This way, Colonel." Spencer shook Fry's hand and drew him inboard.

Samuel took two steps forward and pushed his Colt into Fry's ribs. "Do nothing hasty, Fry. You're one man I'm happy to kill."

Fry took a step back, and his mouth fell open. "Kingston! How the—"

"Doesn't matter. Are my wife and son in the fort?"

Fry's gaze skittered up toward the fort.

"I wouldn't do anything stupid." Samuel pressed the weapon deeper into Fry's uniform. "They must go free, or you die."

Fry nodded vigorously. "They're there."

"Unharmed?"

"Yes."

"Lucky for you." Samuel took the revolver from Fry's belt. "Send your sergeant back to the fort with orders the garrison lay down their arms and line up outside the walls."

Fry drew himself up. "The devil take you, Kingston. My son died because of you. The Costa Ricans killed him like a dog in Santa Rosa. He was gut-shot, helpless, and they murdered him."

"I hardly see what that has to do with me. If you think—"

"If you hadn't stolen the gold meant to fund us, we'd have had more men. More weapons. We'd have won that battle—and Willy would be alive today."

And this was Fry's reason for capturing a mother and child? "Don't justify this. Kidnapping is a hanging offense where I come from. I ought to kill you right now."

"You don't know what it's like!" Fry bellowed. "You don't know what it's like to see a young life just . . . just . . . taken."

"I'm sorry about your boy." Samuel rubbed his chest. Another innocent butchered because of Walker. "I truly am. But all this senseless slaughter stems from Walker's lust for power and the greed of filibusters like you. What did you think? That this land is vacant and yours for the taking? What about the Nicaraguans who've lived here since the dawn of time?" He thrust his face close to Fry's. "You were happy to steal their land. You were happy to make them slaves."

Fry snorted. "These inferior beings aren't good for anything else. It's God's will that they serve us . . . read that in the bible. It works back home in the South, and it's what's needed here."

The gall of this filibuster, the brazen boldness. It was like talking to Louis Greenfell or bloody Lucan.

"Works well?" Samuel's eyebrows shot up. "For who? For you people? Not here, Fry." He gestured to the Euronicas filing in from the engine room. "These men and thousands like them will fight you every inch of the way. As will I." He prodded Fry with the Colt, and Fry wrenched his head back. "Yes, I took Walker's gold. I thought it would finish him, end his naked ambition. But he's still here, isn't he?" He jammed the Colt again and again into Fry's gut, emphasizing his words. "And now, its . . . just . . . you."

Fry stumbled into Padraig, who shoved him roughly back into his balance.

Samuel grabbed Fry's lapel and pulled him so close he could smell the Filibuster's breath. "If you don't disarm your men this instant, I'll hand you to my soldiers, and they won't be as gentle as I am. For the last time: Are you sending that sergeant to the fort, or are you dying?"

"Bastard." Fry's lip curled up to show a blackened tooth.

The silence stretched out, suspending Samuel in time.

"All right. I'll do it." Fry glared at the surly sergeant. "Tell Captain Dawson."

Samuel pitched his voice low and steady. "You've ten minutes, Sergeant. If they're not outside by then, I'll shoot this rat, and I won't stop there. We control the river—both the inlet and the outlet, the forts, and all the river steamers. No more volunteers will get through from the East Coast to reinforce you, yet hundreds of Costa Rican troops are sailing here as I speak. If I must besiege this fort, I'll let the Nicaraguans have the lot of you and settle old scores. They don't take prisoners, you know."

The sergeant turned pale as he nodded.

"Hand your revolver to young Filipe there. You won't be needing it." Samuel whipped out his pocket watch and flicked it open. "You've ten minutes."

CHAPTER TWENTY-FOUR

"You'll never get away with this." Fry speared Samuel with another glare. "General Walker will send troops from Rivas."

Padraig's smirked at him. "I think we just did."

"Walker has his hands full fighting the allied army. He's losing Granada, but even if he comes, a few steadfast men can defend this stone fort, and when the Costa reinforcements arrive, he'll have no hope." Samuel wasn't at all sure of that, but it would worry Fry. He didn't want to kill this chuff; he was sick of the killing and didn't want another death on his tally sheet, not even a bastard like Fry. He nodded to Sergeant Zamora. "Guard him. We're marching to the fort. All of us."

The evening breeze from the lake cooled their climb up the steep hill as darkness fell. Samuel scanned the daunting sheer walls. Thank God he'd captured Fry; they'd never have made it to the top before the enemy barred the gate. The gate was old and weathered but it was still thick, solid, and open.

It was still wide open.

A pinprick of light glimmered at the gate, a lantern spluttered, and orange light flickered on a group of men trudging out. Most wore the blue tunics and canvas leggings of the Army of the Republic of Nicaragua; the rest wore the black-dyed shirts favored by the filibusters before Walker formed the Army of the Republic of Nicaragua.

Samuel smiled slowly. He'd won.

He prodded Fry with his revolver. "Hurry up."

Dozens of defenders formed a ragged line outside the gate, stiff and malevolent beneath their black felt hats.

Samuel waved his men forward. "Cover them." He poked Fry. "Where are they? Sofia and my son?"

A filibuster with skin peeling from his sunburned face took a step forward. "Look, mister, I arrived a few weeks ago from Missouri. I took no part in it. Ain't right locking up women and children. But I know they're in the cottage beside the armory, and they're unharmed."

Energy surged through Samuel. "Where?"

"Last building on the right."

Unharmed. It was going to be incredible seeing them. "Jimenez, watch Fry."

"No, I've got him." Filipe stepped forward; his revolver already pointed at Fry.

Samuel nodded in answer to Jimenez's questioning look and left them.

Huts and storehouses sprawled in the shadows of the sloping stone wall, and only one door was closed and bolted. With luck, Sofia was inside. He ran across the gloomy yard. Soon he'd have her safe in his arms—and baby John. He'd not even spent a week with his son before leaving for New York, but he would make up for it now.

He drew back the bolt and shouldered the rough-hewn door open to a haze of dust and the stench of mildew and urine. Sofia sat pressed against the wall, clutching John, her eyes defiant in the flickering light of a candle.

"Sofia! My darling, I found you." He rushed in and wrapped his arms around her as she squealed, the warm lump of John pressed between them. He closed his eyes and buried his nose in her hair, inhaling the scent of summer rain that persisted despite her long confinement. "I've been trying . . . searching all over. Why did—"

"I knew you would find us." She sobbed in his arms. "That you'd never abandon the quest." Her hand was warm and soft on his stubbled cheek. "Darling, I'm sorry, so sorry."

He pushed her back a span so he could look at her. "What do mean? It's my fault, I—"

"No, let me speak. When you left for New York, I thought you were abandoning me." She shuddered. "I couldn't stop crying and snapping at people. Poor María, I was such a beast to her. I couldn't sleep. I imagined everyone in Clonakilty was staring at little John and calling him a half-breed. I couldn't even baptize him to have the consolation of that blessing. And you were gone."

Her dress was stale and musty, but her hair . . . He buried his face in her long tresses and closed his eyes briefly. It was like being home again. It was simply wonderful.

She sniffled. "Imprisoned in this fort . . . in my own land, I've had nothing but time to reflect on what happened. Oh, Samuel, I lost my mind."

"Sofia . . ."

"I convinced myself to return home to Nicaragua, to Papa and everything familiar. So I sneaked away. Your poor family—and the Kerrs. Oh, I can only imagine the torture I've put them through, running off like that." She kissed him and nuzzled his neck.

"I was nearly driven mad by your disappearance," Samuel whispered.

"Mad, yes." She gave a shaky laugh. "Locked up, I came to my senses and realized I had been mad, quite mad, dragging our son into the middle of a civil war and a plague. Oh, Samuel—I lost my mind without you."

Baby John wailed and squirmed between them.

She released Samuel and leaned back. "Poor baby, are we crushing you?"

Someone moved in the doorway, and Samuel turned to see Teresa with Chavez. Bathed and rested, Teresa looked twenty years younger now, closer in age to Chavez, who he guessed was around thirty years old.

Teresa stepped forward. "You poor thing, what an ordeal." She put a bony arm around Sofia and led her toward the door. "I've medical training. If you don't mind, I'd like to look at you and the baby."

Sofia raised her eyebrows at Samuel. He nodded, and she allowed Teresa to draw her outside and across the square. Samuel followed.

Teresa placed a maternal arm around Sofia. "Now listen to me, young lady. I've delivered my fair share of babies and tended to young mothers, and I won't hear another word from you about losing your mind.

"You can't know what it was like, to be—"

"Oh, yes I can." Teresa nodded. "And furthermore, what happened to you is normal. It's the baby angst. Many women are out of sorts after the hardship of childbirth—and you, poor child, delivering your baby during an assault, and then your husband running off on a wild chase." She twisted to look back at Samuel. "He won't do that again in a hurry."

He gave her an apologetic shrug. She was correct; he'd been a churl, but he would make this right, no matter what.

Samuel's men were moving purposefully around the fort, the flickering lights of torches and lanterns throwing long shadows behind them.

Padraig hurried across the yard and embraced Sofia. "You're safe, thank the Lord."

John wailed in Sofia's arms.

"Here, let me take him. You must be exhausted." Samuel reached out, and touching the hot bundle sent a tingle through him. God, how he loved this boy—loved them both. "I'm so sorry I left you like that, Sofia. I should have been there for you."

John's little scrunched face glowed as if lit within, and he gurgled as his tiny fingers closed around Samuel's forefinger.

Teresa smiled up at Samuel. "Right. Your family will have plenty of time to get reacquainted, but now I need to take care of Sofia and the baby."

Sofia turned her back on her former prison room. "Not here in this dreadful place. Let's go somewhere else."

"He's getting away!" someone shouted from the gate.

Samuel jerked around. "What the devil?" He hastily passed John to Sofia. "Stay here, darling, whatever happens."

He pelted to the gate.

Outside, Filipe stood beside Fry, wearing a hard expression Samuel had never seen before on his face.

And he was covering Captain Blanco with his revolver.

A sudden coldness spread through Samuel's core. "Filipe, what are you doing?"

Three Costa Rican soldiers lifted their rifles and edged closer to Filipe.

"No!" Blanco snapped. "Stand down."

Filipe's face was ashen, and his eyes flickered between Samuel and Captain Blanco. "I'm sorry, I've no choice. I'd no choice all along."

Samuel raised a hand. "Filipe, whatever this is . . ."

"They were going to kill Papa unless I helped them."

Samuel froze as the pieces fell into place. So that was what had been bothering Filipe . . . he was the traitor. He was how Fry had known where to find the stolen guns, why the district attorney had seized the ship in New York.

Samuel's mouth fell open. "You told this bastard when we sailed from America for the Caribbean?"

Fry shouldered the boy aside. "I arranged that surprise on my own. I knew you'd sail that way, so I had the frigate waiting for you in the Caribbean."

Samuel ignored him. His disagreement was with Filipe now. "You were working against us all along. You went ashore first with the captain in Limón"—his nostrils flared—"and it was you who spun the tale that we'd landed to spark a revolution."

Filipe averted his eyes, and his chin dipped. "I was only—"

"And you didn't trip when we attacked Hipp's Point. You fired on purpose to warn them we were coming. The attack on the road from Limón. . ." Samuel weaved a hand through his hair. How had he not seen this before?

A tear trickled from Filipe's eye. "I'm sorry, Samuel, I truly am. They told me that if you captured the river, Papa was a dead man."

He'd kill the little bastard. "What about your sister? And your nephew? You would have let us fail, assuring they'd die in this shithole?"

"He swore they'd go free too, like Papa." Filipe clutched his trousers leg in one hand and twisted the material. "It's been hell, facing these unbearable choices. Whichever choice I made, someone was going to get hurt. I hate myself. But I swear, Fry's contact assured me Sofia and John were safe in Walker's home in Granada—hostages, but well cared for. He said they'd free them as soon as you failed. I swear it. They lied to me."

"Cartago, the attempt on my life . . . Filipe, did you set me up?"

"No, dear God, no. I was passing him a message for Fry, that's all." Tears streamed down Filipe's face. He looked frail and lost. "The bastard took a shot at you. That wasn't me, I swear to you."

Samuel took a tiny step toward Filipe. "Fry's lying to you. But tell me: Why did your father and Walker fall out?"

"Papa never believed Walker would bring back slavery, so when Walker did, he revolted."

Samuel took another step toward Filipe.

"Don't come any closer, Samuel, p-please."

Samuel waved an arm angrily. “You see? Liars. Your father is an honorable man, Filipe. Colonel Valle will never understand this betrayal, even if it’s meant to save his life. I faced a similar choice last year, and I chose to defend freedom even if it cost my father his life.”

Filipe broke into open sobs.

“Don’t do this, Filipe.”

“I’m so sorry.” Filipe slumped, and the gun wavered. “I’ve made a mess of—”

Fry punched Filipe in the head, yanked the revolver out his hand, and swung the gun up to cover Filipe. “Don’t move, or the boy’s dead.”

Filipe doubled over and collapsed, moaning and holding his head in both hands.

Samuel rumbled in frustration.

“Nobody needs to die here.” Fry trained the gun back and forth between Filipe and Samuel and settled on Filipe. “The boy and I are going down to the steamer, nice and quietly. We’re leaving. I’ll release him when I reach La Virgen.”

Samuel glared at Fry. The snake wasn’t getting away with it. He’d stop him or die trying. He tensed to draw the Colt from his holster.

“Don’t!” Fry’s pistol swung to cover Samuel.

Samuel held both hands out. “Filipe, you can still choose to do the right thing. Your father—”

Fry grabbed Filipe’s hair and hauled him to his feet. “Stupid boy, your father is dead. Walker stood him in front of a firing squad as a warning to the rest of the dons. Now let’s go or you’ll join him.”

“No!” Filipe’s agonized scream sent a shiver down Samuel’s spine. In a move Samuel recognized from their training, Filipe twisted and plunged his stiletto knife into Fry’s side. “You bastard.”

Samuel leaped toward them as Fry pushed Filipe away, but not before the revolver spat in Fry’s hand. Blood blossomed on

Filipe's shirt, and he pitched backward. Samuel heard the mechanical cock of the gun cylinder as he barreled into Fry with his shoulder and knocked him over.

The air whooshed from Fry's lips as he hit the ground, and Samuel leaped on him, rage coursing through his veins. This was the man who'd kidnapped his family and caused dozens of men to die in the jungle. This was the face of the tyrant, William Walker. He was going to rip him apart.

He punched Fry in the jaw, and pain lanced through his knuckles. No matter. He pounded Fry again and again. Blood spattered his face, tangy and wet.

Padraig kicked the gun clear and pulled Samuel by the shoulder. "Enough, Samuel. Enough now. Sure, the bastard's unconscious."

Blood pounded in Samuel's ears, and he shook his arm free. This rat had kidnapped Sofia and John, locked them away in darkness and squalor. His knuckles crunched into Fry's nose again, and Samuel glowed inside. Gray spots and pins of light flashed before his eyes.

"Stop it!" Strong arms closed around both shoulders. "Enough. Filipe is shot. We need to help him."

Filipe writhed and groaned on the ground, and a lump formed in Samuel's throat. He couldn't blame the boy for what he'd done. He of all people knew what Filipe had endured, with only poor choices that forced him to pick between his father and justice.

He climbed off Fry's prone body and hastened to Filipe, whose blood flowed through the fingers clutching his shoulder. His head pounded as he sagged down beside Filipe. "We've no doctor."

"Teresa can help." Chavez's voice seemed distant in Samuel's dizzy world. "I'll fetch her."

Samuel cut away Filipe's shirt with the bloody knife. He'd seen enough wounds to know this one wasn't fatal. Filipe was going to be all right; there was always a risk, but he should recover. He pressed his handkerchief against the wound and cradled Filipe's head.

Teresa and Sofia arrived through the gate. Teresa shooed everyone back and knelt to examine Filipe.

"Filipe . . ." Sofia's face crinkled with anguish.

Samuel rose and embraced her, as much to steady himself as to console her. "He's fine. The bullet went clean through, but we must stay back and let Teresa work."

Baby John sensed the tension, for he wailed again and kicked his tiny feet. Sofia began to pace, bouncing John and twisting his blanket in her fingers.

Blanco's men half-carried, half-marched Fry to the very prison where he had locked up Sofia and John. His knife wound would heal in time for the Costa Ricans to shoot him, if they chose too; Samuel didn't care. He'd completed his mission: he saved Sofia and John. He captured the river forts and the steamers, effectively slamming Nicaragua's rear door in Walker's face. If rumors from the west were true, the allied army of Costa Rica, Salvador, Honduras, and Nicaraguan dissidents was knocking Walker around in the west. Lacking access to volunteers and supplies from the east, he would soon be finished.

Teresa gently lowered Filipe back to the ground. "The bullet went clean through. He's a very lucky boy. We'll keep the wounds clean and change his dressings, and I'm certain he'll be fine."

Sofia's eyes glistened as they locked on her brother. It must've been hell to see him injured, and now . . .

He wiped his bloody hands down his trousers and drew her aside. "Darling, Filipe is going to be fine, as are you and John. We're returning home now."

She was beaming. "I know, Samuel, and—"

"But your father . . ." he continued. "Your father's gone, Sofia."

"Gone?" she whispered.

"Walker murdered him. I am so sorry." He looked into her dull eyes and drank her pain.

She sagged, clutching John to her breast. "No!"

Her strangled cry echoed between the stone walls, and soldiers looked over in alarm.

"I knew it, I knew it, I knew it," she wailed, pounding Samuel's breast with her fist. "I told you months ago something was wrong. He never answered my letters, not a word. But you dismissed my concerns. It's your fault, Samuel. It's your fault he's gone."

He held her while the agony of her loss rippled through her, absorbing her blows as penance. Perhaps she was right. Perhaps he deserved this. He'd been selfish, consumed by false guilt over Father's death, and he hadn't listened to her. He drew her in and held her close. Warm tears tickled his neck, and he clung to the hope of forgiveness.

She stilled when John mewled at her breast. "I'm sorry, Samuel."

He kissed the top of her head.

"It wasn't you." She tugged back in his arms. "This is William Walker's doing. He's destroyed our lives—first your father, then Nicaragua, and now Papa." Her soft hand curled into a fist as she stepped back with fire blazing in her eyes. "We'll never have peace while he lives. Neither will Nicaragua. We must destroy him."

Despite the gravity of the moment, Samuel's heart buoyed. This was the woman he loved, as multifarious as a diamond, deep and full of fire in the starlight. She was a fighter. They wouldn't merely survive this crucible; they'd emerge from it stronger.

He reached out and cupped her face in his hands. "Yes, my love, but now is not the time. We must think of John. Nicaragua is no place for him right now. War and disease—it's far too dangerous for you both. We have to bring him back to Ireland."

"But Walker must pay for what he's done."

"He will. Look around you. Costa Rica controls the river, and

Walker's losing ground in Granada. He's finished . . . Slavery is finished. Now, we must go home."

She looked from John in her arms back to Samuel. "You're certain Walker's finished? You believed the same last year."

"It's different this time. Listen, let's go home to Ireland, and I swear to you that if Walker somehow clings to power in Nicaragua, I'll return and finish him."

She embraced him again. "All right. Let's take John home."

Tears welled behind his eyelids. They were safe, and that was all that mattered. Safe from Walker—but not safe from the consortium of aristocrats, not yet. They still had a lock on his money.

The Baltimore papers. Fry must have them. Samuel needed them if he was to force the Earl of Lucan, Colonel Lawrence, and their aristocrat cronies back into line.

He brushed his lips against Sofia's forehead. "Baltimore's papers, darling. I need to find them. I'll be back."

Samuel arrived breathless at the cell where he'd found Sofia and John, and both guards greeted him with broad smiles. Every man under Captain Blanco's command knew the true architect of the San Juan River victory.

"May I borrow your lantern?" he asked. "I need a word with the prisoner."

"Here you go, *Capitán*."

The door creaked open, and the light picked Fry from the darkness against the stone wall, where he slumped with a face crumpled in pain and defeat. The blood rushed in Samuel's ears, and he wrestled back his anger.

Fry lifted a bloody hand from his side. "For God's sake, man, I need a doctor."

He should punch the bastard in the face, but it was more important to scare him. "Kidnapping a woman and child, locking them up in this hole—you don't deserve a doctor. You should hang. A firing squad is too good for you."

"You can't. You wouldn't." Fry's lip trembled. From fear or pain? Samuel couldn't guess.

Samuel took out his tobacco. "Last year, in the civil war, the Legitimists burned six of Walker's men alive in Rivas. The Costa Ricans might do the same here."

"You can't let them." Fry shrank against the wall. "No Christian would allow such savagery."

Samuel wrinkled his nose at the stench of Fry's fear. "You attacked my home, kidnapped my family, and robbed me. I've arranged with Captain Blanco that you'll burn. With green wood, so you'll die slowly."

"Please! I've lost everything: my only child, my home, my freedom. I beg you."

"I'll tell you what." And now he would see if there was still a way out. "If you provide the documents you stole from my home, I'll consider a word with Captain Blanco."

"Yes, yes, please." Fry bobbed his head. "They're in my quarters at the west side, in my trunk. All of them."

Samuel's legs went weak with relief, and he braced himself against the wall. With the papers back in his hand, he could seize the initiative and strike back against the consortium. He'd warned them not to interfere with him or with Nicaragua, and now he'd punish them for it.

He rapped on the door and turned away from Fry. Though alight with hope within, he couldn't forgive what the bastard had done to his family.

"I'll ask Captain Blanco to show you mercy," he said over his shoulder. "But know this, Benjamin Fry: You don't deserve it."

~

The three intimate weeks since Samuel rescued Sofia had bound them more tightly than ever. They sat with Filipe outside the tavern by the harbor wall, Fort San Carlos brooding high above them. Sofia rocked John in her arms as Filipe read the front page of La Nacional.

Hair the color of onyx, golden skin, and honey-colored eyes —the siblings were as alike as minié balls in a cartridge box. The tropical sun hammered down from the blue sky and skipped light over the mint-green lake that stretched to the horizon, as vast as an ocean. The warm breeze brought the scent of peat and fish to Samuel as it caressed his sweat-soaked shirt, though it did little to cool him.

Joyous cries and shouts drifted from the lakeside, where several of the Euronicas were skimming stones across the surface and others horsed about, shuffling their feet in the sand as they threw a jicara above Padraig's fair, tousled head. It was his turn to catch the jar, and though he was taller, broader, and stronger, they ran rings around him, smaller men dark as the land, wiry, spindly, and loyal.

Filipe read President Mora's proclamation in the newspaper: "The main artery of filibusterism has been cut forever. The sword of Costa Rica has severed it." He threw the paper down in disgust. "Why, that pompous ass Mora is hogging all the glory."

"What else did you expect from a politician?" Sofia shifted John on her knee. "Oh, baby boy, you're getting so heavy."

Reinvigorated after three weeks' rest at the fort, Sofia had regained her customary glow and passion. Samuel recalled the pleasure of their bodies pressed together like spoons and stirred below, but this was not the time for that.

He stretched, relaxed now, hardly remembering the tension that had been his constant companion for months. "The Costa Ricans did play a major role in capturing the river. And their attack on Walker in Granada distracted him from our endeavor here. What did Teresa say about your shoulder?"

Filipe lifted his right hand and mimicked a female voice. "'There, young man, as good as new, with two dashing scars to set some lady's heart on fire. You're well enough to travel.'"

"Excellent." Samuel whirled the whiskey in his glass. Catching sunlight, it was the color of Sofia's eyes. "And not a moment too soon. The New York steamship arrives in Greytown the day after tomorrow, and I fear it will be the last. As much as I love Nicaragua, it's not safe for John here, so we must catch that ship back to New York. From there, we'll go home."

Sofia arched her black eyebrows. "The last steamship?" She looked like her old self, the girl he met on his first trip up the river, and beneath her poise and tranquility he spied the old face full of mischief, warm as the breath of summer.

"We've shut the back door. No more American adventurers can join Walker now from the East Coast. And few will want to, not with word of his defeat in every newspaper. General Mora has reinforced the garrison here. We're no longer needed. I want to get to New York and collect payment from Vanderbilt." He puffed on his cigarette and looked at the river steamer tied up at the wharf. "Captain Spencer has agreed to take us downriver at daybreak."

"Sofia?" Filipe ceased turning his glass on the table and glanced from Sofia to Samuel. "Samuel . . . I'm not going."

Sofia's hand flew to her parted lips. "What do you mean, you're not going?"

Filipe swallowed and looked away.

Samuel's back tensed. They'd had enough surprises; Sofia didn't need more. "Filipe, Sofia asked you a question."

Filipe twisted the napkin in his hands and cut his eyes to his sister. "I've made poor decisions in the past, and I must make up for them."

"Well, this certainly sounds like another one," she said with a huff.

"I'm staying in Nicaragua to join the fight until we're truly rid of Walker."

"You're what?" She put baby John to her shoulder. "You can't mean to fight!"

"And then there's the hacienda. With Papa gone, who else can run it?"

Samuel stubbed out his cigarette, and the smoke stung his eyes. Sofia didn't need this, not after losing their father so recently. "You can't stay, Filipe. You're too young. Besides, Walker is on his knees, practically defeated already."

Filipe's brow furrowed. "You said that last year when you took his gold, yet the bastard bounced back and murdered Papa. If he's defeated, I must be here to claim my inheritance, if he's not, I'll fight him."

"Walker may have confiscated the estate." Even a slug of whiskey didn't wash that sour taste from Samuel's mouth.

"Then I'll take the hacienda back." Filipe squared his shoulders. "I can do this, trust me. I've spoken to the Euronicas, and they'll hire on with me to help me work the hacienda." He glanced at Sofia. "Chavez and Teresa too."

Sofia shook her head. "I won't permit it."

Filipe caught her slim hand in both of his. "This is my country, not Ireland. I owe it to Papa to set things right."

Samuel recognized that fire in the boy's eyes. Filipe was as stubborn as Sofia. He fiddled with Father's ring on his finger. "You're too young."

"I'm almost sixteen, the same age you were when you joined the Seventeenth Lancers."

He rubbed the back of his neck. It was true, he'd joined the cavalry at sixteen. And what would Filipe do in Ireland? Great Britain was a harsh place for those of a different caste. He and Sofia had already experienced that, and John would face it in the future.

Samuel looked at Sofia. "Perhaps he's right. Ireland will be hard for him, and I was his age when I first went to war. He has the finest company of soldiers in Central America at his back. Even if Walker rises from his ashes, there's no better force to knock him back down."

Sofia's face tightened. "You won't look for trouble, will you?"

Filipe drew his shoulders back. "I learned from the best." His eyes sparkled as he looked at Samuel for support.

She bit her lip. "And you'll listen to Chavez?"

"Yes, yes." Filipe jiggled his foot. "Please, Sofia, I must do this. It's my duty."

She raised her eyebrows at Samuel. "Perhaps if you go to Chinandega with him?"

He hesitated. John and Sofia were his priority now. "I wish I could. But Nicaragua isn't safe for John or you. Walker may be defeated, but cholera plagues the country. I must take you home to Ireland. If need be, I can return here once you're safe in Clonakilty. Let me speak to Chavez."

He pushed back the heavy wooden chair and rose. It was hard to let Filipe fly from the nest on his own, it would be even harder when John's time came.

CHAPTER TWENTY-FIVE

London reeked of decay, open sewers, and the bitter smoke burping from thousands of sooty chimneys to stain the pewter sky.

"London's always the bloody same." Padraig grabbed the brim of his slouch hat as the wind tossed the trees of Saint James Square in the pelting rain.

"A month ago, you were bitching about the mosquitoes and the heat." Samuel clutched the lapels of his long canvas coat to his wet neck. "Now it's the cold."

They turned left onto Pall Mall.

"I can't believe is almost March. We've been away for eight months." Padraig peered up at a three-level limestone building with towering Corinthian columns. "The Army and Navy Club—well, I never thought I'd see the day. Sure, this place is far too posh for the likes of me."

"Old Nosey, the Duke of Wellington himself, was a patron," Samuel said. "They'd blackball me in a heartbeat. They only want the cream of military society."

"The cream of society," Padraig growled. "Rich and thick."

One of the three archways must lead to the entrance. Samuel nudged him. "Well, let's go stir the cream, shall we?"

The aromatic scent of coffee greeted them in a hallway paneled with imitation marble, and the chatter of voices washed over them. Conversations ebbed and flowed from where officers in bright uniforms piled with gold braid and women in feathered finery held china cups, surrounded by silver pots and trays piled with creamy buns.

A liveried waiter frowned at the puddle of water dripping from their wet coats and looked around, seeking support.

"Let's try the dining room." Samuel led the way to a space richly paneled in hardwood and guarded by a dozen generals and admirals glaring from gold-framed portraits with classical hauteur. It was too late for breakfast and a tad early for lunch; no wonder the room was empty. "Not here. Let's try upstairs."

"I say, gentlemen, you're not members." A waiter standing behind them glared at Padraig down his nose. "You're guests?"

"Why yes, we are." Samuel's public-school accent could be as posh as any aristocrat's when he put his tongue into it. "We're meeting General Bingham, the Earl of Lucan."

The waiter's hooded eyes widened. "The earl. I see."

A passing waitress paused in a rattle of the cups and saucers piled on her silver tray. "His lordship's upstairs in the smoking room, Simon."

"Thank you, my dear." Padraig winked at her.

She blushed. "Third floor, sir."

Samuel pointed to the stone staircase sweeping up from the hall. "That way, I presume?"

The waiter faked a smile. "I'll just check the guest list, sir, shall I?"

"You do as you wish, Simon." Samuel pushed past him and headed for the stairs as poor Simon sputtered.

The *click-clack* of colliding billiard balls greeted them on the third-floor landing. Through an open door, Samuel spied officers and gentlemen in frock coats prodding the colored balls around the green felted tables. He followed the scent of tobacco past the door to the smoking room, which was lined with paintings of battle and hunting scenes. Several club members sat at walnut tables scattered around the parquet floor, smoke from their cigars spiraling to the traceried Moresque decorating the dome.

The Earl of Lucan and a middle-aged man with black sideburns and a broken nose sat in wingback chairs by the marble fireplace at the far end of the room. Lucan's narrow head had thinned on top to a ribbon of gray curling into the billowing sideburns wrapped under his bare chin. Time had not been kind to George Bingham, the Third Earl of Lucan, since the Crimean War. Deep crow's feet folded into his drooping eyelids, and dark bags sagged beneath his eyes like bloody pouches. Devoid of his uniform, brass buttons, and gold braid, Lucan looked more like an exhausted banker than a cavalry commander.

Samuel's heels rapped the parquet as he strode across the room, ignoring the handful of smokers, and planted his feet wide in front of the earl. "Lucan! A word in private if you please."

Lucan scowled at the interruption, and his brown eyes bulged. "Kingston? What the—who let you in here?"

Here sat the man who destroyed Samuel's cavalry career and sent bandits to raid his home. "You, sir, are a churl and a coward. We had an agreement, and you broke it."

Lucan and his companion flinched at the roughness in Samuel's voice and sprang to their feet.

Lucan's face broke into dark blotches, even redder than the veins that webbed his narrow nose. "How dare you burst in here and address me, a senior officer, in that manner."

The hatchet-nosed man swept his hands in the air. "*Two* senior officers. I'm General Helmsley of the Coldstream Guards, and nobody speaks to me like that. I'll have you court-martialed."

"I wasn't speaking to you, and a court-martial is unlikely, since I'm no longer in the Queen's army." Samuel's voice was brittle and cold. He wouldn't lose control because if he did, he might kill Lucan. "I was addressing this . . . this . . . coward."

There were gasps and murmurs from the other tables.

"You will be silent!" Lucan's words lashed like a riding crop. "If you speak another word, you'll regret it."

Samuel pressed his fists to his sides and clung to his composure—scarcely. "Or what? A duel?"

He remembered his only duel: his fifteen-year-old arm flying up in a blur, and the single flat report that punched across Lough Hyne, hollow and fierce, startling the seagulls into erratic flight as the Earl of Baltimore's son toppled to his knees. The grudge born that day, and the Baltimores' thirst for vengeance had traveled the dark roads of three continents to arrive at this very confrontation.

Every eye in the room was on him now, the crass interloper in their midst. General Helmsley made an inarticulate noise as his face purpled. Padraig sniggered behind Samuel, daring him.

"Dueling is illegal"—Lucan's lips peeled into a knife-slash—"and beneath me. Instead, I will have you ejected and arrested."

Still a coward. Samuel was incandescent, and his neck tautened as he bridled. "I have recovered Baltimore's papers—the documents your thugs stole from my home."

Lucan blanched.

"We can discuss them alone"—Samuel cocked his head—"or in front of these gapers." He fired a venomous glance at the onlookers, their bulging eyes and nibbling lips. To hell with them.

Lucan's face crumpled as the stirrings and murmurs in the room ceased and the onlookers inclined toward the spectacle. The silence was so profound they could hear the click of billiard balls from the other side of the building.

Plucking at his collar, Lucan looked from Samuel to the spectators and back. Then he wheeled on the onlookers, his face twisting in rage as he roared. "Do . . . you . . . mind? I need privacy. Get out." He glared at Helmsley. "You too, Peter. *Out*!"

Chairs scraped the wooden floor as the spectators rose,

muttering, pouring their indignation into the tense air, and trudged from the room, stealing glances over their shoulders.

"Preposterous behavior." Helmsley jabbed his cigar in the ashtray and stomped after them.

"He played you for a fool, didn't he?" Samuel's voice was cold, his chin raised in disdain.

"Hmm?" Lucan was breathing heavily, a hawkish expression on his face.

"Fry. He took your money and never delivered the papers you asked for."

"If you mean Benjamin Fry, he has done a great many tasks for me that—"

"Instead, he took them to Nicaragua, believing Walker would reward him more." Samuel noted the narrowing of Lucan's eyes with satisfaction. "Well, I have them, and I did as I swore I would do last year. I released them to the press—"

"I think *not*!" Lucan bellowed. "I shall not permit—"

"Only one page, mind you. For now." Samuel plucked the latest *London Times* from his jacket pocket, and Lucan's forgotten cigar flew from the ashtray when he slapped the paper onto the table.

Lucan snatched it up and read.

Earl of Sligo Found Hanging in his Stables

Colonel John Lawrence, Fourth Earl of Sligo, who commanded the Seventeenth Lancers during the Crimean War, was found hanging in his stables yesterday. His death occurs on the heels of his being named as one of the British aristocrats financing the return of slavery in Nicaragua . . .

"I'm sure you're aware of Lawrence's cowardly act already. Well, now you know why." Samuel hadn't intended Lawrence to die, but showing the consortium what would happen if they trifled with him had been necessary.

Lucan was staring at him, mouth ajar.

Samuel took a step closer. "I revealed Lawrence first because he's the cad responsible for ruining my career, but I didn't want him to die. Suicide was his choice, rather than living in a world that knew him for the monster he was."

Lucan stabbed a pudgy finger at Samuel's sternum. "Do you realize who I am? The power I wield? I will destroy you and your half-breed family. I will—"

"You arrogant bastard." Padraig's face blazed red, and his fists were rising. "I'll show—"

Samuel threw out an arm to restrain his friend. "No. He's mine." He wanted greater punishment for the earl than mere physical injury. His voice was the scrape of clashing sabers. "So tell me, who are you exactly? You're the 'Exterminator,' the murdering bastard who drove hundreds of Irish souls into the cold to starve and freeze."

"It's my land." The veins on Lucan's nose darkened and pulsed. "I can do as I please with it."

Samuel pounded the table with a fist. "You're the bastard who ordered a hundred and fifty of my comrades in Crimea to ride to their deaths, while you retreated and left us to face a gantlet of artillery alone."

Lucan flinched, and his face scrunched tight.

"And you're a mistaken man, misguided if you think I'll forgive you for sending thugs to attack my home and family. Prepare your own noose, Lucan. My next stop is a second visit to the office of *The London Times*."

Lucan raised both hands. "Now look here, Kingston, let's be gentlemen. I meant you no harm. It was William Walker's doing." Lucan inveigled and evaded, like a fox escaping the henhouse. "I'm a powerful man. I can help you in—"

"No more lies." Samuel reached for the Colt in his waistband.

But if he killed Lucan now, another son would seek revenge, and another. Samuel had no right to unleash a new feud.

"I'll give you one more chance, Lucan. For the sake of my children, this bitterness must end." He dropped his hand to his side and stepped back. "You will discharge the debt against my brother's estate, Springbough Manor, from your own funds. Furthermore, you will unfreeze my accounts, and you and your miserly consortium will have nothing more to do with William Walker or Nicaragua."

The bombast bled from Lucan like spilled wind from a sail. He grabbed the table and sank into his seat. This is how he must have felt when he deserted the Light Brigade in the Valley of Death. "Yes, yes. I agree."

"And Lucan"—Samuel lifted a finger—"this time, I'll keep the Baltimore papers safely beyond your reach. If you try anything—if you harm my family in any way—I will publish everything and destroy all of you."

He stepped back and took in the sight of the gibbering earl. Publishing those papers would never be necessary now. Lucan was a broken man—far better than killing him.

~

Samuel woke befuddled and gritty-eyed on a jouncing bed. The room hummed, vibrated, and swayed from side to side as whitecaps churned a black ocean beyond the porthole. Ah, the steamship from Southampton to Queenstown; they were going home.

He reclined against the bulkhead with a slow smile. This uplifting feeling could only be the "channels," as sailors of old called the excitement of sailing the English Channel. The excitement of going home.

Sofia radiated warmth beside him. Her face was sculpted perfection in the moonlight spilling through the brass porthole, and her black hair glistened on the pillow like a splash of obsidian. Her lips were slightly open, and one arm rested across baby John. Her skin, normally the color of pressed olives, was pale in the moonbeams and smooth as polished bone. He could smell the oils she'd bought in London, bergamot and lemon oil, and underneath it, her personal scent of roses and fresh sweat. Slowly, so as not to wake her, he traced a finger down the velvet skin of her side and across the curve of her hip bone, and tingling flooded him, buoying him. Fulfilling him.

She purred and turned to meet his gaze. He bent and opened his mouth over hers, drinking in her warm sweetness, nibbling hungrily and matching the soft movements of her lips. He kissed her neck and slid his hand across her nightshirt. She bloomed beneath his fingertips and surged against him. His body prickled with a warm flush of pleasure.

Baby John mewled beside her, drew another breath, and wailed.

They parted reluctantly as she reached for John. "He wants all the attention. Perhaps Uncle Padraig can mind him for a while later."

He touched her face; it was soft as satin. "The way I'm feeling now, Padraig won't have to care for him too long."

Deep in the bowels of the hull, the engines rumbled as the steamship powered through the waves.

She smiled. "Oh, you're not getting off that easy."

"I'll waken Padraig early, then." He brushed a lose strand of hair from her face. "We dock in Queenstown this afternoon."

The slenderest crinkle appeared between her eyes. "I dreamed of Filipe. Did we do the right thing?"

"The right thing?"

"You know. Leaving him in Nicaragua."

He had wondered the same, but Filipe was old enough to make his own decisions. "I think we did. Anyway, he has Chavez and Teresa to watch over him. And all the Euronicas."

She bared a breast for John and laid her head on Samuel's

shoulder. "Don't be too hard on him. He did what he thought best. He did it for Papa."

"I don't blame him. I was in the same position last year."

She looked up at him with surprise.

"I faced no good choices." He brushed a strand of hair out of her eyes so she could see him. "I could only save Father by supporting slavery, yet I knew he would never have endorsed slavery. That didn't make choosing to fight and lose him any easier."

She placed her hand, soft and warm, over his. "You would've saved him if his heart hadn't failed. He was living on borrowed time. Teresa made that clear."

"I know. Is it selfish to say that relieved me? Not his heart failure, but knowing it wasn't my fault."

"Of course not, darling. That guilt was eating you up. Now you're free."

He tasted salt when he nuzzled her neck.

She kissed him and pushed him away with a giggle. "Don't fire me up. John won't like it."

He cupped a hand on his son's peach-fuzz head, still in wonder at the beauty of such a tiny thing.

"I feel sorry for them, you know." She took John's hand in hers.

"The Euronicas?"

"No, silly, Teresa and Chavez. Their story of love unfulfilled. Imagine being torn from the person you love and not making love to them when you find them again."

It was strange to see the defrocked priest and a runaway nun living together. Samuel wondered if his curiosity indicated a morbid inquisitiveness about carnal sin—a sin he was sure those two would never commit. "I suppose both felt their vows of chastity still bind them. Chavez was a priest, and Teresa was a nun, after all. I know I couldn't do it."

"I know your appetites well"—she nudged his shoulder playfully with her head—"and the Lord himself couldn't curb your lust. But I'm content that they're finally together, as are we. What's the plan when we get home?"

She thought of Clonakilty as home now. The buoyant feeling that filled him, rising like the tide, was bright and levitating, exploding like the sun after tropical rain. "When I returned from Nicaragua last year, I was drowning in grief and guilt. I pushed away everyone who cared for me: Jason, Emily, the Kerrs . . . And you. I want to fix that. I want to throw a party."

"A party!" She sat up in the brass bed and adjusted John, who was latched onto her, his fat cheeks puffing as he guzzled. "My, my, the old Samuel is certainly back. What kind of party?"

He kissed her on the forehead. She was so perfect, unmarred by the creases and blemishes of others. "A christening party, my love. In your church."

"You're serious?" She positively bubbled. "You were dead set against it before."

"I was wrong."

She couldn't reach him to throw her arms around him, so she covered John's head with kisses.

He gave her a wide grin. "It's important to you, so I'm happy to support it. María, for one, is going to be delighted."

She raised her eyebrows.

"Padraig hasn't been to church for years. Our John will give María a second chance at saving a soul."

The sunlight burnished Sofia's golden skin, and Samuel savored the curve of her neck as she bent to kiss John's forehead. Her beauty glinted like a diamond in sunlight, multifaceted, vital and bright. Her lips were plump crescents, complementing her turned-up nose. Even seated, her limbs rested with perfect elegance, as if posed for a portrait.

He'd been in a dark place to have avoided that skin, velvet and soft as roses, but now he was back, and...

A poke of Sofia's elbow returned Samuel to the wooden pew.

The warm air, incense, and candles had lulled him into a daydream, and Father Mulcahy's endless droning hadn't helped either, bless his heart. Unlike Reverend Welby who was a bigot, Father Mulcahy was a true Christian open to helping anybody regardless of their religion.

"—a thousand miles away. Did you hear anything that was said?"

"Sorry, darling, I was thinking about . . ."

She patted his leg. "Just pay attention. It's your son's baptism."

Spring sunshine spilled through the stained-glass windows of Clonakilty's parish church and painted the guests in the polished pews a rainbow of colors. The majority were tenants from the estate, dressed in their finest and firing surreptitious glances at their landlord's family. It was the only time they'd see Protestants in their Catholic church. Samuel hid a smile as Emily tilted her head and stared at the statue of the Blessed Virgin. The Mother of God didn't reside with the Church of Ireland in Kilgariff.

Up front, the old priest's long face was still wrinkled from a lifetime of worry, but he'd put on weight since Samuel last saw him. He stood tall at the altar with a gleam in his eye. And why wouldn't he? It was seldom he got to steal a soul from the Protestants.

Baby John wailed in María Kerr's arms, indignant that the crinkled old stranger had poured water over his head. Or perhaps it was his girly attire that bothered him? No boy wanted to be forced into a white christening gown. The godparents made an odd pair: petite María Kerr, with her mousy brown hair, and broad-shouldered Padraig with his untamable blond thatch and a purple scar across his nose.

As Father Mulcahy closed his holy book to a chorus of *Amen*, a silk-sheathed hand slipped around Samuel's arm, and Sofia drew him down to whisper in his ear. "Thank you, my love. This means everything to me." Her breath smelled like pears.

"Of course," he whispered back. "I was a sod to let this divide us last year."

A smile built on her plump red lips. "What changed your mind?"

He cocked his head. She was beautiful, so radiant and happy . . . That was reason enough. "To please you."

She pulled a face.

He grinned. She wasn't buying it. "Emanuel Chavez and Teresa showed me that it doesn't matter whose missal you carry, Catholic or Protestant, so long as you've the faith of a true Christian. Reverend Welby and school brainwashed me years ago into believing that Catholics were lazy idolaters. Now I know that's poppycock. Their lies don't make my Protestant religion bad."

She elbowed him with a little grin.

"I guess I've grown up."

People stirred and boots rapped in the pews as the most impatient headed for the door. "He's finished, thank God. It's stifling in here, and I'm falling asleep. Let's go outside for some fresh air."

With baby John safe from the threat of limbo, the celebrants made their separate ways home, with only the Kingstons' two carriages rolling to Springbough Manor. In the clean sunshine that follows a sweep of spring rain, the hills were a riot of colors, yellow furze and purple bracken clustered about on a rolling green blanket.

Though the salty winds of the Celtic Sea had eroded the Kingston coat of arms chiseled in the limestone arch above the door, Springbough was still the ancestral family home. The coat of arms reminded Samuel of Father. If only he were here to meet Sofia and John . . . to see how Samuel had changed after recognizing his mistakes: yearning for acceptance by the ruling class he now despised, bending to the religious bigotry drummed into him in school, and his snobbery. He had stopped longing and had learned what true friendship and love was, and now he was finally happy.

Inside the porch, Sofia handed him baby John wrapped in his shimmering white gown. "Hold him, darling, while I take off my gloves."

John made a smacking noise with his mouth and sucked his thumb. Samuel's heart tugged, and he stroked John's dark head; the downy hair was soft as silk. He'd do everything to protect his boy.

Sofia touched his arm. "He's a little miracle."

He lifted her hand, still cold from the winter air, and kissed it tenderly. "It won't be easy, Sofia. You know there are those who'll make it hard on him—on both of you—don't you?"

"It wasn't easy back in that fort, either." Her expression bristled and softened. "These people, the common people, are so kind. Surely the gentry will come around. Regardless, we're here, Samuel. Together. And I believe John will be fine."

He wasn't as sure. It could be a considerable time before the different races and religions lived in harmony here. But people like the Kerrs, the Euronicas, and his own family gave Samuel faith. He'd worked hard for harmony and refused to accept it could never be, and that thought gave him comfort. He held his head high and took a deep breath behind Sofia as she carried their hopes for a brighter future over the threshold.

THE END

HISTORICAL NOTES

The Seventeenth Lancers led the Light Brigade on their fateful charge up the North Valley in the Battle of Balaklava during the Crimean War. Major-General George Charles Bingham, Third Earl of Lucan, commanded the British Cavalry in Crimea, albeit timidly and poorly. Many Irish hated Lucan and called him "The Exterminator" for his mass evictions in the West of Ireland, where reports say he demolished hundreds of homes and evicted 2,000 people during the Great Famine.

For all his faults, William Walker was a remarkable man. He attended the University of Nashville when he was twelve years old, got his first degree at fourteen, graduated as a doctor when he was eighteen, and then became a lawyer. He did oppose slavery in early years, and it must have been ambition that drove him to impose it on Nicaragua. Walker was the only American to assume the presidency of another country. After his removal from Nicaragua in 1857, he made two more attempts to seize control of Nicaragua, and the last led to his execution by the Hondurans in 1860.

Sylvanus Spencer and William Webster themselves devised the plan to capture the San Juan River and presented the plan to Vanderbilt. Spencer, a son of John Spencer, a former U.S. secretary of war, was an adventurer who captained the Transit Company river steamer *Machuca* on the San Juan River before the new Morgan and Garrison management fired him. While, Webster, an Englishman, presented himself Vanderbilt as a gentleman from a good family well-connected in Britain and Germany, he was a conman who'd used a variety of names, including Clifford, Brown, Waters, and Simpson. Webster set himself up in business at Granada as a migration agent but never got along with President Walker, and his venture failed.

Vanderbilt agreed to pay them fifty thousand dollars each if they succeeded. Knowing the Costa Ricans lacked experienced officers, Webster George F. Cauty, who had served as an officer with the army of the East India Company in India. Cauty was an experienced officer who saw action in a bloody the Sikh wars and the 1852 campaign in Burma. I thought it a neat fit to replace him with Samuel for an exciting story. At the time, President Mora was unaware that Vanderbilt manipulated him into this second river expedition.

Colonel Pedro Barillier led the expedition, with Major Maximo Blanco as his chief of staff, and the pair of them performed well.

I used the following books for reference:

Dando-Collins, Stephen. Tycoon's War (p. 279). Hachette Books. Kindle Edition.

Dando-Collins, Stephen. Tycoon's War (p. 154). Hachette Books. Kindle Edition.

Doubleday, Charles William. Reminiscences of the "Filibuster" War in Nicaragua (1886). Unknown. Kindle Edition.

Sweetman, John. Balaclava 1854 (Campaign). Bloomsbury Publishing. Kindle Edition.

Walker, William. The War in Nicaragua (1860) (p. 385). Kindle Edition.

Printed in Great Britain
by Amazon

62016470R00203